Stepping Stonez

a novel by

Candace L. Sherman

Stepping Stonez

Visit our website at www.StillwaterPress.com for more information.

First Stillwater River Publications Edition.

ISBN: 978-1-958217-30-6

Library of Congress Control Number: 2022911700

Names: Sherman, Candace L., author.
Title: Stepping Stonez : a novel / by Candace L. Sherman
Other titles: Stepping Stones
Description: First Stillwater River Publications edition. | Pawtucket, RI, USA : Stillwater
    River Publications, [2022]
Identifiers: ISBN: 978-1-958217-30-6 | LCC: 2022911700
Subjects: LCSH: Women jewelers--United States--Fiction. | Craft festivals--Atlantic Coast
    (U.S.)--Fiction. | Precious stones--Fiction. | Energy medicine--Fiction. | Spiritual
    healing--Fiction. | Dreams--Fiction.
Classification: LCC: PS3619.H4643 S74 2022 | DDC: 813/.6--dc23

1 2 3 4 5 6 7 8 9 10
Written by Candace L. Sherman
Cover and interior book design by Elisha Gillette.
Published by Stillwater River Publications, Pawtucket, RI, USA.

Table of Contents

Introduction

Step back in time while you read this book as it takes place in 2008. That was the beginning of wide-spread cell phone usage. Owning a flip phone felt advanced. Phone stores were not on every corner as they are today. Obviously, we have come a long way with technology since then.

Travel with Vonnette to different fine art and craft shows in the northeast as she tries and often does sell her jewelry. Emotionally and spiritually, she lives in a world of metaphysics. People feel she has special powers; some view her as a psychic, some feel she reads minds, some come to her for natural healing information, some for dream interpretation. Many people admire how she lives life outside the norm and call her a stone whisperer. Vonnette looks at her life as very natural. She doesn't understand how she gets labeled as *special,* or *different.*

Along with her jewelry, she has two books for sale that she's written. Each contain stone healing properties she has channeled. The coffee table book is titled **Dreams Made of Stone** that lists stone healing properties, her conceptualizations of jewelry design symbols and dream messages she received while creating some pieces along with pictures of jewelry she crafted to represent specific stones. The other is a small handbook named **Stone Magic** that lists stone healing properties without any photos in an A-Z fashion.

In an effort to make a living from her creations, Vonnette shares metaphysical information with potential clients. The struggle to make a decent living is one she hopes will soon stop being such a challenge.

This book could be called a how-to incorporate metaphysics into daily life. Perhaps this is a gift-giving guide for women. Hopefully, it is an enjoyable read with great insights!

Events listed in this book are loosely based on my travels; however, it is a work of fiction.

⚜

According to *Webster's Third New International Dictionary*, metaphysics is "something that deals with what is beyond the physical." Today, metaphysics is widely accepted as the study of esoteric sciences. Having heard many times from different sources to write about what I knew . . . I know hand-wrought jewelry, living with and through the arts along with metaphysics. Over the course of my sixty-nine years, I have been asked most often about jewelry and after that, metaphysics. I believe in continuous life. You can't get much more above the physical than that!

In 1976 making a living by creating one-of-a-kind fine jewelry for locals and tourists, I opened my retail business in Newport, RI. After seventeen years, I closed the store to work from my studio at home. I then began traveling up and down the East Coast participating in fine art and craft shows. Winning awards for my designs, I garnered enough confidence to branch out into how I presented my creations to the public. By that time, I had channeled stone healing properties and began to display shortened versions of such on little slips of paper as part of my set-up, which I also reference throughout this book.

Perhaps you are an artist or are friends with an artist, and if so you'll understand some of the angst artists have in both creating and then selling their work.

Being an artist, my day job *is* creating fine jewelry as a goldsmith. Writing, fine art painting, making fascinator hats, painting furniture in a folk-art fashion, sewing and gardening are all part of my artistic efforts and hobbies.

Today, I work out of my home with much of my art and books posted on line. Currently, two of my books are in print and are available on Amazon or through my web site www.clsherman. com. ***Dreams Made of Stone***, the first book I wrote, includes stone healing properties I've channeled along with jewelry I made using various stones that I list in an A-Z fashion. Due to the volume of photos, I have yet to bring it to print but will become available at some point. ***Stone Magic*** is a shortened, paperback version of that first book listing stones and their healing properties in an A-Z fashion but without photos. ***The Crystal Caves***, an adventure book for all ages with sequels that will be coming out soon. Stay tuned . . .

Acknowledgments

For all the women who shared anonymous questionnaire information about their personal life, I give a heart-felt Thank You! Your sharing made the characters in this book come to life.

To all my friends who listened as I discussed the book, I thank you for hearing me and for giving insights that made the book better.

Thanks to all the stone dealers in my life who have assisted my everyday job; you are blessings!

To my jewelry clients, I bless and thank you for participating in my artistic and metaphysical journey! Without your interest and purchases, I might have been living on the street.

To Florence Scovel Schinn and Louise Hay who have each been metaphysical groundbreakers whom I reference in this book, I am eternally grateful they helped to pave the way.

While writing this book, three of my four-legged friends gave me comfort each and every day. I thank them for their unconditional love!

This book is dedicated to every one mentioned along with

Richard Kelley who helped me believe in my writing and story-telling talent and whom I hear in my head as I edit and embrace changes for the better.

With each new editor, I learn more and more in this writing phase of my life. Thank you Karrie Szatek-Tudor, and on.

Rose & Aerous

Tristan

CHAPTER ONE

Newport

October 4-5, 2008

Carved Lavender Jade & Red Garnet Beads

Candace L. Sherman

DREAMS
1. Something about taxes.

2. Alone and aroused sexually, Vonnette did what came naturally.

3. Lavender jade.

4. Deep red garnet.

5. Walking in mud.

Sitting on the closed toilet next to a window overlooking the cemetery across the street as if it were the best chair in the house, Vonnette pulled the window blind open while thinking of stone healing properties for red garnet and lavender jade from her dreams the night before. Pondering what might energetically come her way today from the combination of these two stones, Vonnette was in her own private, contemplative zone.

While watching the view, she thought of how most people couldn't handle living across the street from a graveyard, but then Vonnette was not most people, and she never called it a cemetery. To her, it was a park with monuments. You couldn't walk around Newport, RI, without tripping over an historic cemetery or two. Maybe that's why Vonnette moved to this town in the early seventies. Old graveyards had always intrigued her. In fact, she found them almost comforting.

When she was nine, Vonnette was invited to go with a friend to New Hampshire. The friends' family had a camp up the street from a lake. While out walking one afternoon, she and her friend Natalie came upon a graveyard established in the early 1800's. The older a graveyard was, the happier Vonnette was being in it. Feeling at home with dead people and being aware of spirits since early childhood, Vonnette never really felt alone. Somehow she was at peace with her friends who were invisible to most everyone else. Those two young girls were entertained, happy even that day walking about and sharing secrets among the gravestones.

Remembering back to that childhood time years ago, Vonnette had hope that her comfort zone in graveyards was not really something weird. And maybe, other people had her gift of sight, too.

In adulthood, she had gone through many moments of doubt while sharing her connection with spirits, as it made so many people uncomfortable.

Across the street today, someone was throwing a stick for a dog.

This second-floor window in her bathroom had a birds' eye view of most of the graveyard, including some great old maple trees that crows frequently hung out in.

Seeing crows often made Vonnette think of her great aunt Foffee, her dad's childhood name for his aunt Florence. When Vonnette was fairly young, she and Foffee went for little car rides together in her green Dodge Rambler. When the aunt spotted a single crow, she would almost lose control of the vehicle in an effort to make sure her young charge also saw that one bird. Certain the old wives' tale of spying a single crow alone was a bad omen, Foffee tried to cancel that bad luck out by having someone else see that same crow. To drive her aunt a bit crazy, Vonnette often pretended to not see the single crow when prompted. Little did Foffee know those moments shared in a car would play a significant part later in Vonnette's life.

As an adult, paying attention to whenever and wherever she saw crows, Vonnette always counted how many there were. One crow or ten didn't make a difference, other than there were more secret messages for her. Deciphering those messages was a life-long mission. Feeling the number of crows viewed would give her more insight as to what the day might bring her way, crows took on almost as much daily meaning as Vonnette's dream messages. One crow meant new beginnings, two were for partnership. Three told her there would be connections with other people. Crow numbers and the meanings begin at one and go up to nine. After nine, she would add the single numbers together. Take twelve crows as an example. Vonnette would add the single numbers one and two together to become a number three within the one through nine concept.

Seeing and hearing two crows in her park with monuments, she was hopeful of a good omen for partnerships with clients. And, she was doing a show today.

Pulling back from the scene across the street, she decided her back *had* been hurting her this past week, so she felt the red garnet from her dream was necessary. Healing properties of red garnet associate with the lumbar region and then blood circulation. The human back, or lumbar, is considered to be a major part of the body's support system. When it feels out of whack, wearing red garnet can often help lend invisible support through blood circulation being increased in that area. Lavender jade, also in her dreams, can provide a soothing pillow of comfort when dealing with a harsh environment like contamination from smoke or smog. As for the other dream messages, well, mud always associated with money while taxes usually stood for being physically overwhelmed.

Each day Vonnette gathered whatever stones she dreamed of to wear. The only lavender jade she had in a finished piece of jewelry was mounted as a pendant on black, fresh water pearls. As pearls were not part of her dream last night, she opted to work with a loose stone of lavender jade. Pockets or no pockets in her clothing choice for the day, it would go in her bra. She'd lost stones from pockets in the past but never one placed in her bra. So, when energetically utilizing an unmounted stone, and it was rough to the touch, she would simply put a bit of Kleenex around the stone before placing it in her brassiere.

Somewhere in her late thirties Vonnette became comfortable with admitting this quirk to some of her friends and eventually it translated over to clients as well. It seemed that now she didn't care who knew she often had loose stones stuffed in her bra. There were so many secrets in her world, it was nice to have at least one that she didn't have to guard any longer. Being an artist, most people felt it was just another eccentricity on her part and simply dismissed this bit of information about loose stones in her bra.

The piece of jade she chose for the day was a carved, 3-dimensional peacock with pierced spots. It was about two inches across and overall smooth to the touch. Wear-ability of the jade selected would not be a problem.

Red garnet was an easy fit as well. Vonnette had a simple strand of pear-shaped, red garnet beads placed sporadically on a silk thread separated by oddly spaced knots. It was comfortable to wear and would work with whatever clothing choice she made today.

While walking about the house gathering the purple jade and red garnet beads together, Vonnette began to think about her life, what she called normal and what others felt was outside the norm. Looking at herself she thought she appeared normal. But then, she was constantly told by others, even while growing up, that she had gifts. At least others believe they're gifts and these gifts were considered odd by most people.

What Vonnette believes about these "gifts" is another matter altogether. She doesn't ever remember asking for the gifts. Since she has never been without them, she doesn't know life to be anything else, so for her, these gifts *are* normal. Full on color dream recall, seeing spirits, being able to talk to them, knowing what design a stone or stones wants to be mounted in, and often knowing what someone is thinking are just a few of these so-called gifts.

Feeling nightly dreams tell her how to live her life day by day, she follows up on each message as best she can. Many people involved in metaphysics talk their talk. Vonnette walks her talk much to the amazement of friends and family. To say people don't understand her is a gross understatement. Long ago Vonnette accepted that people didn't grasp her or her life style. Somehow, she felt this life was one she chose on some alternate plane before entering this body, and that perhaps these gifts of hers went right along with that previous plane. Yes, she believes in continuous life. The idea that a choice was made before coming into this body to learn certain things in particular ways explained her supposed gifts, at least to herself.

Along with recognizing her psychic gifts, people told her she was beautiful. Dressed, she'd look into a mirror and would see the same image stare back at her over and over again. There was blond hair that shifted from fairly straight just below shoulder length to being tied up in a bun on top of her head depending upon how she styled it each day. An average height of 5'4" bore out blue eyes with an okay nose, she guessed. Her large breasts were something she never really paid attention to, though others did. That tummy was never flat, no matter what diet she went on. Her big thighs always rubbed together, and those wide calves never fit into high boots. And then there were loads of freckles that someone once told her was from loving the sun as a child. So, what did others see that Vonnette did not? Unsure if she would ever know, her physical self was not where she concentrated her time. Instead, she focused on what could not be captured in a photograph, because beauty to her was not what you could see in a mirror. It was what she visualized in the way of jewelry designs. They all danced about in her head before taking physical form in her studio. As for the psychic ability attributed to her, she never thought of it as a gift, merely something that anyone could do with an open mind. Vonnette spent so much time analyzing her dreams and talking with spirits that she almost forgot how to deal with those around her who were living and in body.

Her magical gifts of transforming metal and stones into jewelry was a true comfort zone and what she chose to concentrate on most in her work life. Clients craved her knack to design something in front of their eyes and almost fell into a spell watching her sketch. Nick-naming her *The Stone Whisperer,* people wondered how she came up with designs for them so quickly once some inherited stone was pulled out of an antique box or pouch and placed into her view. Some story or other was shared about where the stone came from. Aunt so-and-so left this piece to them but wanted the stone to remain in whatever mounting it was in no matter how outdated it might be by today's standards. Any story shared or voice behind it became a background hum once Vonnette began her so-called chicken-scratch sketches while she connected with stone energies. Stones spoke to her and told her how they wanted to be mounted in metal, and while pictures popped into her mind, she sketched. That was the secret zone she entered while drawing.

Often, by the time potential clients stopped talking, Vonnette would also finish her sketches. She then explained how metal would play into the design and the whole piece would then translate into wear-ability for the client.

Almost nightly, Vonnette dreamed about jewelry. Some nights she saw how to create her latest project a bit differently than she had previously imagined. She accepted those dreamed image changes as useful input. Overall, it took some angst out of the equation while making a unique piece. Each day when she sat at her workbench she would pray, asking to do the very best she could while creating such-and-such a piece for whomever whether the jewelry would be for a client or something that would be in a display case for sale.

Vonnette felt things deeply. Tension can and does wreak havoc on the physical. Taking responsibility for creating a piece of jewelry for a client to heart could, and sometimes did, make her physically ill. Therefore, when her dreams suggested specific design shifts, even for clients, she paid heed. All this helped her feel she was working with and through invisible spirits that she was sure only had her best interest at heart.

Since she was a child her dreams were so vivid, volumes could have been written on them, and as a matter of fact she had done just that.

Vonnette first learned how to recall dream messages fully in college. One English professor suggested to lay still when she would first wake and ask her brain what her dreams were. The professor told her to always have paper and pen next to the bed to write even a few words associated with the dream when wakened in the middle of the night. Once fully awake in the morning those few scribblings would usually help her to grasp the whole dream. Figuring out what the meaning was from that message was supposedly possible then as well. Though she had recalled dreams since early childhood, Vonnette religiously did what that professor suggested expecting some major psychic understanding to come her way that had previously escaped her. So, she prayed for understanding of her dream messages along with the correct energy for creating the right jewelry designs to place out for sale and/or for individual clients.

For years Vonnette wrote all dream details down once fully awake in the morning. During the course of the day she would discover what the messages meant one-by-one. Aware this method of dream association with life lacked something, she then chose to write what transpired over the course of the day in her dream journals each night and cross-referenced the days' events with the dreams from the night before. This method of association allowed her to see if specific dream symbols meant something when they repeatedly occurred. Vonnette felt that with each dream she must be getting messages from the other side. That place that's unknown and might exist beyond what she understood of as life here on earth.

Eventually, Vonnette was not satisfied with this cross-reference method. She needed to find a missing link, but what.

Somewhere in her forties Vonnette decided too much time had been spent with paper and pen figuring out the meaning of her dreams. If the universe wasn't going to make things crystal clear to her then she wasn't going to keep writing journals! With that, she also gave up her daily routine of deep-breath meditation and went on long walks instead. Walking helped her work out many thoughts in life and, as a bonus it helped to calm her mind. While working on two brain levels at the same time, she would repeat prayers over and over. One part of her mind recited prayers, the other worked out what her dreams might represent. Instead of waiting till days' end to associate dreams with activities, she now projected dream messages onto the expected days' events. Ironically, her overactive imagination combined with weird dream messages made for stress beyond what she thought normal people endured, and yet, it was all part of Vonnettes' daily life.

Years of living with dream messages and stress had taught Vonnette much about herself and her life. When a nervous stomach happened, and she'd had a nervous stomach since she woke, it almost always meant some connection to sexual attraction or love was headed her way that day. Why would there be any reason for more of those love-type feelings in her life? It seemed a fair question to ask since Vonnette was in her fifties now and had never married.

Who knew why exactly, since she'd had many suitors in her youth. There were a few proposals even, but none ever gelled. Somehow, love had not been a permanent fixture in her life before, so why on God's green earth would something like that begin now? Dismissing the feelings, Vonnette, being empathic, decided she could be picking up on someone else's energy.

To be certain she reviewed her dream messages again determined to discover any possible misunderstanding. One dream was about taxes. Some of her paperwork had not been completed that needed to be sent off to the accountant, but instinctively she knew that was not the dream message. That dream could have been about being overtired, overtaxed.

Another dream was about sex. Being alone in that dream gave her no reason to think a man had anything to do with that one. She did feel that sex often associated with sex, or, it could also represent creative energy. In the end, she dismissed it feeling that dream symbol today most likely represented her creative energy. Suddenly, she remembered there was a famous person that came in at the end of that segment. Having forgotten that part, Vonnette knew famous people in a dream usually suggested help from an unexpected source. Doing a show today could reference help from an unexpected client, and maybe even a good purchase.

Something about lavender jade appeared in one dream. Another dream was about a deep red garnet pin that was being placed in a jewelry display case. While recalling that segment, she knew the pin was made of gold. Jewelry made of gold in a dream is a good symbol. Even though Vonnette was unsure if this associated with her chosen profession, she accepted it as a sign of good things to come for the day.

One other dream had some mud as the core symbol. Mud almost always meant money! But, there wasn't anything she could recall in her dreams that connected with a love interest, so she dismissed that feeling.

Bathed, dressed and stones in place, Vonnette went about readying the house before packing her finished jewelry in the car to leave. Vacuuming, doing the dishes, cleaning the litter box and putting out the trash was part of each day when she was home. It was even more important when she left town for a show, to have the house fresh when she left, so it was easier to organize again upon her return. Luckily, she had a local show today. Any cleaning done now would remain in tack until after she got home tonight.

Uptown on the corner of Bellevue Avenue and Old Beach Road stood an old Tudor style building that housed the Newport Art Museum. Once a year the Artists Guild Show called Art on the Lawn took place there and was something Vonnette enjoyed participating in. Sleeping in her own bed while doing a show was a big plus instead of a strange bed in some distant hotel. Being able to drive just a few blocks in her own town to a show site was also a benefit.

Vonnette grabbed her show jewelry and a packed lunch of tuna and lettuce then headed for the front door. Keys in hand she turned on the alarm, opened the door and said out loud, "Bye babies. I'll be home soon. Be good. I love you." Her normal farewell to her two, four legged feline friends as she closed the door behind her and headed for the car.

Reaching her destination took a mere five minutes. Pulling the car up along the sidewalk next to the same spot that had been hers for three years, Vonnette smiled as she looked at the hustle and bustle already going on. Artists were in process of setting up their booth displays before the opening time of ten. While climbing out of her carefully packed car, Vonnette said hi to three crafters around her. Normally the show was held on the first weekend in September after Labor Day. This year it had been postponed twice due to bad weather making this the final outdoor show of the year for Vonnette.

Fine art and craft shows are normally held on weekends. Some are three days; most are two and rarely, some shows are only one day. "Setting up for a one day show is such hard work," Vonnette thought, as she opened the hatch back of her car. Often artists could set up their booths a day before the show began. This meant that if the show ran Friday, Saturday and Sunday, set up would on Thursday. That turned a three-day show into four days for the vendors. However, being able to set up a day early meant artists could keep their energy up during show hours for the following three days. On the flip-side, there was another day of travel time, hotel fees, meals, and so on. Today was Saturday and all artists had to set up the morning of the show. By the end of the day all artists would be tired and ready for down time both physically as well as mentally. Everyone here today looked bright eyed for six-thirty a.m. as the sun was beginning to shine. All vendors appeared hopeful this show would produce good sales.

Often Vonnette told clients she was like a circus person traveling from town to town with a tent and wares for sale. Educating people about artists and shows was part of her purpose. Most attendees assumed tents were provided and put up by the show promoters. Almost all artists had their own tents, came to set it up, decorate them, and then put out their art for sale. Taking up to five hours to set a booth up along with their artwork in order to be open for business, Vonnette felt information given could only help the public understand what an artist did in an effort to make sales. As all this ran through her mind, Vonnette began to grab the top items from the back of her car and lean them along the side for when she was ready to make use of them. Energetically, she felt thankful she was able to pack her car yesterday and not have to deal with packing it this morning.

Quietly and methodically, Vonnette went about setting up her little 10 x 10' store for today and tomorrow. Taking hold of the bag housing a ten by fourteen-foot blue plastic tarp, she pulled it into the daylight and spread it out on the grass where her space corners were marked off with white paint. The tarp helped lay a flattish foundation for her display tables as well as to keep dampness away. After the tarp came an outdoor rug. Next was the tent. Unfolding that from the center of the rug and making many trips around the four corners of the *EZ UP,* she was eventually able to get it open.

Lifting each tent leg up one notch, the canopy was still low enough for her to easily attach the four tent side curtains to the trusses with Velcro loops. They would become the exterior tent walls for the weekend. Each corner leg would then be raised a couple more notches at a time. By doing so, Vonnette made certain her tent never leaned too far into another artist's tent. Running from one corner leg to another, she did raise the tent to its full extension. Giving herself a silent pat on the back each time she succeeded in getting that not-so-easy tent up, she went back to bring the rest of her display gear out of the car.

Once she emptied the car, she moved it to the very back of the parking lot. Her jewelry was always in sight during set up and breakdown of a show. Since it was the final part of her set up, she kept it hidden yet near her at all times even while transporting the car from one spot to another; today that was a parking lot. Nervous about thieves, some show promoters offered her security coming and going to her car. That was not necessary this day as the parking lot was a stone's throw away from all vendors where everyone could easily see and hear any such scuffle activity from robbers. Gathering the jewelry and her lunch, she locked the car and headed back to her booth. Among show vendors, courteous behavior was to unload any vehicle quickly and then move it to make way for other artists to park and unload their items.

One by one she opened each bag she had put in or just outside her tent to place in specific positions. Sketching and changing her booth layout was something Vonnette did regularly. Once she arrived at the show all bets could be off, though. If the ground under her tent was uneven, the showcases needed to be at a different angle than when level. Today she was fortunate enough to have fairly even ground underfoot. Show cases could go in a straight line. Once the rectangular, collapsible, free-standing table legs were unfolded and placed approximately where she felt they ought to go, Vonnette pulled out the two tabletops that fit snugly over the end posts of the legs. Next came the case corners that snapped into place on the tabletops. Eventually these formed into four Lucite and glass display cases. Two 10 x 10 x 20 inch Lucite display cases were then pulled out of their carrying bags, the bubble wrap protecting them from scratches was removed as she set them up in between the other cases. Being taller, these cases stood out and brought definition to the whole jewelry store image Vonnette went for. Fabric clipped to the outer legs of the display tables gave more definition to the over-all booth look. Light blue curtains went up on the two inner side walls of the tent. Private space near the back of the tent was then created by placing a third row of curtains about two feet forward from the actual back wall of the tent.

Her traveling showroom having been formed, Vonnette took the empty carrying bags and placed them on Christmas wreath hooks in that private back area. She hung concrete weights formed inside wide PVC pipe from all four corners of the tent trusses. Stakes went into each tent leg and the grass. Outdoor ground screws for dog leashes went in just outside her four tent corners. Connecting each of the top tent corners to one ground screw with a Bungee Cord, she hoped it would not only keep her tent in place in case of high winds, but also stop her tent from blowing over and destroying any another artists' tents or wares.

Finished with tent security Vonnette began the last part of her set up, placing jewelry on neck and ring forms that went inside each of the now six display cases. Laying out her jewelry had become a pattern. Moonstones went in the far-right case. Rose quartz was on the left side of the same case. Continuing towards the left came the pearl display, and they took over the top and bottom shelves of that Lucite case. Sapphires, chrysoprase, chrysocolla and lapis went into the next low display. Amethyst, plain gold and lemon citrine went to the left in another low case. Shell and beach stone pieces were chosen to be in the second, tall Lucite display case today and last was the ruby, diamond, and opal low case. There was more than enough inventory for a show; actually, *too* much to display all at once, so sometimes she hid items in the back areas of each locked display case. These items could easily be accessed if someone should ask after something not on display in the front, yet each piece was still under lock and key. Coin jewelry went to the back today and would be used to fill in, when items sold, *if* jewelry sold.

Vonnette was creative and prolific when it came to making jewelry. It was a gift she'd had since childhood. Why her parents didn't see it was a mystery. Anytime she had jewelry in her hands she treated it as if it was gold whether it was costume or real gold jewelry. Revering her grandmothers' costume jewelry was an early childhood memory. Sitting on the floor behind an overstuffed chair she figured out how a piece could be taken apart and shifted for a new look. Those early moments formulated the current designs she called *detachables* where earring drops are removable, pendants can be worn on chains or beads, and pins could double as clasps. All this made each one of her creations more flexible for whomever purchased one or many pieces.

More childhood inspiration came from trips to the beach. After collecting scallop shells, she would carefully wash, let dry, and varnish each one, to maintain any of their natural bright colors. Attaching her mothers' kitchen string to the shells completed each necklace. Her cousin lived on a busy street a few blocks away. On hot summer days Vonnette took her shell necklaces over to sell off a card table while her cousin sold lemonade on another table. Huge sixteen-wheel truck drivers almost jackknifed their rigs in an effort to pull over to buy lemonade and shell necklaces from two young entrepreneurs. It was a gift to create something of adornment. Hooked at a young age creating and selling her wares, Vonnette knew making jewelry had to be in her life forever.

There were times when she didn't actually remember making a whole piece of jewelry. It felt as though some other force stepped into her body and worked through her hands and eyes to form magic. Magic was partly what people craved from Vonnette. Mindful that she, and she alone did not make each piece of jewelry, Vonnette was careful not to get caught up in the compliments people most often fed her.

While placing gold shell necklaces inside her case today, she chuckled and flashed back to that childhood roadside stand realizing she had not come so far after all. Amazingly, she was still selling shell necklaces by the side of the road, the shells today were made of gold and were formed by hand. Some gold shell pieces even had precious stones and pearls alongside. Indeed, her designs and skills had grown since those childhood days.

Finishing the jewelry layout, Vonnette carefully placed small pieces of printed computer paper in front of jewelry groupings. Each blurb was different from another. *Decipher what is important with Lapis. Ruby stimulates the kundalini. Moonstone connects to lunar & feminine energy.* These were all shortened versions of her channeled, stone-healing definitions. They gave enough information for people to feel they had new knowledge. Something they could walk away with as a gift even if they didn't buy something from Vonnette at this show.

Ready to be open for business, Vonnette wiped down her showcases with a cloth dampened with Windex. Today could be a day like any other in one artist's life, but for Vonnette it was a day where she met destiny.

Even for local shows Vonnette sent out postcards two weeks in advance to inform regular clients she would be at a certain place on such and such dates. Never sure they would come to buy, she still proceeded with this ritual. If they didn't come, or came and didn't buy, the card reminded them she was still making jewelry.

Today could be interesting. Sophie Belle was a possible new client who called a week ago. Though she did not ask why or say anything about it over the phone, Vonnette thought it was interesting Sophie Belle had made the phone call and not her fiancé. Usually the man made the initial call and appointment for an engagement ring. The female might be brought in later if necessary. Granted, dealing with the male part of an engaged couple was a bit old fashioned; interestingly, it was still a widely accepted practice in the jewelry world.

During the initial phone interview Sophie mentioned seeing a ring created for her friend by Vonnette. The uniqueness of the ring stood out along with the fact that it had been specifically made for this woman. Sophie felt that was the only way to go with an expensive ring that held as much meaning as an engagement ring.

Agreeing, Vonnette suggested they meet at this show. Most of her creations would be set up. Sophie could have an overall view of designs along with possible stone choices. Vonnette would schedule another appointment later for them to sit down with loose stones so final decisions could be made unless she found something she wanted among the finished inventory. Everything was handmade, so no matter what she might find already finished, each piece would be unique and special.

First meetings for Vonnette were a good indication of just who the clients were, and their showing up on time was definitely a good sign. At ten o'clock, a man and woman walked towards her booth. As they reached her space, Vonnette noticed the woman specifically. Her eyes were wide open, welcoming, and she had a wall-to-wall grin on her face.

Quietly Vonnette said, "Hi, you must be Sophie?"

"Yes, and you are, Vonnette?"

Nodding was exchanged when suddenly the man standing behind Sophie stepped out into the forefront with an extended hand claiming he was Jackson.

Hands shaken all around, Vonnette felt disturbed by the length of Jackson's handshake. His hand was soft and warm. One could almost call it gentle and inviting. Vonnette's hands had calluses, bruises and cuts from her work, so when she felt a softer hand, she made mental note.

Motioning for them to have a look at the showcases filled with her wares, Vonnette kept her mind focused on Sophie while pretending to be unaware of how Jackson focused on her, not his fiancé. Thoughts like "he ought to be tuned into Sophie, not me" crept into her mind. If he was going to be troublesome, then why wasn't her set up difficult this morning? Usually, when the day was going to be a challenge with clients, there would be problems setting up the tent. Today, everything had gone along smoothly.

Sophie broke Vonnette's inner trance and said, "I can see this is going to be more interesting than I had originally thought. This seems magical." Looking outside the tent momentarily distracted, she eyed the rows of other vendor tents and asked if this show had been a yearly thing that she had never heard of until now. Accustomed to people asking this very question at every show, Vonnette told her it had been going on for at least twelve years and that unless she was accustomed to attending fine art and craft shows, it was unlikely she would've noticed any advertisement on such.

Focused back inside the cases again Sophie read some of the papers listing stone properties. Stopping in front of the dark blue sapphire note she read it out loud: "*Sapphire gives the third eye permission to open*. That sounds interesting and like something I could use. Maybe that's the stone I should have in my engagement ring. What's your opinion of using a sapphire in an everyday ring? And; the third eye is connected to intuition, right?"

In a steady, honed tone she used when in work mode, Vonnette began her answer, "Yes, the third eye is associated with intuition, and sapphire is one of my favorite stones for engagement rings. In Mohs scale of hardness, one through ten, it registers in at a nine. Sapphires come in almost all colors from clear to black. The deep blue you are looking at right now is the most widely known, accepted, and appreciated color. Interestingly, sapphire and ruby are the same mineral, corundum. Only the really red color is called ruby though. The pink is sometimes called ruby, but in fact it's considered a sapphire. If you choose a deep blue sapphire as a center stone, I like to then flank it with round white diamonds. One or more on each side looks nice depending upon the size of the center stone and whatever you might want as a band to sit next to it.

"Sometimes I design from the engagement ring on out. Sometimes I do the reverse. People have particular ideas of how they will wear their rings. Some folks opt to wear their bands 100% of the time and engagement rings only when they go out socially. If that's the case, then it's important that the band stands on its own merit. If you intend to wear the two rings together most of the time, then

I begin with the engagement ring and figure the band design out as we go along."

"This is more involved than I thought, but I'm interested in whatever you have as input. Already I like the idea that the stones involved have specific meaning. In the long run that actually makes the ring more important to me. So, what's the next step?"

Glancing slightly in Jackson's direction and only momentarily, Vonnette began, "First we discuss money. Most jewelers calculate the price of an engagement ring to cost three months of a groom's salary. I feel the price of the ring ought to be something you don't have to go into hock over. Rather, it should be one-of-a-kind, catered to the individual and reflect the price you are both comfortable with."

Afraid to linger her gaze, Vonnette looked briefly at Jackson again and then quickly back at Sophie. "Once we have a price range, I can go further into what might work best for you . . ."

Interrupting, Sophie leaned back into Jackson a bit and spoke up so he didn't have to open his mouth. "We figured $15,000- with a band. Is that enough?"

"Yes, that's doable. Now, let's discuss shapes of stones. Do you like round stones? Would you rather an oval, pear, or somewhat of a square center stone maybe?"

"I hadn't thought, but now that you ask, round is very appealing to me."

"Would you like one diamond on each side? That is a very traditional look." Questions came forth in a very practiced fashion as Vonnette had asked the same one's countless times over the course of her thirty-two years in business.

"Well, what might you suggest?"

Looking Sophie over, Vonnette noticed she had on jewelry that did not match. Her gold earrings were smallish with a bit of a delicate dangling silver tip. One ring on an index finger had a peace sign incorporated in it. Around her neck was something that looked almost as if a child had made it. Clothing was a bit off as well. Her bright pink, fitted, silk chiffon top was a button-down blouse and then she had on beige, loose fitting gauzy shorts. After gathering information visually, Vonnette then offered, "You have a slightly quirky manner about you. Perhaps we ought to make the engagement ring a bit asymmetric. Place a good size diamond on one side of an even larger sapphire, then have two smaller different size diamonds on the other side."

Both clients smiled at this statement and had a bit of an *ah ha* acknowledgement twinkle appear in their eyes while slightly nodding their heads.

Vonnette looked them both over and felt something in her gut when her eyes met his for that brief second. Inwardly, she told herself to stop whatever she was feeling and get back to business. Besides, he was the fiancé for God's sake! Maybe Jackson was one of those men that hung in the background while his lady talked. Then, when least expected he would slowly, succinctly, move into the foreground and slide an arm about the lady next to him as a sign of possession. No matter what, his disarming manner threw Vonnette a bit askew. Feeling certain he was a man who could fool around on his mate, this concept became even more apparent to her as the three of them talked. Jackson continued to be more focused on Vonnette than on Sophie. Concentrating specifically on the woman in front of her, Vonnette opted not to be lured into this man's aura no matter how electrifying it felt. This was not her first time around the block with men like this. It was Sophie Belle's choice to be with this kind of man, not Vonnette's.

Inside her head Vonnette repeated, "Stay focused; *stay focused!* You can work on two brain levels at once just as you do on your morning walks with prayers and REM messages."

She listened to Sophie and began to describe possible designs. The distracting energy from Jackson took her physical self into a third arena much like the vibrational force from a vacuum cleaner that once switched on can't help but shake the floorboards under it. Vonnette felt like one of those floorboards right now, inwardly shaking with no known end or shut-off switch in sight.

How could he have his arm about Sophie and be giving off such vibes to Vonnette? Those feelings and questions could only lead to disaster. Giving into chemistry where one person's aura overlaps another's had been trouble for Vonnette in the past. Not only was this not the right time or place, but he was taken!

Brought back from her floating emotional state with a crash, Vonnette heard this man say something out loud. Not that Jackson wasn't saying quite enough silently, thank you very much, now he had to speak verbally, too? Both faces opposite her lit up like children on Christmas morning as they became more aware of one another's presence. Or maybe it was excitement over the obvious connection Vonnette had made with the ring design. They were laughing. What had he just said?

Shaking her brain lose she heard his words in a five second delay, "I think I just met the woman I want to run away with," he said casually as if his words meant nothing to Vonnette while he looked straight at her!

Vonnette stared at him blankly. Inside her head she heard her best friend Cally say, "Yup, you've still got it. Stick Vonnette in a crowded room and every old man and at least one married one will flirt in hopes of it leading further!"

Hearing Cally actually helped. Vonnette's unwilling smile was now under control as she said, "Yes, shall we focus on the task at hand?" Letting go of those flip-flop gut feelings, she grabbed hold of the edge of her display table. It wasn't attached to the ground but acted as a stabilizing force for the moment.

Centering in on Sophie again Vonnettte asked if she had been thinking about what kind of ring she wanted. Did anything so far described suit her design needs? Sophie shrugged and said she couldn't get her friend's ring out of her mind. "Would you really want the same ring style as what a close friend has?"

Sophie's response came slowly as she rolled the thought around in her mind. "I'mmmm not sure I'd want the *exact* same thing, but I did really like it."

"First, I do repeat designs. I cannot make anything exact as long as it's hand made. The most common way to repeat a design is to do a cast method where a mold is made of an original. On occasion, I do work by casting. Normally though, each creation I make is formed one at a time. That's so I can feel the design develop both for you, and for me."

"Yes, I like that idea! Having it be one-of-a-kind is a great thing for us both I think." Excitedly, Sophie began to hold out her left hand as if to picture a ring on the third finger.

Realizing what Sophie was thinking Vonnette suggested, "We have a way to go here Sophie. You are interested in a blue sapphire with diamonds as the engagement ring. I will make the ring asymmetric with three different size diamonds, which gives us a concept, but we need a more specific design for the ring."

"What would you suggest? You had such a good idea with the stones. Can you keep guessing at what I might like for a design, too?"

Scrunching up her face a bit while scrutinizing Sophie more closely, Vonnette went through ideas in her head before answering. "First, I need to ask you a couple of questions. Think about what I ask and then answer me please." Not waiting for a response Vonnette dove in. "What do you do with your hands both at work and at play? Do you like narrow or wide rings or even rings that taper to be narrow in the back? Do you maybe want a couple colors of gold in this design?"

Focusing on the questions Sophie's eyes slowly went in concentric circles before any words came forth. "Well, let me think. I play tennis. I like to sail. Cooking is only something I do because I have to. For work, I am in an office and sit at a computer all day. What rings I have now are thin bands. So, I am unsure if I want a wide ring or not. The idea of different colors of gold had not crossed my mind until you just mentioned it. Where does that leave us?"

Almost before Sophie was finished speaking, Vonnette leapt back in with her concepts. "You have a flair for the unusual but are actually a bit conservative deep inside, so I think we ought to make your rings mainly of yellow gold. Tennis and sailing activities make me think 14 would be the best karat for durability. Diamonds for this piece can either be in white gold or platinum. Platinum is the stronger of those two choices as well as being the most expensive. But, when used for stones and not the whole ring, pricing can be very doable. The stones need to be mounted a bit low so as to not get caught in rigging while sailing or playing tennis. That is, if you wear the rings while you are doing those activities. Honestly, that would be more comfortable for you when you wear gloves in the winter anyway. Perhaps the bottom of the rings' outer edges ought to be straight and of semi-rounded yellow gold. Whereas, the top of the ring will be focused on the center stone. I can make the top flare out on one side, kind of like a half moon shape. Inside the half-moon will be the sapphire. Right next to the sapphire I can place one larger diamond. On the other side of the sapphire I will place the two diamonds of different sizes, one slightly up and one down from the center stone. Then I can overlay another color gold, maybe white, or pink, in a wave-like pattern that will go completely around the ring. When you look straight down at the ring from the top, you'll notice that on the opposite side of the half-moon shape, there will be an invisible straight edge created from the stone line-up. That means a straight, or flat, outer edged band can easily rest next to the engagement ring.

"The band can have a few small diamonds and sapphires mounted asymmetrically, but flush with the surface of the metal. That will give a bit of a repeat element to the wave pattern without actually duplicating it. This should not be wide, maybe five millimeters I think. The engagement ring will then sit flush on either side of the band. In other words, you do not have to match the engagement ring up to the band before replacing them on your finger when you take them off at the end of the day, or for washing your hands, or whatever. The two rings will work well together, but with two straight edges on the band, you can comfortably wear it alone if you want.

"If I made the band so that it followed the other edge that has the half-moon, you would have to either be careful each time you replace the rings on your hand, or tac solder the bottoms of the rings together. That would mean you could not wear either of the rings alone.

"That said, I think we could also make a plain band, too. Maybe three millimeters wide so when you choose not to wear the engagement ring, you will still feel as if you have one ring on containing stones and then a plain band together. Having three rings you can wear them all at the same time as a stack, each one separately, or two at a time. Being able to mix and match everyday rings such as engagement and wedding bands I find gives you options, a variety if you will."

During this rather rapid speech Vonnette was creating what she called chicken scratch sketches on a white piece of paper. She drew the engagement ring, the stone band, and then the plain band. While staring at the paper she didn't see the faces of the couple standing in front of her as she spoke and sketched, but after she finished with her explanation and sketches, she realized there was no sound. Glancing up, the look on Sophie's face caught her off guard; it had turned a bit colorless. Even Jackson looked a bit ashen as he dropped the possessive shoulder grip he'd had on Sophie. Both their mouths were open slightly as if time had struck them momentarily dumb. Eye contact with Vonnette broke the moment.

Sophie nodded and began to speak slowly. "Yyyeeess, yes, . . . that sounds like me and great. That's why I'm here. You come highly recommended as a woman who sees what will work on people. Your reputation for psychic powers proceeds . . ." Not finishing her sentence, and suddenly back into normal speech, Sophie turned slightly to Jackson and asked excitedly, "Isn't she great?" Without allowing time for or expecting a response, Sophie turned back to Vonnette with, "What else do you know about me? Are you reading my mind right now? How do you do that? Am I giving off a particular energy that you can see? Gosh what gifts you have!"

"Here we go again," Vonnette thought. "I have gifts. These gifts are normal everyday knowledge. Yes, I'm different. Some say I'm special in that 'Oh she's *special*' kind of way." Seeing spirits and having pre-cognitive dreams along with understanding the healing powers of stones is not for everyone. Even seeing designs around stones was not something that every goldsmith could do, so yes, being able to connect with what people desired for jewelry designs was one of her unique talents. Perhaps some of it was her ability to read people's minds. Maybe it was straight-up observation. Still, there were people who acted as though all of these were some sort of mystical powers.

Many years back Vonnette had consulted a palmist during a visit to New Orleans. He had told her a few things about her past when she stopped him and said, "I'm not someone that needs you to prove your gift or powers by what you see that happened to me as a child. Instead, please tell me what specific lines on my palm mean. I've never been able to find certain lines listed in palmistry books." Pointing down she asked about a couple lines in particular.

The palmist was more interested in the star formations on the heel of her palms that overlapped into the center arena. It seemed those stars meant she could read people's minds. He was sure she already knew that fact.

Vonnette nodded and said, "Yes, in fact I do, do that with people I'm around consistently. Maybe that's why some of my boyfriends have gone running and screaming out of reach over the years. That certainly explained how my mother and I could have half conversations and still know what each other was talking about."

With stars on her palms and the ability to read minds, Vonnette never felt she did anything other than pay attention when she sketched designs for clients. "Why do people have to label everything? I mean, if you pay a little attention each and every day, then wouldn't we all have the same knowledge?" she wondered.

Coming back into the present moment and putting her hand up slightly as if to stop an oncoming vehicle, Vonnette interjected, "Before you get into some hocus pocus concept, let me say I have had my business for over thirty years. Part of what I do comes from experience. Some part of all this is a gift. I must have nailed your desires. If not, you wouldn't be so quick to label my artistry as psychic."

Jackson still had an odd color to his face since he'd seen the completed sketch. He opened his mouth as if to say something when Sophie cut him off again before he could speak.

Unsure of what was going on between them, Vonnette dismissed it as a couples' little nuance.

"You are the person I want to make these rings, very much so. I've heard about you over a couple of years now. Some people call you 'The Stone Whisperer.' When I was proposed to, I knew right off that I needed to come see you."

Vonnette smiled, feeling complimented until Sophie continued, "It's just that you have a way with jewelry. Everyone I know that has a piece of yours cherishes it so much! They all say you have psychic powers and can tell what kind of jewelry someone ought to have! Here, today, you have proven that fact. I stand in awe of your talent. And, I don't even have a creation in front of me yet. Your words and sketches come through with such connection!"

Surprised, and caught slightly off guard Vonnette took a moment to respond when Jackson finally got control of his voice and spoke first. "Sophie, I don't think it's a good idea for you to push this kind of hearsay onto Vonnette. We came here for a specific reason. You need to concentrate on that task, don't you?"

In some odd way, he was standing up for Vonnette. Something that was not a normal experience. As he spoke, Vonnette's stomach flopped again, and she noticed for the first time that Jackson was actually a bit older than Sophie. Not that that was a bad thing, or for that matter anything unusual. It's just that somehow after her phone conversation with Sophie, she'd thought they would be closer in age. Maybe that's why he was not giving any real input as to what the ring design might be. Maybe he felt this was her thing and was willing to go along with whatever her decision was. But why did Vonnette feel the way she did physically? He was attractive to her. Standing about five inches taller than Sophie, Vonnette guessed he would be about five foot eleven. His wavy dark hair with piercing, steel blue eyes made Vonnette's heart pound as it did whenever she fell in love. With that emotion, she had gone a bit off her professional game. Determined not to let whatever was happening inside get the better of her, Vonnette focused again on the two people in front of her as she heard Sophie trying to defend herself.

"Please know I didn't come here to offend you, Vonnette. You must be aware of what people say about you?" Her words came with a sheepish facial expression.

"Oh, you're not saying anything I haven't heard before." Vonnette offered in a matter-of-fact dismissal way. "I feel we all have gifts. One of mine is to be able to see how you are presenting yourself today both with clothing and jewelry. Toss in the answers to my questions on what you do with your hands, stir in the concept that we all want a bit of flash with an engagement ring and there you have it! It's nothing really other than observation and years of experience. Parts of what I do are experience. Maybe some of what I do is a gift," Vonnette said while looking at both of her guests, "*However* . . . we need to concentrate on what you are here for, engagement and wedding rings."

"Yes, that's my point exactly! That's why I am here, for rings that you have a great impact on not only because you make them but also because you make them so special with your other talents of psychic energy!"

Moaning in disbelief at this last statement, Jackson rolled his eyes and stepped backward slightly. Bringing his hand up to rub his eyes in frustration, he seemed at a loss for words and looked suddenly very uncomfortable.

Deciding she needed to put an end to all this talk, Vonnette had to think quickly. She knew what people thought and said about her. Yes, she could read people well enough when it came to designing jewelry. Psychic energy or not it was something she wouldn't get into in great depth with new clients. Thoughts of how we've come a long way from burning witches at the stake and yet we still have not come far enough not to label people raced through her head. Clearly, this woman was proof of that.

Instead of going wherever Sophie was heading, Vonnette began, "What we are discussing is very important. I understand you want my input on multiple levels. That's fine with me. Let's continue with the bands. I will take down all your information, name, address, phone number, finger size as well as the width and length between the knuckle and the webbing on your left-hand ring finger. I'll take these measurements into consideration with overall width of stones and gold for comfort in your finished piece. Next, I will go in search of stones that match up in color, and size for our discussed concepts and your price range. Once I have stones in for you to look at, I will give you a call for us to meet up again.

"I'm on a very tight show schedule at this very moment. Hope you are okay with my waiting until I have a block of time to look for your stones in a calm manner. You told me no date has been set as yet for your wedding. That suggests to me that you are okay waiting for the ring with such meaning to be finished and on your finger. We will readdress the design issue when we next meet to look at stones. You see, sometimes when stones are in front of you, the design shifts, so we'll finalize all that when we have stones you like.

"I will get started as time becomes available. Usually in your price range and choice of center stone, I like to get Pai Lin sapphires. They are the best available today. Round white diamonds will set off the main stone very nicely, and I'm sure you will be happy with your choice. For diamonds in a ring that is worn daily, I tend to choose VS1 to SI1 quality. That means they have either a very slight imperfection not visible to the naked eye or have slight imperfections still not likely anything you can see without magnification. Color quality for the diamonds I choose will depend upon the blue tone of the sapphire. Also, I will get smaller stones to fit well into your band idea. By selecting all stones at the same time, they will match in color. When it's time for you both to choose from the stones I select, we will firm up the design concepts.

"What we haven't spoken of yet is what Jackson would like for his band. Or if he wants one at all? If you would like a band, and maybe one with stones in it, now is the time to tell. Speak up!"

Almost leaping forward Sophie excitedly exclaimed, "My fiancé doesn't want a band, at least he doesn't want one yet."

Aware of other people milling about the booth, Vonnette,

Sophie and Jackson moved slightly to the right of the tent interior to let others have a better view of the jewelry on display. Vonnette wrote down the pertinent information on a sales slip, thankful that Sophie was the contact name and phone number given. The less exchange she had with Jackson the better. Since they were not choosing anything today to purchase, there was no need for a deposit of any kind. She tried to dismiss them from her selling arena for now when Sophie began again.

"Please, I hope you understand I did not mean to offend. I wanted to come to you because of your gifts. You displayed them so perfectly with me today. I mean, you even get that the thought of wearing an engagement ring twenty-four-seven is not who I am at all. Having options such as a plain band, a stone band, along with an engagement ring is fabulous! I am very pleased with your suggestions and look forward to your finished design work so very much!"

While nodding in total disbelief Vonnette watched as Jackson placed an arm about Sophie's waist while pulling her out of the booth. Turning and smiling Jackson calmly said, "Thank you for your time and valuable input. We will wait for your call. Good luck with the rest of your show. We are leaving now."

Vonnette watched this couple walk away from her booth wondering what that was all about. Sincerely, why on earth would such a couple be in her face that way this day? Why would they be getting married? Maybe on some level he was committed to her, but on some other level he clearly was not!

People milled about the show throughout the day. Most were happy enough to come close without entering the tent. Some did come in for a closer look.

"Scrumptious! That's what your pieces are, scrumptious! You have a real gift."

Smiling at the stranger, Vonnette watched her walk away from the front of her booth. The woman seemed uplifted as she left. It was interesting how many people left in a better mood as opposed to how they were when they arrived at her display area. People could call it a "Storefront," especially if they had played that game as a child.

While picturing an over-sized cardboard box with the word STORE written near the top, Vonnette reflected on her own childhood. The box was a bit larger than the size of a 1950's refrigerator. A three-sided square shape cut out functioned as the selling counter in that makeshift storefront. The folded down cardboard had something placed underneath to act as support. Only small children could comfortably stand at that counter. Canned goods nicked from household pantries along with empty boxes of cereal like *Cocoa Puffs,* or *Sugar Pops* were piled up behind the sales counter on a small table stolen from somewhere in the house. Vonnette and her neighbor friends used to shop and count out change for one another as they took turns being the shopkeeper or customer.

In her fifties now, Vonnette welcomed people into her ten-by-ten foot traveling storefront. Looking about she thought that in a way the booth set up today was even similar to the one she played at as a child. Her overhead sign read, "Goldsmith" instead of store, and a countertop was created from the display cases not from cardboard. She stood or sat behind these cases waiting for people to come and look over what she had for sale. Although items for sale were different today, she was still playing the same childhood game. Wondering to herself she spoke slightly under her breath. "We play house, doctor, and store as children. Is it possible we have everything mapped out even before birth, and what we play at as a child is what our adult lives actually become? Or perhaps child play is the groundwork for us not to take life so seriously."

Blankly staring out into the small group of people touring the show, Vonnette muttered while shaking her head as if to rattle herself back into reality, "I am alone entirely too much!"

Vonnette smiled at her next possible client, one she hoped might buy a finished piece from the cases in her booth. For over seventeen years she designed and created custom, one-of-a-kind jewelry from a physical storefront in Newport. Clients couldn't understand her reasoning when she closed the store and began traveling and participating in shows. Truth was, she had to spend too much time inside heads other than her own to create those individual designs. Perhaps all that connected to the star shapes on her hands the palmist had told Vonnette about years back. She had to reach inside a clients' head when they first came in to discuss what jewelry they might be looking for. Later, while choosing stones she would have to be back inside their heads. A third time came when showing stones to those clients. Creating the actual piece was the fourth. And a fifth time came about when the piece was delivered to make sure it was actually what her clients wanted. Being inside another person's head this much was exhausting both physically and emotionally. Vonnette wanted people to buy the creations bubbling forth from inside her own head now.

Cally had asked Vonnette once why on earth she was letting go of her staple, money-making work of custom designs. Being her best friend, she wanted to lend support while she felt Vonnette was soooo good at custom work! After Vonnette explained how many times she had to climb inside someone else's head, Cally understood. Explaining that situation to friends was one thing. Conveying the need to step away from custom work was not something Vonnette shared with clients. If they wanted a special design she could, and most likely would, still make it for them. One thing was certain, Vonnette was exhausted from all her years of doing custom designs. Today proved that point. The main source of income from this show might be from the custom job she could eventually create for Sophie Belle. She was already exhausted from talking to them today about their possible design order.

Occasionally during the day, Vonnette pulled jewelry from a locked display case for someone to try on to look at more closely. Long moments when no lookers were in her booth brought reflections of childhood choices that tumbled over into modern day along with her stone choice for the day. Red garnet aligns the lumbar region of the body while balancing iron in the blood stream. Lavender jade offers comfort in a harsh environment. Sophie and Jackson shook her support system and created a harsh emotional environment. Thankfully, the stones she chose to wear today had helped thus far.

People who knew her work began coming through the show. They admired it and bought! Though sales seemed to be on the smaller side of riches, enough sales happened to make the day worthwhile for sure. At least the items she sold she had chosen to make from inside her own head. Mud in a dream usually indicated money. Her mud dream had come to fruition. And the fact that she did not have to pay for a hotel room at this show gave the sales more of a financial oomph.

Regulars stopped by. These were people whom she had either made jewelry for in the past or who had bought finished pieces from the showcases and had repeated business with her at some time or other. Vonnette felt that once people became clients, those people would always be clients. Even when those people stopped in for a visit without making a new purchase, she enjoyed seeing them.

"Great to see you. Are you enjoying the last piece you bought? Oh, how nice that you wore a piece of mine today. You know, seeing something I created after it left home is similar to when a child comes home from college. It's wonderful to see them, but you're also happy to have them return on their new path of being away from home. Speaking of which, what are your children doing these days? Where have you been on vacation lately? Sorry to hear of your recent illness, operation, or loss. Glad to see you again and hope you enjoy the show. There are some wonderfully talented people here this year." Conversations such as these gave Vonnette an opportunity to share and to remain connected with her repeat customers.

Two such clients presently in her booth had bought a few items over the course of a couple of years. Normal pleasantries were exchanged when it became obvious they wanted to talk about something other than jewelry.

"Our daughter is living with a man quite a bit younger than she in Colorado. I believe I've mentioned that to you in the past," came the first indication from Sarah as to where todays conversation would lead.

Nodding in agreement Vonnette felt no need for words yet.

Looking toward her husband for support Sarah continued, "Well, we were wondering if perhaps with all your talents and gifts you could give us input as to how we might get them away from one another?"

Eyes widening and blinking in disbelief, Vonnette took a mini step backwards feeling the sudden need to be out of energy range of these two people. Brows furrowed, Vonnette tilted her head slightly to the right as if she was going to give an emphatic "No." Then, as her mind began to shift, Vonnette spoke slowly in order to hold their attention. "This is not my field of expertise."

Since Sarah was about to interrupt, Vonnette put her hand up in what seemed to be her stop sign for the day. "What I need to ask is why on earth you would think to come to ask me for this kind of assistance?"

Waving her hand in the air slightly as if swatting an invisible fly, she continued. "On second thought, never mind, I don't want to know. Do you feel your daughter is in some form of physical or emotional danger being with this young man?"

Obvious concern began to sculpt new lines on Robert's fairly smooth face. "Sorry Vonnette for coming and interrupting your show. We received your postcard for the event and thought you might be able to give some valuable input on how to handle this relationship that seems to be draining our daughter. This young man is very controlling and doesn't like it when Holly comes home to visit us. He feels it takes him awhile to get her back in line after she returns to him. At least that's what she's told us. That, along with how she seems so tired when we see her makes us feel this man is not good for her. Maybe you can't do anything. It was a thought that came up over coffee this morning after Holly left to head back to this guy. Our hearts are breaking as we watch our lovely daughter sink deeper and deeper and then further away from the bright star we've always seen her to be. That might be parental prejudice talking, but you've met her, and somehow, she's just sinking. We don't know what to do."

Sarah spoke, but Vonnette didn't really listen. Once people discovered Vonnette's investment in metaphysics they often thought she would be able to magically turn things around in their lives somehow. Maybe they gave her too much credit for her supposed talents. Maybe they were looking for a port in the storm. Maybe they needed to say things out loud to someone who wouldn't judge them and knew she was a good listener. Vonnette decided she would give them a tool for providing safety for their beloved daughter, but that would be it. Once there was a break in conversation, Vonnette dove in to share her idea, and as she did, she imparted more than one tool with them. She was in the end, a sensitive and an empath. Vonnette had not learned how not to lend a hand when possible.

While handing a piece of paper and pen over to the couple she said, "I'm going to give you a great tool that could make a difference. Write it down and see. If nothing happens after doing this for, say, two weeks, then you need to move onto either accepting this relationship or going to some form of a counselor." Not waiting for their response, Vonnette began. "Picture your daughter bathed in white light. White light is pure energy. Once you *really* visualize that, then put flexible mirrors all around that white light that face outwards. In other words, it's as if you've placed a Mylar balloon around that white light facing out towards other people. Fully visualize that and then say . . . 'Spirits go before Holly, make her way safe, perfect, and clear. Please don't let anything I consider even remotely negative come near her this perfect day, (name the date) under Grace and in Divine right perfect and healthy ways' . . . . You can both do this each day for a two-week period. It doesn't matter if you do this exercise together or separately.

"Some feel this method of utilizing mirrors outside the white light keeps out the good as well as the bad. If you feel that way, then picture the mirror element as if silver sparkles are sprinkled all around the exterior of the white light you've pictured. This type of sparkling flexible net is a terrific form of protection. And, this is a sincere call for Divine protection. The white light specifically, I mean. The mirror element is to reflect negative energy back at whatever may be coming at Holly at any given time. I especially do this before I leave town to do a show and want to make sure I arrive safely. I'm suggesting a two-week spell to see if two things happen. One, that Holly is safe and that she has some time to think clearly on her own about where she wants her life to go. The other part is for the two of you to find a space where you feel peaceful about Holly being protected, *and* for you both to calm down about where Holly might be heading in life."

"But how will that get rid of this boy slash man?" Came Sarah's plea trying to enlist Vonnette in the plight to save her daughter.

Distress was beginning to play havoc on Sarah's face as well as her husband's. Being a young, fifty-year old woman who had a great figure and wonderful, flowing black hair that went down the middle of her back, Sarah was accustomed to having people assist her in whatever her need was at any given moment. Claiming she didn't know how to do anything, Sarah generally never even had to ask for assistance; people simply offered their help. Sarah's husband Robert was out of town often for work and appreciated any assistance Sarah received from those in their close circle. This was not the first time Vonnette had been enlisted to give Sarah help. However, it was the first time she had been asked to do something so unrelated to her own career. Getting rid of someone was not part of Vonnette's normal skillset and not something she ever hoped to be asked to do again. Feeling this couple's emotional pain, Vonnette thought she might be able to give input that could provide some form of relief from their present emotional struggle.

"I cannot help you with that, Sarah. Honestly, I don't believe anyone can or should help you get rid of the boy. My belief is that if the universe shows Holly this boy is not part of her correct path, then she needs to be the one to take action. Don't you realize that we all have contracts in this life while here on the earth plane? Perhaps these two have come together for a specific reason."

"Yes, to kill my daughter!" Popped out of Sarah's mouth spontaneously. Both Vonnette and Robert looked at her but opted to dismiss this outburst as concern. Hysterics wouldn't solve anything at this time other than to provide more drama to an already stressful situation.

"Here's the deal. You both know I believe in the energy of stones, but there's nothing in the stone world that can act as a deterrent in a situation such as this. My feeling is that the more you put up roadblocks for the two of them the more you will drive these young people closer together. I'm sure you have already surmised that. You ought not try to put a wedge between them with criticism because that simply reflects on the two of you. It will also attract criticism from others, including Holly. My suggestion is, rather, to see if in some way you can embrace them together."

There was a momentary look of horror on both faces across from Vonnette along with visible gasps for air.

"Just give me a minute here. By being normal with them both you may show Holly he is not who she really wants. And I mean show her by example and support, not by judgment. What you are looking for today from me is some form of magic or witch's spell to make them fall out of love with one another. There's nothing I can do on that front for you. I would strongly suggest you do not pursue any of that line of thinking either. In my opinion we each have lessons to learn by coming into the physical body. Why we have certain experiences and how we learn from those experiences help us each develop into and become who we are as an adult. And that all contributes to our individuality."

The anxiety displayed on their faces seemed frozen in place. Desire for these people to have something else to ponder when they left her booth made Vonnette continue. "Often when people give actual physical gifts it triggers emotional reactions. That reaction resonates on some plane that needs to be looked at and/or addressed. Maybe the gift-giver heard a claim of a specific need. Maybe that gift provided an opportunity to heal an age-old wound. Perhaps the giver knew instinctively of something the receiver never even voiced interest in and yet was fantastic. The giver as well as the physical gift can then become special. You see, whatever the reason the physical gift causes an affect becomes another opportunity for inner growth.

"Seemingly, the opposite is also true here, Sarah. Say your

emotional buttons get pushed by another; ironically, that person can provide great gifts, too. Will you accept what someone says to you as truth? Will you change because of what someone said? Will you recognize that person as a bully, one that as a child held you hostage but as an adult you now have different emotional tools with which to cope? Tools that help you respond differently today. In other words, Holly needs to decide if this man is a gift of great love . . . or a gift for higher learning.

"I've learned wonderful things from loves that ended for one reason or another. Of course, at the time I felt I would never get over the emotional hurt. When I did I thanked that person in prayer for adding a new facet to my existence.

"One relationship in particular for me was like an old coin I thought I lost through a hole in my pocket. When I least expected it, that coin would reappear in my pocket. Figuratively, this man found a way to get back through the emotional hole I had. It was up to me to sew that hole up to stop him from ever finding his way back once I was completely finished with my lessons from him.

"So, in all this you may have to sit back and wait for your daughter to discover how this man fits into her development. As painful as it can be, you would have it no other way if the shoe was on the other foot. Maybe you lived with someone while you were young. Did your parents feel about him as you both feel about Holly's lover now? Trust your parenting skills and hope she will learn and grow well. If he is physically abusing her that would be another matter altogether! Mental abuse is also difficult. Only the individual involved can put a stop to any of it though be it alone or through the help of others."

Realizing the couple was actually listening, Vonnette carried on: "While you came here today ostensibly to discuss your daughter, I need to point out that you both have a great opportunity for personal growth, too."

They looked at one another quizzically, then back to Vonnette. They had been so stressed out when they came into her booth, but now were standing before her simply dumbstruck.

"Perhaps you each have control issues. Maybe you haven't learned to trust your daughter's ability to make good choices in her life. However you might view this circumstance, it's an opportunity for you both to trust your skills. You've given to your daughter what you know how to give and most directly, unconditional love! Show your support now unconditionally. See if that doesn't open up a new doorway for her.

"One thing you might try to shift this energy of great concern is to send Holly an actual gift every so often that has sentimental meaning, like family Christmas ornaments. I mean, her name *is* Holly. She'll connect with them emotionally. This man might see that as a threat and try to turn her sentiment around somehow. All that gives her more opportunities to see him through different colored glasses. You might find something that sparks a really good memory around the house as you clean one day, Sarah. A time shared when you and your daughter had such fun that it is sure to spark a fond memory for her as well. Send that off and tell her it's to remind her of good family times as she creates her new family. That'll show her you are respecting her choice to move on but with a sound base from your life shared.

"Whatever you do in gift giving please make sure it is something that comes from the heart and is not something sent out of manipulation. If you do that she'll see through you and a wedge could be driven that may not ever be fully repaired between you.

"Speaking about gift giving . . . a person who is abusive usually gives gifts out of guilt. That's where your gift giving can shine a light into Holly's world. You'll help her to see the difference between a gift shared from the heart and one given either from guilt or need for control. In the meantime, you both have to shift your parenting style to one of support instead of guidance. She has opted to take the lead in pursuing an independent life. If and when she needs you to lean on, she'll ask. Until then, I've given you a great tool to work with. Here's the thing . . . the angels in heaven hear a mother's prayers before most others. Surrounding your daughter with white light is very powerful and has the pure energy of love. I'll repeat, the mirrors facing outwards are to help keep out unwanted energy, to have negative energy bounce off the mirror and go back at the giver. It might seem simple, but it's actually an intense visualization technique. When you add in, *Spirits go before her, make her way safe perfect and clear, please don't let anything even remotely negative happen to Holly on this perfect day under grace and in divine right healthful ways*, you are adding prayer into the equation of visualization. Honestly, you cannot get much better than that! You can even picture Holly having fun with work colleagues. Picturing her happy with others can be powerful, too. And . . . when you focus on the positive with your visions, you will be seeing Holly's life as half-full, instead of half-empty. That will always be a good thing to concentrate on no matter what and can help create something positive in her life. You know what they say, 'Like attracts like.' In this case, you'll be looking at positives and focusing on that side for Holly. She can, and most likely will, follow suit into an optimistic life.

"Please let me add one more element to this scenario. Only use the mirror part for a week or two at the most. Here's why: white light is powerful and filled with love. Mirrors can and do keep some stuff away. For that reason alone, you must only use the mirrors for a short time. Continue then with your prayers by simply using white light.

"With everything we've spoken of here today, you have new tools for your parenting skill set. And remember, it's never about the destination. It's always about the journey. Holly has begun her passage in a life of free will. As parents, your job is still to guide but in a new, open arm way. No matter how you look at it, you all are on a new course in life's lessons. How you choose to step forward is up to each of you!"

Apologies for having interrupted her show were exchanged and accepted along with farewell hugs. As this couple was leaving, Vonnette made mental note that their physical bodies had relaxed a bit from when they first entered her selling arena.

People reach out to other people in times of crisis. Obviously for Sarah and Robert, this was a time of crisis. Certain they were feeling incapable of protecting their daughter, Vonnette was hopeful she had provided a new tool to use as parents this day. What they did with this energy was up to them. How they carried it forward was also up to them and part of their learning experiences while here on this planet.

After Sarah and Robert had completely left her booth, Vonnette drank some water and sat for a moment to collect herself and reconnect with the energy of the show. Though deep in thought, she noticed another of her repeat clients approaching her booth. It was Abigail. Standing up as she came closer, Vonnette smiled in greeting. The two women reached across the display cases to touch hands hello while asking how they each were?

Abigail had a very effervescent personality and was in her mid-twenties. Her shining, light brown hair was always trying to do its own thing much to the chagrin of Abby. Being a chef on large yachts with unruly hair could be an issue when you were supposed to be among the barely seen, and not heard, society.

"I haven't seen you in about a year I think Abby, right?"

"That sounds correct. Listen, I'm so glad you don't have anyone in your booth just now. Goodness knows I don't want to interrupt a sale, but I wanted to touch base about something we spoke of last year."

"What, pray tell, was that?" Vonnette asked. "Seems you and I get off the beaten track every time we connect. In a good way!"

"You mentioned to use something in the shower when I felt overrun by life. Try as I might, I cannot recall how it all went. Obviously, I didn't follow through with your suggestion at the time. Otherwise, I would recall it now. Do you mind telling me again please?"

"I don't mind telling you again, Abby, if it can help. I'm sorry to hear you are feeling life has been overwhelming and/or bombarding of late." Without waiting for or in need of a response Vonnette dove in. "Get yourself some apple cider vinegar. It doesn't matter if it's from the health food store or the grocery store. Sometimes it's in plastic bottles, sometimes in glass. If in plastic I take the whole bottle into the shower with me. If it's glass and it drops while you're in the shower, you've put yourself into a bad position. So, if it's glass get a plastic spray bottle similar to what you use to spritz your ironing or plants. You can even get that at the dollar store. Fill it up with the cider vinegar and take that into the shower. Wet yourself down and spritz the vinegar head to toe. Rinse off with clear water while saying, *Please remove any and all negativity within or on this body at this time and allow me to continue moving forward into the light where I belong under Grace and in Divine right healthful ways.* After a few days of doing that shower regime, you should feel a shift happening: it may be emotional, it may be physical, or even both. The shift can also be about the way other people respond to you. You will feel the change, though. Most people who do this tell me it begins to happen within three days. Each time I do it, it's different timing. Everyone asks how long they ought to do it for? In general, I suggest to do it until you begin to forget to do it, which should happen after about a week. Two weeks, maybe, if you are really under some emotional rock."

"It's so simple. I'm surprised I didn't recall the procedure. Sorry," came Abby's contemplative response as she wrote all the information down.

"Abby, there is no right or wrong way when doing something like this with vinegar. The main thing is to always rinse off with clean water afterwards and ask for everything to happen in healthful ways.

"I read somewhere a long time ago about a woman who kept praying and asking over and over to gain a certain amount of money by such and such a date to pay her creditors. She then had a bad car accident and received money from the insurance. The problem there was she forgot to ask for the financial help to come in from divine right and healthful ways. So, please, please make sure you always ask for things to happen in divine right and healthful ways!

"If you are more of a bath person instead of one who takes showers, then pour some vinegar into the tub. No need to measure. Still rinse off with clean water after a soak. If you don't, you're defeating the purpose which is to cleanse off your auric field. Most likely I explained all this before, but in case you don't recall, your auric field is the space and energy found directly outside your body. It's electromagnetic energy that usually has different colors depending upon your emotions and/or how you're feeling towards life each day. Sometimes holes develop in our auric fields when we are bombarded by life. Using the apple cider vinegar for some reason not only cleanses the auric field but also repairs holes in it. Don't ask me how or why, I simply know it works.

"Sincerely, I usually have a bottle in my shower in readiness for the next time I feel life is handing me too much. After I wash my hair I often open the bottle and pour some over my head. Don't worry about it possibly damaging your hair; it's actually good for it. But again, rinse off saying what I gave you. It also puts a stop to any of what I call vampire energy."

"Not sure if you could call it vampire energy. Lately I have had numerous people in my face gossiping. There have been many moments in my life where I have joined in quite heartily, but this past year I have tried to stop myself from gossiping. I don't know; maybe what I think of as gossip could just be people venting. Would you call that vampire energy?"

"No, not at all. Vampire energy concerns someone who wants more and more of your time and energy. Normally they keep asking for your help with something and then won't take advice on how to stop whatever, or make shifts in their lives. If they did, they would be taking responsibility for whatever is occurring in their world. Somehow they want you to take their responsibility on. You'd feel the difference in vampire energy compared to what you're experiencing because you'd feel drained energetically as if that other person is sucking the life out of you as they continuously ask for you to help them with something or other all while knowing they won't take any help you offer. They just want *you* to give and give. They take and take.

"Anyway, as I said, this is not what you're describing to me. Gossip is gossip. Sometimes it's out of concern for the party or parties involved in whatever conversation. Usually though, it's meant to make the presenting person feel better about themselves. At least that has been my experience.

"Interestingly enough, both situations can be made better by rebuilding your auric field and taking apple cider vinegar showers to help you remove whatever gunk you're carrying off it. Once you are finished with the apple cider vinegar showers or baths, give me a quick call. We can go over everything again because there is a great stone combination that can work towards the end you are looking for."

"I have a pen and paper here now if you have the time to tell me about the stones. Really, I would appreciate it so much. This has been eating away at me lately, so any help would be greatly accepted."

"Okay. To learn the difference between gossip and simple conversation . . . wear amazonite. When you comprehend what you as well as others are doing while engrossed in conversation be it gossip or not, switch over to gray pearls and blue chalcedony. This combination helps you to process and air verbally in a new and healthful way with a shield of protection. One thing that is vital at this juncture is to ask yourself, 'What is it I am supposed to learn from this experience?' Usually an answer will pop into your head soon after asking for guidance."

"I don't have the stones you are talking about. Hope you don't hate me Vonnette, but this is the only reason I came to the show today. I'm not shopping. There was a list in the paper of participating artists for the event and I saw your name. That's when it hit me that I ought to run over to ask for your advice once more. Hopefully this time I will get the message and the cleansing I need. When I finish the apple cider process, I'll give you a call. We can figure out a way for me to get the stones I need to end the gossip. Love you. You're the best!" came Abby's voice as she ran away from the booth waving and throwing air kisses.

An elderly couple entered the booth. They looked at a cuff bracelet made with labradorite and blue topaz in 18Ky gold. It was obvious to Vonnette they had been married for many years by the way they physically related to one another. It was familiar, kind, knowing and secure. Like a comfy pair of sweats that you know cover and even flatter your bodily flaws. Guessing they were maybe in their early seventies, Vonnette waited to see if they'd go for the bracelet today.

The wife commented on her appreciation for the bracelet but claimed it was too fancy for her present lifestyle. One thing lead to another and they asked to see a pair of earrings. She next moved onto a necklace that had rose quartz beads with a matching stone drop mounted in 14K pink gold. Apparently, clasps were difficult for her as her husband moved over to assist without being asked. A confirmation head nod over to Vonnette completed that thought. While pulling out his cheater glasses he remarked, "I am the clasp fastener in our house." With her head bent slightly so he could see more easily what he was doing, his wife chuckled. Once done, they both moved over to the mirror Vonnette was holding up. Both parties took in the view of it about her neck.

Somehow this still wasn't what the wife was looking for. The necklace came off as she glanced again into the display cases. "Can I try on this ring over here please?" she asked pointing to a beach stone ring with a black pearl set off to one side.

Handing it over the counter, Vonnette described the ring. "This is a beach stone I found out at Sachuest Point where the waves roll all the stones smooth. When I go out to the point, I comb the low tide shore. The black spiders come out to patrol their territory and keep a watchful eye on invaders like me. They duck for cover as my feet crunch the stones, hoping I won't be the cause of their last moment in time. It never ceases to amaze me how Mother Nature changes our shoreline twice daily with the tide. What magnificent power she has in her belly. Being an artist, I see this as creativity in its finest.

"The ocean lure has gone on since time began. It's fortunate I live here so I can visit her regularly to recharge energetically as well as artistically. I love collecting stones that are either white quartz, or this darker, very rich black stone I have named 'triple black.' Making jewelry with gold and these stones is so unexpected. The beauty of wearing something like this is that there's already a worn surface, so it can be knocked about a bit without worry of damage. Along one side of the beach stone is a black saltwater pearl. Black on black is such a classic! Making a ring asymmetric is a passion of mine. You can wear the ring facing in one direction and then turn it around for a different look. Also, by making it asymmetric you know it is hand-made and not one of a thousand out there somewhere. Combining something like a beach stone with a pearl is fun, don't you think?"

Not waiting for an answer Vonnette went on talking about the ring. "The gold is a combination of white and yellow. The smaller dots sprinkled about the beach stone are in 22Ky gold to give a nice contrast to both the pearl and the beach stone. To me, these gold dots represent the spray from the waves as they hit the shore. They're almost like air bubbles, only in gold."

Momentarily, Vonnette had lost herself in her storytelling going on well beyond what these possible clients might want or need to know, yet there she was in her own world once again.

The wife smiled up at Vonnette and then held her hand out for her husband to view. When she did so, the ring rolled a bit off to the side as it was obviously too large for that finger. The man asked Vonnette, "Is this something that can be altered if we decide?"

Nodding a "yes" Vonnette left them to look at the ring and talk together.

"What size would you think she ought to have?" he asked while still holding onto the under part of his wife's hand making sure the ring did not drop to the ground.

"Shame on you!" Vonnette said in an almost scolding teach-er-like manner. "There is no reason on this earth for you not to know your wife's ring size. I bet you don't know her shoe or dress size either, do you?"

There was no sound from either of them as they glanced at one another. She displayed hope. His face hinted at an admission of ignorance and guilt by scrunching his nose up a bit.

Without waiting for them to respond verbally, Vonnette added, "Well, discoveries are made all the time. Please realize that your wife knows all these things about you."

A tell-tale nod came from the wife along with a knowing smile. Embarrassed, the husband looked sheepishly at his wife and then back at Vonnette.

Vonnette tried to cool down the hornets' nest she had stirred up a moment ago. "This is easily remedied. You can have a great time discovering all these things about your life mate. It can be a game. Go into her closet to find clothes and shoe sizes. Pay attention, though, as we women have a bad habit of shifting dress sizes rather quickly. We also hold onto older clothes in hopes of being able to fit back into them really soon. My suggestion is to always choose a piece of clothing you know you've seen your wife wear recently. Do the same with shoes. Please realize you need to do all this when she doesn't know you are doing it. If it's not done in secret, then the wonderment at the time of gift giving is lost.

"When it comes to discovering your wife's ring size, you can do a couple of things. For one, you can ask me to size her right now and then place that in your memory bank. The other way is to take a ring of hers you know fits, place it on one of your fingers and remember where it stopped. Say it stops here on your pinkie knuckle." Motioning to the top knuckle of her own left pinkie, Vonnette formed an invisible circle with her right index finger. "Just remember that spot and when you find a ring that you want to buy for your wife, ask the attendant to size that spot on your hand. Chances are good you are going to be very close if not exact!"

Vonnette was always surprised at how little men knew about their wives' sizes. Yet wives knew everything about sizes for their man.

While still admiring the ring on her finger, the wife began removing it claiming she didn't like her hands with all the arthritis-shaped knuckles. As she handed it back over the counter to Vonnette, she looked a bit sad.

"Women in this country are so tough on themselves, be it their weight, wrinkles, or the knobs on their hands!" Clearly this woman wanted something today in the way of jewelry. Becoming animated, Vonnette continued, "Personally, I don't understand where this came from. We need to pay attention and get rid of the lack of confidence we women have! One thing to keep in mind is this; when you wear a statement ring like this on your finger, people notice your ring, not your hand, or your arthritis. By the same token, when wearing clothing made of a beautiful color in a great fabric that is flattering to your skin tone, people compliment that choice. No one notices if it's too tight in certain places. They remember the outfit, color, fabric and how flattering it was. Over all the years I have made jewelry women have complained the most about their hands. My suggestion is for you to wear a great ring and then wave your hand about during conversation. Watch as people stare at the ring traveling through the air. It's as if you are about to do a magic trick. If you think of being a maestro, then the experience can be very entertaining. So, if your arthritis is holding you back, I say don't let it! Wear whatever rings you want and draw attention to the rings. Start having fun with your jewelry again!"

Fearing that she came off too dictatorial, Vonnette thought there was need for some levity at this juncture, so she began to go for it. Looking at the husband Vonnette said, "I'm sure you know all the hot spots on your wife's body when it comes to intimacy."

Both parties on the other side of the display cases turned beet red. Vonnette loved it when she knew she had a client's undivided attention. Talk about sex in an unexpected place and time and everyone will stop to listen.

"Well. Now you simply need to expand that knowledge a bit to know what works *on* her body in the way of clothing and jewelry. You are in the perfect place for learning the latter!" Vonnette expressed as her hands and arms opened wide showcasing her wares for sale. "I am a goldsmith who loves to create fine jewelry that can be worn in different ways. Most of my pendants are removable from the beads they are displayed on, so they may be worn on a chain, another strand of beads, or even a silk cord. Many of my earring drops detach for different looks. Pins can often become clasps with the right strand of beads. I love it when I can make something versatile for my clients. If something goes a bit out of style, or you change your look around with, say, a new haircut, you can then shift my jewelry designs to accommodate that as well. Which means you won't get bored with my jewelry. You also get the best bang out of any dollar spent with me."

Realizing their delight in her fun conversation, Vonnette pushed a bit further. "One thing I love to do with a couple in your age group is to show the wife what will happen when I do one thing." Grabbing a long strand of light green, 5mm, fresh-water button pearls out of a case she walked around the other side of the display to lay the strand over the woman's head. She let the strand lay down against this woman's jersey for only a moment before taking what was now the bottom end of the thirty-two-inch strand of pearls in hand. Vonnette then pulled the ladies jersey out slightly at the neckline with her left-hand index finger and tossed the end of the pearls inside with her other hand.

It all happened so fast the woman had no idea what to expect. Giggling over the coolness of the pearls, she shook slightly which made the strand go straight down.

Noticing the husband's complete attention focused on the strand of pearls that had disappeared inside his wife's clothing, Vonnette chuckled and said, "So there you have it. Men love it when a woman has a bit of mystery about her. After many years of marriage there is much you still have to discover. Right now, it's a form of playfulness." Facing the husband Vonnette asked, "Where exactly does that strand of pearls end under that jersey? That's what you want to know. But the fun is guessing where they end. Am I right?"

Nodding but not diverting his eyes from his wife's jersey, the man couldn't believe how in a split second this conversation had taken such a turn. Currently at a loss for words, it was the wife who took over verbally. "Well, didn't we learn some new things today? This has been the most fun we've had in some time. Who knew coming to an art show would provide such an experience? I think we can take this strand of pearls if you don't mind."

Giggling, the woman slowly and purposely removed the pearls from inside her jersey, tantalizing her husband.

He grabbed hold of his heart region with his right hand and buckled his knees a bit to continue with the playfulness happening between them.

Laughing outwardly, Vonnette took the pearls and wrapped

them up for the couple glad she had realized they were fun enough to handle such a moment with her and her jewelry designs. As she wrapped she thought, "Reading people might be one of my gifts. If only I could read people into higher priced jewelry instead of lower priced each and every time I did a show, then I would be a happy camper with all of my supposed gifts!"

Breaking the moment, she now said out loud, "I'm going to give you some additional information on pearls."

Noticing how the husband was suddenly all ears, she knew he was thinking something was about to be said that referenced sex again.

"Over many years I've had quite a few different experiences with pearls and how people have certain misconceptions. Once, a woman brought me a strand of pearls in a jar of olive oil."

The look on each person's face was questionable.

"When I asked her why the olive oil? Her answer was that since the pearls would not be on her person, they needed to be coated with oil to remain lustrous. In fact, she almost ruined her pearls by doing such a thing. I had to clean the pearls in a strong solution as soon as possible to get rid of that oil and then give them a firm rinse in clean warm water. Thankfully, it was during the wintertime. My radiators were on. Placing the pearls on top of the radiator on a clean cloth towel dried them from the inside out before I restrung them. Don't fret, I knew just how long to leave them on the radiator. Left too long on there and they could have been destroyed! That woman had a good train of thought but an incorrect carry through. You see, pearls do get more lustrous from wearing them against the skin while receiving natural human oils. When they are off the skin, they ought to be in a nice room temperature environment, not in anything that could chemically alter the color or texture. Since we are discussing it, please do not place your pearls on a radiator at home. I'm a professional and know how to treat stones and pearls.

"While I have your attention on care, let me also say that you ought not ever wear your pearls in water, such as when swimming or taking a shower. Another woman came to me who wore her pearls in the shower certain that since pearls came from water, they needed to be in water all the time to remain nice. The water was actually rotting those pearls from the inside out.

"Pearls do come from water but most importantly, they come from *inside* the protective element of a mollusk. Once they are removed from that protective shell organism, they need to be away from water. Pearls that are drilled through the center to be strung are made weaker with that drilling. Usually the cord they are strung on is silk, but they can be strung on nylon, too. No matter what, if the cord gets wet and doesn't have a chance to dry quickly it rots, as does the pearl from the inside out. So, what I am saying is this: do not wear your pearls in the shower or while swimming. Do not place your pearls in olive or any kind of oil when not in use or while waiting to be restrung. Also, please spray your perfume and hairspray above or below where your pearls will lay and do that before your pearls go on your body. Hope I don't sound like a tyrant. I simply want you to enjoy your pearls for a long time to come, okay?"

"I'm grateful for the information. Doubt I would have thought of placing my pearls in olive oil, but I might have thought water wouldn't harm them. All in all, I think what you've just shared was good for me, especially about my perfume."

"Well, the chemicals found in perfume can be harmful to the pearl and its luster; whereas, the oil from your body adds to the luster. That makes for a win, win situation for pearls. I even place perfume well above the wrist region in case I decide to wear a pearl bracelet during the day. Happy to know my information didn't fall on deaf ears."

Turning slightly, Vonnette focused specifically on the husband. "Speaking of ears . . . I'm sorry to disappoint you, kind sir. I feel you were hoping I was going to share another sex reference before you left." His face turned a bit red as he waved his hand in a motion of dismissal.

Vonnette chuckled and added, "Perhaps not knowing when and where your lovely other half is going to wear this new strand of pearls will fill that desire for more."

Everyone laughed knowing Vonnette was correct.

"As I stated earlier about my pieces being worn in different ways, let me suggest what else can be done with this strand of pearls. It's long enough that you can double the strand and wear it more as a choker, or, you can wrap it about your wrist to be a bracelet if you like.

"I'm a bit spoiled since I'm in the business and have multiple strands of pearls. Being able to toss one about the neck and another one on my wrist suits me on certain days. Let me show you how this clasp works in case you want to do any of the things I've suggested."

Specifically showing the husband how the clasp worked as he was, the self-proclaimed fastener in the family. He informed Vonnette he had worked with one of these types of clasps before on another necklace his wife had at home.

After paying for their purchase, the couple left hand-in-hand. Vonnette took note that they were like two teenagers as they walked away.

She wasn't alone in her booth long when a familiar face came in with a short bob hairstyle. It was Lucy Mae. This woman was about the same age as Vonnette. Mainly, she came to try on earrings that would display below her hairline to draw attention to her wonderfully long and slender neck. Knowing her penchant for earrings, Vonnette began to look in her cases to see what was made that Lucy might like.

Lucy saw Vonnette begin a search and knowing what she was looking for, waved her hand at Vonnette in a no fashion. "Sorry Vonnette. Earrings are not my point of interest today. It's rather this ring." Lucy Mae held up a gold ring that had been squished almost in half.

Lucy handed the ring over the counter. With one quick glance, Vonnette could see that this was an older ring, not only due to the style but also from the wear of the now thin shank. Amazed the gold had not split in two from being bent so, she glanced over to Lucy's hands to see if there had been any damage from the ring being obviously jammed in such a way.

Realizing where her eyes had gone, Lucy enlightened her. "No, this didn't hurt my finger when it happened. It was during the night while I was asleep actually. When John's mom passed a few months back this ring was part of her legacy. The thing is, both times I've worn the ring this has happened and I have no idea how. The first night I took it off before I crawled into bed. It was across the room on top of the bureau. When I got up in the morning it looked like this. The family was all in Philadelphia for the funeral. Not wanting John to know it had happened, I took it into a local jeweler there who straightened it out for me on some metal stick thing."

"Yes, that's called a mandrel."

"Okay. Anyway, he did make it round again claiming that since the back of the ring was thin, he was able to shift it back into shape slowly, carefully. While looking the ring over, he asked me if perhaps I slammed it somehow in a car door."

"Interestingly enough, that's what I thought when I laid eyes upon it just now, that you had gotten your hand caught in a car door and the ring went wonky." Vonnette added.

"Well, that idea would make sense but no, as I said, this misshaping thing happened the first time during the night while it was sitting on the bureau. I put it away after that jeweler made it round and only pulled it back out this week to wear to a dinner thing. This time it went weird while I was asleep and it was on my finger!

"You know, if my finger was damaged in some way when I woke I would naturally think it was my fault, but here it is all bent up and nothing is wrong with my finger. I can't figure it out. This time though, I almost couldn't get it off my finger due to the odd shape. With some ice and good soap, it did eventually come off.

"I'm wondering if there is something I need to do to make it more secure? Would you consider fixing it for me? Maybe the back of the ring needs reinforcing on some level."

"Lucy, far be it for me to step on toes here, but it's apparent your mother-in-law doesn't want you to have this ring. That's why it keeps happening during the night. That's when she visits."

"No. Seriously? Do you think that's possible? Really?"

"Yes, I'm quite serious. The saying goes, 'You can't take it with you', but here's the thing - there are times when material objects can be controlled by a spirit after they have left this plane, and this seems to be one of those times. Doubt you want to hear this Lucy, but I think you need to do some energy clearing in order to keep the ring."

"That could explain it. Honestly, she didn't leave the ring to me. She left it to her niece, but Anne hates green. Anne knew I loved the ring. I commented on it so many times while my mother-in-law wore it and she recalled those lovely comments. After the will was read where she got the ring and I got a simple strand of white pearls, we traded. Anne will get a lot of use out of the pearls. I already have two strands so didn't need another. We were each happy with the trade.

"I can't believe you picked up on that whole scenario! It never occurred to me that it was John's mother coming in to destroy the ring rather than let me enjoy it! What can I do?"

"I'll tell you what, I'll take the ring, carefully straighten it out and make certain there are no cracks from being bent like this twice. While I have it, I'll see if perhaps it can be cleansed of her energy. If the energy doesn't want to let go, then I might suggest you do another trade of some sort. But, before we go there, let me see if I can do what's necessary first."

"Gosh Vonnette, that'd be great! I very much appreciate your help with this. Sincerely, I've always loved and admired this ring and would hate to give it up."

"You might need to if she has such a hold on it that I cannot get it clear. I'm guessing you and she didn't like one another?"

"I liked her, but she never thought I was right for John. She was forever bringing old love interests into the house when we went for visits. He didn't catch on but I did. Once, I tried to explain what she was doing. John thought I was making things up, that it was simply a small town where everyone knew one another and that was the reason these other women were being invited over. I knew better, though. Sad, but true.

"I had hoped that once we had our children she would get over whatever. She did love our kids; I'll give her that, but she never warmed up to me. Such a shame as I always looked out for her health, even from a distance. Guess she liked me as a nurse but not as a match for John. Oh, well, her loss."

"You and John have been a good match. At least every time I see you together you appear to have a really good connection. So, yes, I think it was her loss. In the meantime, let me see what I can do for you and the ring. I'll give you a call when it's done. My schedule is a bit crazy. Hope it's okay that it won't be right away?"

"Yes, that's fine. Knowing where it is, is good enough for me at this moment. Thanks for your input. I began to think I was losing my mind with this happening twice. As I said, the first time it happened, I didn't tell John. I simply found that jeweler and got the ring straightened out. When it squished again, this time while on my finger and in need of immediate attention to remove it, John thought I had done something to it, so his feelings became disjointed. Wait till I tell him his mother is doing this crazy thing to the ring!"

"If I were you, I wouldn't suggest that, Lucy. You know, mothers and sons have a special bond. If he thinks his mother didn't want you to have the ring, he might cringe every time you wear it. Best continue to say you have no idea how this has happened. Then, let's see if the energy can be cleared to the point where it won't happen again, okay?"

"Okay. That actually makes sense. I'll follow your guidance here and see. Appreciate all your input and efforts in advance. Then, if we can get this all worked out properly, I'd like to get a pair of earrings made to go with the ring in some manner. I'll wait to hear from you on all fronts. Thanks."

Vonnette wrote up a sales slip about the ring repair, handed it over, and waved bye to Lucy.

While wrapping the ring up in tissue paper and putting it safely away she shook her head at the ring and said, "Don't try any shenanigans with me, Mom! I've got your number and know how to deal." Amazed the vibrant green tourmaline, or any of the tiny surrounding diamonds had not fallen out or been broken from having the mounting bent so, Vonnette placed the ring alone behind one of the neck forms on display. It was as secure as she could keep it until home from the show later that night where she would lock it up inside the safe.

⁂

About an hour before closing time a woman showed up in the booth dressed casually with a simple pair of trousers and decent, but casual shoes on. Nothing stood out on this woman in particular. If she'd made an effort, she could be quite attractive. For whatever reason, no effort was made. After taking a quick purveyance of the display cases she asked, "Do you do custom work?"

"It depends totally on what it is you are looking for in the way of design. And, if you have stones for me to work with or not."

From inside her purse, she pulled out a small, black, drawstring fabric pouch. Opening that up she removed a well-worn simple gold ring with a red stone in the center. While glancing down at it, she smiled a little and then handed it over to Vonnette. "One of the prongs has broken so obviously, I need that fixed. I'm also wondering about changing the style of mounting at the same time because the back of the ring is so worn."

While the woman considered what style mount she might have in mind for a new ring, Vonnette took the opportunity for a closer look. Reaching underneath the display cases for a ten-power jewelers loupe while having the ring in full view of the possible new client, Vonnette pulled the loupe up to her right eye while closing her left. Bringing the ring up close to the loupe until it came into full focus, she was able to see the stone clearly. Feeling she had the information necessary, Vonnette began. "This is an imitation ruby mounted in 14 karat yellow gold. If you want me to remount this because of sentimental reasons, I am happy to do so. I have done so many times in the past for other people. Let's face it, most of the time there is a monetary value to jewelry but sentiment is the true value."

While Vonnette spoke, the woman standing across from her began to twitch. After maybe a full minute she was able to speak. Quite upset, she began to speak louder than necessary. "But it can't be imitation! This was my grandmother's engagement ring. She left it to me in her will. I know it's real. You are mistaken!"

Taking in a slow breath to give them both a moment to collect thoughts as well as emotions, Vonnette spoke in a low voice. Actually, it was almost a whisper. Sometimes when she spoke softly and a client spoke loudly, they would come upon common middle ground.

"When your grandmother was young, gold was twenty-six dollars an ounce. It was the depression. People often had to choose between a ring made out of plated metal that would eventually turn their finger green or buy a genuine gemstone. Most people opted to go for real gold with an imitation stone. Plans would be to have the synthetic stone replaced later when money became available. If children came along, money had to go in that direction instead. Time wears on. Sentiment along with finances most likely kept the ring as it was in the beginning, and then it got passed on down. I'm sure the sentimentality of the ring carried on throughout the years. Your grandmother most likely thought only of that, not the monetary value. In all the years of my being in business, I've had this kind of thing happen numerous times. I could be wrong; this is only a ten-power loupe, not a gem scope. But as I've already stated, I will remount the stone for you if you would like since it does hold such sentiment."

With that last statement, the woman grabbed the ring out of Vonnette's hand, placed it back in the black pouch, yanked the drawstring taught and then placed the pouch into her handbag. Anger had her face in a knot as she turned and flew out of the booth and away from the show without another word spoken.

Shaking her head, Vonnette had no time to consider what else she might have said to that woman to have her not leave in such a mood because as that woman left her booth one of Vonnette's favorite clients approached her. Grace was a petite, five-foot woman with bright purple hair and an energetic personality to match. Over the years this wonderful woman had come into Vonnette's storefront as well as attend her shows. There would never be a dull moment when Grace came for a visit no matter how short or long.

"Grace, how great to see you! Think it's been about six months or so since our last go-round?"

"Maybe, maybe. Not for lack of thinking of you, though. Always get my husband going when he knows I am about to visit you. It's good for his mental health. It makes him stretch."

Outwardly laughing, Vonnette stood waiting for whatever was going to come next.

"He likes to tell our friends how you send me notes in the mail. He calls them love notes and claims he has never heard of a jeweler sending cards the way you do."

"Thank you notes are important to me, Grace. Most likely he knows that."

"Oh yes, he just enjoys having something to joke about. Joe is forever telling me he's never heard of anyone having their own private jeweler before me. I just tell him he's lucky! Seriously, most people have their own doctor on call. I have my jeweler on call. For me it's a win-win situation. For him it's also a win because he never wants for gift ideas. Seriously, I wear everything you've made for me. Don't believe in putting something away in a safe deposit box as you well know. My family had most of these gemstones tucked away in a safe for years. Inheriting them and having you make them all into pieces of jewelry I wear and enjoy each and every day makes me happy, and helps me remember my family fondly." Her hands were now flashing about with four large, multiple stone rings, and she then reached for her neckline where a three-stone pendant hung off a white gold chain. "We believe these stones came from debts that were somehow settled with stones instead of money during the depression. You made the single earring collection my dad had into that great flower pin arrangement for me back when I was still working at the hospital. Remember?"

Nodding, Vonnette did recall the grouping of earrings she had placed together that had various sizes and kinds of precious stones. Grace wanted them grouped together in some manner, so she could wear them more often. None of the earrings were a match to one another. Many of them had small diamonds in some form of surround to a center stone. By creating an interwoven basket of gold, Vonnette was able to attach the earrings coming up and out of the basket. Once finished, it looked like a flower arrangement. The new cluster pin did make a statement and became quite a conversation piece, even more so after she lost it once.

That was the first time a client had shown Vonnette the power of praying to Saint Anthony. Vonnette was raised in a Congregational church. Though she was aware of teachings on angels, the concept of praying to angels or saints had never occurred to her.

One day Grace thought she had fully clasped the flower-basket pin when in fact she had not. It was on the lapel of her suit when she got up from her work desk to hike to a meeting. While carrying a lot of paperwork in her folded arms, she walked a common staff route through a basement corridor. After her meeting ended, Grace gathered up her paperwork and stood to leave. Who knows why, but she reached to touch her pin only to discover it was no longer on her suit. Figuring it had come off by getting caught in all her paperwork, instead of panicking, she began the prayer . . . *St. Anthony, St. Anthony, please come down. Something is lost and can't be found. Please bring my flower-basket pin 'round.* Repeating that prayer as she retraced her steps, she had hopes of, but sadly had no luck in, finding the cherished pin.

Over the next two days Grace kept repeating the prayer. One thought kept running through her head and that was to contact the custodian. A quick note was sent off to him describing the pin and its sentimental value to her. Unfortunately, he had not seen it. Shortly after that, she gave up on ever seeing the pin again.

A week later the custodian knocked on her office door. Some nice gentleman walking in the same basement corridor noticed something shining when he went up the stairwell. Stopping and retrieving it from under the stairs, he realized it was a pin that was marked as being gold. Taking it to the custodians' office he discovered it belonged to one of the hospital staff. At that point the man turned it over to the custodian for delivery to the unknown woman. Grace had her pin back; she felt it was due to her prayers to Saint Anthony.

Leaving work that night she noticed signage that there was a celebration in Saint Anthony's name being held at a church near her home. Feeling the need to pass along a good deed she stopped into the church and made a donation.

As a matter of fact, that was not the only time Saint Anthony had come to the lost jewelry rescue for Grace. Shortly after Vonnette had made up a ring combining two slightly different sized white diamonds, set on either side of one big yellow sapphire where all stones were mounted in yellow gold, the largest center stone went missing. That yellow sapphire had a deep-belly cut, and the manner in which it was mounted with two diamonds flanking it, it looked like a canary diamond. While volunteering at a church consignment shop one day, Grace glanced down at her hand and realized the center stone was gone. There were many rough edges to counters and display cases in that tight space filled with clothes and bric-a-brac. Certain she had hit the stone just right so that it had come out of the ring, she was still hopeful it was not crumbled into a thousand pieces on the floor. Standing absolutely still she began her prayers with great hope and belief. After repeating the prayer to St. Anthony many times, she began to look over the exposed areas on the floor. Nothing stood out. Her heart went into her throat as she thought, "What if someone came in today, noticed it, and took it? Maybe they didn't even realize it was real. Or, maybe they thought it was a canary diamond instead of a sapphire."

Believing in the greater good of people entering a thrift shop, she forced her focus instead on what had been dropped off that day in the way of clothing. There were three large piles that no one had really gone through. Methodically, she began to lift the items in the stacks of clothes one at a time and shake them out. Midway down the second pile there was a shiny object sparkling up into her face from a brown suit jacket. It was the yellow sapphire!

Bringing the ring and the loose stone into Vonnette, Grace told her saga of the sapphire that had gone missing while volunteering.

Telling Grace that she was obviously not meant to lose the sapphire, Vonnette was thrilled it had happened in a contained space where it could be found.

Grace told her it was due to the powers of Saint Anthony.

Discussing the need for alternate measures to contain this sapphire, they agreed to tack solder the large, three-stone ring to the other flattish ring Vonnette had also made that contained a few different size diamonds together. Soldering the two rings meant they would no longer float around on Grace's finger separately and possibly be exposed to being hit without her realizing it. Since remounting that sapphire and tack soldering the rings together, nothing else bad had happened to them, thank goodness!

Snapping herself out of memory lane and back into the moment, Vonnette asked, "Grace, did you stop over to say Hi? Or, are you here for a specific reason?"

"Gotchya. I'm looking for a gift for my husband to give me. It's our fortieth anniversary you know. Let's try on some rings!"

With that, Vonnette began to pull out one ring after another for her. Grace took notes on kinds of stones and prices to pass along to her husband. When she tried on the yellow gold diamond and yellow sapphire "star" band, she was happy. It was tight going over the knuckle, just the way she liked her rings to fit. The small, top-quality diamonds and brilliant cut sapphires were flush-mounted asymmetrically around the eight-millimeter flat band in what Vonnette called bead mounts. Tiny prongs were raised up out of the gold band and then pushed over the top of the stones. With a special tool these bits of gold later would become rounded, bead-shaped prongs. It created a feminine image that was kind of lacey and comfortable to the touch. Unlike regular prong rings this style stone mounting could go completely around the finger without feeling bulky. Clothing would not catch on this type mounting, either, where prongs can, and often do. Pierced out spots in the shape of "paisleys" finished the overall band design. Creating holes in wide bands was something Vonnette liked to do. The holes would give the finger a chance to breathe and dry out after the washing of hands, even if the ring wasn't removed while doing so.

Grace kept trying on the band and then tugging to get it off. Combining other possible new rings with her own alongside the band had her finger swell from all the pushing and tugging.

Realizing how swollen Grace's finger had become, Vonnette said, "When a ring is too tight, spray a bit of Windex on the finger just above the ring at the knuckle and the ring will slide off." In case Grace purchased the ring, and it got stuck on her finger at home, Vonnette felt the information about Windex could help. Pulling out her bottle of Windex from under her display cases, she spritzed a bit above the ring while holding a paper towel underneath Grace's finger to catch the runoff. Giving a head nod to remove the ring now, Vonnette bent over to replace the Windex bottle on a shelf below her display units.

Expressing disbelief at such a simple resolution, as so many had in the past, Grace tugged at the ring. Being soaked with slippery Windex the ring flew off her finger, out of her hand, through the air and dropped to who knows where. The ring was suddenly out of site. This had happened so quickly and while Vonnette had momentarily turned away from her trusted client. So, she didn't see the ring go airborne. It only took a split second. If Grace had been someone Vonnette didn't know so well, her eyes would have been glued to the ring. She would have seen it go up in the air and onto the ground. As it was, she had no idea in which direction to even look for the ring.

Horrified, Grace looked at Vonnette, then to the rug-covered ground, and then back at Vonnette. "Oh no, I can't believe that just happened. I didn't think the ring would actually come off with such ease. And then it literally flew off my finger! Vonnette, I am sooooo sooorrrrry! You said the Windex would work. I am so sorry. I am so sorry!"

While shaking her head, Vonnette was already coming around the end of her display cases to look for the ring. Two women put their heads close together bent over to peruse the rug-surfaced ground to search for the traveling band. Grace kept apologizing. It got to the point where Vonnette found the whole thing funny.

Standing upright momentarily gave them both a chance to get the blood back to proper flow. Vonnette told Grace, "Listen, I'm not worried yet. We'll find the ring. I'm glad it happened with you rather than an unknown person. So, don't worry. We'll get it back in place. Obviously, the ring wanted to go on a journey today."

Chuckling together, Grace said, "Let's do the short version of the Saint Anthony prayer and look some more, okay? I use this version all the time. *St. Anthony, St. Anthony Please come down. Something is lost and can't be found. Please bring the gold, sapphire and diamond band 'round."*

Silently at first, they both repeated the prayer and continued to look. Vonnette lifted the fabric that hung off the display tables to have a clear view of the ground where it might have disappeared. Following suit, Grace lifted fabric as well and kept looking.

Mainly, each woman concentrated her search around where Grace had been standing. While repeatedly reciting the prayer out loud now, they each slowly expanded their search area. Vonnette went behind the display case area to look. After lifting some of the bags under her counters, she looked closely on the ground. Without knowing why, she stopped for a moment and turned to look behind her. Lying there, next to one of the rear legs of the bar stool height chair she used at shows, Vonnette saw the ring.

"Got it!" Came her claim while lifting the ring up in a victory stance.

"Thank God! Vonnette, where did it go to?"

"It was all the way back here behind the chair, Grace. I'm surprised it didn't hit me in the head as it flew past. Guess that Windex worked better than even I could have imagined."

"That and Saint Anthony!" Came Grace's response. "Do you trust me to put the ring back on, or would you rather I not? I completely understand if you would rather I not play any longer."

"Not at all Grace here, play away. If you lose it again you're buying it, that's all." Both women stood laughing, happy the ring had returned from its short journey.

Pushing her arm out in front of her as far as it would reach, Grace turned her hand from side to side to look at the ring. Play-time continued as she tried the band on with countless other rings from Vonnette's cases. Two additional times Vonnette used Windex to get everything moving. Each time Grace very carefully slid the rings off and on to make sure nothing else went missing.

Keeping the conversation going was never a problem between these two women. While Grace was playing, Vonnette opted to share more information about Windex. "You know, there was a day when a man who never stopped talking came into my booth at a show. Seems he had a ring stuck on his finger for ten years. While enjoying his lunch in the makeshift restaurant at the other end of the show, he got into a conversation with someone who had just purchased a ring from me. While she sat admiring the new ring on her hand, as you've been doing with this band, he went into his saga. He told her of his torment of not being able to get the ring off his hand for so many years. The woman suggested he come to see me certain he would get help.

"He came, and as I stated, he never stopped talking. He couldn't understand why he had listened to this woman to be visiting with me at that moment. He claimed he had tried everything to get this ring off, short of having it cut off his finger.

"Opting not to interrupt him I simply motioned for him to place his hand over the counter near me. Placing a paper towel under his finger as I have done repeatedly with you today, I spritzed his finger with Windex. While he was still speaking, I motioned with my eyes and head for him to try the ring. He did try. In total disbelief, the ring came off. For that moment, he completely stopped talking. Looking at me, and then the plastic container of Windex still in my hand, his face took on a weird image of terror. I'm sure he thought I was a witch and that this was some form of black magic! Leaving my show space, he didn't say anything else. Not even a word of thanks.

I'll never forget his facial expression as he walked away seemingly afraid to turn his back on me. I shook my head and let the experience go. What else could I do?"

"That's fantastic! And you know, in a way it is magic! I mean, who would ever think of using Windex to get tight rings off your fingers? I wouldn't, and I'm certain others never have either. How did you come up with the idea yourself? Maybe it is black magic!"

"No, Grace, it's not magic. Simply something jewelers have known for some time. There is a chemical reaction between the ammonia and the swollen finger I am sure. Combine that with the soap that's in window cleaner and voila`! As I said, that man left my booth with that weird look on his face and never even muttered a word of thanks. Oh, well. Anyway, as I look at your finger with all these rings on it, let me just say, when in doubt, overdress! That statement covers so much in the day-to-day, doesn't it?"

Two women were taking turns making one another laugh while playing jewelry dress-up. Once Grace had three rings on along with the diamond and sapphire band. She waved her hand in front of Vonnette and exclaimed, "You know I am not of the school of less is more when I wear jewelry. No . . . more is more, and more is even better when I'm here with your jewelry Vonnette!"

"Grace, your fingers are not like a Tressy Doll where they can be made longer as her hair could be. Do you remember the Tressy Doll?"

"Yes, I do remember that doll and her hair. There must be a way to extend my finger length so I can fit more gemstone rings on at once!'

"Sorry Grace. I wish I did know a way to do that for you. You crack me up! If you hear of something to extend fingers you must tell me.

"Think you'll have to go home and tell Joe you found, lost, and then found the anniversary gift you want. He ought to get a charge out of that story.

"Speaking of rings going missing, did I ever tell you about the times rings have gone missing in my home?"

"Don't think so, no. Did your kitties take them away to play with?"

"No, not that I didn't think that at first. One of my rings has a green moonstone and a druzy psilomelane. It's a sizable piece. There was a time I wore that ring almost every day. That's saying something because as you know I change my jewelry each day. At that moment, I wore that one ring quite a lot. Suddenly I couldn't find it. I normally string beads in my dining room where there is good natural daylight. When I string, I remove my rings, so they won't get caught in the silk cord. The last time I could recall having seen the ring was in that room sitting on the dining table.

"Feeling one of the cats had taken it, I crawled on the floor to look under furniture and my radiators. I must have checked under the old-fashioned radiator in that room five different times thinking I just didn't see it the last time I looked. While on my belly, I felt around behind each of the feet on that radiator as well. Moving around the house, I checked under every possible cubby and radiator.

"Nothing.

"Following your lead, I did the Saint Anthony prayer repeatedly. Still nothing. Obviously, I was sad at the loss. Not that I don't have other rings, because as you know I do! It's just that when you love something and enjoy wearing it you feel such a loss when it's no longer around.

"After about a month I thought about it again and looked everywhere once more. Certain the universe had some reason for keeping the ring away from me, I spoke to the powers that be. I offered to cleanse the ring and not to wear it for a month if they returned it to me. Thinking that if I had been wearing it too much they would give it back to me with the pact I made. Still nothing happened.

"Another month passed. I thought about the ring off and on still willing not to wear it for a month if it was found. Then, one day I was stringing again and a couple of pearls dropped off the dining table onto the floor and rolled over under the radiator. I got down on the floor to retrieve them and low, there was my ring sitting front and center under that radiator where I had looked so many times before!"

"So this pact of yours worked better than St. Anthony."

"Maybe it was the combination of St. Anthony *with* the pact that worked. I'm not sure. What I do now when something goes missing is to cover all bases. I say the St. Anthony prayer and make a pact not to wear whatever, for however long I feel is good for the moment. Thought you would find my usage of St. Anthony fun!"

Laughing again, these two women clearly enjoyed one another.

"That laugh of yours. It gets me." Grace giggled. "Just hearing you laugh at the other end of the phone makes me forget some of my daily struggles. But it's not about the laugh alone. It's the fact that you think all the time! Seriously, I would not have thought of making a bargain with the universe to give my ring back."

Clearly mystified, Vonnette asked, "Doesn't everyone think all the time?"

"Not the way you do! You look to understand everything that happens. You never dismiss an incident as an accident. If you come upon an old drunk man, you feel it's a reminder of what happened to you as a child. Somehow that makes you realize how far you've come since that time, and you take charge of the emotional side of the situation. I don't know anyone else who thinks that way. Most people would see a drunk person and think it's a drunk, leave it at that. You wonder if something special happened to form that day in that persons' life where they became a drunk, or if it was simply a one day thing. You would have made a great detective."

"I do love watching detective stories on PBS. You never know, maybe in another life. In this life, I'm still trying to make a living through my jewelry art. The rest is, I think, simple curiosity. Being curious about life keeps my mind wondering, constantly!"

Laughter once again took over between these two women. There was a strife-filled moment in the middle of their visit due to the band disappearing as it had. Overall, it was a fun ending to the day. That feisty, purple-haired woman always brought an interesting moment Vonnette's way and today was no different.

"You know, you mentioned something about cleansing your ring before wearing it again after having lost it. Did you mean washing the dirt off?"

"No, not cleaning dirt off. That's not what I mean by cleansing. We can all cleanse our jewelry. I list a few different ways to cleanse jewelry in my coffee-table book. I know you have the book because I gave it to you. Guess you haven't read pages 269-271, at the end of the book?"

"That book of yours is my bible! Almost daily I pick it up, look at the jewelry, and read something or other about a piece of jewelry I find interesting. How you come up with design after design blows me away! I'll admit, though, I haven't read the back pages of the book yet. Didn't think there was any need."

"Guess you should pick up *Dreams Made of Stone* again and flip to the back to discover why I included those pages without any jewelry photos, Grace. Possessing high emotional energy most of the time, I feel it's necessary for me to cleanse my jewelry pieces at least once a year. Sometimes more often if I wear something a great deal."

"I don't recall ever talking to you about that before. Is it something I need to do with my rings? I mean, I wear these pieces all the time. You know that. Now I'm feeling nervous that I have not cleansed them other than to get rid of the grime."

"Grace, if you're in balance, then your rings will be as well. When you feel out of balance, then you might feel the need to do what I suggest.

"As a very simple rule, though, cleansing jewelry is a way to remove negative gunk that energetically can get stuck in metal and stones. When you clear that out and recharge your pieces with the sun's rays, your jewelry seems to be lighter and happier again. It's a personal call, always. In the meantime, you're retired. You don't have the strife of the work world now. You also laugh a lot with Joe. I think your emotions are in a good place. Look the book over and then decide what feels comfortable for you."

Recalling how the diamond and sapphire band flew off her finger and needed to be found, Grace and Vonnette wound down their conversation while sharing another laugh or two. It was closing time and all artists were getting their booths ready to be shut up for the night. Realizing Vonnette might want to head home, Grace left after they exchanged a heart-felt hug.

Different day this, Vonnette thought as she began to pack her wares thankful it was closing time. Once finished placing her jewelry safely away, she began to prepare the tent for overnight. Lifting anything that might get wet if left on the ground and it rained, all hooks on the rear, tent tresses were now completely occupied. Draping curtain bottoms over her chair during the night meant the moist ground would not affect them either. Covering display cases with white cotton blankets, a plastic sheet that painters use for drop cloths was then draped over the tops of the blankets. After securing the blankets and that plastic sheet with a couple of clamps, she had done what she could to stop moisture from getting inside her display cases, the now empty neck-forms, her packaging or her sales slips overnight. She then pulled down and began to zip the tent sides closed. Each of the exterior four corners had a clamp that went over the zipper tab to keep it closed. This temporary storefront was as secure as she could possibly make it to walk away from for overnight.

Vonnette tended to do this same nighttime preparation even at her indoor shows. On some level, it kept her in sync whether a show was indoors or out. One outdoor show sealed the deal on this kind of organization. During the night, men had used power machines to clean the walking areas in preparation for the following day. Those leaf-blowers blew all kinds of junk up underneath her tent. From that show forward it was simply easier to lift things up off the ground for overnight and sweep out in the morning if necessary no matter where her show was located.

Though tired, she stopped to talk to a couple other artists before heading to her car. Each one wanted to know the same thing. "How did your day go financially? Do you know what the weather is supposed to be tomorrow? Do you think tomorrow will be a better day? One can only hope." Questions and input among vendors could encourage an insecure artist. Everyone doing a show needs input of how it's going for those around them. If one artist had low sales while other artists sold well, it could be their artwork, price range, or the weather. Often when it's too hot, or too cold, attendees won't try on or buy clothing or jewelry. Usually at least one artist who cannot contain him or herself speaks up on how terrific the sales were that day; however, what price range anyone might have sold in was not normally shared.

Thankful she didn't come across any artist of that ilk tonight, Vonnette headed for her car. She drove up the street a couple blocks to stop at the health food store for some ready-made soup and then went home. Unlocking the front door, she happily greeted her two cats. Smiling down at them she said, "See, I told you I wasn't going out of town this time. We all get to sleep in our own bed tonight. Let me get my jacket off and I'll make up your dinner. Thankfully, I picked up some soup so I don't have to think of what to make for me. It was an okay day financially with promises of more income for the near future. Not that you both care, but it makes a difference to me. I promise that even with all my financial issues you'll never go hungry."

Glancing at the clock on the microwave over the sink Vonnette noticed it was 7:30.

Her living room and kitchen area were an open concept. While pulling out dishes for the cats' food and one for her soup, the phone rang. Almost tripping over her little black cat Rose, she reached the phone in the living room. A practiced greeting of "Hello, Vonnette's Designs" was spoken as calmly as possible while she turned, walked, and pulled the extra-long phone cord over to the kitchen. Phone receiver was automatically cricked between her ear and right shoulder while Vonnette held the phone base in her left hand until she reached the kitchen counter. That's where the phone cord stopped. Determined to finish getting food ready for her two, four-legged children, she pulled the coiled cord taught to reach what she had begun. Without realizing she had done so, she placed the dishes on the floor and was then a bit frozen in place. It had only been a matter of maybe ten complete seconds to get the phone in position and the dishes on the floor. No time really for anyone to have said anything important. But then her stomach began doing flip-flops as *he* spoke. She knew who it was with "Hello," before he had even said his name. Why on earth would he be calling at such an hour for business, unless it *wasn't* for business? This would not continue!

Firmly, she began. "Listen, I don't know exactly why you've called, but let me say that I just walked in the door and haven't had dinner yet. You're interrupting that. I would appreciate your calling back at some time that is more appropriate for working hours."

Starting to pull the phone away from her head ready to hang up certain this dismissal would end the conversation, Vonnette was surprised at what came back at her.

"Please don't hang up." Jackson spoke loudly and urgently. "This doesn't have to do with your work. I need to explain something to you."

Vonnette was sure she had heard every possible explanation, or line, and didn't want to open herself up to any more thank you very much!

"Just one moment of your time is all I ask." Jackson pleaded.

Placing the phone back up to her ear Vonnette thought, "Sure, that's what they always say. Why don't these unavailable men get some new material?"

Taking her moment of inner thought as a sign to go ahead, he began speaking so quickly it was like a jackhammer turned on, and that once in motion was impossible for anyone to interrupt him. "After meeting you today I felt something I thought I would never feel. I promised my sister I would go with her to meet with you and act as a ruse, but then I looked into your mysterious blue eyes and was a goner. Sophie felt it was weird to talk with someone about an engagement ring alone. Her fiancé is in Iraq as part of his time in the Army reserves. Though I'm sure you have people talk to you alone about engagement rings all the time, my sister is a bit old fashioned. She wanted support while making decisions. That's why I didn't really give any sort of input whereas; if Tom was there I'm sure he would have wanted to say more than I did. Living out of town most people here don't know who I am. So, for a moment in time Sophie felt it was a great disguise."

Vonnette felt her knees begin to buckle. With the phone tightly gripped in her hand, she could only think of her need to sit before she fell over. Her head was pounding as was her heart. Weak-kneed, she backed out of the kitchen into the living room area and sat on the outer edge of the couch. Yet, how Vonnette sat was almost cat-like on the edge of the cushion where she could easily spring upward at a moment's notice. She had to admit this was the first time she'd heard this one!

"Wait, was this a story, or was he really her brother?" She silently questioned. "Was that actually what he had just claimed, or did she blank out and hear what she wanted to hear?"

After taking time to breathe, Jackson continued now at a slightly more normal pace. "I'm forty-seven years old. Sophie is thirty-nine. We had one brother between us in age who unfortunately passed away. Because of that loss, we've become very close over the years. I did marry once for a brief moment. We both realized we got married for the wrong reasons and divorced amicably. My work is consulting with computer software. I travel often, mostly here in the Northeast. My home is in New Hampshire, and I own the house outright. After living alone for over twenty years, I was certain I would never feel anything special for a woman again, until today. I've tried many online dating services but have not had any luck and gave that scene up some time ago.

"Would you consider going out with me? I noticed you didn't have an engagement ring or wedding band on today. Figuring that could be due to the work you are in I made a few inquiries while at the show. Hope you don't mind. Trying to be subtle I couldn't help feel I might have a chance when no one claimed you were dating or involved. While walking about the show today, I heard someone say it closed down at six, so I have been calling the number on your business card every ten minutes since then. You did say the number you gave Sophie would get you at home."

Pausing only to take another breath he tried to go on when Vonnette stopped him. "I don't know what it is about men. You all feel the need to qualify everything about yourselves. Let me ask something to be absolutely sure after your monologue. Are you really Sophie's brother? Remember, I can and will check up on this, so be truthful!

Furthermore, until I do check up on this information, I won't want any further contact from you."

Did she honestly just intimate she would go out with him? Those words so easily escaping her mouth, came as an utter surprise. The moment caught her completely unaware!

"Yes, I am Sophie's brother." Silently, he waited for her to respond, afraid pushing any further might make Vonnette hang up on him.

"Jackson, I've heard every line imaginable, except this one, if it is a line. First, I need to finish this show, then I have three more shows on back-to-back weekends. I get a week and a half off, if you can call it that, from shows I mean, and then one other show. Because I have to do normal work in between actual shows there's not a lot of time for me to do the investigative work necessary to give you an answer. You said you travel as well, so maybe you will grasp my need for time. Once I do figure out if you are telling me the truth, I need to ponder if I will see you in that way." Holding the side of her head not connected with the phone, Vonnette wondered if she could get answers to the questions swimming around in her brain in *any* time frame.

"You tell me when to call back and I will make it a date." Jackson had replied so quickly Vonnette didn't have enough time to take a full breath. "Before you do any checking I have to tell you I wasn't kidding today when I said I just met the woman I want to run away with!"

Vonnette blushed and was glad to know he couldn't see what kind of effect he'd had on her. The silence spoke volumes to Jackson. It seemed as though their auras overlapped even over phone lines.

They agreed to be in touch in about seven weeks' time. After completing this, and her next four scheduled shows, she'd have time to check up on his story as well as have a bit of time to think!

They hung up and Vonnette sat motionless, stunned by the call. What a day. She needed food but no longer wanted it. While still sitting on the edge of the couch she said out loud, "Thank you God! I believe Jackson is telling me the truth. I mean, seriously, who could make up a story like that? I have to believe you sent him to me. Not sure I can deal with the stomach flip-flops attached with spending time with him though."

Vonnette went over the days' events in her head once more along with dream messages from last night.

Mud was about money. There had been a few sales of jewelry today along with a couple of her books, and possibly an order from Sophie. Oh, yes, and hopefully a purchase from Grace.

Taxes in one message, being over taxed. She had been over taxed meeting Sophie and Jackson. After this last phone call she was even more over taxed by Jackson!

Lavender jade has a soothing affect when dealing with contamination or a harsh environment. Yes, there was Jackson, but also the couple who somehow thought that Vonnette could separate their daughter from a scheming young man. Then there was the woman who was upset after discovering the inherited stone from her grandmother was synthetic.

Red garnet helps iron in the body be more easily assimilated. Vonnette needed to have better iron absorption with the days' emotional turmoil. Remembering, she had given advice to Abigail of how to use apple cider vinegar today and thought, "I must begin using apple cider vinegar again tomorrow."

The sex dream might have meant just what it suggested. Jackson had stirred something deep within Vonnette on many levels. Some things she thought *she* would never feel again, a chemical as well as physical attraction!

Her dream messages had been a way of guidance for so many years. A way to know she was on the right path each day. Another person wouldn't pay much attention to such messages and yet, for Vonnette, they were comfort as well as confirmation she was not alone. One eyebrow went up as she thought . . . "Interesting day!"

Talking to the cats now she said, "Funny kids, you wouldn't believe what just happened even if I told you. For that matter, I don't believe what just happened. I'm going to bed, so I can be fresh at the show tomorrow." With one clap of her hands, it was if Vonnette said, "Enough thinking." She got up off the couch, put the uneaten soup in the fridge, turned off the lights on the first floor and climbed the stairs to bed.

CHAPTER TWO

Northampton

October 11-13, 2008
Set up Friday the 10th

Carved Bone and 14Kg Golden Beryl Ring

DREAMS

1. A huge bowl of cereal to eat. Some famous person was in that dream, too.

2. A bone elephant sculpture had a headpiece over his forehead with a golden beryl mounted in the center.

3. Visiting with other shop owners to discuss the impending evictions. Everyone was upset and angry with the building owner. Vonnette had a plan. Explosives were in hand and there was a man who knew how to set her plan into action. While in the basement of a building, he planted the bundle of joy in the proper place. He then informed Vonnette the explosives would go off in 6 weeks.

Impatiently Vonnette told him, "I wanted them to go off immediately!"

He explained that a woman who knew astrology told him things would be different if they waited until then. Going on, he shared how this woman could read signs of the universe written in the sky that no one else could read.

As if she could suddenly see those same astrologic signs marked in the sky, Vonnette thought waiting wouldn't be such a bother in the long run. The reason she had wanted to push the bomb through now was to make sure no one would see the explosives in the meantime and pull the plug. But if this woman knew things, maybe they should wait and have better timing for the job. Her partner in crime was in the middle of setting up and connecting the timing wires when Vonnette awakened.

Saturday, October 11th, Vonnette rose out of bed trying not to make noise that might disturb the friend she was staying with feeling edgy from the one full dream about explosives. Sliding her feet into a pair of purple, felted-wool slippers always brought the feeling of home when she traveled. She then headed off to the shower. Once back in her temporary room she applied lotion in her usual way beginning at her feet and working her way up to her arms without applying any cream to her breasts. Somehow, ignoring her breasts with skin cream for most of her life helped Vonnette not to think about being molested as a child. Vonnette never felt appreciation for that part of her body as her breasts were the main attraction for that ugly man. This day, Vonnette did recall those moments in time and felt that being molested took something away that was forever lost, her childhood innocence. Hoping that anything was possible slipped away along with any belief that all people were good. That void where purity lived was then filled with a feeling of dread that anything can, and most likely will, be taken away. She shifted into adult mode at such a young age to nurture that wounded child deep within. Perhaps it was also at that time Vonnette lost her ability to ever fully control her food issues.

She was never too overweight, but it was something Vonnette paid attention to throughout her life. Once, while discussing her fears of being plump in therapy, Vonnette was informed that being overweight meant there was more of her to see. Meaning she wouldn't fade into the woodwork as she might have hoped. Vonnette knew from experience that people didn't linger their glances in her direction when she was chunky. And, being slightly overweight gave her another excuse not to engage herself socially and/or in the dating world, especially when she felt nothing lasted anyway. There it was, Vonnette's insecurity about her physical body along with her reluctance to pay any attention in particular to her breasts.

There was no rhyme or reason why, but today she applied lotion to her breasts. Maybe Vonnette wanted to let her breasts know that being molested had been a long time ago and she was letting go of the whole experience. But then, she felt a lump in the upper quadrant of her left breast. Vonnette shook her head loose of all molestation memories and came crashing back to the present.

Panic was the first emotion that struck her when she found the lump. Straight up fear that could have stopped a speeding train in its tracks. Every year when she went to the doctors, she was asked if self-breast exams were part of her monthly routine. Truth was, that fateful day at age eleven had tainted her on ever paying any real attention to all parts of her anatomy, especially her breasts. Making a joke of not doing self-exams rather than face the horror from childhood that made her not appreciate her body, she now wished such a thing was performed regularly. Yes, it had been years since Vonnette had been molested, but some things just never left her. And today, all those memories came flooding at her.

Vonnette opted not to tell the college friend she was staying with about her discovery. And though she could have easily called any other friend to receive emotional support, she made no call. As much alone today as she had been years ago when molested, Vonnette felt completely off-center.

Lots of reading on the subject years back lead Vonnette to believe that most people who were molested had it happen over and over. Self-hatred, guilt, shame, and loss of a childhood were often subsequent results from such sexual assaults. Being a sensitive, that one experience taught her how to live in a grown-up world very quickly. There were countless years before she shared that horrid day with anyone, and she suffered even more years to experience some form of closure on the attack. Emotionally connected to her childhood molestation this morning, and being a sensitive, Vonnette feared how long she might suffer psychologically before she could go beyond finding this lump. Would she even get through the experience alive was the real question that craved an answer?

Sitting on the edge of the bed alone, shaking, holding this moment of terror close to her heart was where she opted to remain for now at least. Her yearly mammogram wasn't scheduled until sometime after this show. Being the trouper that she was, Vonnette dressed and left the house for the tristate fair grounds to do the one thing that always grounded her . . . work!

Seven times Vonnette applied to the Paradise City Fine Arts Festivals only to be refused or wait listed until she became brave enough to call and ask why she wasn't juried in. She had been accepted once after she had placed that call, but the festival organizers wait listed her for following shows.

Jury process for these high-end fine art and craft shows could be brutal. Vonnette spent a lot of money on professional photos that were mailed off on a compact disc along with jury fees before a set deadline. Jewelry was the most competitive field in the show circuit today. Usual wait-time was three months before hearing if she had been accepted or not. Being on a wait list meant that when someone who had been accepted in whatever field dropped out due to health, death, or even disinterest, the show promoters would then call someone from that same field to see if they could participate. This was one of those shows for Vonnette. She had been called in off the wait list to fill a spot left open by another jeweler.

The organizers positioned booth number 197 across from the silent auction tables, a staple at most high-end shows. Each show promoter wanted to be sure to give back to the community that attended their event. Being October, the cause du jour was breast cancer. While setting up yesterday Vonnette didn't pay any attention to those tables. A month back when called in off the wait list, she was asked to make a donation and so she did. Since breast cancer had been the cause of her moms' death, she was happy to donate a long strand of jasper beads. Little did she know how much more personal that donation would be now that she had found a lump on herself.

"Thank God set up for the show was yesterday," Vonnette muttered as she slowly went about placing her jewelry in the display cases. The world somehow seemed to be operating in a blur, as if everything moved both in slow motion and was slightly out of focus.

Vonnette tried to distract herself from the lump once she was finished setting up her cases. How could she continue through not only this show but also two more shows she had scheduled on back-to-back weekends if the lump was cancer? The month had turned into four, back-to-back shows since the first weekend was rescheduled from an earlier date due to bad weather. Even this show wasn't on her original calendar. There was still a fifth show scheduled in November. If she allowed herself to think about the lump, she most definitely would freak out and be unable to continue.

When applying to shows Vonnette always looked at a calendar to see whether there would be enough space between shows if and when she was accepted. Time was always necessary to recuperate physically as well as to make new jewelry. If the shows were scheduled too tightly together, she wouldn't get any rest, or be able to make anything new. Once home from this show she would have three days off, and then would pack for the next show in New Jersey. Parts of her show set up would be left in her car in between shows to save on her own physical wear and tear. Clothing and food would obviously come into the house along with her jewelry. Interrupting her train of thought and without warning, her overhead track lights flickered a couple times, and then went out completely. Investigating around the back of her tent curtains where all electrical wires had been plugged in, she found her backdoor neighbor plugging and unplugging cords into the main extension box where four booths shared one box for electricity. He apologized for undoing her lights certain that would be the end of the stern, displeased look upon Vonnette's face.

Unhappily she said, "My lights need to stay off now until they cool down before they can be turned back on. So, for a half hour I won't have booth lights, thanks."

Knowing it wasn't his fault, she couldn't help her disdain or frustrated anger. Turning back into her own booth, she felt tears well up. Looking out of her dark booth onto the breast cancer auction tables across from her, a black cloud descended. Biting her lip to stop from completely falling into an emotional hole, she thought at least no lights was a form of distraction. Perhaps the fact she didn't have lights on in her booth hid her and the red face she had from fighting back tears.

A suggestion made once by a psychic Vonnette visited on occasion was that when lights flickered around her at a show or when the scent of lilies came to her for no reason it meant that her mother's spirit was visiting. Simca, her mother, was born in the month of May when lily of the valley bloomed in the northeast, so the idea of being able to smell lilies when her mother's spirit came to visit made sense to Vonnette. Flickering lights today were from human sources, not dead relatives, and there was no scent of lilies.

Sitting alone in her booth and feeling all that came with that emotionally, Vonnette sank way down. When her mother had breast cancer, Vonnette felt Simca's emotional pain deeply, and yet, in this instant she knew on an even more serious level what having a breast lump entailed. She reached up and touched her long blonde hair that today was tied up in a bun on top of her head. Most women with cancer lose their hair. Her mother had lost hers. Wigs were uncomfortable on Simca. She chose to wear a lightweight fabric cloche instead. Hair was not the only thing her mother had lost, however. She gave up her right breast as well as all the lymph nodes the doctors could gather on that side of her body. Eventually, she regained the movement in her right arm after months of physical therapy, but it had been a sincere physical as well as emotional struggle.

Twenty odd years ago cancer was dealt with differently than today in 2008. Watching anyone go through what her mother did was too much! Back then Vonnette told herself that if diagnosed with cancer and such an operation was suggested to her as a cure, she was going to live whatever was left of her life to the fullest without surgery. Though relationships between mother and daughter had been a struggle at the time of her mother's diagnosis and surgery, Vonnette never stopped loving Simca and had great respect for how she fought to stay alive. Simca had cancer at a much younger age, however, Vonnette was the same age now that Simca was when she passed. While wondering if being the same age was a message from on high, she experienced a sudden flashback. Friday morning, yesterday, the main portion of her drive to the show venue in Northampton was spent on route 90, better known as The Mass Pike. While enjoying the vistas along the side of the highway, Vonnette suddenly heard her name yelled out as if someone was sitting next to her in the car trying to warn of imminent danger.

"VONNETTE!"

To say she was shocked would be putting it lightly!

Swerving, and almost driving off the highway into a ditch, Vonnette gripped the steering wheel so tightly she would have strangled and killed it if it was a living, breathing thing!

Where did that scream come from? It wasn't as though she had never heard voices before, nor was it the first time she had heard her name called out by an invisible force. This was the first time she had experienced her name being shouted out while driving along an interstate at high speeds.

She slowed down.

Maybe the voice brought her out of the trance-like state she'd been in while enjoying the country views. Maybe she was thinking something she ought not to be. What was she thinking when that happened? Nothing came to mind as being anything of value.

While her heart still pounded, Vonnette maintained her slower speed with a death grip on the wheel; finally, she asked out loud, "What?"

No one responded.

Though the remainder of the drive was uneventful, Vonnette had pondered why her name was screamed out. After arriving at the show venue and while setting up her booth for the show, Vonnette kept wondering why her name had been shouted out.

When finished with her pre-show prep work yesterday, Vonnette met her college friend for dinner, happy for the distraction away from the highway screamer along with her all-inviting spare bedroom.

Sleeping in a strange bed the first night was always a challenge. Normally, Vonnette pulled out her travel compass before climbing into bed to reference where north was. Years back, a message to sleep in this direction had been given while meditating. Sleeping with her head in the north produced clearer dreams. When in hotels she was willing to sleep across the bed, at a diagonal, or even with her head at the foot of the bed to be in the right position. In a friends' home, however, Vonnette usually slept where the bed and pillow were placed thankful to have safe shelter.

Perhaps she ought to have pulled out that compass as her sleep

Friday night was fitful at best. Waking many times only to glance at the iridescent green clock in her flip phone left Vonnette blurry eyed in the morning. Total dream recall was not there. She hated it when dreams felt like fragments. Except for that dream about explosives.

While staring at the donation table right across from her today, Vonnette wondered if the experience of her name being yelled out yesterday could be a warning that her number was being called. Maybe that was why she was having a flashback today, to realize that this would be her exit point through breast cancer at the same age her mother had gone. And the explosives from her dream would in fact reference her discovering the lump today along with a death sentence actually happening in six weeks, or six months.

A group of friends Vonnette occasionally meditated with had serious discussions about death. One person wondered if others agreed that an exit point could be chosen before entering a body. Another member of the group suggested that more than one exit point for any given life was possible. That perhaps as individuals it was up to each person to decide which exit might be taken and at what time.

Vonnette believed strongly in continuous life; however, there were moments in her present go-round where she questioned her beliefs. "Faith was a funny thing," she thought, "as it comes and goes. You reach the end of your rope and suddenly find there's more length to that cable than you knew." Hopeful that rope had more length today, Vonnette was determined she would make it through this event and all the rest of her scheduled shows until the mammogram appointment in Boston gave her the answers necessary. Then, she would decide whatever on how to move forward with any health treatments. Emotionally gathering her strength together, Vonnette knew the importance of focusing on the day and the show.

One thought lead to another, and before she knew it Vonnette had stopped thinking about her name being called and instead, pondered her own story, her brand. Telling a story about artwork at a show is supposed to be a good thing. Most people love a good narrative. People can then become emotionally invested and buy. That purchase can then turn into a conversation piece as there is now a story behind the acquisition.

Her father used to tell stories at the dinner table. Some entailed someone with whom he had worked that day, or were even about the client he had just helped out. He was a plumber. Clients became invested in his story of his having two children at home that could use whatever these people might want to get rid of. Usually it was something he'd spy collecting dust while replacing a furnace or hot water tank in their basement. Once he brought home an old jukebox that was tall, boxy and lit up inside when turned on. A 38" vinyl record would play when a coin was placed in a slot. Vonnette's sister and her friends held dance sessions after that music box came home. Sitting on the cellar stairs Vonnette watched with glee as the teenagers did the swing. Maybe that's where some of her interest in ballroom dancing came from today. She'd grown up being in one ballet class after another but never felt fully connected to stories told through ballet. When she began taking ballroom dance lessons a few years ago she did discover something. Ballroom dances told stories of two people lost in one another's arms while moving gracefully across the dance floor. Yes, there was an element of that in ballet, too, but somehow, with ballroom dancing Vonnette grasped the story much more clearly. While standing in her booth Vonnette remembered that, in telling stories to his clients, her father managed to succeed in business.

Exactly what to say to people and then how much to say was where Vonnette felt insecure unless someone showed specific interest in one piece or another. When people did ask questions, she could go overboard maybe telling too much of a story; as when cereal is poured from a box into a bowl, and sometimes too much comes forth, sometimes too little. In other words, Vonnette could pour out too much when a client asked questions about her jewelry and its metaphysical connections. Even discussions of healing through color, or how to cleanse the auric field with apple cider vinegar could come from being asked about her fine jewelry creations.

All this information came hopefully before someone forgot why they were attracted to her jewelry booth in the first place. At shows she would watch male jewelers grab potential customers' attention with some tidbit of information, and they made sales. Vonnette lived in her own thoughts so much that many of the social skills to encourage people to invest in her story were lacking.

Whenever Vonnette went into that dark place where she questioned why she had such difficulty making ends meet, finding her brand, or getting people invested in her creations, her best friend Cally would remind her of how few true artists throughout time became rich from their talents. Statements like that always brought Vonnette back into a place of calm dismay. It wasn't that Vonnette didn't make sales, and sometimes really good sales at shows. No, her problems were caused from sales that always came close to covering her expenses but never going higher than her bills. Always two weeks behind, or even one month late on most payments at home was a sincere concern. Payments for her shows had to be made; otherwise, she couldn't do the shows or make any money. Her mortgage was paid on time, or she wouldn't have a place to work or live. Everything else was on a late schedule that was never really any kind of schedule. It was more like, okay, I have a certain amount of money, I can pay such-and-such today. That decision was always made according to whomever was screaming the loudest. Extra cash for frivolous things like clothes was not a concern. Even food purchases came after the cats' meals were covered.

Shows brought self-doubt to the forefront if no sales happened, and were even more distressing when a near-by artist made sales hand-over-fist. Trying to find her story during slow shows was a challenge. Today Vonnette was facing another show and this one had the added element of horror that comes attached to the word *cancer*. Should she tell that story she wondered? And if she could muster that story, would she even survive the emotional telling of it?

While pondering her inner emotional torture, two potential clients approached her booth. Her hope heightened as she recalled one dream message with a famous person in it. When a famous person appeared in a dream, help usually came in from an unexpected source. Maybe these people would be her unexpected source today.

Unfortunately, they walked on.

It had been at least twenty minutes since that rear neighbor had unplugged her lights. The bulbs had cooled down sufficiently enough to plug them back in. At a show in Maryland last year, Vonnette had seen a bright light from across the venue building. After asking that artist what type of lights he had, she was given the name and number of a business in New Jersey that made them. The bright white light that came off these particular bulbs was so perfect for showing off jewelry. Natural daylight presented stones at their best; this white light seemed as if the sun had kissed, and was now trapped inside, each piece of her jewelry. Vonnette bought three of those lights for her booth. Three bulbs were enough to showcase all her displays if set up in a straight line. These expensive lights took about five minutes to warm up and were thankfully back up to full strength before three bubbly women approached her booth chatting and laughing. Laughter like that was infectious. Vonnette found herself following suit without the benefit of knowing why. Upon closer examination, she realized these women were three distinctly different ages with similar mannerisms. Either they had been close friends, the kind where your actions overlap without intent or they were related.

Coming to a full stop at Vonnette's booth, their laughter slightly subsided as they glanced at the jewelry. Each woman focused on something different.

"Wow!" "Did you see this ring here?"

"Oh my, look at this pendant!" Seemed to come all at once from each woman in front of a different jewelry case.

Standing closest to the eldest woman, Vonnette unlocked a case and pulled out the ring she seemed most interested in. It was a hand-wrought, 18Ky gold ring with a 14mm white, fresh water button pearl mounted in a bezel. Six small, round, Persian turquoise cabochons also in bezels were mounted around the pearl's outer gold ridge. The turquoise did not face up, but towards the outer sides of the other fingers. This woman seemed overjoyed at placing the ring on her hand. The two other women came in tightly together for a closer look.

"Gran, that suits your hand. It fits, too, doesn't it?"

"Yes, it does fit. I don't know. The colors are me, but I think it looks a bit like a land mine."

Oblivious that such a statement might offend the artist, Vonnette simply smiled to herself in acknowledgement. Although the three women were engrossed in one another and the ring, Vonnette opted to interject herself at this time. "Don't mean to interrupt your conversation, but I made that ring to be a bit like a land mine. I'm pleased you see that in the design."

All of the women turned their focus to Vonnette and seemed to go quiet to ponder what she had said. Continuing, Vonnette added, "Yes, this may sound dumb, but I was thinking about women and men, and their relationships in specific when I made that ring. Relationships can be like a land mine in how they lay in wait to blow! The trick is to stop yourself from exploding and hope your partner does the same. If we could each be reminded how easily a relationship can be blown to bits, perhaps better care would be taken during difficult moments."

"Golly! I cannot believe it. You just came out with part of what we have been discussing all day between us. Do you believe it?" the youngest member of the group asked glancing at her two companions.

The grandmother of the group, with the ring firmly on her hand, nodded and began to smile from ear-to-ear. "This is a perfect ring to bring home for my husband to see. It would serve as a reminder of how lucky he is I haven't blown him into smitherines over all our years together!"

All four women, including Vonnette, laughed at this comment.

"Well, Mom, I think you ought to get the ring. Dad would even find it fun to brag about to all your friends." Laughter continued. "He could say how he could be blown up at any minute if he didn't keep all his ducks in a row! That *is* his normal sense of humor," the mid-aged woman said. In some small way, she was attempting to explain her father while looking straight at Vonnette.

"Tell me something more about this ring," the elder woman asked.

Although unsure if healing properties were what she wanted to hear, Vonnette carefully began to explain. With each sentence spoken, she would analyze looks on the faces opposite her, and then decide if she should go onward because emotionally she was walking on tinder hooks today. Anything could and already had upset her between the lump found and then her lights having to be cooled down before she could really function for the show day. "White pearls are great for balancing feminine energy. Turquoise is the stone for birth, or rebirth if you will," Vonnette said. Feeling the three women all paid close attention, she began to speak a bit more loudly as she connected with her personal belief system. For this moment, she came into her element and cancer was not welcome there. She read their faces as being a bit quizzical and felt that was her sign to go on. "Rebirth happens when you know you have been working on emotional things for some time and finally connect the dots. Turquoise helps you see what you have connected and then guides you into that new path or pattern in life."

All three women stood seemingly mesmerized by the words that Vonnette had just shared. Experience told her they needed time, so Vonnette gave them a couple seconds to catch up to what their brains were processing.

When a full minute passed, they all three looked at one another. The youngest spread her arms out and angled her shoulders as if to say, "Well?"

The middle-aged woman looked at her mother and said, "Mom, you *haaave* to buy that ring! No kidding!"

Another moment of silence passed, and the elder woman made a decision. The ring was to be purchased. As Vonnette began to take information from her charge card and wrote down her telephone and license numbers, she also pulled out a box for wrapping. The three women were engrossed in the ring while everything was readied. When it came time to actually wrap the ring, the grandmother waved her hand and said, "No need. I'm going to wear it. But thank you for offering to wrap it. Since we have your ear, and you have ours, can I ask you a couple of questions?"

"Certainly," Vonnette said, thankful for the distraction. "Ask away."

"Well, I'm guessing that without realizing it you nailed something that we've been discussing today. Carrying that forward, what would you tell me if I asked about relieving stress?"

"Perhaps I should warn you that once I get going I can go on and on ad nauseam. Let me begin with this point: I didn't nail you or your discussion, you did!"

These three women exchanged looks of confusion and then attention went back to Vonnette as if to ask, "What do you mean?"

"You automatically focused in on the ring that you are now purchasing. I am simply an artist channeling designs and stone combinations. With each creation I am hopeful the right energy comes through to help others receive the healing energy they need. Years back I began to feel the energy present in stones, and as such, there were days when I ought to work on specific pieces and days when I had to ignore those stones and concentrate on something else. Eventually, I channeled all the stone properties you see displayed here in the show cases along with many more stones. As a matter of fact, it took me eleven years to complete the list of stones I felt necessary for today's public consumption. During that same time span, I wrote a book with stone properties that have specific jewelry matched with the stones discussed. Some of my day and night dreams that helped me decide how to mount something are also incorporated in the write-ups. Long story short, I don't take credit for what usually comes forth. I feel I am a vessel that is fortunate enough to work spiritually with stones and gold to create something that assists people in their life path.

"Now, you asked specifically about stress. There are all kinds of stress. All stones work on some form of stress. If you are dealing with emotional trauma that has manifested in your shoulder area, then kunzite is a great stone to work with. If you have been emotionally slaving over something that has taken a very long time to process, then perhaps bone is the right way to go. Trust me there is an end-less supply of where I can go with this conversation.

"Should you rather, we can also get involved with things like Bach Flower essences, or lavender oil baths, meditation, yoga, or long walks. If you can give me a little more to go on, I can give you more information. Don't feel you have to go into specific detail as that's something I don't want to know or even carry around with me."

"My name by the way is Edna, my daughter here is Tia, and grand-daughter there is Coco." Everyone exchanged head nods in acknowledgement. "It's fascinating you are touching on things I have been curious about for some time now."

Glancing up and reading the sign overhead that said *Vonnette's Designs, Newport, RI,* Edna continued, "I think if we lived closer to one another we would be fast friends. What I am specifically work-ing on, or have been, is that my husband has colon cancer. He's a vibrant man and yet feels that if it's his time to go, then he will. Whereas, I feel we ought to do whatever is necessary to continue on with life. We've had a good relationship for many, many years. Although, he has never known what sort of gifts to give me in all those years, he normally just gives me money now and tells me to buy what I want. What would you suggest from that in the depart-ment of a stress-release kind of stone?"

"Edna, that's a lot to deal with for sure. First, I would comple-ment your husband on his taste in women. Even without meeting him I can see from the three of you that your life has a unity and that is partly due to his being in your lives. Now, as for you specifi-cally, generally, men don't know what to give women. Men find us fascinating though they don't understand us. Often treating women as a fantasy, they don't see the reality until after they're married. In honesty, the reverse is somewhat true as well, except we don't usu-ally fantasize unless it's in a sexual way, and that might happen after we're married."

Chuckles came from these three women.

"To be specific, with each age there are different things women need as gifts. There ought to be a gift giving guide so men would know what direction to go in for their women. I suggest you make some specific time for yourself. That could be a weekend spa trip to someplace nearby, or you can change your own bathroom into a spa.

"Buy a head pillow for the tub and a book rest that goes across it. Some scented candles that soothe you. A great book you have been intending to read. Some form of bath salts or bubbles. Top everything off with a plush robe and slippers you buy specifically to use at these times. There's nothing like putting your feet into a nice pair of slippers after a bath. Cinderella lives!

"Tell your husband not to disturb you for a certain amount of time. If he's not doing well on his own at that moment, then make the time for you when there's coverage from your daughter, or granddaughter. Make sure you don't bring a phone into the bath with you. If you like, bring a glass of good white wine. Between all that and the warm water, you ought to feel you have a new lease on life for at least a couple of days.

"Something like lavender oil in your bath can bring a lot in the way of healing energy. You can even find clarity of mind. There can be an association made emotionally that connects you with your past and how now to have positive moments in your day.

"Years back, an English doctor named Bach created flower essences. Believing he felt different after drinking water from a running stream surrounded by specific flowers, he developed a process to extract their energy to promote emotional healing. Personally, I have worked off and on for years with a woman in Newport who can diagnose what will work with your energy to bring forth positive shifts with Bach Flower Remedies. So, if you ever get to a point where you might like to try such a thing, give me a call and I'll hook you up. "Meditation, yoga and taking long walks can be good for your soul right now as well. These are all ways that not only help to clear the mind, but will also assist with your emotional shifts."

Without leaving them more than a moment to ponder her words, Vonnette moved to the display case two spaces over from where she had been standing. Unlocking it, she retrieved a transparent natural crystal pendant that was pink with a faint hint of a purple cast to it. It was hung on a black silk cord and she handed it over to Edna. "Since the burden of your husband's illness weighs so heavily on your shoulders, you might find this kunzite pendant useful, too."

All three women pulled their heads together again to gaze upon the pendant. Edna looked up, tilted her head to one side while pulling the pendant to her chest and said, "Thank you. You heard me, and saw me. Everything you just said except for the jewelry and flower essences is something I think I've known in my mind but didn't have any idea how to give myself permission to do. So please tell me, how does this stone work?"

"Kunzite helps calm known and unknown anxieties as well as lessen shoulder trauma. There is a lithium base to this mineral. Don't worry, it's not something that rubs off or seeps into your bodily system. But, a core element, lithium, does assist to bring a sense of spiritual calm into your realm. We all carry burdens in different ways. Shoulders carry most everything emotional. That's why when we are stressed our shoulders often climb up around our head. This pendant has a kunzite in its natural crystal state and then there is a faceted rhodolite garnet, which is the pink tone garnet. Pink garnet helps you make peace with what is in your world today, change what no longer suits you, then helps you gather strength to go outward again. The design in gold on this piece is what I call *Leaf and Vine*. Vines and leaves in nature grow towards a light form, normally the sun. Personally, I feel humans grow towards the spiritual light. Is that enough information for you?"

"It's as though you read my mind! You have given me a great gift today above and beyond the jewelry you have created. I feel I now have permission to take care of myself even though this is a time to pay more attention to my husband. Thank you from both the top, and the bottom of my heart!" Handing the pendant back to Vonnette, she said she would like to take it as well as the ring, and the pendant could be wrapped. "Before you give me a total, why don't we all find something? It'll be my treat!"

Coco then asked if Vonnette could "do her" the same way she had done her grandmother?

"What attracted you first when you saw my booth? Wasn't it this ring over here?" Vonnette queried without taking time to consider Coco's question about 'doing her.' Happy to have any diversion, she pulled out a 14Ky/w gold ring with a largish, odd-shaped white pearl. There was a smaller blue aquamarine off to one side of the pearl. Overall, the ring was asymmetric in design.

"Yes, actually, I was attracted to that ring. What healing properties does it possess?"

"We discussed white pearls with Edna. They bring forth a balance to feminine energy. We all get out of balance from time to time. Usually it comes from trying to make everyone else happy, something native to most women. White pearls help create an inner balance with feminine thought that you can then take forward into your daily life. I personally wear white pearls a lot!

"Now, the aquamarine is a different ball game. I'm guessing you are considering a long-term relationship?" Not waiting for a response Vonnette kept talking. "Because aqua is the stone that works on partnerships. That partnership can refer to dealing within the self, with a family member, even a work situation, a new loved one or maybe something like alcohol or food. Often I find that when a young woman is attracted to aqua, she's contemplating a life-mate partnership. Aqua helps you focus on what partnership truly means to you. When you've got that straight within your own mind, then making those thoughts known outwardly from the heart comes more easily.

"The fact that you are drawn to a ring with both a white pearl and an aquamarine tells me you need to remain centered while conveying your ideas on where this relationship is going. While everything is happening with your grandfather, the rest of your family, and a specific love interest, it's still vital to remain centered on what's important to you. Though we are a me-oriented society right now, aquamarine does not suggest focusing on yourself in a selfish way, but to know from a firm inner and grounded place what's vital to keep you who you are and not lose yourself in any relationship."

The break in conversation lasted a mere second when Coco began to say, "Oh my gosssh! I have no idea how you did that unless you can read minds as well as make exquisite jewelry. I haven't told anyone about what has been going on in my life because we all needed to concentrate on my grandfather."

During this explanation from Vonnette, Coco kept sliding the ring on and off different fingers. Eventually the ring came to rest on her left-hand index finger. Now she looked at her mother and grandmother in amazement. "Did either of you know I was contemplating marriage with Rick?"

Both older women slightly nodded while simultaneously saying, "Well, we kind of figured it was the next step. He seems to worship you."

"This day keeps getting more and more out there for me, I don't mind telling you." Turning to Vonnette, Coco said, "I think this ring has to come home with me. Does it matter that it fits my index, not my ring finger? I mean, you did say aquamarine is good for partnership. Usually that would indicate the ring finger, right? I'm sure you could shift the size for me, but I don't want to be without it."

"No, that doesn't matter. If you like the ring on that finger, it's good for you. Actually, I designed it for an index or middle finger anyway. Though I never know when I design a ring for a certain finger if it will end up there, I trust the process. Over many years of working with stones and jewelry, I feel very strongly that energy comes to us mainly from the left side, and then energy is given out on the right side of our bodies. This moment plays perfectly along with that theory. You'll formulate information about your partnership and then convey it outwardly from the right side."

While all three women gazed upon the ring and considered the confirmation of the new serious take on Coco's relationship, Vonnette slid over to the end case to grab the pendant Tia had eyed as she came into the booth. It was a 14Ky gold starfish with a Ceylon blue sapphire attached to the side of one tentacle. It hung nicely on a strand of small round blue onyx beads and showcased both the pendant as well as the beads. Vonnette felt it was larger than what

Tia was accustomed to wearing simply by looking at the jewelry she wore today. Her thought was that perhaps the interest Tia displayed was connected more to the design and the sapphire for its healing energy rather than overall pendant size.

Handing it over to Tia casually Vonnette said, "I know this is where you need to be today, Tia. Although, I feel it's not a size you would normally be drawn to."

"No, you're absolutely right on both accounts. Guess there is no escaping the concept of you doing me now? Thought I could just be quiet and blend into the background here, but with the pendant in my hands I think you have to continue. It is what caught my eye as we entered your booth. So please tell me about it."

Without waiting for anyone to become comfortable, Vonnette dove in. She was on a roll with this group. Amazingly enough, these ladies wanted to hear whatever it was that Vonnette had to say. It was energizing when people wanted to hear her tell a story. So much so that she never stopped to think of how people normally wanted to label her as *special*. At least she didn't feel that was happening with these three women even though twice now she had been asked to "do them."

This group could actually make her day at the show financially even if they didn't buy everything they were looking at, not that she had that in her head as she showed her creations and discussed healing properties with them. It was more important that their presence and interest plied Vonnette out of that dark emotional space she'd been in all morning. That alone was worth so much more than any financial gain!

Completely focused on Tia and the necklace, Vonnette felt inspired. Words began to shoot out of her mouth quickly. "Let's begin with the design of this pendant and work our way upward. The starfish has five tentacles, a number I term as wealth. That can refer to wealth of spirit or it can be actual financial wealth. For today, I think it means wealth of spirit. You don't trust your instincts. You would rather stand in the background and hold onto your thoughts. With your father being ill, you know it's time for you to stand up and be counted. You're no longer just a daughter or a mother. Neither of those elements are ever a 'just' in anyone's life. Mothers do so much and don't usually ask for anything in return. They are forgiving and emotional rocks for everyone else. In this time and space, you have an opportunity like never before. You can affect all three generations of your family, stand up, be counted, and give the input you need to with your dad's being ill.

"Though you are filled with doubt, instinctually you know what he needs to do for his health. Your opinion matters. Everyone is looking for someone to take the lead in this event including your dad. Give your mom the break she needs and give direction to everyone involved. Once you trust your instincts, you will then take your personal life to new heights. It'll be a very liberating experience. And that's how the darker blue sapphire will help your third eye to open."

Pointing now to the space between the eyes and a bit northward on her own forehead Vonnette almost didn't take a breath. "You need that extra boost because of the trauma you've been hiding since childhood. Since that event you've hidden all your intuitions. The starfish has its tentacles reaching outward with the sapphire on purpose. It's so you can spread your intuition out in many directions at once and trust the ideas that come forth won't steer you wrong."

Everyone was now staring at Tia wondering what she had hidden that they did not know?

Without stopping for them all to catch up, Vonnette went on, "Last are the blue onyx beads. They help when you have really faced your fears and are ready for the world to see the true you. Protection from negative thoughts will be provided while you shift into a positive frame of mind. Let me add, when I get going like this I almost have no control. Words pour out of me. Hope I didn't out you in some unsafe way."

For the first time in almost five minutes Vonnette took an actual deep breath and waited for these women to catch theirs. Looking from one woman to the other, she tried to guess if what she said was overload or if she had really nailed Tia.

Certain Tia would be the first to speak, she was surprised when Edna grabbed the piece out of Tia's hands, handed it over to Vonnette and said, "Okay, yes, Tia needs this to be wrapped as well."

Tia's eyes teared up. This was something Vonnette had experienced many times before. Reaching out and touching Tia's hand lightly she said, "Tia, when someone cries in my booth I know it's because they made a firm connection with one or more of my creations. I take it as a good sign, not a bad one. So, what I'm telling you is, your emotions are safe in here today."

While bending over to grab another box to wrap this pendant, Vonnette waited for the family dynamics to get going in full.

Edna spoke again. "Tia, I have always known something happened to you when you were a teen, yet you would never talk to me about it. Today has confirmed it for me. That said, I know in my heart you have more going on inside you than you are ever comfortable portraying. This artist has given you, and all three of us actually, an opportunity to communicate in deeper ways than we have been for years. With your dad being ill we have each been walking on eggshells. This needs to stop! Maybe this pendant will help you to do that. I'm buying it for you, and happy to do so. Please use it in the spirit it is intended, to come out from hiding!"

That was all Tia needed; three tears escaped and fell down her cheeks but with control still a major issue, she then gathered herself together enough to say what was necessary. Beginning slowly, she spoke in a soft voice. "It was Vance Mom. You know. My boyfriend in high school. He felt so connected with enlisting. I knew he would not complete his years in the service and told him so one day. He lit into me verbally like I had never experienced before! He said I didn't know what I was talking about and to keep my thoughts to myself!

"Through his bodily expressions, it seemed as though he was going to attack me physically. I was really afraid, not only physically, but emotionally, too. Vance was so into joining the service once he left high school. I was positive, though, it would be his *last* mission in life. After screaming at me for nearly an hour, he did hit me across the face. I didn't blame him really. He was so worked up at that point I don't think he knew what he was doing. After he hit me he fell to the floor of the car in a lump. Maybe on some level he felt I was right. For whatever reason, he couldn't stop himself from joining the service. That was the last time I ever came out with my true instincts to anyone for fear it would bring nothing but torment, bad feelings, and possibly death."

All women pondered what had happened so many years ago.

There was quiet then.

Unsure if she should interject here or not, Vonnette did speak. "This moment seems to have more in store. Hope it's okay that I add something. I know you are feeling very emotional, Tia, but I believe your Vance is here with you."

Suddenly it seemed as if there was no air in the ten-by-ten-foot booth because these three women quickly breathed in, and held it.

"If he had sandy colored hair, stood about eight inches taller than you and had an army uniform with stripes on his sleeve, I think denoting sergeant, then he is standing in front of you, Tia."

Making room for this new invisible person, the three women got even closer to one another almost becoming one body while trying to see what Vonnette saw.

"Sincerely, I don't normally see spirits attached to other people unless there is some form of heightened emotion. Well that, or if someone asks me directly to see if a spirit is about. Honestly, I have enough spirits dancing in my world to keep me busy. In other words, I don't *try* to see more spirits. He wants to connect with you, though, and hoped that if he showed himself I would help. So, if you don't mind I will lend a hand for you, Tia."

Nodding a bit unsurely, Tia stood so still she could have been a mannequin. Tears became frozen on her face as if they, too, were shocked by this sudden turn of events.

"He wants you to know that he's not with you all the time but likes to check in occasionally. On some level, you're a bit of unfinished business for him. He's sorry for striking you that day. He knew deep down that you were right about his not returning. And yes, he did feel driven to join the service. This is to say he knew that what you were telling him was true, but he didn't want to face it at that point. Today is his opportunity to tell you he's sorry for that, and that you were the one person he could always trust to be truthful with him.

"He's smiling now at Coco and wants you to know how happy he is you found something with another man that he was unable to give to you.

"He doesn't hold any grudge or ill will for what you said, or that it came true. When he has checked in with you in the past, it was to try to get this point across. Perhaps you knew when he was there because he made sure your song came over the radio. I don't know what that song is, but you do. What he's showing me is the kind of jukebox you find in a diner mounted on the wall next to the table. That's how I know it's a song. He wanted you to feel comforted whenever you heard the song, to know he was about and not to be scared by his presence. When he comes to visit in the future, you will hear that song and, hopefully, will think good thoughts.

"After today he won't come visit for some time as the urgency will be gone. He is placing his arm around your shoulder."

Two women stepped further back from Tia to make room for the invisible man.

"He's smiling at me in thanks and is waving bye."

The three women came back together and hugged in the booth. All three had tears in their eyes. One said, and then all agreed, "I have chills."

When they took a break, Vonnette leaned towards them and in a soft, soothing voice said, "When you came into my booth today you were all laughing. Now you are all in tears. I hope you won't hold this against me?"

All three women smiled and giggled a bit nervously. They were suddenly aware of what they had just experienced and each woman shook her head side to side.

"By the way, when you have chills after someone says something to you, it's direct confirmation. It's the other side's way of letting you know that what you are hearing, reading, or connecting to in some way is correct. Some say it's like being touched by an angel when you feel the chills like that.

"And, although this man Vance was here for a short visit this day, he has been around you many times, Tia, in an effort to convey his apology."

Certain these three women needed a moment or two to gather themselves emotionally, Vonnette opted to tell a story while she wrapped the starfish pendant. "One time a young woman came into my store looking for a gift from her father to her mother marking an important anniversary. The presentation was to take place at a surprise party that the husband and daughter had planned. For sake of the story, I'll call this woman Sharon. She was married. Her sister had not met her husband. As Sharon shared, I discovered this sister would not be in attendance of the coming party. It made both her and her father sad. I couldn't understand why Sharon was imparting this information about her family with me. Shrugging it all off to the element that jewelry is sentimental, and this was to be an emotional time for the family, I simply listened. All the while, I was showing her possible ideas on what the father might gift his wife.

"Suddenly, a transparent young woman appeared next to Sharon. Since they had similar features, I guessed she was the sister who must now be in spirit. The spirit began to speak to me rather quickly. Since that always happens in my head, I asked her to hold on, that I would get to her needs once her sister and I finished our business.

"A wonderful necklace had been chosen for the mother with pearls and diamonds. As I stood wrapping it, I pondered just how I was going to approach the subject of the sister being among us. Obviously, I needed to handle this carefully. You never know how people will react when you suggest a dead person is trying to communicate with them."

Holding her hand out towards Tia, Vonnette added, "Case in point today."

Beginning slowly, I asked Sharon if her sister was maybe two inches shorter than she?

"Sharon replied, 'Yes.'

"Was her hair a bit wavy and shoulder length?

"'Yes, but how . . .'

"As I went further into a physical description, I wanted to make sure this spirit was in fact Sharon's sister and that the woman in front of me knew beyond a shadow of doubt I was seeing her sibling. I then suggested I knew what I was going to say might sound nuts, but that I often talk to spirits. However, they are normally people I knew in this life. Today, your sister has joined in your gift search.

"Sharon tried to wrap her brain around what I was saying to her and asked, 'Seriously? This is hard to believe. But your description is true.'

"I then told her that the sister had something she wanted to say and had been waiting for our business to be finished to speak. If you don't mind, I will give a go at whatever she needs to say.

"'Okaaaaaay...' Came a tentative response from Sharon while asking, 'Should I be nervous here? You said this isn't normal for you.'

"Just as I've told you ladies here today, I suggested how I rarely see spirits attached to others unless there is a specific need. I was certain Sharon was getting weirded out, but I asked her to let me say that I had never met her or her sister. I mean, Sharon had simply walked into my shop to buy a gift. We'd never met before. How would I know her sister? It wasn't like I could instantly call anyone and ask about her background.

"Of course, at this point I was hoping the sale I'd just completed would remain intact. She could have gotten so upset that she might demand her money back and go running out of my store.

"But Sharon was a bit curious, though I could also see she was very tentative. She opted to let me continue at least for the moment, so I did.

"First, I said, 'She wants you to know the man you married is wonderful! She couldn't have chosen a better life-mate for you if she tried. She is thrilled you both found one another and wants you to know you are going to be happy in your married life together. Though I'm not certain why this was a vital message for you, I'm guessing you do.'

"Next, I told her this was going to sound as if I was tooting my own horn, but she wanted to agree with the necklace she chose as a gift for their mom. Other than that, her sister said she would be at the anniversary party with everyone.

"I apologized. I wasn't sure if I had freaked Sharon out. That seemed to be it. The spirit smiled and nodded her head in agreement.

"This must have been Sharon's first experience where a spirit communicated to her and she began to ask, 'Seriously? How? Um, why? I mean, I don't really understand what just happened.'

"Explaining to her that throughout my life I had spoken to spirits. That it wasn't something I publicized, but rather something that happened. Nervous to have come out in this way to a complete stranger, I repeated how I normally saw spirits I'd had connections with in my life. Every so often, though, I did see a spirit attached to another. Hearing those spirits speak is not normal for me either. Sharon's sister had been quite adamant that I convey what she said. Sometimes I understand why spirits want to say something. Other times I don't get it at all. But then, the message wasn't for me, it was for her. Just as today the message was for you, Tia. Hopefully, Sharon comprehended why her sister said what she did that day. What she did with what I shared on her sister's behalf was completely up to Sharon.

"Remembering now, I did even ask Sharon not to feel obligated to share information or confirmation of what her sister had conveyed to me. I mean, the information was not mine, it was Sharon's.

"Sharon felt it'd be good to remain in the store for a moment or two to talk about this experience since it all seemed so other-worldly.

"Her sister had a brain tumor that no one knew anything about. While playing Lacrosse one day in high school, she passed. Though graduation day is normally a joyous event, the loss of a beloved sister shifted the whole family's emotions for that time. Oddly, these girls were ten months apart and due to scheduling ended up starting school the same year. Sharing the same friends, they were a bit more like twins who spoke about what boys could be interested in one or the other. When Sharon met her husband in college, she wished so much that she could be sharing the experience with Patti, but she was no longer living. By the time Sharon's wedding came along, the family had all had enough time to grieve and now they danced, laughed and enjoyed their relatives being together. The wedding was maybe the first time they had been together and participated in some fun since Patti had died.

"This surprise party for Sharon's parents' anniversary was to be another such joyous moment. At least they hoped it would be. Still, Sharon and her dad had been feeling sad that Patti wouldn't be there.

"Amazingly, and thankfully, Sharon took what I said graciously and felt it was a gift! Even though she wasn't sure if she would share it with her family or her husband, she couldn't thank me enough and claimed she was in my debt!

"Honestly, I was happy she was not freaking out. It's always a challenge to know whom to share with and whom not to. Most people cannot handle this kind of information well.

"She left the store with her purchase. I didn't give it another thought until a few weeks later when her mother came into the store wearing the necklace I had wrapped up that day. The mother was a lovely woman and the necklace and surprise party I'm pleased to say were each a great success. Thinking she came in to see about my making earrings to match, I couldn't have been more surprised when she pulled out some photos to share that were from the anniversary party.

"Group shots attendees had taken with different disposable cameras showed a white shape alongside the main family members. Of course, I knew this was the lost daughter slash sister but didn't say anything in case Sharon had not mentioned my seeing Patti that day in my shop.

"Turned out Sharon had told her family about the visitation while making the necklace purchase over a recent brunch when they were viewing all the photos given from others as well as their own shots. In each one taken of the immediate family, a white shape appeared. I guess she had approached the topic nervously.

Thankfully, the idea had been received well. So much so that the mother stood before me giving confirmation of my statement that the sister would be attending the anniversary party, too. Once the family began discussing this openly over breakfast, each member admitted feeling something, some energy at the party but were uncertain how to describe it. It was a gift in the end for them to know she was not really gone from their lives.

"And, maybe that's my point in sharing this other event with you today. To let you know that life continues. I would have thought the young man showing up here this day was maybe a grandfather who passed while in the service, except his uniform was more current. When he began to speak to me, I knew he was here with you Tia and wanted help conveying something special.

"I'm not sure if spirits connect with jewelry and I see them because of the sentimental attachment, or if I see them because the person on the other side is simply trying to find a way to make a point through any source they can find. In other words, I'm blessed these visitations from outside sources don't happen all the time or I would have to live in a larger home!"

Chuckling at the space joke, Edna then spoke for the three of them again. "We have cherished our time with you today, more than you could possibly know. Apparently, we all have things tugging at our heartstrings and were afraid for some reason to share. Thank you for opening a door for us to communicate in a new way along with the gift of knowing you. Who knows, maybe you and I knew one another in a past life that we are so connected today?

"I'm thinking maybe you are something of a stone whisperer by the way you were so able to tell what each of us ought to have from your creative collection of jewelry. Is that something you are comfortable hearing?"

Edna was actually taking Vonnette's opinion into consideration. That was something she was unaccustomed to and it touched her deeply. "Edna, I am what some people call a sensitive, an empath if you will. Long and short of it is that I can often feel what others feel. Sometimes I know what they are thinking maybe even before they think it. How all that connects with stones and jewelry is a bit of magic I guess.

"When picking up a stone, I often get an image in my head of how it wants to be mounted in metal. As I create the piece, shifts might happen. Those shifts I thought when I was young ought not to be made. With age, like good wine maybe, I have learned these changes made the piece better than I had originally envisioned. And I trust that outcome now. Of course, there are night dreams that also show me designs. And I do often create those, too. Since I pray over my creations as they are being formed, I also believe they find the right homes where the correct energy comes forth. Long winded way of answering your question. I don't know if that is being a stone whisperer or not, but that is what often happens.

"Maybe by being a conduit with stones and metal, I give over to others an energy not normally found in jewelry.

"Maybe it's simply that I am more tuned into stone energy than most people and as such can hear their energy cry out in certain ways. Guess that is what a stone whisperer is now that I'm thinking about it." Vonnette shrugged her shoulders and chuckled wondering why she had never made that specific connection until today between stone energy and her being able to hear, see and create through it.

"This has been a very special day." Edna said smiling. "I think we need to go and have a glass of wine and enjoy this moment. Can we bring you anything?"

It was Vonnette's turn to shake her head, no. She did thank them all for their kindness and appreciation of her creations. Handing over the three wrapped packages, Vonnette added a couple more notes before they left the booth. "Edna, you need this kunzite pendant on occasion. You'll know when that is. One or both shoulders will begin to tighten up and bother you."

Smiles were exchanged between both women.

Turning a bit to the right as she handed the package to Tia, Vonnette added, "Tia, your necklace had to be wrapped. The tulle outside the box is stretchy. You can slip the box out of the wrap, remove the pendant, and slip the wrap back over the box. Maybe you want to leave the box out on a dresser as a reminder, that in general, you are a gift to those around you and, in specific, within yourself. You are a gift! I'm hoping everything else that was shared here today will sit well with you over time and not be a burden in any way."

Tia smiled slightly while pulling her tiny shopping bag to her chest while mouthing the words, "Thank you" to Vonnette.

"Coco, your ring is something you need to wear and connect with even as the day progresses. Your partnership with self, friends and family is important to get right into."

Three women left Vonnette's booth to continue with their new-found emotional connections. Their bodies were brushing against one another as they walked up the aisle. People gave a wide birth as they approached from the opposite direction. It was a magical connection for the three generations that others were able to feel on some level even if they didn't see it.

Vonnette smiled as she watched them walk together and was hopeful she had just met both new and future clients. It was fascinating how these three women had been an emotional as well as a financial lift for Vonnette this troubling day. For quite some time after they walked away, Vonnette had shifted her fear away from cancer. Instead, she was busy thinking about how well-suited her creations were for these women and what she would now be able to write out checks for once she returned home. Her overhead lights had thankfully been in full strength during their visit, and her inner lights were also bright.

⁂

After lunch-time a couple that was perhaps in their mid-sixties walked into Vonnette's booth. Noticing the woman was wearing a wig, Vonnette wondered if it could be due to some form of cancer. The wig had seemingly shifted to one side. Perhaps the slip was due to not having any hair underneath to help keep it in place. The woman focused on a simple blue chalcedony pendant hung on a strand of black onyx beads. Vonnette pulled it out of the display case for her to try on and then asked if the woman knew how to deal with pearl clasps?

She didn't.

Vonnette went around the counter to assist with the necklace. Demonstrating how the clasp worked, she also explained how it was a bit of a safety catch. Should the clasp tongue come lose it would remain hooked on the end crossbar of the other side of the clasp. Necklace firmly in place, Vonnette went back around the cases to grab the mirror and hold it up for the woman to see.

Adjusting her wig a tiny bit once the mirror was in front of her, she then put her right hand over the pendant and stroked the beads. Smiling at how it felt and looked, the woman seemed pleased. She asked the price. It was given. The woman pulled out a charge card and handed it over to Vonnette.

With a quick wave of her hand the woman dismissed the idea of a box and bag for the necklace. "I'd rather not have anything else to carry about today, but thank you for the offer."

Vonnette pulled out her sliding credit card machine. Placing the charge card in its slot along with a carbonless duplicate set of sheets in place over the card, she then pulled the top slide over all. Many a time Vonnette had hit the other end of the metal and plastic stand only to crunch her knuckles. Somewhere along the years of being in business, Vonnette had heard this kind of credit card machine called a knuckle-duster. After removing both the transfer papers as well as the card, Vonnette then placed both paper copies in a small clipboard and handed that across the counter along with a pen for the client to sign and jot down a phone number, license number and address. Vonnette asked to see the license to make sure all information written was correct acknowledging to herself this method was not what she had done in the past. Once this task was complete, Vonnette took the bottom copy and handed it over the counter along with the charge card for the woman to put in her handbag. The top paper had the original signature and was the one all shop-keepers held onto in case of a question sometime later.

Until that moment the male counterpart of this couple had been quite uninvolved and quiet. Suddenly he spoke, and not in a friendly way.

"Is that your only method of accepting payment?" He asked sounding miffed.

"This, cash, and personal checks are my methods of accepting payments, yes." Vonnette replied in as calm a manner as possible unsure of where this man was going with his attitude and question.

"Well, I hope you know it's unsafe running a credit card in that way. Keeping a printout of the card face could in fact be dangerous for my wife's account. People steal those printouts all the time. Then they take off with the information and run up charges. If that happens due to her purchase here today, I assure you, we will be back in touch!"

Hearing this, the wife gave a very slight wave in Vonnette's direction and walked away from the booth.

Much to Vonnette's dismay, her husband had obviously not gotten his pound of flesh and remained in place. His voice became louder as he became more animated. "You are not taking me seriously. I can tell by the look in your eyes. These credit cards are a hazard. As a merchant, it's up to you to protect your purchasers and their information. That's a very serious job! Too many times these cards and sales slip copies are not handled properly. When that happens, *we* take all the risk, and *you* are gone from the area. I'm sure you feel we won't come after you. Trust me, I *am* keeping track and *will* come after you if there are any unknown charges."

"Sir, if there are unknown charges to your account that is between you and your bank, not me." Certain this fell on deaf ears, Vonnette felt she had to stand up for herself in some manner before he walked away laying all this possible future guilt on her.

Suddenly the man realized his wife had left the booth and was actually out of site. He began to walk away. As he did so, he turned and kept yelling at Vonnette about her hand in all this, whatever all this was.

Left to her own thoughts yet again, Vonnette went over past

efforts of finding alternative credit card machines. There were newer machines available. Vonnette had looked into them over the last few years. The card companies wanted stores, or vendors, to buy and/or rent the machines along with all the supplies of paper and replacement parts. These were a bit smaller in size than her knuckle-duster and had a tiny printer inside that gave a paper receipt. In a way, the new machines looked a bit like tiny adding machines.

Asking other artists how they felt about their machines, she heard repeatedly that they were a problem from the get-go. The sale would not be complete until a batch was run at the end of the day. That meant each artist had to call in all charges once back at the hotel. If a charge was over the card holders' limit, there was no recourse because that person was long gone. Calling in for an approval at the time of a sale with those machines was frowned upon and often times artists couldn't connect with an actual person if they even suspected the card was stolen or fraudulent. That was assuming that any flip phone worked at the location of the show. Standalone phones at shows were forever occupied so, there was no resolution there either.

Vonnette also had to call in for approvals on her sales at the end of each day from her home or whatever hotel she was staying in. Since she was given a credit limit of twenty-five dollars by her card company, any sale over that amount would need an approval code before the financial transaction was complete. Vonnette didn't sell anything under seventy-five dollars, which meant she had to call in for approvals on all sales. Currently, Vonnette took down license numbers, addresses, as well as phone numbers. It was a tried and true method of keeping someone in her booth long enough to realize if, in fact, they were who they claimed to be. Normally, people who knew they were over their limits, or who were using a stolen card, wouldn't stand still long enough to give over that much information. Instead, they would want to be away from the booth and what they might have purchased as quickly as possible. If a charge run that day was refused by the credit card company due to the person being over their credit limit, or if the card was stolen, that person would in fact end up with free items. Then, Vonnette would be out her goods along with the money. Sales from Vonnette's booth happened over the course of, say, half an hour. In that amount of time she could assess whether the client was honest, antsy, or impatient and sense if the patron might be a risk.

Only once did Vonnette have a serious problem with her credit card company. And that happened before she took all the extra information she did write out now. While still in her storefront, two people who made a purchase later reported their card as stolen to their bank and refused to pay for the purchase they made at Vonnette's store. Two months after the purchase, the card company took money out of Vonnette's already skimpy business checking account to cover what the bank had paid her without ever claiming they were doing so or why. After calling the card company, she was told the people claimed the item was purchased after they lost the card. The card company assumed their clients were being truthful.

Given the amount of the sale from what the bank had removed from her account, along with the date of that purchase, Vonnette chased down all information possible on that supposed sale. After locating the card receipt and sales slip with a full description of the necklace, she decided it had been too long since the purchase for it to have been fraudulent. Vonnettte decided she wouldn't allow the card company to steal from her.

Vonnette was able to recall what the couple looked like after reading the description on the sales slip of the item in question. Spending time with clients as they made a purchase, Vonnette always studied their faces and somehow, she could recall their images long after a sale. This ability could be described as another one of her gifts. Vonnette continuously made jokes with repeat clients not seen for some time on how she recalled their face as well as what they purchased, but not their names. Figuring there was only so much room in her brain, Vonnette told them that what she did retain were the important elements for her. People always laughed and forgave her for not recalling their names once she shared that little story with them.

Incensed and armed with the signed receipt and full description of the necklace on the sales slip, Vonnette drove over to the charge company office within her bank. Sitting in a small, closed office with one older man, Vonnette would normally have felt trapped, and at first she did feel small and insignificant. Somehow, the more he spoke, the more arrogant she felt this officer was. That's when she decided she would not be molested by him regarding her money or her creations. Telling the charge card officer, she had waited on the couple herself, and as such, recalled the sale very well. She described the couple and asked if her description matched the card owner's. He had no idea what they looked like and tried to dismiss Vonnette. Pulling out the signed, card receipt along with the full description on the sales slip, the officer had no choice but to take note. While watching his facial expression shift from one of dismissal to one of almost dread, Vonnette carried on. Asking exactly when the card went missing, she was told he didn't have that information. Having no idea where her inner strength was coming from, she would not back down. "If you don't know when the card went missing, then you don't know if in fact this purchase was made by the authentic couple or not. Why then would you feel you have the right to remove money from my account? You don't even know if the signature on my imprint matches theirs. If it does, then the sale was proper."

She must have hit a note of recognition because he then opted to make a phone call. Giving the date of the purchase over the phone to someone, he nodded in silent agreement as to who knew whom. Someone on the other end of the line gave the bank officer a few more details on that call and more nodding ensued. The credit card officer asked for a physical description of the couple and signature matches.

When the card manager hung up from that call, he faced Vonnette once again and had new information. The common method of charge sales slips at that time was where three carbon copies were placed in the sliding credit card machines. One copy for the client, one for the store and one for the bank. Seems there were also microfilm copies of those bank receipts. Signatures had been compared by whomever was on the other end of the phone just now. The signature on Vonnette's receipt looked valid. It became clear that the couple had made the purchase from Vonnette a couple weeks before their claim that their card had been stolen. The card officer assured Vonnette the money would be restored into her account within twenty-four hours. Then, the officer dismissed her from his office space.

Although proud of herself for standing her ground and actually getting a positive result, Vonnette was not finished. She had to say something to calm the anger stored inside over being taken advantage of in such a way. "So, without doing your homework, you decided to take money from my account. Did you figure I wouldn't notice? Did you think that I would let this event slide? The credit company was played by these people who claimed their card had been stolen. By claiming their purchase was made after the card went missing, they wanted to get something for nothing. Your company chose to believe them over me. Your company chose to steal from me. Your company decided I would accept whatever you dished out, and, I guess you discovered today that's not the case. Please take note. I pay attention and won't lay down for this kind of behavior."

Leaving that office with her head held high, Vonnette fought that battle and won because of her careful attention to detail. After this experience, she decided to take more precautions when accepting a charge card for a purchase. Taking license numbers, phone numbers and whatever Vonnette could think of on each charge slip for future security became part of her new method.

After two or three months, she made sure the information on these newer carbonless papers was destroyed through the bank shredders. By holding onto the receipts for that length of time, she would know the paper trail was no longer necessary for proof at the bank, or if the client wanted an additional piece of jewelry. If more jewelry was called for, Vonnette had all the information on hand along with an actual signature on paper. Feeling this to be the best method for accepting credit cards today, Vonnette opted to stick with it until something she felt was better came along.

Wasn't it interesting, she thought, how quickly these kinds of memories came to the surface when faced by an aggravate such as this last husband in her booth. When she shook him off as a momentary disturbance, she let the memory of that customer trying to get their jewelry free fall away as well. They were all blips on the radar screen for now.

⁂

Two vaguely familiar women came into Vonnette's booth. One woman was white, had slightly graying, chin-length wavy to curly hair. Her friend was African American with the kind of honey colored skin one could honestly say would look good in any color stone jewelry. They each had nice feminine figures.

"Hi, do you remember us? We met you in a show this past March in Florida."

At first Vonnette felt her powers of observation had escaped her. "Sorry, traveling as much as I do, you look familiar, but I meet and see so many people in a year."

"Maybe this will help; we asked about the show and how much it cost to enter? We make straw hats and thought Florida would be a great place for us to attempt shows. My name is Susan, and my friend here is May."

"Hi Susan. Hi May. As you're talking I'm remembering having a conversation with you. Did you in fact get into any of the shows in Florida with your hats?"

Happy that Vonnette remembered them, May said, "No, we still haven't applied to any shows. Applying to and hopefully participating in shows is on our to-do list. For now, we are building our inventory up and going around to shows to see where we might like to apply. It's amazing. There are so many shows! It's difficult to choose which ones to enter. Some we've investigated are a bit lower key than what we figure we ought to be looking for."

"I definitely understand what you are saying. In the hat category I think you can figure you will most likely be accepted into whatever shows you apply to as long as your photos are decent. In my field, there are so many people applying it's been a challenge to know if I will be accepted or not. Seeing you in Florida and now here in northern Mass. means you are traveling a fair distance in your search. I hope it's at least been a fun pursuit for you both?"

Susan interrupted the train of thought before May had a chance to reply. Looking into one of the display cases she asked to see a ring. After moving over to the case where she stood Vonnette unlocked it and reached in for a navy blue, natural crystal ring with a faceted navy blue stone next to it. "This one?" She asked and received a nod.

Removing the ring from a clear plastic stand that held it upright, she then handed it over to Susan. Vonnette automatically placed a flat, black, velvet disc on top of the display case. Vonnette always made the effort to keep the glass unscratched. When Susan took the ring off her hand to return it, the velvet would prevent any possible scratches from stones and metal on her pristine glass surfaces. Surprisingly, many people saw the velvet pad and still placed jewelry on top of the glass case, an occurrence Vonnette could never grasp. An explanation followed about how this ring had a natural, uncut sapphire crystal in it along with a faceted sapphire alongside. Deep blue sapphires connect with the psychic ability we each have. You can easily say blue sapphires have a connection to the third eye.

While Susan looked at the ring in her hand May added her two cents. "Susan, you are so connected to the third eye. This could be a great ring for you!"

Turning the ring over and over again, Susan did eventually place the ring on her finger to admire it. Once she removed and handed it back over the counter to Vonnette, she asked to see the Herkimer diamond ring that was sitting next to where the sapphire ring had been displayed.

As Vonnette replaced the sapphire ring into its little stand and inside the display case, she then removed the Herkimer for her to try on. "I see you're drawn to natural crystals, Susan, because both rings you've asked about have that as a core element. Perhaps you are finding your way in the metaphysical world. Let me say this is not a stone for the faint of heart. It's doubly terminated, meaning it's pointed on both ends of the crystal. This mineral comes from Herkimer, NY. Generally, smaller crystals are found and sold from that mine. Obviously, this is a nice large one. This stone energetically brings in a huge electrical charge to the brain. Think of the conscious and sub-conscious mind going in different directions at the same time. You'll then have a taste of what this stone is capable of energetically."

"Holy crap!" Embarrassed by her spontaneous outburst, Susan quickly looked about to see if anyone heard her and then continued, "Oh, God, I should not have just said that. I'm sorry! But it is much larger than I had initially thought. Between that and the energy you claim it to have, I was caught off guard."

Everyone laughed.

"Why is it called a diamond?" May queried.

"That's something I can only guess at. I believe it's because of the clarity, along with the crystal structure being close to that of a diamond, but honestly I'm not sure."

Feeling a kindred spirit connection with these female artists, Vonnette went off in a slightly different direction. "If you are in the midst of learning to live in the metaphysical world, maybe one of the first questions you can ask yourself is, 'Are you living your life authentically?'"

May stood nodding her head with a slight smile on her face; she seemed connected with the question, but it was still Susan who answered.

"You know, I'm not even sure what the Hell that really means! Oops, I did it again. Pardon my French. But seriously, when you are living any old way, aren't you living authentically?"

"Not a problem, Susan, with your explicative. Actually, we're all living authentically if we believe in our choices. As an example, say you're a thief who robs people for a living. You come home at the end of the day, or night, just like someone who works crunching numbers in an office. You're tired and feel done in from your long day, or night. You are working from theft-to-theft just the same as most people are living from pay-check to pay-check. Isn't that person living authentically?"

Both women looked surprised as to how the conversation went into the direction of talking about thieves. Though Vonnette recognized their facial expressions, she continued in hopes that her tale would connect up in the end because sometimes she wasn't sure herself where a conversation would go.

"Generally, we do not like to think of a thief as having a home life let alone a nice life at our expense. So, the thought of their living authentically is not something we want to have in our heads. But, at the end of the day, they may be living as authentically as you or I.

"The thief's job is to take belongings you believe are yours. You paid for them, aren't they yours?

"Well, it simply boils down to what you think of as authentic and if belongings are actually yours. The truth is, yes, you bought and paid for them, but they aren't really yours. You've paid to borrow them for some period of time. If you have a cat or dog in your home, you'll get what I'm saying here. Our animals remind us each and every day that our stuff is temporary. The tail wags and wipes the coffee table clean of any and all bric-a-brac, to say nothing of nice glassware. The stealthy feline climbs up into a bookshelf that houses some antique baubles along with your latest read, and even with the cat's great agility, the cherished item goes flying to the floor never to be the same again! Do you love your animal or do you love the stuff? Usually it's both. In the end, you should be saying the living creature wins out over stuff. If you're not claiming that then you're not being driven by the heart. Instead, you're living as a collector. Today is about authenticity which connects the brain to the heart. And if you're a collector you know the thrill is in the hunt. Having stuff about after you find it is really about collecting dust.

"By the way, you cannot take that collection with you when you leave this plane. Oh, except for tattoos. But then I feel you leave your body when you die, that your soul continues on to another plane. If in fact that's true, then you still don't take the collection of tattoos on with you.

"Anyway, I digress.

"Today when people ask about living authentically, they usually mean in the world of metaphysics. The word 'metaphysics' alone takes us into another column of study for another day. For today, let's simply say metaphysics is the study of the unknown. Obviously, that covers a lot of territory. Authenticity is about being true to yourself and your beliefs whatever they might be. And this can be a huge task each and every day no matter what you do for a living, what you collect, whom you live with, or who your friends are. Most of us do not think of ourselves as thieves, and yet . . . we steal moments from our day as we look out a window, or snack on something we know we ought not to. We tell white lies to protect ourselves or our friends from criticism.

"What I might suggest is that if at days' end you can look into a mirror in your mind and claim you were as true to who you feel you want to be, then you are living authentically. If that didn't happen, then perhaps you could ask yourself who or what you want to be in this life?

"Being a metaphysician working to live as authentically as possible each and every day, I believe we are in school while we are humans on this earth plane. On some level, we graduate when we leave here. Looking into the mirror each day can be a challenge if you take it as seriously as I do. It might also be the thing that gets you to the next grade level. Maybe telling those white lies is something that's eating you up inside. Maybe that's thieving you of all you want in this go-round of a life. If so, then that's not living authentically. You can choose to change that element internally. I won't claim to have all the answers nor will I say you are not living up to your potential. I also won't tell you what happens after we check out of this life.

"I do think it's important to love yourself and question what's going on internally. You need to ask the hard question as to whether you are a thief. Ask, too, if you judge people who are living as authentically as possible no matter what their career choice is or their internal belief system is. Only you can tell if *you* are living as authentically as possible each and every day.

"Certainly, this was a strange segue for you to suddenly find yourselves involved in. Here's why I've gone off in this direction. When you choose a stone like Herkimer to work with in its uncut state, your mind takes off into parts unknown. Just as I did now as a demonstration. So, if you want to expand your consciousness, this is a good stone for you to work with. If you simply want to feel *whatever* intuitively, you can go with sapphire. Each are interesting choices."

"It's fun talking to you. If we didn't come here with a mission today, we would most likely never leave your booth, but we have to go, carry on, or whatever."

"I'm so sorry if you felt I was rambling."

"Honestly, I think I could listen to a lot more. But we do have a limited amount of time here to figure out if this show is one we want to apply to or not. I'm taking your card again. I'll keep that stone ring in mind. Thanks for everything. I'm sure we will meet again, perhaps on the show circuit or maybe through the metaphysical world you have enlarged for us today. And then we can go deeper into everything!"

"If you can't stop thinking about the ring, Susan, then perhaps you are supposed to have it. If so, then give me a call and we'll work out the rest over the phone."

With that, Vonnette watched as Susan and May left her booth to investigate the rest of the show, all while wondering how she got so off track in conversation. Maybe by getting off track she lost a sale. Maybe by handling that huge Herkimer ring her brain went into uncharted territory. What she did know was that she hadn't thought about the cancer donation booth across from hers in over an hour. That in itself was a great gift.

⁂

When Vonnette was packing up her jewelry at the end of the day, she went over her dream messages. First up was the dream about a huge bowl of cereal and a famous person. Maybe cereal represented some form of wealth. Being able to feed oneself is a form of plenty! Famous people symbolize a sign of help from an unexpected source and that had happened in financial ways today. The three ladies buying four pieces of her jewelry was unexpected and had most certainly pertained to her financial situation.

Bone and yellow beryl appeared in one dream. Wearing bone when feeling bombarded by life helps absorb shock to the emotional system. Finding the breast lump was a lot of emotional bombardment. Vonnette *did* need to have some of that shock absorbed. Yellow Beryl helps one have wisdom in sharing. How and what Vonnette shared with clients throughout the day had connected with that stone. Even though she had not packed any bone or golden beryl from her personal jewelry, Vonnette thankfully had a piece of each in her finished inventory to place upon her person this day. Yes, she was energetically connected with the stone messages from her dreams.

Being across from the silent auction donation table for cancer was an emotional strain, but it didn't dampen her ability to rally when called upon by clients. Perhaps that table and the possible reference to having cancer herself connected with the dream about explosives being set but not going off. Or, maybe that dream represented how Vonnette felt when the booth-mate unplugged her lights. The saying, *that which doesn't kill you makes you stronger* kept circling her brain. The dream could also have had something to do with the man who wanted to run ragged over her about Vonnette's use of a knuckleduster for credit cards. She never lost her temper with him, so no explosion on that front either. And then, she had sold something to his wife so that could be called an overall win.

She remembered the explosion dream also had a reference to astrology in it. The astrologist claimed that six weeks was the correct time for the explosion. That six-week time slot may be reflective of her mammogram being rescheduled sooner.

As Vonnette finished these thoughts about her dream messages, her mind turned to one of her friends. Adele was into astrology, much more so than Vonnette. After looking at Vonnette's astrology chart one day Adele told her it made perfect sense she was so into her dreams because Pluto was in her 12th house, the house of dreams and the subterranean.

Vonnette always suggested to others that she knew enough about astrology to get herself into hot water and hoped that no one would hold her accountable for whatever connection she might suggest to them about character traits she assigned to a specific person with a particular astrological sign. Pluto and the 12th house of dreams and the subterranean . . . who knew if that was the reason she had such recall of her dreams or why she felt they were meant for daily guidance.

People asked Vonnette to decipher dream messages for them while wanting to know how she could seemingly interpret them so easily. She never implied it was due to where Pluto was in her astrology chart. Instead, Vonnette told those interested that she wasn't sure where her understanding of dream messages came from. Maybe it was the fact that her mother had some interest in interpreting her own dreams, and that from early childhood dream messages were discussed openly between mother and daughter.

One close friend asked about a repeat dream she was having. Wendy never lacked for companions. People enjoyed being around this woman who looked great and made each person feel interesting. Certain she would have children in this life, she felt let down when the universe seemed to have other plans. After a full hysterectomy, Wendy continually dreamed about a large hen house in which she was a chicken. There were loads of eggs in these dream sequences along with one rooster who strutted about the yard seemingly very proud. He kept all the hens happy. Wendy did not like that rooster, so much so that when the rooster approached her in the dream, she would feel shaken, and wake in a full sweat. After a couple months of having this recurring dream, Wendy asked Vonnette if she had any insight about her experiences.

"Wendy, this is not a difficult dream to interpret. You're going to hate yourself for being too in your own head not to see the meaning. But here goes . . . . Since your full hysterectomy you've lost a purpose of having children you were certain were to be yours in this lifetime. Dreaming of eggs being all around you must feel on some deep level that everyone else can still have children except you. The strutting rooster represents your husband. He could have children with someone else if he chose to. Subconsciously you're feeling resentment towards him right now. That's why in your dream you awaken when the rooster comes near and then you feel off once awake. It's classic, really, when you think about it."

"Oh my God!" came Wendy's voice over the phone. Wendy felt Vonnette's interpretation was correct and agreed she should have gotten the hidden meaning of the dream when it was really simple. Once Wendy understood the dream, she stopped having it.

Interpreting other people's dreams could be so simple for Vonnette, yet it would drive her crazy when trying to interpret her own. When Adele, her friend who was into astrology, told her Pluto was in her house of dreams, Vonnette needed more information. After inquiring as to just what that meant, Adele informed her that Pluto was the planet of karma.

Karma can be confusing at the best of times; the concept though, could really be quite easy to comprehend. Karma means that what is given out, comes back. As an example: if someone screams at another, then others will scream back. A rather simplistic description, but the point is valid. The thing about karma that no one completely gets is that karma never gives an announcement of when it's going to come along.

Vonnette had asked, begged, even for answers about what had happened at the end of a relationship over six months ago, yet no answer that she understood came to her. Certain she had made peace with the final event of that break-up, she'd begun online dating again. Careful not to jump into another emotional commitment, she developed a method of screening men to see if they actually had anything in common with her before having a first face-to-face with whomever. Any dating, but especially online dating, could be made up of lies. How could she know for sure if someone was telling her the truth? Vonnette relied on her own intuition when prospective dates answered loads of questions. At least that's what she hoped for. One man did not seem to be her type, but she felt it worthwhile investigating simply because they both made items by hand. He was a woodworker. She saw that as a starting point.

His lack of patience showed up quickly when Vonnette was unwilling to connect in person immediately. Doing a complete turnaround from his previously kind and interested nature online, he screamed at her in writing one day. What he wrote didn't make sense to her at first, but he came across with serious passion during his tirade. Rereading his message, she came to comprehend that different women he'd met online were all looking for Mister Perfect. He felt rejected by Vonnette due to her not wanting to connect with him immediately in person, so he was angry. He commented that he shouldn't have been honest on his profile page; she reminded him of other rejections from his online dating scenarios, so he made her a target of his anger.

Normally, Vonnette responded to all dating site generated e-mails, feeling it the courteous thing to do. Unsure what she could possibly say in response to this particular e-mail left her at a loss. She would not take responsibility for what had happened between this man and all of his other online contacts. Why continue with something when he lost his temper so easily online all before they had even met face-to-face?

While thinking about the karmic plane she wondered if this situation might have been an answer to her other circumstance. Six months earlier her last serious relationship with Joseph had been confusing. It had had her up in the air and completely off balance emotionally.

For years prior to meeting Joseph, she'd had visions about an event, a wedding. These visions all began while she worked in her garden one day. Living across from the cemetery, her park with monuments, Vonnette excused her sightings thinking that perhaps the people involved were now deceased. Maybe their remains were planted across the street and they were coming over to give her visions of a joyous day in their past.

Although she dismissed the visions at first, Vonnette was surprised when they kept coming to her. Each time she had an apparition, it was ghostly and transparent. Not long into these repeated quick, snippet-type sightings, Vonnette realized the wedding taking place was not from some gone by era, but rather a more current time. Clothing was her first real clue. Attendees were all in modern dress. When the people at the wedding finally came into full focus, Vonnette knew it was her wedding because she recognized most of the attendees! At that point she also began to see the dress she wore to the wedding, not a typical wedding dress, but a tea length one made of white cotton with multiple layers, or tiers, that formed tulip shapes. Though she did try to see the grooms' face, she was dismayed that it was never visible.

Time progressed. The wedding scene came to her repeatedly. Her latest visions also included a log house that had been built next to a road that lead up a mountain. Quite different from where she now lived, the kitchen could always be seen along with the exterior front porch that had a wooden swing built for two. During one of those such visions a voice from inside her head said that the house existed in New Hampshire, a forty-five-minute drive from Mount Washington. She'd never been to Mount Washington and as such had no idea if her images were correct for that locale.

Then, one day while looking in a few storefront windows at a downtown cluster of stores known as Brick Market Place, she noticed a man trailing behind her. Catching her completely off-guard when he approached, Vonnette noticed this man stood taller than she by about four inches. He had black hair with touches of salt and pepper and wore blue jeans, blue tee shirt and clogs, and although in casual dress, he looked attractive.

Once they began talking, he said he was looking for a hand-made gift for his mom. She would be seventy-eight that coming week. Even though he lived in Pawtucket which housed many fine artisans and wonderful galleries, he felt Newport was the perfect place to find that special gift.

As she looked in the same store windows as he had, she felt

flattered that he suggested she might help him choose something. It never dawned on her that he was watching her ass more than any window dressing along the street. Instead, she felt they both shared an interest in the arts, so when he asked, she opted to have a cocktail with him after the shopping effort was complete.

Unbelievably, and against all her normal standards, she followed a man she did not know in her car to a near-by lounge he knew of for a drink.

That was the beginning of an intense relationship lasting only a few months. It surprised Vonnette at how quickly they became close. Speaking on the phone a few times a day, in e-mails as well as in-person dates left them both craving more of one another. Chemistry had them in her grip and was not letting go.

Joseph didn't recall his dreams, yet he didn't feel that Vonnette's choice to live by the messages she received was strange. They hadn't discovered many common interests as yet other than their love of handmade items.

Vonnette felt this man was possibly *the* man of her garden wedding visions. Grateful to have a face to attach to her images, she became surprised when they all disappeared as the relationship carried forward. Vonnette thought perhaps the visions did not need to continue now since Joseph was physically in her life so, she let them go.

As Vonnette readied herself for a big show in Connecticut she had not participated in before, she had a serious attack of nerves. Explaining this fright to Joseph, she thought he understood her level of stress.

He didn't.

There had been red flags in the relationship before this moment that she had chosen to ignore, like the uncertainty she felt as to where his income really came from. He'd said he worked for a liquor company in sales. That could explain why he always had bottles of booze in the trunk of his car. If so, then why was he able to take bottles from that reserve whenever he wanted? Wouldn't it all have belonged to the company he worked for? And, if he did work for a liquor company, how could he have so much cash on him all the time? Since the relationship was so new, she chose to put these questions on the back burner believing they would sort themselves out over time.

While in the uneasy two weeks prior to and preparing for the show in Connecticut, Joseph chose not to call her or e-mail numerous times each day, the pattern he'd established thus far. Although Vonnette could call him, Joseph had asked her not to since he was on the road dealing with sales. It was accepted early on that all calls would be placed by him when time permitted and was yet another red flag. Sudden withdrawal of his attention sent Vonnette into an emotional tailspin. Feeling betrayed and alone, she slipped quickly into that familiar black hole territory where insecurity rules.

Finally, a full week and a half later his next call came, which was one day before she had to pack and leave for the show. By that time Vonnette felt taken for granted and was filled with frustration. Exclaiming to herself as she saw his number displayed on her flip phone, "Nice thing, once he got involved with me, called me every day, sometimes three times a day, he left me high and dry for over a week? Just who does he think I am? Apparently, he thinks I am at his beck and call!"

Answering and hearing Josephs' voice on the other end of the phone after that week's absence she felt incensed and everything came out of her mouth as a scream. Reading him the riot act about leaving her for over a week without a call, she didn't know how to contain the rant.

"Dammit!" She expressed to him. "I'm an independent woman!"

Unable to stop or control her screaming that day, she was amazed that even after he hung up on her, she felt even more angry and hurt.

Well after the phone call with him ended, she kept talking out loud to who knows who? "Maybe he's not accustomed to independent women. Maybe he thinks I'm somehow less than he, or that my work is less important than his. Whatever he thinks, he's wrong!"

With no time to dedicate to this man or the situation, Vonnette finished packing and headed off to her show.

While at the show, Vonnette replayed everything that had recently transpired and decided she'd been quite wrong to scream at him in that manner. No one deserved such treatment. Even if that was how her parents used to respond to one another she knew better than that at her age. Nothing ever gets resolved with a tirade.

After returning home from the show, she did try calling to apologize. He eventually took one of her calls and claimed to accept her apology; however, he did not want to see her again. That was it. It was over, whatever *it* was.

Over the next six months Vonnette replayed those events in her head. She always believed she was wrong to have screamed at him but correct in what she had said. It was high time she stood up for herself in this universe and received better treatment than what he had handed over to her that last fateful week and a half.

Falling in love during that four-month time frame had thrown Vonnette off balance. No wedding visions and no partner to talk all this over with left her even more out of tune with her inner self.

When she had chemistry with a man, she would normally lose her sense of self in the relationship. Determined not to let that happen this time she went overboard in making sure he understood she was not waiting around for his affections like some lapdog. If he really loved her unconditionally as he'd claimed, he would have forgiven her tirade and gotten in touch again to make amends. At the end of the day, wasn't this where good make-up sex came from? Frustration, anger, and a tirade with an apology does usually make for great sex.

Supportive friends told Vonnette to forget him. That he was not worth the time and effort she was putting into understanding what had happened. But Vonnette felt there was a reason for everything, and she needed to comprehend what had transpired in order to move on. Moreover, she'd had all those wedding visions that suddenly stopped. How could she reconcile that in her mind let alone her heart? Though Vonnette never shared details of her repeated visions with him, she knew about Joseph's desire to be in New Hampshire after retirement and that connected with the images she'd seen of the log house built into the side of the mountain.

When she was fully ready to let go of that liaison and whatever had really happened, the karmic answer was then staring her in the face. Insecurities and emotional imbalances caused Vonnette to fly off the deep end with Joseph. Maybe she had pushed him away before he'd had a chance to leave on his own. That was something she might never know. If karma was where the universe handed back whatever she had handed out, then this online dating site man screaming at her was a karmic answer to that day when she had screamed at Joseph. And, why would anyone pursue such lunatic action willingly? Vonnette didn't want to ever be in touch with that online screaming man again just as Joseph had certainly felt about her all those months ago.

Vonnette told herself that karma had shown her how she had treated Joseph and how in turn she did not wish to be treated by this dating site man. Finally, in her mind, the dots connected. Now able to grasp what and why things were happening, Vonnette knew that if she didn't like what she was receiving, then she had to look at how she had treated others in the past, recognize it, make some internal shifts and hopefully move out of that particular Karmic Hell. She'd heard that karma can and often does carry forward into future lives if it's not dealt with front and center in this one. So, Vonnette dealt with this bit of karma in order to get it over and done with. Her karma this day was to walk away from the screaming online man just as Joseph had done six months ago. Thankfully, this time she had not been in love with the bodiless man she had only met online. But karma had given her the answer she craved whether she liked it or not. Looking inward, she scrutinized how she had treated another and how now she had been treated in kind.

Karma is a tricky bedfellow that way.

With that thought Vonnette finished packing up her goods for the night and closed down her booth for the day. The full day had presented her with gifts of distraction on multiple levels. Clients liked and bought her finished jewelry. Even her lights being unplugged provided a much-needed moment of peace before launching into the meeting with the spirit attached to Tia. Recalling

Candace L. Sherman

how she stood up to the credit card person years back gave her a bit of pride as she had stood tall against the man questioning her methods of payment today. There wasn't anything she could do about her lump until sometime in the future. No, cancer was thankfully not her main form of mental activity this day. Having the cancer donation tables firmly planted across from her booth for the whole weekend was still a challenge. But, Vonnette instead chose to focus on deep thoughts about her dreams and where her mind took her with each message throughout the remainder of the weekend. As in her dream last night, Vonnette wouldn't allow the emotional explosives to go off while at the show this weekend.

CHAPTER THREE

Morristown

October 17-19, 2008
Set up & cocktail party Friday 17th
Actual Show: 18-19

14Kr/y/g Amethyst & Lemon Citrine Cuff Bracelet

Candace L. Sherman

DREAMS

1. It was a three-day art show where no one was coming in through the doors. All the vendors were upset and didn't know how they could continue.

Vonnette forgot the show schedule on the third day and didn't come in until it was literally ending. The show promoter was not happy with the fact she had not attended her booth all day. Booth-mates claimed it had been dead, so she had not missed anything no matter what the promoter had said to her.

At the closing of the show Vonnette noticed two kittens and a puppy coming out of the neighbor's garage area. One kitten was mostly gray and fluffy with a bit of white on its face, the other was a completely black one. Even though Vonnette had a black and white cat and an all-black cat at home, she felt quite attached to the black one that approached her. When the puppy came over, she realized it was a black Labrador retriever. The black kitten, the black puppy and Vonnette were in a petting fest. All three were intertwined and loving every minute of it. How could she possibly leave these new friends behind when she left the show? What on earth would she do with another cat and then a dog, too?

2. 14Ky/r/g gold cuff bracelet with a large cushion cut lemon citrine (lemon quartz to some) and triangular cut amethyst. Both stones were mounted in bezels with the opening of the cuff sitting on the top of the wrist instead of the bottom. Seeing this in her dream and knowing she had such a bracelet in her finished inventory, Vonnette felt certain someone was going to buy it.

Once fully awake, Vonnette went into the studio to choose a pair of lemon citrine earrings and an amethyst ring to wear for the day. Stone healing properties rolled around in her mind as she laid the days' jewelry out on the bathroom countertop. Handle inner and outer issues in a different creative way by wearing lemon citrine. Be insightful by connecting the intuitive crown chakra with protective forces by wearing amethyst.

Next was clothing. While choosing a pair of socks, she noticed a new pair draped flat across the top of other folded pairs. A ladybug design was woven into them. They were still on the tiny plastic hanger with the cardboard fold over bearing the makers' label and price tag. These socks reminded Vonnette of a movie message . . . "Ladybugs, lots and lots of lady bugs!" This was a line from *Under the Tuscan Sun* where the main character was told she was being sad yet again! The character actor went on to explain that as a child she would go to a field to catch ladybugs. Once there she couldn't find any and out of frustration would eventually fall asleep in the grass. When she woke, there would be ladybugs all around her. Coming across a new pair of socks with ladybugs on them that she hadn't noticed until today, Vonnette felt must mean something!

Maybe it would become a ladybug kind of day for Vonnette where she would relax and things around her would fall into place. She didn't know why but she felt awake, had energy, and happened to be happy. Why did she feel different, she wondered? The clocks had been turned back yesterday as part of daylight savings time. But she doubted that could be it. Maybe she had finally gotten enough sleep, or cried enough. Whatever the reason, Vonnette didn't care. Getting back to work and out for a walk became her focus. That sense of normalcy, of what having a purpose in life suggested; lump or no lump, a shift had happened. Losing herself in work and halting that feeling of sadness would begin while out walking. A new pair of socks would at least give an emotional boost that the day was a new beginning.

First up today: bathe, dress and then e-mail all the lovely women that had given support this past week. "Giving thanks to all is a great way to begin a day," she thought. It fed her soul.

To All My Dear Women Friends,

For those I wrote, e-mailed, phoned, or saw in person last week, thank you from the whole of my heart! Thank you for your kindness and well-wishes. I cannot begin to say how fortunate I feel to be included in your thoughts and prayers. You helped me get through a very difficult and emotionally weak moment.

I'm unsure what happened, but today I feel like myself again with a positive attitude!

Maybe I've had enough sleep.

Maybe I cried my last tear (doubtful there, but a high hope).

Maybe it's the time change.

Maybe it's something astrological.

Why is not important. I am writing to ask for your continued positive thoughts. I am on the mend psychologically. The mammogram appointment is still weeks away. It's a new day and a new week. Though the sun has not peeked out from behind the clouds this day, I'm seeing it in my minds' eye. Hope your day is filled with inner sun as well.

Love, Vonnette

One mission complete, now on to that walk. Getting out in the fresh air mattered. She was never concerned about how far she walked. Gray skies above didn't affect Vonnette's mood. In her heart, it was a clear day full of possibilities.

Since she never figured job prices for two clients the day before, she decided that would be a top priority today. Making the phone calls for those estimated jobs to schedule consultations would come later on.

Remembering one of her dream messages . . . One kitten was gray, but also had white on it. Gray in dreams indicates marking time. White denotes all around success. Black in dreams could be a bad omen, or maybe that money would come in to bring her accounts into the black. The two animals she grew attached to in the dream were not fully grown, but were old enough to leave their mother. Animals in infant stage might cross reference to the jobs she was giving estimates for but had not yet created. Holding onto that last train of thought, Vonnette felt she ought not worry about the show. It might turn out like her dream message where no one attended, which would translate into no sales. However, money could come in from some other source today. And, she trusted that source would reveal itself over the course of the day.

Concepts such as these ran through her head as she walked. Maintaining a positive belief system was vital and a mainstay. Today Vonnette felt she had come back to some sense of that normalcy. With the word "normal" in her head, she reminded herself of a couple of birthday cards she received last week. Since they had arrived so far ahead of her actual birthday, and due to her depression, she hadn't opened two cards for three days. One card said, "Thank goodness she *wasn't* normal." That made her smile.

Holding good thoughts, Vonnette felt that card message could translate into her breast lump not being a normal shape for cancer. Maybe it was something like a cyst.

Back from her walk and while figuring prices in her jewelry studio, Vonnette watched her favorite birds, crows, being quite vocal across the street. The crows flew about the large central maple that was still dropping its leaves. That one tree in the very middle of the graveyard was always the last in the neighborhood each fall to fully lose foliage. "Maybe it's a nice umbrella for the spirits," Vonnette thought while watching the crows fly in and out of the tree branches.

There were three crows which indicated union. By e-mailing her friends, Vonnette already had union, or connection, in her day.

Once finished figuring job prices, Vonnette packed her car with show equipment in preparation for her drive to Morristown, NJ. How to pack the car had become a practiced skill. Though she had a compact car, a Prius, she still managed to fit her whole booth display and the tent inside. With the hatchback and the rear seats folded down, the car had an internal height with space necessary for all her equipment. Everything had a particular place. As the seasons changed, so did what and how she packed. When she first started traveling to do shows, she sometimes had to take everything out of the car and repack so the whole lot would fit. Today, she was able to fit even more inside the car since her ideas on placement had become such a skill.

Packing for an indoor show Vonnette needed her usual booth set up. Display cases, rug, curtains, collapsible tables, fabric skirts, a step stool and over-sized photos of finished jewelry that would hang as backdrops were packed. Since Vonnette had never partici-pated in this New Jersey show, she also included a dolly in case she had to carry her booth display some distance instead of unloading on site. Better to be safe than sorry on that front. There were a few indoor shows where she still utilized her tent, but this show pro-vided pipe and drape on three sides for each booth. What color that drape might be she did not know, so her own curtains could be vital to help her stand out in a crowd. Happily, since she didn't need her tent this trip, the foldable dolly and a small, fully-formed wooden table fit behind the passengers' seat where her folded tent would normally have been. The table could be used as an actual sales counter or for informational hand-outs like business cards, or maybe even a guest book to collect new names and addresses. What use that table could serve would be decided once she was at the show and setting up her booth.

Nervous about delicate, detachable glass parts for display cases and lightbulbs, Vonnette carefully placed those bags on the floor behind the driver and passenger seats. A small canvas bag full of extension cords was placed over the rear floor hump. Once in place, longer items like tabletops could overlap and further protect these items. Every inch of the car was accounted for. On one side were foldable tabletops, her collapsible, tall, booth chair and a couple of Lucite display cases. Her rolled up 8x10' carpet filled the center sec-tion along with the long curtain rods, tracks for the overhead lights, and a duffle bag filled with clothes.

Over the years, Vonnette had become smarter about the actual neck forms for displaying her jewelry. Originally, she placed all forms in one bag; together they took up valuable space inside the car, so she created bubble wrap homes for each unit that she then placed inside the two Lucite cases. These cases also had a bubble wrap nest with Velcro closures for protection before going into their own zippered bags, so they would not be damaged if jostled about in the car. It was a bit like Russian nesting dolls where each bubble wrap piece fit inside another larger piece that was then placed inside more bubble wrap and a yet larger zippered bag.

Grouping as much as possible in canvas or oversized zippered plastic bags, Vonnette then color coded all to be easily identified when unpacking and re-packing. Proper placement of all these bags in the car had come about due to space, weight balance, and visibility. A big canvas bag contained papier Mache boxes ready for wrapping sold jewelry could be placed anywhere within the car once packed due to being lightweight. Sales counter items like sales books, pens, notepaper, business cards, velvet pads to show jewelry on, Windex and paper towels would all be in one large bag that today fit between the legs of that extra table. One very heavy canvas bag full of items she never knew if she would need housed screw drivers, a hammer, duct tape, masking tape, bungee cords, hooks to hang her photos and signs from, safety pins, fishing weights for when the wind blew curtains all around and then floor wedges in case her space was not on level ground. Gobs of clamps of all sizes went into that same bag and were utilized throughout her booth. Curtain rods created her three, fabric walls and were held in place with clamps. Other clamps gripped hold of display case fabrics. Still more clamps held her overhead tracks in place so she would have lights. That heavy bag went in the very rear of the car and today was placed on top of the dolly.

Other items were put on the floor in front of the passenger seat, and then on top of that seat as well. Once done, the car would have a full load with space enough up front for her, some drinking water and her handbag.

Happy with her placement, Vonnette pulled out a forest-green, flat, bed sheet. Spreading this out over the top of all that was packed in the back made it easier for her to see out the rear window due to reflections off plastic bags. Climbing into the driver's seat she quickly checked the rearview mirror to make sure her view was clear. Vonnette then fit the well-worn, kid leather gloves she used for loading over the ends of the track lights and curtain rods in case they slid forward they would not damage anything on the dashboard GPS. Hearing crickets in the yard while loading, she wondered what they might mean this day? Next, she headed inside again to finish packing food that would complete the center isle in the rear of the car. She would then be ready to leave at any time.

Vonnette decided to call clients after reaching the show hopeful there would be time and energy then to discuss both monetary and time estimates if orders were placed.

Getting on the road early was best as it was going to be a very long day. It would be about a four-and-a-half-hour drive. Making the hotel the first stop in New Jersey would mean she could unload personal items. After which she could find her way to the show to set up her booth, head back to the hotel for a quick wash, and change of clothes, and then return to the show venue for the opening night cocktail party.

The George Washington Bridge crossing was, thankfully, uneventful. Actually, the whole drive went along smoothly. There weren't even any weird hold ups along 95 in Connecticut. That alone was a great gift! Finding the hotel for the weekend seemed easy as well. Twenty minutes after her quick unload at the hotel, Vonnette arrived at the Morristown Armory for the show called The Morristown Craftmarket.

Vonnette parked and went in search of the check-in desk where she was given a show packet and told to get her car in line for a drive-in that would take place in twenty minutes. Inside the packet was an 8x10 sheet of paper with her booth number on it. Instructions on another page said to put that 8x10 sheet on her dashboard before driving inside as it would provide necessary information for the men giving directions. That slip should also be left on her dashboard throughout the weekend for easy identification in case she parked incorrectly and someone needed to locate her. Also inside the 9x11" manila envelope were instructions for the New Jersey sales tax percentage, the show schedule, time slots allowed for vendors to be inside before and after hours for set up and break down each day, and a printed name tag on a long lanyard cord expected to be worn at all times during the show that identified each artist and/or helper and separated them from possible buyers. The packet included information as well on when artists would be able to drive in safely at the end of the show to reload their cars and leave.

While heading back to her vehicle, Vonnette felt timing today had been perfect! Being able to drive up to her booth to unload was much easier than having to dolly everything inside.

When she was instructed to pull inside the one floor building, she realized men were positioned at every turn to guide each vehicle into place for the unloading process. Once there, she was instructed to quickly remove all contents and place them into her designated 10x10' space. No time was given for unloading really. She was hustled and whistled at to move faster and then basically yelled at to move! These same men gave instructions on how to maneuver her car back out of the narrow aisles created by all the pipe and drape-lined booths to reach the outside of the building. All floors were smooth concrete. Vonnette found them slippery to maneuver and drive around corners. With some patience and time, she did eventually make her way back outside again to park, but by then she was stressed and tired. Somehow she had to muster enough energy to keep going.

When Vonnette reentered the building on foot, she took longer than expected to set up her booth. Her having to unload so quickly meant everything ended up in a jumbled pile in the center of the booth. Normally she placed all packed items near the back of, or just outside her space until ready for each bag. Cars were constantly going up and down the aisle leaving no place outside the booth to store items. Also, at the rear of her booth was a single curtain dividing her space from that neighbor. Most shows had double curtains there providing a bit of storage room for each artist. This show gave no such space. Shifting bags from one place to another was exhausting. Thrown off by the unexpected car fumes, and the yelling of directions happening all around her, Vonnette found that each time she placed her display tables and cases, they seemed to be in the wrong position. Then, the cement flooring had uneven spots, so packed shims would in fact be necessary.

Behind, and underneath her display area were temporary shelves where Vonnette stored gift boxes, bags, scissors and more. Soon enough, she placed all her sales books, ring sizing tools, velvet pads, pens, calculator and hand mirror for easy access. Eventually

Vonnette made the space her own and felt a bit more balanced. After testing all the lights to make sure they worked and were properly positioned, she unplugged the lights and pulled out two, white, lightweight cotton bed blankets and placed them carefully over the tops of her display cases that she had readied for her jewelry once she returned from changing back at the hotel. Walking out of the building, she stopped often to glance at other booth displays to gather inspiration for possible future show set-ups.

While reaching the car, driving, and arriving back at the hotel, Vonnette thought she would now have time to make those phone calls to possible clients with their price quotes. Calling the first person on her list, Vonnette gave the quote estimate. That client wanted to ponder the expense at least overnight. Not a problem. Vonnette knew her prices were in a financial category where people had to think about their investment. Her next client said yes to the estimated quote. Numbers were exchanged over the phone for credit card information. Deposit for custom orders was half up front with the balance due upon completion. Finished with the phone calls, she had just enough time to shower, change clothes, and return to the show venue for opening night.

People came through the show prepared for a social event complete with cocktails, hors d'oeuvres, art and artisans. Most attendees were dressed in upscale office attire. Artists tended to dress up a bit for shows, too, when a cocktail event was involved; however, it was never a challenge to distinguish an artist from a show attendee.

Many people walking the show did stop at Vonnette's booth claiming they would be back the next day to shop. Vonnette thought how people who say that have clearly never been in retail because if you're on the receiving side of such a comment it sounds as though they're saying, "I have a bridge for sale." Artists call these people IB'S. It's short for *I'll be back*. At the end of a show day when another artist asks how you did, it's easy to respond with, "I had many *IB's* today." Some people visit these types of shows solely as entertainment. Artists cannot normally distinguish the difference between buyers and tire kickers unless there are shopping bags in hand.

An older woman came up in front of Vonnette's booth with a much younger woman alongside who realized there had been an unscheduled stop and waited to see where this might lead. The elder woman was speaking before she stopped and continued on even though she was browsing. Feeling she was suddenly inside a private moment, Vonnette didn't say anything to these women; instead, she stood and smiled in hopeful readiness.

"You know, some women marry when they are quite young mainly to procreate. It's good as they have the energy necessary to spend time and do things with their children. Sometimes when those children are older these same women find themselves at a loss. Not just because the children have grown and left home to find their own way, but because they no longer know who or what they are without children to define them.

"When that happens, they might leave their husbands who have settled into such a routine they no longer inspire their wives to be all they can be. Those men usually feel it's their time to be children again and expect their wives to dote on them. If these wives leave home and their marriage, they often find they are quite happy being alone to discover, or should I say, rediscover themselves.

"Of course, there are women who meet their soul mates when they are young. These women find their male counterpart helps them to rediscover their inner womanhood when she feels lost, but these men are few and far between.

"So many of my friends settled when they got older. Settled for existing in a world that no longer inspired them to be more, more than anything they could have imagined for themselves. Somehow they accepted a life-style chosen at a young age that no longer fits. Or maybe their relationships work because their husbands knew them in their youth as well as sexually because some women are afraid to step out of a sexual comfort zone.

"Thankfully, there are other women friends of mine who are changing as are their sexual interests. Of course, their men have grown, too, mentally, emotionally and sexually. With women, though, these changes in sexual energy come out in such creative ways they almost cannot contain themselves with all that is happening inside their heads!

"Interestingly, there are also women who didn't marry young, nor did they have children. Often these women are the ones who give such great inspiration to the women who've been married forever. These women have been self-sufficient, know how to be alone, with friends, and yes, even with men when they want to be. It's all on their terms. This seems very appealing for the women who decided to leave their nests as it were.

"Some women find true love at a later age. Those women are either married at the time, or unmarried and find their other half in such peaceful ways. They know the struggle for power is useless; that's for the young. Men don't define them; rather, their men become partners in life. Men who have minds, cravings all their own, but who also want to find more meaning to life than simply existing. *These* men feel there's more to life than work, home, children and a smattering of friends. Those men find life interesting and always provocative. These are men that will drive women forward to seek out a male.

"Of course, I am speaking in terms of heterosexual women, dear. If you want, we can go into the direction of bi or homosexual women, too. I have friends on all fronts and enjoy their company and minds equally."

"Gran! You can be so embarrassing!"

"Don't mean to be, sweetie. Just trying to expand your mind. I do have friends of many ilk's and very much cherish each and every one. Without my women friends I doubt my marriage would be as stable as it is today. These women provide the colors in my life that make it really inspiring. Not that your grandfather doesn't contribute on that front. It's just that women can and do grasp one another often even without words. It's effortless I guess is what I'm trying to say. And sometimes with men you need to explain everything, or leave it be.

"But, as I've said, men are a wonder all in themselves and can inspire us women in many ways. So, my dear, some women are very fortunate indeed to have a partner in life to give them a hand in creating not only a physical family, but who also have a spiritual well-being that transcends emotions and inspires them to be more, or everything! I only hope you have found such a man."

"Did you find such a man in your life, Grandma?" The telltale look on her face suggested she fully expected her grandmother to claim her husband to be this man.

"I did, but he was not the man I married." Busy studying pieces of jewelry in the cases, she didn't notice the mouth gaping open on the young woman next her.

Vonnette watched this conversation take place with mild amusement. Able to tell when someone was speaking from the heart, she knew this woman was doing just that. Desiring to make a point to her grandchild, she used a bit of shock therapy to cut through the sweet syrup that young women often feel as they approach marriage with wide eyes. Eyes like a young doe standing in the middle of an open field during hunting season who never thinks that danger lurks without notice. This young girl had that wide-eyed deer look right now, obviously caught in the headlights of an oncoming car at dusk known of as her grandmother.

When she spoke again, she did so slowly, deliberately, as though each word out of her mouth would find its own way to detoxify what she'd just heard come from the woman she thought she knew. "Grandmother, am I to understand you correctly, that Granddad is not the man you feel was your soul mate?"

Without looking up, her grandmother answered quietly and with a smile growing on her face like an imp with a secret that everyone wanted to know, "That's what I said, and that is the truth."

Looking at Vonnette for perhaps the first time, the grandmother asked if she might see a ring from the case?

Pointing, in an effort to confirm which ring but not to disrupt the continuing conversation between these two women, Vonnette opened the case and decided as she removed the ring from the plastic stand that the conversation had halted, so she said, "This is an oval amethyst cabochon, with a faceted pink tourmaline along the side."

Wondering if this conversation could lead anywhere with these two women, she began to explain the stone combination and how the design was something she called "*Harvest*." Where sheaves of wheat in gold come up and around the stones.

"Asymmetric designs are a favorite of mine. They lend themselves so well to rings. You see, as an artist I get a bit bored from time to time with anything that might be totally symmetric and as such stagnant. Also, when you go into a standard jewelry store, you find symmetric jewelry. Not that all symmetric pieces are boring. It's just that by having something asymmetric you know it is definitely handmade and hopefully one-of-a-kind. You can wear this ring facing one direction one day, and turn it around to have quite a different feel the next."

Clearly still feeling stunned, the granddaughter was trying to process what she'd heard without any luck. "Grandma, I don't understand what you just said. Why did you tell me this when I am on the verge of marrying?"

Laying her hand with the ring on her finger on the top of the showcase, the woman turned to look fully at her granddaughter and replied with dignity: "Obviously, this is the right time to tell you about the facts of life, and I don't mean the birds and the bees, although that should be part of this discussion."

"Grandmaaa!" The girl said in a singsong embarrassed way.

Continuing on as if not interrupted, "I think it is the perfect time, my dear, for you to hear all this as you have always thought your grandfather was my soul mate, and it made for a comfortable mental state. Maybe now you can open your mind to other possibilities that exist on roads not taken. Your generation didn't invent the wheel, nor did it discover what true love is. In truth, I have no idea who did discover that, if you want we could go to Adam and Eve, but I'd rather keep this conversation into some phase of reality for the moment."

"Well, thank God for that!" The granddaughter was having an emotional meltdown in a matter of minutes.

Facing Vonnette again the woman said, "You know, I think I will take this ring. I noticed you have what some stones mean written in the cases. Would you write down what these two stones stand for please? I'd like a remembrance of this day, this liberating day." With that she rolled her eyes off towards her granddaughter in an effort to let Vonnette know to whom she was referring.

Vonnette busied herself under the counter with sales book and calculator figuring out the New Jersey sales tax while motioning to see if this woman wanted the ring wrapped or not.

Shoulders went up and down instead of verbally answering.

Shrugging of shoulders always gave Vonnette a feeling of power. The shrugging meant the client didn't think one way or another about a piece of jewelry being wrapped. By wrapping her item, it showed extra care, and to Vonnette, that was important.

The ring was handed back and Vonnette began the ritual of wrapping it in a plain, light brown paper mache box. Each box had her gold and black label on it that said, *Vonnette's Jewelry, Newport, RI,* in a beautiful script logo. Lifting the lid of the box she pulled out a piece of white tulle, a glittery gold leaf, and a bit of well-folded white tissue paper. Opening up the tissue, she then laid the center gently open back into the box. Taking a piece of sturdy white paper, she created a tube that fit inside the ring as though it was a cigar, and the ring, a cigar band. Placing the ring in the center of the box, she folded and tucked the remaining white tissue paper over the top of the ring and closed the box. Wrapping and tying the tulle at the center top of the box, she then added the glittering leaf into the knot. Finishing the look, she created a bow with the tulle. The end effect was very pretty and feminine. Wrapping her packages up was a magical dance that Vonnette took great pride in. It was the completion of a sale and she felt why not make that as pretty as possible?

Opening a black plastic bag with her gold logo hot-stamped on it, Vonnette placed a business card inside and then the ring box as the two women watched with delight and exclaimed in unison, "That is so pretty I can't imagine taking it apart to remove the ring!"

Smiling, Vonnette felt she had completed a bit of magic not only with her wrapping but also in getting the two women to agree upon something. "You don't have to destroy the wrapping to remove the ring. I came up with this type of gift-wrap so people could keep the box and wrap in tack. Tulle is a bit stretchy, so you can slide the box out of the tulle, remove the ring, and then replace the tulle bow over the box. Some of my clients have a box or two sitting on their dressing tables. At least that's what they tell me."

Momentarily distracted, the young woman spoke with softness in her voice for the first time. "I can see how having one of your boxes sitting on a dressing table or bureau would make a woman feel like she was special and feminine."

Making eye contact with and smiling at the young woman, Vonnette felt her own power as an artist, as a woman, and also as a storyteller. Looking into the elder woman's eyes with that same all-knowing smile on her face Vonnette said, "If you wait just a minute I will happily write out the stone healing properties for you, along with the design symbolism if you like."

Nodding, the woman didn't feel the need to utter anything just then. Quietly, she stood and watched as Vonnette began to write out information on both stones in her new ring. Fascinated, she then asked, "Is this information on healing something you've come up with on your own, or have you read it somewhere? I know I've never come across anything like this before myself."

Looking up again Vonnette replied, "I've channeled these stone properties over many years. Do you know what I mean by the term 'channeling?'"

Watching her nose wrinkle spoke volumes to Vonnette.

Not waiting for a verbal answer, Vonnette continued, "Channeling can mean a few different things. One is where you allow a spirit to come through your body, to use your mouth and communicate things to people sitting in front of you. Though I did do that over the course of a year, I didn't enjoy the feeling of some other entity having control over me along with how it might be affecting the other person. So, I stopped doing that.

"The kind of channeling I grew to be comfortable with was where I would go into deep meditation while pieces of paper sat in front of me on a table. I'd written a stone name across the top of each piece of paper. Losing myself in meditation as each definition came through, I then wrote it down, I didn't have any idea what had been written. Simply, I would just grab another piece of paper and write out more information. Sometimes maybe five definitions would come through. Most times, though, nine came in.

"I never recalled what was written because my own spiritual self was in the background while seemingly another entity was writing. Never good at memorization, I would put the written information away until sometime had passed.

"Some might call this method of channeling automatic writing. I differentiate them because what I know of automatic writing is that, yes, you do allow another entity to use your body to write out whatever, but here, I was allowing my brain to communicate with whomever while I wrote and wrote. My brain seemed to be in the background, but was certainly still in the mix.

"Sometime later, after I had channeled different properties, I would then create a new piece of stone jewelry and write down how I felt as I worked on the piece. You know, what kind of emotions I felt, and so on. Later, I compared what I had written about the new piece of jewelry with what notes I had from one or another of the channeling sessions. Inevitably, these feelings would be very close to the written definitions. It was a personal way to cross-test the information I had felt while in process of making something with what came through during channeling sessions. When placing these channeled definitions in a loose-leaf notebook, I wondered if I would ever make use of the information.

Slowly, I tested the properties out on myself again by wearing certain stones when I felt a certain way to see if anything shifted once the stones were in place. Eventually, I followed up by doing more testing with willing clients. When people were attracted to certain stones, I would pull out my notebook and ask if they wanted to read the information on each stone's healing abilities to see if they matched up with what was happening in their personal life just then. Everyone surprisingly seemed interested enough to read and answer simple questions. Needless to say, the properties did match up each and every time.

"As far as I'm concerned, this information comes from another place so I don't take credit." With the upward swing of her right arm in a circle she said, "It's all out there in the ethers, information I mean, if we want to tap into it. I chose to tap in I guess. I could go on ad nauseam as this is a great part of what I do in my day-to-day existence. I pray for answers. Pray for the right energy to flow through me as I create a new piece of jewelry. Pray for the divine right combination of stones and design. Pray for the right client to buy the piece who has the correct energy for each finished product."

"So you ask to be a tool with your design and stone work?" The youngest woman questioned.

"Yes, that's it exactly. I feel we are all tools in our own way for higher energy to work through us. It's up to each of us to decipher what's important and use the mental, psychic, or physical equipment at our disposal at that moment to find balance and make something out of nothing. Making jewelry since childhood is a gift I could not imagine being without. I've grown with my talent. When I was able to connect my spiritual side with creating jewelry, so many things bonded for me as an artist, woman, and human."

Vonnette now made a swirl motion with her right hand over her display cases. The two women while watching even the simplest arm movement seemed mesmerized. Vonnette decided to continue. "You see, even as a child I had visions and nightly dreams. My mother had occasional dreams that she recalled as well that she felt connected her to the other side. Once, she saw her own deceased mother in a dream standing in a garden with bare feet. She knew it was her mother, yet only saw her from her feet up to the knees. The garden was full of blossoming flowers. When my mother woke, she wondered what message that dream might hold.

"Perhaps that was the beginning of a lifelong quest for me as I have wondered about my dream messages forever. Usually I discover they hold answers to specific questions I've had about daily life. Combine that with my fascination with jewelry, and you have a great combination of a creative craft, creative imagination, and spirituality. And voila`. Here I am in this package! To that end, I've written a book that contains some of what we're discussing today. The title is *Dreams Made of Stone,* and it's for sale right over there."

Pointing to the end of the showcases at the simple wooden table that had found its use today, Vonnette was happy she had brought it. Being a perfect size to house her coffee table book standing open on top, people could peruse the book while deciding if they wanted to buy it. Or, it could even entice them to take a more serious look at her finished jewelry for sale while here at the show. The lower shelf on that simple table held five books ready for purchase.

Both women turned and walked over to the open book on display and began to flip pages. "Guess you can add three of these books to my total for today, please," The grandmother said. "And forget about writing down the stone information you started. I'm sure it's all here in the book." Looking at her granddaughter now she said, "I'd like us each to have this book to commemorate our day together. And please take one home for your mother who couldn't come along with us this wonderful day."

"Yes, as a matter of fact the stone healing information you're looking for is all there as well as the design symbolism. You both might find some of the book information crosses over into the conversation I could not help but overhear about women finding themselves and their soul mates. Not directly through the written word, but rather from stone combinations that assist you to find what your mind and heart are searching for in life.

"Would you mind if I put the three books in one bag?"

Simultaneously both women shook their heads no as they continued to flip through pages of the book while standing at the end of her display cases.

Vonnette enjoyed it when people became invested in her designs and her book.

The grandmother walked back in front of Vonnette and began, "Would you say I was correct in what I said earlier about women and men?"

"Actually, yes, I quite agree. Not to sound like an old sage, but I have lived alone a long time. Watching married friends go through their stages of life with their partners has been very educational. I've heard the stories of love at first site, or even second site, and then if you'd like I can give some examples of that in my own life at younger ages."

Both women nodded in agreement.

"Personally, I've found that the men I chose at a younger age were selfish. It's not their fault, nor does it mean I didn't learn great things from being with them, or for that matter without them later on. All that helped me to be who and what I am today along with all my spirituality and creativity. You see, I feel that sexual energy and creative energy are one and the same. Maybe I had to have my sexual energy focus mainly on my jewelry creativity. Perhaps that meant there was not enough room for a physical male in my every-day world all those years.

"One thing is certain to me; women do go through 'stages' as my mother used to say. Men do as well, but they grow comfortable with life being the same, and expect it to always be. I think that's why most men don't like it when their spouses rearrange the furniture in the house."

Laughing out loud the two women were captivated by this artist sharing her slant on life.

Egged on by their interest, Vonnette continued. "I feel women have so many thoughts coming at them at any one given moment and that we need input from many sources to make shifts in our world, which ultimately make us who we are each day. We might find massage relaxing and fulfilling today as a way to find peace of mind, body, or even provide some answers to questions that are plaguing us. Simply put, when anyone is relaxed, answers can and usually do come without force. Even though we all know this, we still push ourselves to the nth degree to see if we might force something out. Then, tomorrow, we might find that reading a good book gives the foresight we had been craving.

"Whatever direction is taken to find our path of possibilities is a good thing. Any good man will recognize our need to shift energetically and will give positive support along the way. This is not to say that men don't crave some of what we do, too, and it is our duty to help them out as well if possible.

"Well, I could go on and on about the differences between men and women, but the simple truth is, we as women all need to feel that our internal shifts do not mean we are no longer of interest, but rather that as we change we become more interesting to our partners, whomever they might be. Any friend of mine who has had a lasting marriage has a relationship that shifts with time. If you want I can associate all this back to jewelry and call our shifts and changes stepping stones in the course of life."

"You are so right," said the grandmother. Turning towards her granddaughter now she verbalized, "That is why I have stayed with your grandfather all these years; it's that he found my changes interesting."

Turning back to Vonnette she added, "And by the way, why don't you call that your next book, *Stepping Stone, or Stones*?"

Nodding, Vonnette replied, "Well, thanks for the suggestion. That'll actually be my third book title. The second book is a paperback pocketbook with only stone properties listed. It's small, so you could leave it in the car or even in a handbag to use when you go into a store and discover you are experiencing an attraction to a particular stone. You can then look up the properties to see if it connects with who and what you're going through at that time. That book is called *Stone Magic*. I didn't bring any of those books with me on this trip, sorry. The third book is loosely based on my travels about the country doing fine art and craft shows like this one. I had titled it *Vonnette's Gifts*. Perhaps I'll rename that one, *Stepping Stones*."

"Grandma, I'd like to know more about all this stuff you began talking about before on not marrying your soul mate. Who did you meet that *was* your soul mate? For that matter, why didn't you marry him instead of Granddad? Going one step further, what made you choose Granddad if you knew he was not your soul mate?"

"Sometimes sweetie, soul-mates are put in your path to bring about change. Sometimes they are a true heart connection that everyone likes to attach to the term. For me, that man was very fun and enlightening. As time progressed, I realized I was looking for something more than what he could offer me. When I met your granddad, I was ready for him. He was comfortable and yet challenging at times, something I was craving. It's a good thing to be challenged as a young woman. You then feel better as life shifts. Having children, and then when the children leave home, it becomes yet another change you can and do look forward to especially if your life-mate is supportive. These are the kinds of things your grandfather has brought to the marriage for me. Of course, it doesn't hurt I still find him physically attractive, but then that could be due to the fact that he challenges me both mentally and spiritually."

All women laughed out loud at this comment. "Grandma, are you suggesting the man I'm marrying is not of this ilk?"

"No darling! Only you can decide something such as that. I'm simply pointing out that getting married does not solve problems. It actually creates new ones you don't expect. If you have the right partner, making your way together is fascinating, fun and even unexpected. Marrying the right man can bring out things deep inside yourself that you only had an inkling were there. Some of that can be good. Some of that can be very challenging, and then some of that can be life altering! What you choose to do with all that is up to you and you alone. Please do not get married if you feel this man doesn't accept you unconditionally as well as challenge you on many levels. During difficult times, total acceptance and unconditional love are necessary components to your relationship. I only want the best for you. What I chose has worked very well for me. I don't need to divorce my husband to change and develop as the years go on as some women do. I'm lucky. That's something I can and do wish for you, that you will be one of the lucky ones, too!"

"Okay, guess there's more for me to ponder with all this information today. That's why I love spending time with you. You give me information that takes my mind into a different place. But I'm still wondering, don't you feel then that you married a soul mate? I mean, if you two work as well together as I feel you do. . . ."

"If you're marrying the right man, he will bring your mind into different realms as well. And yes, in fact I do believe I married a soulmate. However, ours is not the kind of relationship that most people associate with that term, so that's why I said I didn't marry my soulmate."

Seemingly satisfied with this last statement, they smiled at Vonnette as they said good-bye. Everyone thanked one another for the input, information and a lovely creation that would be appreciated for years to come.

"Maybe I'll wear this to your wedding."

"Maybe I'll snitch it from your dressing table when you're not looking," exclaimed the granddaughter as they walked away.

"If you do I'll know who took it and just where to find it again, so don't lets us go there. Instead, let's appreciate it as a turning point in our connection to one another today."

Waving over their shoulders to Vonnette, they left her sight.

Smiling to herself Vonnette took the personal check and sales receipt from her hand and placed them into her shoulder purse for safe keeping until she would be back home to deposit it.

These two generations of women had a great interest in life, her creations, and even one of her books. Maybe she should have brought her other book on this trip, but she didn't know the crowd and what they might be interested in. Maybe she could have sold three copies of that just now, too. But then, she might have only sold the smaller books instead of her coffee table book. Second guessing herself, she decided everything was fine just as it was. Vonnette felt happy that her dream of not making any sales at this show was false. The purchases just made didn't cover the expenses for the show; however, they would pay for the hotel room. There were a couple more days to see if she could gather enough to pay the show fee, gas and time invested, as well as the cat sitter.

Exhaling, she sat on her chair pondering who and what the rest of the show would bring her way. All in all, a deposit was given today over the phone that, thankfully, brought her accounts at home back into the black again. She had dealt with the two women who just left her booth in a different and creative way by wearing lemon citrine. And, sharing information with them had been done in a protective and intuitive way with the use of amethyst. Focusing on work, creativity and spirituality was a nice emotional shift for Vonnette, which also provided a great ladybugs kind of finish to the day!

⁂

It was Saturday, a new day and anything was possible. Surprisingly, Vonnette slept fairly well the night before. Dreams had escaped her. Not having messages to ponder throughout the day could be a gift mentally as well as emotionally. Only time would tell that for sure.

While waiting for the show doors to open, Vonnette conversed with booth mates a bit. Light conversation could at least fill time.

"Have you done this show before?"

"Do you think I can expect good sales?"

"Do the people in this area support the arts?"

"How did you do last night with the cocktail party?"

"Can you think of any shows you've done thus far this year that might be good for me?"

Most artists had the same questions at the beginning of any show. At the end, their concern was in getting packed up and on the road home as quickly as possible so, conversation then was usually kept to a minimum.

Once the doors did open, everyone went back into their assigned booth spaces and fussed over their displays until someone stopped in the aisle to interrupt them.

The first such person for Vonnette was a woman in her mid-forties with bright red hair. Quite attractive and well dressed. Greeting the woman with a broad smile, Vonnette held good hopes of making a sale. Unfortunately, this woman was the kind of person who can energetically suck the oxygen out of any room. When those types of people come to a show, they treat the artist like a trapped animal, so that the artist has to listen to their woes whatever they might be. In this particular case, it seemed she had just lost her husband due to illness. Although a sad situation on any front, it was not Vonnette's job to make things right for her. Vonnette's good hopes of this association leading anywhere positive were quickly squelched.

Having a lot of experience in retail, Vonnette knew how to deal with people who wanted to drain energy. First, she visually sent massive amounts of white light towards her solar plexus while silently asking the universe to remove this woman from her space. White light used in this manner was straight out positive energy. Within five minutes of white light being psychically blasted at her, the woman said she had to go and meet up with someone. Grateful she was leaving within five minutes instead of an hour, Vonnette said, "Good-bye," all while hoping this woman was not a sign of what the whole day would be about.

People in the position of taking energy instead of sharing energy cannot be allowed to hang around, or the reason Vonnette was there would be lost. Sincerely, there was a financial investment in participating in each show. There were jury fees, booth fees, travel costs that include gas, hotels and food. If Vonnette gave her energy up at the start of a show day, she could potentially lose a lot.

The next woman to stop in front of her booth was also nicely dressed. This woman was well taken care of, perhaps in her mid-sixties with almost no wrinkles. Her hair was short and well maintained. The jewelry she wore today was elegant, simple, and classic in style with clean lines and a few well-placed diamonds. Vonnette noticed she was looking at the "Moon and Stars" cuff bracelet that had two layers of gold, pearls and diamonds. While asking if the woman wanted to see the bracelet, Vonnette was surprised by how quickly this woman never lost a beat in her reply.

"No thank you. It would be like holding a puppy."

"I'm sorry, I don't quite get your reference."

"When you hold a puppy you want to take it home no matter what it looks like, or what your situation is at home. That's how I would feel trying on your lovely bracelet. I already know it will look and feel great. So, no thanks, I won't be trying it on today."

Both women laughed as Vonnette watched her walk farther up the aisle glancing into other booths. That comment alone could be why she'd dreamed of kittens and a puppy yesterday.

While doing a show such as this, artists need attendees to ask questions at the very least. Questions can turn into sales if not today, then perhaps in the future. Questions would also keep an insecure artist sitting alone too long in their booth from having an emotional meltdown. Vonnette didn't want to be alone with her thoughts about cancer, so she reached under her displays to pull out a booklet filled with word-search puzzles. Feeling something mindless was in order that could be either picked up or put down at a moment's notice should someone want to try on a piece of jewelry. Perhaps the remainder of this show would be one where she worked on her word puzzles instead of showing her jewelry. Sitting in her tall chair she began a puzzle.

Most of the day went by in this fashion. People stopped, looked, and gave compliments only to move onward. Some claimed they were looking today, would come back tomorrow to buy. After hearing that same comment last night during the cocktail party, Vonnette didn't have any high hopes of people returning today or tomorrow.

There were evenings where Vonnette had done well when a cocktail party began the show on a Friday night. Attendees to such an event had to pay. Some of the fees were usually donated to a local charity. Promoters hoped the early viewing of artwork would help promote sales. After having a drink or two, and feeling their liquor, people would often encourage one another to spend. Generally speaking, one day of a show would be better financially than the other. If there was no cocktail party to begin with, that better day would usually be Saturday. When shows ran longer than one or two days, Vonnette knew people could have too much time to consider a purchase. When people had too much time to think about making a purchase, they would often decide not to buy.

Having a lot of time in her booth without questions being asked or showing her jewelry gave way to thoughts of too many shows that turned out like this for her, where Vonnette did not pull in the kind of money she thought she should have. Shows where male jewelers would make good sales while hers would be meager at best.

Walking about her booth, Vonnette wondered under her breath, "Why is it women love buying jewelry, or anything for that matter, from men rather than women?

"Why don't I find a nice gay man to do shows with me? He could have fun playing with the jewelry as well as joking with the women who come through."

Too much time on her hands let her mind go into that negative thought process.

Since finding the breast lump, Vonnette had been making decent sales at her shows. There was no rhyme or reason to it. Perhaps the universe was giving her money and distractions away from cancer. Or, maybe, finally, it was her turn to make sales at shows.

So far, lack of sales at this show was proving to be all too familiar. When money became tight and there was no idea where the next dollar was coming from, she tended to look at the dark side of life. What Vonnette discovered during such dark moments was that if she was willing to take a hard look inside, deep inside her soul, she could and generally did find something positive in anything. A friend called her Pollyanna. Perhaps choosing to focus on something, anything constructive in the face of despair, was her own way to play the glad game. The one that Pollyanna played where no matter what happened there needed to be a reason why what was taking place was a good thing. Wondering what she would find as a positive at this show, she watched and waited to see.

Try as she did, her mood kept sinking into that dark abys. Suddenly feeling trapped at this show with meager sales and nowhere to go brought her mind back to that fateful childhood moment. The time and space where as a child while trapped beneath a full-grown man, she was afraid to move and yet struggled to get free. How did that time slot come up so easily over and over again in her mind? How did that day translate into this space at this show? Vonnette had never made the connection before about being trapped in her booth to being trapped that one day. Thinking about it again right now helped her make a connection she had not seen before as to how it wasn't just that one day. Such as when men had confined her in a car wanting sex while on a date. They'd block her from any escape when her answer was no. Some climbed on top of her using brute strength to get their way. Once, a man had trapped her; at least he thought he had. Being quite thin at that time, she wiggled her way onto the floor of the passenger seat and curled up into a ball. He was big and couldn't get at her tucked up under the dashboard, so in the end, he gave up and let her out of the car.

Pollyanna was not in her head now!

Struggling emotionally to hang on, she told herself that she was an adult! That what she was recalling were blips in time. "Look at how far I have come! As an adult, I did what that child could not. I forgave that molester, and others. I didn't forgive for the sake of the abuser, but rather for me. It was important for me to let go of the hatred I had for the man who first abused me. Who he went on to be was no business of mine. What I carried forward from that fateful day *was* my affair, however."

What Vonnette had brought forward as an adult were bad food choices along with selecting the wrong men to love. Almost any stressful excuse would send Vonnette hunting for man-made sugar, chocolate, or ice cream. Electing to be a food addict when feeling emotionally trapped was a difficult mirror to stare into. Food is fuel. Simply, it keeps the body going. Sugar was not a necessary element to that end, and yet, sugar was her weakness.

Vonnette knew her addiction to processed sugar only too well, and that her sweet tooth connected with feeling her life was not sweet enough. Having that understanding and being able to do something about it were two entirely different things.

Only Vonnette could decide when and if she'd learned her lessons and moved forward. For some weird reason, thoughts like these today also reminded her about the crickets she heard while at home. No idea why she made the association, she thought of how when crickets move, they usually spring forward. At this turn, would Vonnette do the same, move forward, or would she sink back into poor food choices tonight.

Head too far down this emotionally negative reflective rabbit-hole and Vonnette could find it extremely difficult to climb back up and out. Having been there so many times she knew the warning signs. Standing up out of her chair she began to move about. Shifting jewelry inside display cases put her mind in a new place for a few minutes. After that, Vonnette began to reorganize her sales items like sales book, calculator, paperclips, pens, mirror, boxes for wrapping, and so forth. Busy work did help.

Glancing up every so often from straightening her items, she found herself focusing on the people looking at art in other booths. A couple was looking at and talking to the artist three booths up on the right who made paper lampshades that attached to laminated wood bases. He made the shades out of brown or white rice paper, painted on them and attached them to the wood frames. The whole look was a cross between Asian art and the Arts and Crafts movement styles.

Next door to her left were three women helping one another decide upon hand knit baby items. Each woman was busy talking about their latest family addition and how this or that piece would be something fun for that particular baby.

Accessories could be a good judge of who might buy. Vonnette began looking to see what women were wearing for shoes and carrying for handbags. She used these elements as straightforward indications of whether the people attending the show today were her kind of clients or not. People viewed thus far were a mix. When people came through in sneakers, tee shirts and ripped jackets, Vonnette generally felt they were not her clients. Women who had nice handbags and shoes, who spent money on such items, could and usually did have nice jewelry as well. Jewelry was an accessory along with shoes and handbags.

Though, back in Newport she couldn't use the same formula to figure who would be a client. People at home came to Vonnette in sneakers, high heels and everything in between. The same held true with handbags. One good client used to come to see her jewelry in old yard clothes, ripped and very badly stained. Anyone else seeing him with Vonnette might feel he could be a problem, and actually one day a woman had been in her store shopping when this very man came in. She was nervous for Vonnette being left alone with him thinking that he was some sort of bum. When after entering her store, he almost immediately went down on his knees to look at jewelry on a lower shelf, that woman mouthed to Vonnette her nervousness while pointing downward at this man who, thankfully, didn't take notice of her actions. Vonnette smiled back at the woman and mouthed, "I'm good. It's okay." While also making the universal hand sign for okay. He was a great client and very considerate to all of the arts and artists!

At shows, however, Vonnette could almost predict what people would ultimately be interested in her jewelry by what they wore and carried for handbags.

A man approached her booth. Telling herself to remain focused and positive, she quickly looked over his clothing. He was well dressed, though casual. He wore a beige, hip length suede jacket over a brown and beige striped shirt. His two top shirt buttons lay open. His brown corduroy pants had cuffs. Brown tassel loafers completed the look. Vonnette watched as he perused her jewelry cases. This man moved about like a cat rooting in a litter box, pacing back and forth, back and forth, then side to side. It had been Vonnette's experience that men born under the sign of Cancer tended to move sideways. Having no idea if in fact he had been born under the sign of the crab, Vonnette felt that perhaps he needed to move like this in order to make an important decision.

Asking if he needed information on anything, Vonnette stood in the central section of her display area to easily reach whatever he might suggest interest in. Seemingly distracted, he took a moment or two before looking up and making eye contact. Even then he took his time to speak.

"I never know what to buy. It's important that I choose a gift today. It's my thirtieth wedding anniversary this week. That seems important enough to warrant a piece of jewelry. A friend suggested this show, that there would be interesting jewelry. Something my wife would not find downtown could be a nice thing. I've never come here before and don't know how all this works, but guess it's kind of like going into a store."

"Yes, it's exactly like going into a store except that we have come to your neighborhood. All the artists displayed here today travel about doing this kind of show. We come from all over. Personally, I'm from Newport, Rhode Island."

"That's a pretty place to be. If I lived there I'm not sure I would travel here to do business."

That statement had been repeated to Vonnette over the years. Hearing it today, she thought, "Leave it alone." Sticking to her Pollyanna attitude, Vonnette opted not to be defensive about having to travel to make a living; instead, she chose to focus on what her business was at this moment: to see if she could make a sale. And, sharing that information with this man, a possible new client, was simply not necessary.

Still moving side-to-side, he eventually came to settle in front of one case that had a strand of lemon citrine and light green fresh water pearls in it. "What is this stone?" As Vonnette opened her mouth to respond, he answered his own question. "Oh, I see here, lemon citrine. Is that suitable for my anniversary do you think?"

"You know, years ago someone came up with a formula for what you ought to give as a stone for each anniversary. Today that kind of thinking is considered old fashion. Also, there are stones being discovered all the time, so the list became very dated. That said, why don't I ask a bit about your wife before I answer your question? Let's begin with what color hair does she have?"

"Well, she used to be blonde. Lately she seems to be heading in the direction of redhead, I guess."

"Okay, that skin tone ought to work with this combination of lemon citrine and light green pearl. Does she wear gold jewelry, silver, or white gold? Or do you even know?"

"Hmmmm, umm, I think she normally wears gold jewelry. I gave her a gold watch once. Yes, it was gold gold, not white gold."

Striving not to sound pushy, Vonnette asked her questions and gave this client time to answer in an effort to give honest input. Answers to her questions would provide insight as to what this man's wife would not only like but also would actually wear in the way of jewelry.

Snapping her back into the here and now came, "Yes, now that I think about it she does wear yellow gold jewelry."

"There's one more question before I wrap this strand of beads up for you and that is, does your wife wear beads? Some women only wear pendants on chains, some wear both pendants as well as beads. There are still other women who don't wear any form of necklace. Those women usually wear a lot of earrings and rings. Normally these women claim that if they cannot physically see the jewelry, they do not understand the point of spending money on it."

"Ah, this I know, she wears beads!" Knowing the answer right off got him quite excited and animated.

Playing along with his body motions Vonnette replied laughingly, "Then I believe you pass the test!" Vonnette offered the strand of beads over to him for inspection. He chuckled as well but had a doubtful look. She decided to enlighten him. "From what you've said, your wife has a bit of a pink skin tone and that shade means she would feel comfortable being either a blonde or a redhead. If her skin tone was pale, yellow or brown, the red hair might not suit her. If her skin was a more yellow tone, then these beads would make her look a bit ashen. Something no woman wants to experience. Having a good pink skin coloration, she'd be able to wear this strand of yellow gold, lemon citrine and light-green, fresh water pearls. So, you see, my questions did suit a purpose."

"Color me impressed! First, that you know to ask such questions, and second, that I knew the answers. This has been enlightening!" His words came forth along with a genuine smile.

Handing the beads back to Vonnette, he gave a yes nod of the head that he wanted to purchase the strand. Vonnette removed the tiny price tag, wrapped them, placed the box in a bag and then wrote up the sales slip. After his charge was rung up, she handed the bag over. He went on his merry way walking in much more of a straight line than he had done while in her booth.

As she wiped down her display cases to remove finger prints and to ready them for more possible clients, Vonnette pondered how that man discovered he knew more about his wife today than he thought and that must have made him feel positive about his purchase. She supplied a stranger with an opportunity to realize something he didn't know until he came into her booth space today. Added knowledge was a gift that Vonnette passed along to him. "Perhaps he'll recall this day with some fondness," Vonnette thought as she watched two women approach the booth to her right that was selling ceramic wear in the form of bowls, plates and vases.

Each piece in that booth was a nice, cobalt blue color with some form of an animal figure worked into one edge somewhere as a permanent 3-D attachment. Frogs were on some items. Fish were on others. They gave a nice, yet subtle difference to the overall finish for serving platters and bowls.

While observing one of the women who had stopped at that booth, Vonnette thought her hair looked like an unfurled birds nest. It lay limp and crinkled along the back of her neck and shoulders. Perhaps it had been up in a bun with hair spray holding it in place. And when she took it down without running her fingers or a brush through it, her hair remained slightly stiff as if it still wanted to be in that bun. She justified staring at this woman's hair as a way to stop her brain from thinking of cancer yet again.

Picking up her word puzzles as she sat down, Vonnette opened to her working page. She smiled at the neighbor artist across from her selling acrylic bird paintings.

Inspiration suddenly hit her.

Artists will sketch on almost anything, and Vonnette had her word puzzle booklet on her lap just then. Opening to the inside back page that was blank, she began sketching a bird's nest made of gold twigs with three golden eggs inside. Writing quick notes with tiny arrows, she marked down that one egg could be in white gold to symbolize white eggs. One or two eggs could be in yellow gold to represent brown eggs. The nest would become a very three-dimensional ring sitting a bit high up on top of the finger. Some gold strands could filter down from the nest. And those would form the band and be much the same as how twigs spill out of a bird's nest in real life. Stopping the sketch briefly, she thought about how a bird forms a nest. She jotted down additional notes for later reference. *Make the nest out of different colors of gold and different sized gold twigs. Soldering each together will help make the nest look more life-like while making it sturdy enough to wear without worry.*

Sitting and staring off into nowhere for a few seconds, obviously lost in thought, she then began sketching once again. This new design would be another bird's nest piece. However, it would not include any eggs inside. Instead, this ring would consist of a diamond, or some diamonds somewhere on the top outer edge. Also, along the top outer edge would be a bit of gold tubing that would house tiny bird feathers. The titles of these two rings would be the *Full Nest* and the *Empty Nest*. Titles that came forth like this always made her chuckle. Successfully she moved her mood out of the gutter and back into a Pollyanna space.

A few years back, Vonnette made little gold chickens and roosters to represent the Rhode Island state bird called The Rhode Island Red. Originally, that breed of rooster and chicken came from Little Compton, RI. Cross-bred to create a good egg layer as well as to have more breast meat to feed a family during the depression, it became a bird people world-wide now have in their chicken coops. Eventually, someone had the bright idea it ought to be the state bird, and so it did. When the fiftieth anniversary of that claim to fame rolled around, Vonnette noticed no one had ever made any representations of that bird in gold. Something she could and did remedy. One such rooster design had a chef hat on his head and a large soup ladle stuck to one wing all made of gold. His name was *Oven Roaster* to represent the Rhode Island culinary art school called Johnson & Wales. All her gold chickens and roosters in that series represented activities that took place in her home state like boating. *Charlie, Rooster of the Sea* held a tiny sailboat in one extended wing. With many Rhode Island vineyards, Vonnette made another rooster with a bottle of wine under one wing and a corkscrew in the other. His name was *Coq au Vin.*

Names for these fun creatures came to her as she completed each design in gold, and in turn, each one made her laugh. The Tennis Hall of Fame is a big part of Newport's history as well. That rooster stood ready for the next serve and was called *Raquetear* due to all the people who play tennis and take it so very seriously they become disheartened when they don't win.

Inspiration came along at the most unexpected moments. Seeing that woman's hair in the booth next door gave Vonnette the thought of making a nest in gold. One idea had blossomed into two designs. When the titles came to mind, she thought of all her friends who had children who were mostly grown now and either leaving home or about to leave, making the parents empty nesters! Yes, Pollyanna does live!

One thought rolled over in her mind to formulate another as Vonnette recalled her sister asking once how Vonnette could work at home and not be distracted by other things like gardening or laundry. She told Aurelia, "When you're interested in what you're making, you want to get into the studio even if the laundry needs doing, or the garden weeds call. Creating the next piece of jewelry is always the best fun!" This day was a perfect example of that kind of thinking. A few minutes ago, she had been pondering no sales and cancer. Now, she focused on two new nest designs.

Why hadn't Vonnette thought to do a nest in gold before when she had spent so much time creating all those chickens and rooster pieces of jewelry? For that matter, simply paying as much attention to crows as she did even when out walking, one might expect a nest design to have come up long before now. But then, that's how inspiration works, there is no time line, it comes when least expected.

Today, Vonnette had heard crickets when she left the hotel which reminded her again of the crickets she'd heard in her garden as she packed for the show. Observing crickets became another easy fit into her crammed world. When not leaping forward, crickets tend to step slowly from one side to another. They seemingly do not move backward. Symbolically, their presence foretells of giant leaps forward coming in. Once or twice while doing outdoor shows, crickets appeared on top of her display cases. Delighted, she would point this creature out to whomever walked into her booth. That may not have been the brightest idea, though, because those people then lost their train of thought and focused on the cricket instead of her jewelry. Earlier, while thinking of crickets, Vonnette wondered if she would stoop to poor food choices. Being in a creative space now, she hoped hearing the crickets this morning connected to the nest designs. Maybe these sketches would symbolically be her giant leap forward, and not a slow step to one side or another.

Maybe these sketches would help her stay out of the dark thoughts of molestation, date rape, food issues, lack of sales and cancer. Being creative did usually shift her mood. Suddenly it didn't matter to Vonnette that the day had been slow financially. She had come into her own rhythm in a wave of creativity that would carry forward once she returned home.

A woman in her later fifties to mid-sixties stopped to read some of Vonnette's notes on stone properties. No time to continue her inspired thoughts and visions, Vonnette watched the woman read with anticipation. Looking up after she'd moved the length of the booth and having read most little notes inside the cases she asked, "Do you believe all these notes here. Or is this an effort at selling?"

"I believe what is written. These are healing properties I have channeled. Do you understand what I mean by channeling?"

"Being a child of the sexual revolution, yes, I understand the term channeling. We all used to meditate back then. Some people felt they were channeling spirits. Some even felt they had been someone famous in another life. Personally, I never had any experience like that. Maybe that's why I'm questioning your notes."

At that moment in conversation, the woman's face turned beet red and she suddenly looked weak. Knowing this look well, Vonnette quickly asked if she was going through the change?

Almost reeling in place the woman did come to focus again and replied, "Yes, I am. Having a tough time with it as well. Sorry. Don't appreciate it when a hot flash comes on so suddenly with nowhere to put your head down or hide. Don't mean to make you feel uncomfortable."

"You're not making me feel uncomfortable in any way. If anything, I understand what you are experiencing."

"That's impossible! You're too young to have hot flashes, aren't you?"

"Don't think our bodies have a timer. I began the change in my forties. Had red eyes all the time. Thought I had pink eye. Kept going to the eye doctor and getting different scripts. Each time I got a new prescription I threw away all my eye make-up. Honestly, I tossed so much eye make-up away it would make your head spin. I felt it was all contaminated and as such wanted to get it out of reach. Oh, well, spilt milk and all that. Turns out I had dry eye during the beginning of my menopausal experiences. It took a client's visit to straighten me out on that, thankfully. I was apologizing to her for my embarrassing pink eye when she asked if I was in the change? Having been there herself with the same eye situations, that client told me to buy some saline solution and put drops in my eyes numerous times a day, that it was simply dry eye and the saline would take care of it."

"Did that work? Was it really that simple?"

Chuckling mainly to herself, Vonnette informed the woman, "Yes, it really was that simple. To this day I make sure I have a travel size container of saline drops with me while on the road, especially if I'm flying somewhere. Don't know why but planes dry out my eyes like nothing else. That was the beginning of my new understanding of alternative methods to deal with menopause."

"Okay, I'll bite, what alternative methods? I mean, if something simple like eye drops helped you, maybe you know of something that'll help me." Her face was beginning to have a bit more normal color again. After a few sips of water from her container a certain amount of her physical stability returned as well.

"After a lot of reading at the time on almost anything I could lay my hands on as well as information I garnered from the health food store near me, I finally found something simple that was worth trying. It was about different food combinations. No idea today where I read this, or if I even read it in one article or a few different ones. What you need to do is eat a bit of salmon, some walnuts, and some tofu every day for a week or so. After that first week, you can cut back a bit until the flashes return. That way you'll learn the magic portion that works with your body.

"Here's what worked for me. Not saying you have to do this; it's just what I did. I ate a few walnuts with my fruit for breakfast. At lunch, I ate a bit of tofu with salad, a sandwich or whatever, and then had some salmon for dinner. There were days where I reversed the tofu and salmon. When I explain this to others, they ask if the three items have to be consumed together or not? I ate them separately and it worked. After about a week I began to switch out foods and then did my three foods in one day as the flashes appeared again. Immediately, the flashes subsided once more. It was amazing! I stopped having any kind of difficult hot flash after those food choices became a regime.

"I know there are natural hormones in tofu. Research I did at the time was how Asian women don't usually suffer from breast cancer as often as we do here in the states. My mother got, and eventually passed from breast cancer, so hormone replacement therapy was not an option for me. Having some natural hormones in the tofu I thought was fine though. With all the hot flashes and general physical suffering I had gone through, I couldn't believe how simple and effective this cure was!"

"I've not heard about this at all. You don't recall where you read this?"

"No, I don't. I do remember reading that walnuts have some hormonal thing going on as well as the tofu. Salmon, I have no idea about other than it's a good fish to eat with the right fats for your heart. Discovering it was also good for dealing with my menopausal symptoms was a plus. Between the shift in food choices and the saline solution for my eyes, I was golden! The only remnants I have to deal with now are the dry eye if I eat very salty foods." At this moment Vonnette had her hands outstretched showing how exuberant she felt about what she had just shared.

"I'm on the fence about believing you here, but you know, it's worth a try since it's food related. And, I'm in such a difficult physical place these days. While I'm at work I can't ever tell if I'm going to need the air conditioning on in the middle of the winter or what. It's driving my husband to distraction to say nothing about my co-workers! If this does the trick, I'll make a deal with you. I'll buy something from you, okay?"

"I won't hold you to that deal. You can buy something from me if you like. I simply passed along information that worked for me when I was in similar circumstances. Most of my flashes were of an embarrassing nature. Dealing with the public as I do, talking to a possible client and turning beet red in the middle of a conversation was not good. There were even a couple of times when I thought the rescue wagon would need to be called due to how weak in the knees I went. Water was shooting out of every pore in my body and fainting felt imminent. Food was my chosen way up and out of that period and it worked. What you do with that information is up to you. Perhaps you'll pass it along to someone else in need if it works for you, too. If you decide you are in the market for a new piece of jewelry, it would be great for you to consider giving me a call. I can e-mail some photos for you to look over of what's finished and ready for sale at that time. Let me know if there's a color or a specific stone you are interested in then, too. That'll help me to concentrate on what photos I send. Here's a card. I'll write menopause on it, so you can make the connection later of who the card came from."

Now, the other woman chuckled. "Thank you so much for the information and possible cure for my debilitating hot flashes! I very much appreciate the input. It's interesting that the reason I stopped was to read your stone properties, and yet I'm leaving you with some possible natural menopausal assistance."

"My stone healing properties attracted you and you received information on food healing. It all works together really. Healing is healing!"

They said good-bye, and off she went.

They had shared a nice moment together even if there was no sale from her today. And, even though Vonnette had returned to a conversation about breast cancer, it was mainly to help this woman in finding a way out of her menopausal issues. So, the cancer element had not overwhelmed Vonnette mentally. Their conversation had also provided a momentary distraction; something so very welcome at this emotional time in Vonnette's life.

⚜

Leaving the show at the end of the day to head back to her temporary hotel home, Vonnette found the skies had opened up and rain was coming down quite heavily. No way to dodge getting wet, she tried to cover her hair a bit with her jacket and walked to her car. People all around were scurrying, trying to duck the rain. Vonnette knew no matter how hard she might try, she was going to get wet, so she took her time.

Driving was another matter. It had been a very dry season. When rain falls that fast after such a dry spell, it tends to form large puddles that cannot find a quick home. Watching vehicles ahead of her maneuver through and around puddles brought images to mind of overflowing washing machines. Dirty water was churned as car tires created foam-like bubbles. No clothes to clean here; the suds were left to eventually find their way to a sewage drain or pothole.

Vonnette felt a bit like these puddles tonight. Being bright and hopeful all day exhausted her. To only make one sale was disappointing. Emotionally still filled with fear, Vonnette knew her expenses for the show had not been met.

Would she meet the overhead necessary by the end of tomorrow?

Could she hold onto a positive attitude if no additional sales came forth?

If she didn't make sales tomorrow, she would at least be busy packing up her gear and heading home, so the long day in itself would be a distraction. She'd had a productive day once she began to sketch. Maybe this was not as bad a show as she had thought. New jewelry ideas gave her something positive to hold onto through the long night alone with her thoughts of financial and health fears.

⚜

Sunday morning found Vonnette tired and not looking forward to the long drive home after closing time. Thoughts of sleeping in her own bed tonight did lift her spirits a bit. She took an extra-long shower and dressed. Since she would not only be doing the show, but packing and then driving, she wore very comfortable clothing. Black stretch pants with a nice, clean, oversized cotton jersey along with some coin jewelry suited her for the day.

Even though artists know the hours of a show long before it happens, they can't ever count on how they will feel once there. Perhaps this particular show location would be cold. Maybe the heating system would be jammed on high. A few times at shows Vonnette had to deal with a leaking roof. Taking such elements into consideration, Vonnette always packed at least one or two alternative outfits. Today was one of those alternative outfit days. Everything on her looked okay, but nothing stood out in her clothing. Her jewelry choices were subdued as well. Always conscious of her personal jewelry, she knew on the final day of the show, it would be removed and put away before packing up all her gear for fear it would catch in something or other and could either be a detriment to her physical self or maybe even be ruined.

Upon arrival at the show, she looked for food. Thankfully, a food vendor had been positioned near the rear of the building. He didn't have anything fancy, just coffee, muffins and sandwiches for later on. Even though Vonnette packed food and water for every show, there could be unexpected moments such as this where her energy level was so low that she needed to consume outside food. Years back Vonnette had given up coffee. It made her jumpy and also caused migraines. At this moment, coffee could have been just what the doctor ordered energetically. Going backwards was not an option. So, much like the crickets, she moved slowly and steadily forward choosing a corn muffin as well as a sandwich wrap for later. Even though there was sugar in the muffin, she hoped some of that burned off in the baking process. She needed energy. If a little baked sugar combined with flour and eggs did the trick, then she was onboard. The muffin calmed her stomach a bit, and eventually the complex carbs kicked in and provided the energy necessary.

Once she set up her booth, she ran to the bathroom. While walking back to her booth space, Vonnette overheard another jeweler claiming he'd had the best financial day ever yesterday.

Vonnette's heart sank.

Reaching her booth once again, she felt that Pollyanna had left the building. She had no idea when or if, Polly might be returning. Necessary smiles for the day would be a challenge after hearing about the other jeweler. Though she was thrilled someone else had pulled in good money here, it wasn't she who pulled in that money . . . sooooo.

The show doors opened. People came in looking as if they had slept in their clothes and were in serious need of caffeine.

Two teenagers stopped into her booth asking if she had any belly rings?

Smiling, she told them she didn't have such a thing.

A man stopped briefly while remaining far enough out into the aisle that Vonnette felt it would be rude to speak to him.

He walked on.

Three younger women came and looked while their conversation was in full swing. They spoke about their night out on the town the previous evening. Their look about the booth was so brief Vonnette felt certain they could not have actually seen what she had in the way of jewelry. She guessed it was good they were merely tire kickers because she felt they were not her typical customers anyway.

The morning passed mostly this way, with people wandering through her booth area as if they wore blinders and could only really see what was directly in front of them. Noticing no one carrying shopping bags, she thought of how there are times when artists hold purchases until the client leaves the show. Normally though, when no bags are in sight, it means people are not buying. Standing on her feet with a smile on her face as people walked by had her feeling not only emotionally down, but also physically down. The crowd flowed steadily. So, even though she felt it wouldn't matter with these people today, she had no time to sit and do puzzles.

Recall of her dream about not showing up on the third day of the show due to forgetfulness danced in her head. Though Vonnette felt she ought to have done exactly that today, to come in when the show ended and feign forgetfulness as her reason for missing the day, she continued to smile at passers-bye.

It was painfully apparent no more money was coming her way at this show. Try as she might to focus on the two new design ideas as positives, she felt she could have come up with the same concepts someplace closer to home where she didn't have such expenses to cover. No, her glad game did not work today. Pollyanna had indeed left the building. Tired, she felt let down by the general public in this area that she had heard such good things about.

People claimed Morristown to be an upscale community. Reportedly, people here loved the arts and had the means to buy whatever they found interesting. Three books, one ring and one strand of beads sold didn't hold that concept up in Vonnette's mind. Maybe she didn't have the kind of art these people were interested in. Perhaps they were of the mind set where they didn't buy from someone they had only seen once and didn't know anything about. It didn't really matter. This show was a wash for Vonnette. Unfortunately, expenses had not been covered and she felt disappointed. But then, Vonnette had done shows where nothing at all had sold! If her glad game worked today, she would have held fast to the fact that she had actually sold a few items.

Doubtful she would ever apply to this show again, she tried to remain focused on what she would need to do in the way of packing to be ready when she could drive her car in at the end of the show. Being one of the first people inside the building to load up and leave quickly became her new motivation. And when the time came for her to get on the road, she hoped she would still be awake enough to drive the four plus hours, straight home. If not, at least she always had her own pillow in the car. That enabled her to stop if necessary and put her head down for a few minutes. Since childhood she had been able to rest for a few minutes, maybe ten or fifteen even, and feel refreshed enough to carry on. This might be one of those days where those ten minutes were vital for her to make it home safely.

Unfortunately, this show had turned out just as she dreamed; no sales on the last day.

Surprisingly, she was in fact able to be one of the earliest people to get her vehicle inside to pack up and leave. However, because

Candace L. Sherman

Vonnette got in so early, others that came in behind her, boxed her car in. She couldn't exit until some of them were packed and ready to leave. Patience, never a strong-suit, became her new commander. Waiting in her car became almost meditative. Resting her eyes while they were wide open, she did feel as though she had somehow slept. Then, when able to get out of the building again, Vonnette left for home never needing to put her head down as she had thought might be necessary.

CHAPTER FOUR

Providence

October 24-26 2008
Set up Thursday the 23rd

Pink Stick Pearls & Pink Spinel Rose Ring

Candace L. Sherman

DREAM
Something about wearing a pink blouse that was transparent enough to see some of the bra through it.

Shows within a certain traveling distance from her home were what Vonnette termed as home shows. These allowed her to sleep in her own bed at night. The Fine Furnishings Show was held in Providence, RI, a mere 45-minute drive from her house and therefore, a home show.

As Vonnette readied for the show today, she bathed and thought about her dream message. Pink was usually a good omen. Excited, she dressed, opting to wear her question mark styled earrings with pink pearl drops along with round, pink pearl beads and a pink stick pearl necklace. She pulled out her pink spinel ring, too, because she felt it went along with the dream message, so why not wear it. The design was a stylized gold rose with a faceted pink spinel in the center.

Vonnette usually only wore one ring at a time. Sometimes she displayed one ring on each hand. In her way of thinking, one ring could speak volumes alone rather then so many rings that no one could decide upon which one to look at.

Clothes, well, they always had to be comfortable when doing shows. Today, Vonnette chose a pair of white, stretchy knit trousers with a light green, long sleeve jersey for a top. Normally, she chose clothing of plain fabrics to showcase her jewelry. Printed fabrics would compete with her jewelry designs. People didn't ask about her clothing at shows. If they did, then she would shift the concept of what she wore because having people focus on her jewelry meant they were paying attention to what she wanted them to pay heed to.

Something Vonnette learned years back was not to have anything in her booth other than her product lest people became distracted and asked about the very thing that wasn't for sale. Her love of fresh flowers helped drive that lesson home when she had a vase of fresh flowers in her booth at one show. People either asked about the flowers or the vase instead of her jewelry!

Local show, her own home with her own bed each night, great. Pink in her dream, today could be a good day on some level. With that thought she said good-bye to her cats and headed off to Providence.

Early on her drive she spotted five crows searching for food along the side of the highway. Five crows stood for riches. Fifteen minutes later she saw seven crows fly overhead. Seven was news from a distance. Maybe it meant she would meet people who lived farther away than Rhode Island at the show. Almost at the parking garage she noticed four crows fly over. Four crows symbolized birth.

Today was Friday and, happily, she felt rested. Set up was yesterday and, thankfully, Vonnette didn't have much to do to be ready for the opening time of ten.

After she set up her jewelry, Vonnette did her normal pre-show run to the ladies' room because during the show she never knew when the next opportunity would present itself. Some shows send around booth sitters. It's a kindness so artists can come out from behind their small restricted space, stretch their legs to maybe get lunch and have a bathroom run. These people do not know any artist's product though and cannot give the information necessary to make a proper sale, so Vonnette left her booth only when absolutely necessary.

Back in her booth and ready for the day, the doors opened and the show began.

Indoor shows where cars were parked in a covered garage, such as this one meant there was no need to pay attention to weather reports and wondering if people would come out if it was too hot, too cold, raining, or even snowing. Something each artist had to take into consideration for outdoor shows. Indoor shows had other challenges. There would be a charge to park as well as a fee to get into the show, something minimal, like a three-dollar per person charge, or as high as twenty-dollars a head. Usually children were admitted free. Normally, outdoor shows didn't charge for admittance.

This day started off slow. Well, it was Friday and most people would be at work. Maybe after lunchtime it would get busy.

Organizing her booth space underneath the showcases was going to take a few minutes so, good, there was something to do. All right, finished with that, now what?

After pulling out word puzzles, Vonnette sat down and opened her paperback leaflet. Sketches done in New Jersey on the back pages had been removed. They were safe in her studio pinned to a wall until she could find time to create the nest rings. Those sketches would not be a distraction. Today was in any event, a new show. One where pink was in her dream. Yes, new show, new people, new opportunities! While sitting with her puzzle, she glanced up every so often where if too engrossed, a possible client could be missed entering her space.

Some man began to talk to Vonnette from outside her booth range not wanting to come closer lest he be mistaken as a possible customer. He spoke about what brought him to Providence today and how he happened to get to the show. While wondering how to put a stop to this non-conversation, her phone rang. Putting her index finger up in the air for the universal sign to wait a minute, Vonnette answered, "Hello, Vonnette here." A man on the other end gave his name, but Vonnette couldn't hear it thanks to the man outside her booth still talking. More words came over the phone that Vonnette didn't really catch. Asking the man on the phone to hold a moment, she tried to excuse herself from the outer conversation by saying "Good-bye" to the man across from her. Going back to the phone, she covered her free ear in hopes of hearing what the man might be saying only to find that no one was there. The line had gone silent.

Feeling her unsuccessful efforts to disengage the person standing outside her booth from continuous chatter may have caused the phone conversation to be cut off abruptly, she feebly asked, "Hello?" This was a last stitch effort before she hung up her on end.

To her complete surprise, she heard a voice respond! "Hi, yes, I'm here."

"Oh, great, I thought I lost the connection."

"Sorry, that was my fault. I accidently dropped the phone."

"No problem. If I heard you correctly, you said something about a piece of jewelry I made years ago for your deceased mom? Can I ask your name please?"

"Yes, it's Justin and actually you made a few pieces for my *grandmother* over time. We always called her Mum. This piece is not one of those though. It's something we grandchildren had bought as a gift for her, but I'm thinking she never wore it. Guess it wasn't her style. My grandmother has passed. Originally, my mother was the push behind our buying this other piece for Mum. Anyway, as my grandmother spoke so highly of you, we, the grandchildren, thought it might be nice to have you make this into something for our mother to wear now. It's a pin with pearls in it. My mother loves pearls. We thought she would enjoy it as a remembrance. Here's the thing, she doesn't wear pins, so we thought maybe if you could switch it over to a pendant. That could work for her."

Vonnette's curiosity was peeked. "Justin, may I ask who your grandmother was?"

"Yes, I don't know if you remember your clients, but she was Melinda Bronson."

Suddenly, and without warning, Vonnette broke out in tears. Unable to contain them she apologized numerous times over the next few moments of strangled conversation with Justin. "How unprofessional," she heard herself mumble at one point. "I am so sorry for your loss and for my reaction that I cannot seem to contain."

Tears can be contagious and Vonnette felt Justin's words choke up a bit on the other end of the phone. Total strangers sharing a sad moment over a telephone together. "How odd was this," Vonnette wondered? Looking up every so often from her lap Vonnette made sure no one was coming into her booth. "I thought the world of your grandmother. I had no idea she passed. I feel at a complete loss for words just now. What can I possibly say to you? Please forgive my reaction."

"Honestly, my brothers, sister and I didn't want to contact you right away when we were all in Newport together because we didn't want to get weird with you, and yet here we both are. Mum spoke highly of you whenever she shared her latest purchase from you with us, her *treasures* she called them. But I also know she was not a regular customer. I guess I thought you might not even be sure who she was. So, I didn't expect this reaction from you at all. It's nice that you are this touched by her passing. Thank you."

"Justin, if I got the paper I might have known and could have attended whatever service you all may have had. However, being on the road doing shows as much as I do, I don't have time for the *Daily News*." As Vonnette replied she visually searched for something to ground her energy to be coherent for the remainder of the call. Finding nothing, the only thing she could think of was to grab a paper-towel from the roll she had on hand to wipe down display cases. Dabbing her eyes and running nose she continued, "I knew your grandmother was not doing any better physically when she last stopped in to see me about six months ago. I felt awful seeing her bent over from the pain. But what happened between then and now if you don't mind my asking?"

"Don't worry about the service. We had a small ceremony with just family members. But I'm interested. You knew she was ill? There was such a time where she was unable to get around that I had no idea she was in touch with anyone to talk about all this with."

"Yes, I knew."

"She got some odd thing that affected her bones. I won't go into detail but that, topped off with the other physical issues she'd been dealing with over the last five years, seemed too much for her. We were all there with her in the end and she went quickly. So we were glad that she didn't suffer. Her quality of life these past few years had diminished so drastically. Mum was ninety-three you know, and still lived on her own. I'm touched that you liked and cared about Mum and are this upset over the loss."

Vonnette began to tear up again, then apologized again. "Thank goodness no one was in her booth," she thought. When she finally did speak again, she said, "Your grandmother was a delight! I enjoyed our visits very much. Melinda loved my jewelry and all the channeled stone properties I list. We had great discussions about anything and everything. I have thought of her often over the last couple of months, but sadly had no idea that might have been a sign that she was leaving this plane. I'm usually more tuned in than this. Gosh, I can't seem to let go of the fact that she is gone.

"Okay, let me be professional for a moment." Clearing her throat in an effort to sound coherent, Vonnette continued. "Please let me know when you might next be in town, and yes, we will connect to see if there is anything I can do to help in your search for this pin to be changed and made somehow different. It's not something I normally do, work on other people's designs I mean. However, for your grandmother I will at least take a look and see if I can help. In some small way, I would feel it was a final thing I could do for your Mum."

"Thank you for all, and yes, I'll give a call when I get back down to Newport. For some reason, I was left in charge of this deed since my sister lives in Hawaii. It will be nice to meet you in person after hearing about your talents from Mum."

After a few final words, they got off the phone.

Sitting quietly alone Vonnette thought of her now deceased client and their many past visits. She began to cry again. It was a show day so that had to end! In an effort of getting her emotional act together, she forced her mind into another place. Pulling out her word puzzles again she tried to push these sad thoughts out of her head without success. But why was she sooo touched by the passing of this woman? All in all, Vonnette believed in continuous life which meant Melinda was not gone, gone. Melinda was no longer in physical form yes, but she was still here and there, and could suddenly appear to Vonette from wherever there is.

Since finding the lump in her breast Vonnette had been self-centered. Not selfishly, but aware of her-self and her needs and that put her mind into a place where she was not tuned in with the universe enough to recognize a message was coming through about Melinda. Why else would she have been thinking of her off and on over the course of the past couple of months? Tears kept welling up in her eyes. It was a challenge but she did keep reminding herself to concentrate on the word puzzles to get out of that emotional place and be mentally present for the day at this show. A whole day lay ahead for her and at this moment, her emotions had won out over work. Suddenly she remembered seeing seven crows on her way into the show this morning prophesizing news from a distance. In fact, she did just have a call with news from Justin. He had said he lived in Brunswick, Maine, and that was a long drive away.

Vonnette thought, "Pay attention and the universe does give messages."

While drinking some water, she checked her eyes in the show mirror and decided they were not any worse for wear. "Okay, nose and eyes are not red. Got to be thankful for any small thing right now I guess. Think I need to get a hold of myself and be more centered. I might have known Melinda was leaving this plane if I had only tuned in to someone or something other than my own health lately."

Around that time a couple wandered into her booth with smiles on their faces. How lovely it was to be reminded that a smile goes a long way each and every day to improve a mood. The couple held hands as they came along the aisle. Looking straight at Vonnette, not her jewelry, they asked if she was in fact Vonnette?

Though nodding yes, Vonnette displayed a quizzical look. People approached her and often asked if she remembered them. Vonnette didn't recall this couple.

They were perhaps in their late forties. She was very attractive with long, extremely black hair and piercing green eyes. Maybe she was five feet six because she stood a bit taller than Vonnette. He stood, at least six feet two, had light wavy hair, a tad longer than maybe he was comfortable with as he kept pushing it back off his forehead. They both had on nice clothing, medium to higher price range, Vonnette guessed. Their jewelry was not anything she recognized. It was tasteful, but looked as if it came from a standardized jewelry store. Not that there was anything wrong with that. Simply, Vonnette used her visual scan as an observational way to distinguish that they had most likely not been clients, at least not yet.

Placing their hands out to shake, they introduced themselves as friends of Paul & Marie Post. They were Jack and Joely. Hands shaken and smiles of acknowledgement exchanged, a question seemed to lurk on their faces. Vonnette ignored it at this moment to see if it would manifest without prompting.

Pleasantries were shared about their mutual friendships. Slowly, the couple began to look over the showcases of jewelry on display. Jack stopped dead in his tracks as he gazed upon a lapel pin. Motioning for his wife to come and take a look, they each read the printed stone property placed just below the pin: *Chalcedony acts as a shield of protection.*

After opening the display case, Vonnette removed the lapel pin and handed it over to the man without being asked to do so. While placing a black velvet pad on top of the display case for the pin when he was done holding it, she began her psychological search. "You seem connected to this pin. Are you in the midst of something trying, maybe at work?"

Quickly the couple looked at Vonnette, at one another, at the lapel pin, and then back at Vonnette as they responded in unison. "How did you guess that?"

"I trust and believe the stone healing properties displayed in my cases. They give me insights. Even more than that, as a couple, you are connected on many levels. That leaves a possible need for protection to be either from work or, perhaps, extended family issues. Not difficult to figure really with the process of elimination."

"You are absolutely spot on with the work issue." Jack said, and with a new sympathetic ear he went on. "I have been struggling with the idea of leaving my position because it has become such a challenge emotionally. My wife is giving me support in whatever decision I might make. It's just that I have been at this job for four years. Right at a time when I should be advancing, I'm instead contemplating moving on to another company. People who came into this organization after me have made my job very difficult with their cutthroat methods. The company never used to be that way. When I came onboard, the owner ran the whole business and there was consideration for employees as well as clients. I'm on the fence as to leave, or stick it out a bit longer and see if things shift again."

"That's a decision only you can make." Vonnette replied. "Let me give you a hand to decide if this lapel pin is for you or not. Do you feel the need to shift from who you are internally in order to remain with the company? In other words, do you feel the need to become defensive, offensive, or a straight out hard ass?"

"Good question. If I'm honest, I think if I stay I do have to become a bit of a hard ass so I won't get lost in the office shuffle."

"Are you comfortable with becoming that person? Is it within you, or is that something you feel is a step away from your character?" Vonnette's questions definitely had Jack's attention.

"Think it's within me to be hard, but it's well hidden. Not sure how comfortable I am with the concept that I need to be different to remain in the company. My thought usually goes in the direction of why do I have to change?"

His wife nodded in agreement while he spoke these last words.

Feeling she now had what she was looking for in order to advise him about making the purchase or not, Vonnette began again. "Here's the deal with chalcedony; you will feel protected from outside influences as well as from others making decisions for you. That includes my input of how to use chalcedony to say nothing about those around you telling you how to do your job. If you leave and move on, you might not need to be protected from outside sources. Inner thoughts are another matter. You have to decide if you want to shift your ideals to remain in that company. But in a normal method of ladder climbing one usually has to shift from being a co-worker to being a boss. That can mean you have to stop being a best friend to now inspire others to complete their work in timely and efficient ways. If this is a shift you can embrace willfully, not out of defense from those around you pushing you, then maybe you should remain. If that goes against your nature, then perhaps leaving will help you find a position where your methods are appreciated.

"The additional design to this piece has peaks and valleys in how the gold is shaped along one side. In my term of looking at symbolism I see this as how we look at life, with ups and downs. Your work situation is just that, at least right now it is. For today, it's your decision to make the purchase or not. And, that decision is a small example of what you need to consider about your career."

Round about then a man stood two booths up the aisle and was trying to catch Vonnette's eye. He leaned to one side and waved a bit. Though she had noticed him, she had opted not to get sidetracked while attending a possible new client. Still, she wondered who he was and what he wanted?

Energy focused on the couple, Vonnette could see there was still a question lurking. Thinking about it, that look had been on their faces since they and Vonnette all met a few moments ago. It seemed they now felt comfortable enough to ask.

Almost in unison, they admitted their mutual friends had suggested Vonnette was a possible source for them in whatever they termed their hour of need.

Vonnette had known Paul and Marie for many years and felt certain this suggested meeting was for her to give them some form of psychic input. She simply said, "Ahhhhhh."

Almost apologetic while blushing a bit, Jack looked like a child caught with his hand in the cookie jar just before dinner was to be served as he felt the sudden need to explain further. "You helped me without my even asking the question first. So, I guess Paul and Marie were right."

Vonnette chuckled a bit and added, "You are the one who helped yourself today. There seems to be a nice connection between we three, but you were drawn to the stone you needed even before you read the healing properties. I created the piece and chose to have it out on display today, so that's my part in this shared moment. However, you made the connection yourself!"

Looking at one another again they voiced an "Ahh ha" together. Jack added, "We didn't know how this might work. Neither Marie nor Paul told us anything along those lines. They simply told us you knew things and might be a good connection."

"Well, as I've said, I did have a hand in this since I made the pin.

By the way, lapel pins can be and are worn by women as well. Say there comes a time when you, Jack, are not wearing the pin, your wife might wear it with her outfit that day. If you would like to take it home, I will wrap it up for you."

In a bold stroke, she was asking them to make a decision. This was a show. Someone else could walk into her booth, distract both Vonnette and this couple, as the man across the aisle was attempting to do now, and by doing so the sale might be lost. Vonnette was learning in subtle ways how to close a deal, and that was a good thing! Once their minds were made up, the pin was wrapped and Vonnette handed it to them over the counter.

"Thank you both. By the way, I am a catalyst, not an answer. Inevitably you have the answers inside that you're looking for. Maybe now with the use of this chalcedony lapel pin you'll be able to pull those answers to the forefront and enjoy the process of change. Some people find change a challenge. Even I can, and do, emotionally fight shifts, but usually in the end, I feel change is good."

"Before we leave, can you give me a book title where you've acquired the stone properties from?"

"Joely, that's an easy fit. I wrote the book. Literally. I have copies over here." Walking to the other end of the display booth she pointed out her two books to the couple. "The coffee table book has the stone properties along with pictures of pieces I've made that work with the healing energies. This smaller paperback book is something that has no pictures, just healing stone definitions. It's something I feel can be left in your car, or a handbag, for when you view a stone you feel immediately drawn to. If you'd like to buy a copy, I will happily sign it for you."

"Yes, please, give us the stone properties book. It says here on the cover these properties are channeled. Sorry, I've heard this term before but honestly have no idea what it really means."

"Not a problem. Channeling is where you sit and perhaps go into a deep meditation. During which time, you allow some other entity to come through you. It's a bit unnerving because you don't have any idea of exactly what's going to happen. It's especially scary if you're someone who likes to remain in control of your senses. If you are, then this kind of experience can be a nightmare."

"You did this in order to write this book? Seriously?"

"Yes, Jack, I did do that, but it wasn't to write a book. It all began quite simply. Meditating is something I practiced daily for many years. Looking for answers to life along with deeper meanings, I got into it more deeply than maybe some people do. I don't know. It was okay. But looking back at the whole time I was practicing that form of meditation I was uncomfortable with allowing another entity the use of my brain and body.

"All my books have developed from those days, though, because all my writing has stone healing energy at the core. So, it was good and informative especially since I question everything!

"Anyway, I began to channel for people, giving advice. It was yet another thing I felt was not in my realm. Usually it was health advice in some form of natural healing where color could be utilized, herbs, acupressure and the like. Between channeling and doing psychometry for others, my hope was that they would get some healing out of the experience. Perhaps they did. Eventually, my gain was to channel the healing energies specifically listed in these two books. Each stone is listed alphabetically. Even when there are more than one color or name for stones, I've listed each alphabetically under the main heading, as in rhodolite garnet is placed under garnet.

"Over time I tested the properties out on myself. When I created a new piece of jewelry, it was easy to not pay attention to whatever I'd written or could even remember for that matter because each stone property would be given along with about ten additional stones. I'm not one who can memorize. Doubt I could ever be an actor due to that fact. Actually, I have difficulty remembering names of people, even clients! My point here is that blind testing stone energies on myself was easy. In time, the properties were verified with willing clients. I say willing because I always asked if they wanted to read the healing properties of whatever stone or stones they seemed connected to just as you did here today with the lapel pin. If they expressed interest, I pulled out my notebook and let them read. Normally, the connection was so strong that people either teared up or actually cried.

"After years of that confirmation process, I decided this had to be the base for my future books. I don't take credit for the properties listed, just for being the channel that wrote them down and tested them out to see if in fact they worked."

"So, you're no longer channeling that entity?" Joely asked.

Smiling outwardly, Vonnette was smiling inwardly, too. "Well, that's a good question and honestly, I can't say one way or another there."

Very quizzical looks came over the two faces opposite her.

Vonnette wondered if she could, and then opted to try and explain. "When I'm working, creating, there are lost minutes in time. It's where I feel as though I step to one side and someone else takes over. Mind you, this doesn't happen all the time. But when it does, I look at my work afterward and wonder just how it shifted. This began when I was in college in painting class and eventually it spilled over into my jewelry work. When I began to practice deep meditations, I started with automatic writing. That's where you sit with eyes closed, a pad of paper and pen and simply write. You begin with one word, maybe writing it over and over again. When you're really meditating, your writing shifts in style enough so that you no longer recognize your own penmanship. After a period of doing that and reading what had come from those moments, I began to feel okay with whatever was coming through and felt it was not trying to abuse the situation. So, when I opted to channel for others it was a continuation of a theme. Like when I'm in the studio and lose minutes."

"Then why did you stop? You did say you stopped, didn't you?"

"Yes, I stopped. The reason was as I said, I became uncomfortable allowing another entity to use my brain and body especially as guidance for others. When in my work element, other energies come in an almost natural way. I accept that force because I feel I create for the good of whomever ends up with the piece. Why not accept input for the greater good?"

"Oh, yes, you did say that already. I'm sorry." Joely had been hanging on every word Vonnette shared. "Guess I got so engrossed in the story I forgot. I'm not sure I would ever feel comfortable doing such a thing. But you did this over a period of time and still feel as though it happens without your knowing it while you work? Yikes! I think you're brave. I'd walk away from my work if that ever happened to me. I'd be fearful of whatever came through, that you refer to as an entity. I mean, how do you know if it's friendly and doesn't mean you harm?"

"When all that happens now I don't question it as much as I did when I was younger maybe because in general I believe things happen for a reason. And, these experiences have happened over many years allowing me to feel some level of comfort in stepping to one side for whomever to come through. Sharing my body and mind for moments doesn't seem so odd when it's while I'm deep in thought. It's rather exciting that another spirit wants to come and literally create through me."

"Wow, this is fascinating stuff. No wonder Paul and Marie suggested we get in touch with you! Can honestly say I've never met anyone like you before."

"Hey, Jack, I'm not much different than either of you, not really. I think we all have situations where spirits stop in for visits. Maybe I'm just tuned in enough to know when it happens. Maybe I'm curious about things you don't think about. For me it's normal to question continuous life, spirits, angels, ghosts, and the healing powers of stones!"

"Well, you've given me a lot to think about today," Jack said. "These are all new concepts. I don't know about Joely, but for me definitely. Think we will be back in touch at some point if you don't mind. There are bound to be more questions."

Looking between the two, Vonnette nodded her head. "I don't mind having further conversations with you both. Keep in mind that once you begin to go down this road, people will never look at you the same again. I guess what I am saying is that before you embark, make sure it's the road you'd like to travel. Your new lapel pin ought to help you feel confident in making any decision about your work situation as well as having further inquiries into the unknown."

Standing wide-eyed, Joely said, "I've had so many questions pass through my head as you have been talking. They were so quick they've all left my brain at the moment. I would love to get together again, too. That is if you don't mind our questions?"

"We all begin somewhere when we are on a new path in life Joely. There was a moment where I was in your position, too. I mean asking loads of questions. You're being here today, Jack, confiding in a complete stranger, is a new path and has brought forth a new tool, if you will, to help with your work situation. Sometimes the things we wonder about can bring in weird energy, as with maybe people who abuse your both being novices. That can be trickster energy. Trickster energy can come from humans as well as spirits and is something we need to grasp early on in our research so as not to be dragged into it unknowingly. This study of the unknown can be an interesting journey though, and something that might be taken with us when we leave this plane. I'll look forward to our next visit. For today, thanks for listening with an open mind as well as making a purchase."

Turning to leave, Joely quickly turned back into the booth space with her right hand up. It was as though she was in school and raised her hand to ask a question.

Recognizing that kind of inquisitiveness, Vonnette stopped and waited.

"I just remembered one thing I was going to ask. You mentioned a word a while back. Think it was psychommm . . . something?"

"Oh, yes, psychometry."

"Yes, psychometry. That was it. What is that?"

"We all have energy, that's a given, and I'm certain you follow me on that, right?"

"Yes."

"Well, we leave traces of that energy on things, inanimate objects like jewelry for instance, or even keys. Keys are a big one in fact, and something that many psychics use to tune into your spirit guides.

I know, I'm getting ahead of you with that term of spirit guides. We can discuss that at another time. Anyway, objects that we hold or have on our person a lot contain trace energy from us, and that energy can be felt and/or seen by someone who is sensitive when they hold your objects.

"Apparently, something clicked inside when I said psychometry. Or you would not be asking me about it. Before you get involved with doing this as a parlor trick with friends over cocktails or dinner, please let me warn you off from doing so. When you muck about with energy from others, you need to have an arsenal of protection about you as well, such as ways to wash off any negative energy someone has left as a trace on these items. It's best that you hold onto that thought as something for your future. After you've learned more. Okay?"

"Hmm. You know, Vonnette, it was as though you were reading my mind as you said not to do this as a parlor trick. I had thought it could be something fun to do with friends. Guess not."

"No. Joely, using psychometry is like having a key that you've no idea what lock it might fit. Once the correct lock is found, you still have no idea what's behind that door. Please don't be a Pandora and experiment until you do some serious homework on how to protect yourself first. It can be fun, as when you first play with a Wee Gee Board. But then you never know what you might see that someone doesn't want you to know. Think of all the movies out there where someone begins to see a murder or something happening that is connected with a friend. You would be horrified if you ever saw something weird associated with a friend. Honestly, that can be a door not worth opening. Better to be safe than sorry.

"However, if you cannot get this concept out of your head, you can try something within the safety of your own home. Take hold of some family treasure, preferably something that belonged to Jack's family because if it's your family piece, you might know the answer to any question so nothing gets discovered. Hold the item and blank out any thoughts of who it belonged to. Remain empty of preconceived ideas of who owned it, what their life was like, where they lived or anything. Just breathe deeply. I am visually oriented, so I get pictures in my mind when I do most anything. You may be scent oriented and would thus get a fragrance of one sort or another. If that happens, don't question it, just let the smell come forth. When you do psychometry properly, you should end up with some form of vibration from the object that associates with whatever deceased person owned the item before it came to your husband.

"When you are done, you can ask Jack to confirm or deny whatever you saw, heard, felt or smelled.

"Does that answer your question, Joely?"

"Yup, it does, and thanks for all the input. Think I had best not rush in. You know what they say about fools. I could easily fall into that category with my enthusiasm here."

Pleasantries were exchanged and the couple left her booth. Vonnette was feeling positive again about the day and thankful she had stopped crying before Jack and Joely had come into her selling space. It was also great that she was centered enough to give proper advice on how to do psychometry. Otherwise, she could have lead Joely down a bottomless pit of uncertainty.

The aisles were empty. Thinking it might be close to lunchtime when people attending a show normally took a break, Vonnette was not hungry, but felt like moving. Walking around the end of her booth, she looked up and down the row and noticed only other artists. Music piped in from overhead speakers played an Argentine tango. She began to move about as if she had a dance partner and was on a dance floor with her arms up in position. Totally unaware other artists were staring, she enjoyed the song and the movement. Being constricted in her small booth space for such long stretches of time was no way to stay physically fit. This was at least an enjoyable moment and break in the day.

Seemingly out of nowhere, a man stood in front of her. Where had he come from? He looked a bit familiar. Yes, he was the man trying to gain her attention earlier. The moment was broken and she stopped dancing. Three adjacent vendors applauded her dance. Laughing a bit, she bowed to them and then focused on the very tall man standing in front of her.

"Hi, do I know you?"

"No, but I'd like to know you," rolled out of his mouth nonchalantly. "My name is Tony Brown. I design and make wood side tables. My booth is over one aisle and up three spaces on the left. Yesterday while we were setting up, I noticed you. Someone mentioned you live in Newport?"

"I do, yes."

"Yesterday there was too much on all our plates for me to interrupt our schedules. Today, now, it's sooo slow." Tony began looking about as if to see who might be able to hear his words and then, almost in a whisper said, "The reason I wanted to talk to you is . . . you're a walk-in, right?"

As he spoke, Vonnette began to feel her face redden. Uncontrollable blushing that happened at inconvenient times such as this gave away some of her privacy. Vonnette thought a moment and then replied slowly, "Okay, you've just caught me off guard. Not sure what to say."

He smoothed the moment over by asking, "Would you walk with me to my booth? We can talk a moment without anyone overhearing."

Nodding, Vonnette grabbed hold of her display case keys and wallet and then followed as he motioned the way to his booth with his left hand outstretched as he walked a bit sideways. Perhaps he was single. There was no wedding band to say one way or another. But then, some men chose not to wear bands especially if it could get caught in tools and affect their fingers. Being a woodworker, that concept would certainly fit. Jewelry was something Vonnette noticed on everyone with whom she had conversations. What type of jewelry a person wore helped her figure out what kind of person she might be talking to. Without any visible jewelry, there was no help in that department. Unsure where Tony wanted to go with this conversation, she opted to keep her mouth shut and decide what to say and do as they walked and talked.

"About five years ago I was in a really bad car accident. Most people gave me up as dead. Being in a coma-like state for days they were not far off I guess. I remember leaving my body, seeing it from above and not feeling attached to it. I went through the tunnel and met a bunch of people I've known in this life who have passed over. I then came across a guy who said I could return, or switch my life on earth with another soul. It didn't matter one way or another to me at the time. Though I didn't say anything, I do recall shrugging my shoulders as an expression of detachment. Suddenly there was another male figure in front of me waiting for my decision. As I looked at him, I somehow communicated mentally telling him to go for it. After a long period of recuperation, I emerged from my coma as I stand before you today.

"Time has progressed, and there are people I've come upon that *he* knew well. People I didn't remember at first. Everyone felt that was due to the coma which gave me loads of leeway time with high hopes to recall. Most memories of people have come to me, but some have not at all. I can't make it happen. There are things I remember from his life. Guess most would call it my life. Normally, my own existences play heavily into my daily routine." Tony spoke quickly, as if there was not much time to say what he needed to with sincerity. "Honestly, I didn't recall I was someone else for almost a year. Now it's weird; I feel like two people who've had different experiences in the same body. Usually, I feel like twin souls exist in here together. So, when I say he or I, I guess I really mean we or us. Has it been the same for you?"

"Let me begin with, you are not the first person to say I am a walk-in."

Artists sitting alone in their booth could be bored and might listen to a nearby conversation. In an effort to keep her exchanges private, Vonnette looked around, spoke openly but with a softness so others might not overhear. "I was told many years back by a woman I had met briefly that I was a *walk-in*. I'd never heard the term before and that's saying something since I am big into metaphysics. Because I was curious about the phrase, she simply explained it this way: *it takes a walk-in to recognize a walk-in.* You are the second person who has asked me, so perhaps I am a walk-in.

"I don't mean to rain on your parade here, but my experience has not been like yours. I had a really high fever once in college that lasted a few days. It began as something they called the Hong Kong Flu. What it turned into, God only knows. My roommate had gone home for the Christmas holidays. On my own and running a very high fever, I simply didn't think about eating or drinking liquids. I heard voices while I was awake. Honestly, I felt as if people were right next to me in bed, which would have been something since my bed abutted an outside wall at that point. Friends felt I was hallucinating and didn't think any more of it than it was due to the high fever. Physically, I kept sinking downward.

"Eventually I was taken to my parents' home and nursed back to health. Returning to college again after winter break, my boyfriend got into serious trouble with the police. From that point forward life became an even higher challenge than it had been before. Emotionally I didn't feel capable of handling anything. Actually, I doubt I felt I could handle it all before being that ill but somehow did muddle through.

"Constantly feeling overwhelmed by life during that time frame, I tried nonetheless, to take one day at a time, but looking back I realize now things were off, way off! Over the course of that following year, I functioned but didn't live normally. Beyond that I cannot describe it. A friend told me one day that he heard me laugh for the first time in a year. It was a strange time for me, almost like living in a fog. I remembered people for the most part.

"Once, I was talked into attending a high school reunion. While there, I knew I didn't recall most of the things my closest friends from that period did. Chalking it up to those events not being as important to me as they were to them, I let it all go; that is, until many years later when I met the woman who called me a walk-in for the first time.

"After meeting her, I began reading up on the concept to see if it fit me in any way. One book suggested two souls could have a contract from before the time of your birth. Should you want to step out because life was too much for whatever reason, that other soul could step in and take over wherever you had left off. If that did happen, the second soul had to deal with all the trash the first soul had amassed along with making their own way in this new, but already happening existence. Understandably, that new soul might not recall all former activities of the previous soul.

"This is quite different from any form of near death experience where the same soul returns to the original body. Long winded way to say yes to you. So yes, I guess I am a walk-in.

"During that time when I did my research on walk-ins, I found people often called such experiences step-ins in books. I continue to call it walk-in as that's how I first heard it termed. However, I do not recall going through the tunnel or meeting all the people you suggest happened to you. Maybe that was what happened while I was hearing people next to me in bed. Years later I did a very deep meditation and found that tunnel though, along with faces of those I knew, but my deceased mother stopped me from going further."

Nodding with seeming understanding, Tony stood quietly as Vonnette continued with her personal explanation. "I believe I've made peace with the two souls concept today. The difficulties that that other soul had, some are still with me. Thankfully, there's much I have managed to work through. It's not often I stop to think about being a walk-in now. However, it does feel as if I've had two lives in one. One where I don't recall people or places much, and one where I hope I face my struggles in new and different ways.

"It's always hard to explain how my life is different. One important way is that now I discuss metaphysics much more openly than I ever used to. The fear of being called a witch due to my thoughts on metaphysics is somewhat in the background today. Not all the way gone, but I am more comfortable discussing my beliefs with others who seem fascinated."

"That's an interesting slant on being a walk-in," Tony added.

"Something I have not heard before. Would it be possible for us to talk more about all this in the future?" Tony had that look of sincerity on his face and Vonnette felt there was no malice in his heart. "It's just that no one I know understands me when I get going on this concept. Having mentioned it once or twice to friends, I realized they were squirming in their seats waiting for a clear exit to appear in the conversation. Somehow, they all look hurt if I talk this way. I'm not trying to upset anyone. Guess I'm simply trying to understand what happened to me!"

"I feel we are spiritual beings having a human experience," Vonnette added feeling more comfortable in this conversation with Tony. "The end of what we call life is just a new beginning of a whole new existence. Maybe we all exist on one planet or another in whatever life-form possible to survive. Like maybe a planet where life can only exist in a gaseous state, there we would merely be vapors. Here on earth we are in a solid format we call human, animal, mineral or vegetable. When we leave here, who really knows what shape or form we take?

"I mean, I see spirits that are in a transparent human form. Maybe I see them as human because that's what I knew of them while they were on this plane. People think I'm crazy when I talk like this too, but it's all part of metaphysics really as a study of the unknown. If I were into science, I would be trying to prove what I am suggesting. After doing countless past life regressions, going for psychic readings, palm readers and the like, I don't have to have something in black and white to make me believe. To me, it's as real as you and I are at this moment Tony.

"My experiences in past life regressions came to a halt when I saw many people from this life in a former one. Of course, they looked differently than how I know them today, but I could still recognize them. It helped me to correlate how our relationships were then, to how they might be similar in this current existence.

"I feel we bring new people into our human experience each time we are incarnated to help us learn new things. Then there are always people who are in their first or second incarnation. Often these people have a difficult time doing what I call normal, trivial, manual things like hammering a nail into the wall. We all need to have patience with those people just as we need patience with walk-ins. There is transformation happening on all fronts if we open our eyes to the possibilities. I know we could talk for a longer time about all this and so much more, and perhaps we will in the future, but for now I have to get back to my booth.

"Your pieces are interesting, by the way. Hope the show is good for you."

Nodding in agreement, he gave her his card so they could be in touch and watched as she walked, waved good-bye, and headed back around the corner towards her miniature home for the weekend.

Vonnette felt this connection happened for some reason. When they got together again, they would get further into the concept of each being walk-ins. Who knows, maybe they had a cross over moment for some specific reason. Their conversation was seemingly extensive; however, she did not remain in Tony's booth long. While there she had noticed his pieces of furniture were unique in that he used unusually shaped pieces of wood. Most of his work had smaller, square, flat tops. They could be used as side tables in either a living room or bedroom. Carved bits of ebony or teak in animal shapes along the legs added a great slant to his art. They agreed to touch base before the show ended. Sometime in November they would discuss their connections in the world of walk-ins.

While coming around the aisle's corner to approach her own booth, Vonnette saw a distinguished gentleman looking at her jewelry. He had a deep-gray, three-piece suit on. Perhaps he still worked in an office environment though he looked to be of an age beyond retirement.

Making eye contact she smiled and apologized for being absent whenever he had stopped.

Smiling back at her he said, "If you make all this jewelry then you have a good eye. I've enjoyed perusing your wares while waiting for your return."

"I do make it all, and thank you . . ." her voice trailed off a bit as she watched him looking deeply inside her showcases.

"Do you remount stones that belong to other people?" he asked.

"That depends on the stones and the people." Vonnette added coyly while still smiling.

"I have a diamond that I would like to have remounted. Can we discuss design possibilities now, or are you too busy attending your booth?"

Scrunching up her face a bit she told him, "If you don't mind possible interruptions I will be glad to talk with you about designs."

After pulling out a white gold ladies ring with an approximately two-carat-round diamond in it, he handed the ring over the counter to Vonnette. He explained he wanted this to be made into a different ring with a combination of both white and yellow gold. He no longer wanted it to look like an engagement ring. "Perhaps it would be nice if she could wear it on an index finger?" he pondered in a very low voice as though Vonnette wasn't even within earshot.

As she held the ring and turned it about a few times, Vonnette also grabbed her 10-power jeweler's loupe. If there were any major issues with the stone, like internal flaws, cracks or chips, she would need to know that up front. Always cautious with work, any possible issues would need to be discussed before sketches or further conversation took place.

Everything looked in good order. Sketches were being drawn after a few moments of slight discussion about his lady friend. A design both artist and client felt would work for her was decided upon. Working under her temporary sales counter on a calculator, Vonnette figured out an estimate for him. Pulling out a sales book, she began to write the order up when he asked for an appraisal. Glancing up at him, Vonnette stopped writing and told him she would be happy to give him an appraisal once the piece was finished.

Shaking his head, he said, "No, I want an appraisal now."

Putting down her pen on top of the sales book she questioned, "Why would you want an appraisal now?"

"I need an appraisal now as well as when the item is finished."

Standing quietly a few seconds Vonnette tried to wrap her brain around his reasoning and then spoke. "Are you concerned the diamond in your ring today will not be the same one when the ring is re-made and returned to you?"

"Yes." Feeling suddenly defensive his body stiffened.

Without hesitation Vonnette responded, "Well, here's the thing; you will need to go elsewhere to have an appraisal done first, then drop the diamond off with me to be remounted. Once the piece is finished, you would then take the new mounting with your stone in it back to the first appraisal person to make sure the diamond is the same."

Watching his head shake, no, she stood waiting for his verbal response.

His words came out stiffly. "No, I want you to do an appraisal now and then again when the piece is made new."

"It's clear you are getting frustrated with me. Let me go at this again from another angle to see if we can end up on the same page. I do appraisals at the end of a job if you decide you want me to make the piece. I would have the stone out of this mounting at that time to weigh it as well as see it without any prongs covering any possible hidden imperfections, and it would be cleaned then, too. What you are asking me to do now is an appraisal before the diamond is out of this mounting and then do up another appraisal after it is in a new mounting. All that would be in an effort to prove the stone did not get changed, or switched out in the process. Correct?"

Nodding clearly, Vonnette knew she had him comprehending up to this point so felt it was safe to continue. "Yes, that makes sense if the appraisals are done by one independent party. If I do an appraisal now, as well as at the end of the project, I could lie to you today, as well as at the end and tell you it's the same stone. That is, of course, if I were that type of person that switched stones, which I am not! If you do not trust me I understand and don't want your business. You most certainly can take whatever time you need to ask around about my reputation. Make sure no one has reported any switching of stones before, something, which by the way has never been in question over all the years I've had my business. You can ask past clients of mine, other people in business in Newport, or even the Better Business Bureau."

Standing quietly, this man pondered all that had been said and then made the connection he needed to make. "I don't want to take this to another person for an appraisal. I want the job finished, and to know it's the same stone then, as the one I have right now."

Speaking with a touch of sympathy and softness in her voice Vonnette went forward. "I totally understand your concern as well as your predicament. Guess the bottom line is whether or not you think I'm capable of doing the job in the way you would like along with trusting I will return the same stone to you as what you have right now. One thing I can say that might make you feel a bit more comfortable is that I would only suggest you take the diamond elsewhere for an appraisal first if I was honest. If I were dishonest, I would have gone along with your first request for an appraisal now as well as at the end of the project. You would not be any the wiser for sure as I could switch stones and use a really good fake. Except that that goes against every fiber of my being. So, you can trust me or not." Shrugging her shoulders a bit she added, "Sincerely, it really makes no difference to me."

"I think you're right. You could have taken me for all I'm worth by doing what I asked. Guess you must be an honest person to have explained this to me and then made sure I understood what I was asking. Think I will go ahead and have you do the design we've discussed. Now, might I ask what kind of turn-around time we might be talking about?"

"That depends on a few different things. One is my show schedule. Another element concerns how many orders I have in front of yours and how long it takes me to finish those up. I will also have to get in a part for the diamond. If I were to take a guess, and it is a guess, I would say the new ring will be finished in about five weeks. That is all said without looking at my schedule and work orders. You can do one of two things at this point. I will write up a sales receipt for you today as well as take half of the estimate as a deposit. The balance will be due upon completion. On your receipt, I can either write up what you are dropping off today, or write up that I need to call you when I'm ready to do your job. That means you would have to drop the ring off to my home studio at a later date.

This concept is to ensure the idea I have less time with your stone to switch it out on you."

"You've been patient with me by explaining how all this could go wrong and what to do about an appraisal. Actually, you've been very forthcoming. So, the answer is, I am going to trust you to do the job agreed upon and that you won't switch the stone. Thanks for the additional offer to hold onto the stone longer though because it just convinces me further of your honesty."

With a nod of her head in agreement while writing up the information necessary on a receipt, Vonnette filled the now empty space with chitchat. "You know, in a few years the questions you have been asking will be even more important. Industry magazines have articles about lab grown diamonds they've been making. In the beginning this process was to create diamonds for the industrial purpose of battery life extension on things like transport trains. The stones they're coming up with now are small in size. Somewhere down the road I feel these stones will be larger and will not only be used for such things as batteries, but also in the jewelry industry. Thankfully that day has not arrived as yet. When it does, the need for trust with your jeweler will grow to epic proportions. Seriously, the people you buy from and/or deal with for remounts and repairs are going to be scrutinized so much more than today. I doubt these newly grown diamonds will be readily recognized as fake the way we can easily see a cubic zirconia today for what it is. Hope I'm not talking you out of your order. Simply put, I am trying to inform you how in the future it will be even more important to know who you are working with for all diamond jewelry."

"No, you haven't talked me out of my order. It's interesting though that your industry has come so far as to be able to create new diamonds in a laboratory."

After finalizing this work order with a deposit, Vonnette felt they had reached the same page in the end and could part company. As he walked away, she thought of how being a family jeweler had changed over the years. It used to be that the jeweler uptown knew the clients coming through the door and could make good recommendations. Most people trusted that jeweler so much that they brought their children in when ready for fine jewelry needs as well. Today, who knew whom to trust?

While Vonnette stashed his ring for safekeeping, a woman came in to browse. This woman attended every show Vonnette had done in Providence thus far. She came to look at whatever was new and wonderful, often trying on some necklace or other. Upon handing it back to Vonnette she would intimate the need of her husbands' approval before making a purchase.

When someone came year after year and repeated the same action without making a purchase, Vonnette really learned not to pay much attention to them. Could this year be different? Doubtful.

When the path was clear without anyone else in the booth, the woman began to ask about a necklace that had a natural, light pink blister pearl above a green prehnite cabochon and a faceted pink sapphire mounted with open filigree swirls of gold. Vonnette told her it was one of the newest pieces she had created. Asking without thinking, "Do you want to try it?" slipped out of her mouth. She almost kicked herself as soon as the words were spoken. How very thankful she was when the woman thought a moment and declined the offer. That woman usually brought her husband to see whatever her latest idea of great jewelry was. He never bought from, nor did he connect with, his wife's strong desires for fine jewelry, at least not in Vonnette's booth. Maybe she had champagne taste but a beer pocketbook.

Three older women approached the booth as that woman walked away. They were bubbly and full of smiles as if there was a secret between them that would be very fun to know. Vonnette smiled, too, as they reached her space, glad to have a new distraction from the woman who just left that never made a purchase. One of these three women made specific eye contact as though she knew Vonnette.

"Hi, don't know if you remember me or not, but I came to your show in Newport with my husband . . ."

"And bought a strand of pearls!" Dawn had come instantly.

Vonnette had spent a certain amount of time with her husband and her before showing them the long strand of pearls and how to make life interesting sexually when the strand disappeared inside her top.

Smiling in acknowledgement, Vonnette began her connection with all women. "Yes, how nice to see you again. It looks as though you ladies are enjoying your day together."

"We are," came the response in unison along with some giggles.

"Actually we all came to see if you have any more of those really long strands of beads to show us. My friends didn't believe me when I shared your input of what to do with long pearls. So, I dragged them here to see for themselves what I have experienced first-hand."

She and her friends had wide eyed anticipation. Though it was fall, they each had on round or V-neck tops, so showing beads would be easy. If they had on turtlenecks, the bead demonstration would not work so well. Vonnette looked them over while deciding what color skin tone they each had and then searched for long strands of beads to go with. One woman had a very peachy tone which was set today against a light green top. The other woman wore a navy-blue jersey and had a very pale, white skin color. Vonnette pulled out a couple long strands of beads and a strand of pearls as she began to speak. "I like to take into consideration your skin tone before I make any type of jewelry suggestions. If the color of your skin fights the color of the beads then you won't ever feel comfortable with them, nor will you receive any compliments on them. Which translates into your not wearing whatever you purchase. I'm not the kind of artist or sales person who wants that for you. I trust and feel my creations go to the right homes, are appreciated and are worn! I think of them as my children who are being adopted by you. And, I love it when they go to good homes that will watch over and enjoy them!"

All eyes were on what Vonnette was pulling out from behind the sales counter. After putting the black velvet pad on top of the display case, she placed three strands of beads on top that each formed its own pile. Anticipation was apparent on their bright faces.

"I'll begin with you," she said facing the light-green jersey woman. After reaching down to grab hold of her mirror, she went around her displays to be directly in front of this woman. Placing the mirror on the floor, then leaning it against the legs of her show case units, she took hold of the 48" strand of 5mm amethyst beads to begin a jewelry conversation that would end with a relation to sex. "Your skin has a nice peachy tone to it. I could, and still may show you some other beads that'll work for you like coral, or even natural colored peach pearls. For now, though, I'm thinking you're comfortable with color judging by the great green top you have on today. So, I have chosen amethyst. It'll work against your skin as well as almost all colorful clothing you might choose to wear with it. That is, of course, if you choose to buy this strand today."

Not waiting for any response Vonnette continued, knowing her audience waited with anticipation. Demonstrating how these beads could be worn by holding them up in front of her own neck, she went on, "As you can see this is a long strand of beads. Actually, it's long enough to go around your neck three times if you are in favor of wearing chokers. Obviously, you can wear it doubled, either as even strands, or one shorter than the other. But what I showed your friend and her husband was the mystery element of having a longer strand of beads, especially as it associates with sexual innuendo."

With great ease, she slipped the strand of beads over the green jersey woman's head. Without hesitation, she then grabbed hold of the bottom part of the strand while slightly opening the top of the woman's jersey. Sliding the strand gently inside the top and releasing it, she then took a slight step backward to allow the other women to view what she had done all the while taking the mirror in hand. It was as if Vonnette had just performed a magic trick due to the complete attention all three women were paying to each move she made. Spellbound, they stood as she held the mirror up for each model to join in the view while she continued on with her talk. "You see, men love a mystery. Honestly, we all do. But when it comes to sex, we can sink into a routine over time with one partner. What I've found is that by demonstrating our prescience for sexual curiosity, a simple strand of long beads can send a partner over the edge. As you move about, your partner will wonder just where that strand of beads is inside your jersey, top, or dress. Not knowing creates the best fore-play imaginable. Your friend here knows. If not, she would not have brought you all here to join in the fun."

Still holding the mirror up Vonnette watched these three mature women giggle with their own thoughts. The green jersey woman made fun faces as she moved and shook her body a bit to make the beads move about under her top. Giving them enough time to visu-alize themselves and their mates enjoying this new game, Vonnette chimed back in, "You can wear the strand as a long one inside your top or dress. That works quite well on the mystery element. Then, as I've already said, you can also wear this doubled with one strand as a choker, leaving the other length to drop inside. You can wear different strands of beads with a couple being of choker length and the rest long inside your outfit for another look. Again, it drives men to distraction wondering just where those beads are inside your clothing and just what the beads might be touching."

More giggles from all.

"One thing I did not go into with your friend was this." As she spoke she placed the mirror under her left arm and reached over to remove the long strand from inside the jersey and lay it out in the open, fully exposed. "When you leave a long strand of beads like this to dangle as you move, even exposed on top of your cloth-ing, it will make your man crazy. He'll see the beads move over your breasts and (in a whisper) nipples."

That was it, these women completely lost control. Chortles galore, so much so that it was difficult for Vonnette to finish her demonstration. After waiting a full three minutes, she was then able to carry on. "You need to pay attention when you wear a long strand of beads exposed like this, though. When you stand up you can easily catch the beads in a table setting or even the decorative element of a table. When you bend over the same issue comes to the fold. You have to place your hand in front of your mid-section to hold your beads in place. However, the effort is worth it because your man will be watching your every move wanting to be those beads. No Viagra is necessary with this kind of sexual foreplay ladies."

More chortles, giggles and outright red faces from each woman let Vonnette know she had a captive audience who knew she spoke the truth. It was as if she knew their spouses first hand, which of course she did not.

Of all the years Vonnette had been in business, she had worked hard to establish new and different ways to wear her creations. Trying ideas with jewelry out on herself in public showed her these methods with beads drove men crazy. As these women quieted down a bit, she shared that once, while attending a large formal party, she put on a simple plain dress with a scoop neck. Multiple strands of pearls she wore that night began with a choker length and ended with a forty-five incher. Any strand that was longer than where her neckline sat she tucked the beads inside the dress. Men around her were clamoring trying to figure just where all those beads ended inside that dress. They were each very vocal about it.

Upon hearing this last statement, the women couldn't get their hands on a strand of beads fast enough. Looking in the mirror at themselves with a strand inside their top sealed the deal for each. Anticipation grew as they were anxious to get home to see if their new purchases worked.

Vonnette carefully wrapped each strand, wrote up each sales slip, collected payments, and then placed a business card inside each bag. Each woman could then call Vonnette if they wanted to experiment with new and different strands of beads. As they walked away from her booth, they were in a bit of a huddle. Shaking her head from side-to-side, Vonnette thought how she had a hand in their new sexual experiments and hoped they would be as happy afterwards as they were right now.

Without time to think any longer about these women and their sexual exploits, another woman entered her booth space. A green sapphire ring had caught her eye. There were two white diamonds flanking that center stone. All stones were mounted in 14K yellow gold. Asking to see it, the ring slipped over her knuckle without a problem and sat beautifully on her third finger. It was obvious she was in love with the ring. Looking up at Vonnette she claimed,

"My husband would have a fit if I came home with this ring in tow. Divorce would be immanent."

Being in an uplifted and frisky mood from her three ladies and their beads, Vonnette didn't lose a beat and suggested, "It's all in the presentation."

Quizzically the woman looked at Vonnette and asked intently, "What do you mean, presentation?"

A bit impishly Vonnette smiled and scrunched up her shoulders to say, "My jewelry looks good without anything else on. Each piece stands on its own merit so well that partners cannot refuse."

Beginning to choke a bit before she could verbally respond, the woman claimed it was an interesting concept, one that she had never tried before. Uncertain she was ready to have this new method of communication with her partner, she reluctantly handed the ring back to Vonnette and left the booth space.

Once again Vonnette was alone and thought of how fascinating it can be traveling and doing shows. She never knew who might attend or what energy different people might bring to her day. Some people come to look, some to buy, some to share what they do in the way of their own art, and still others who do not ever know why they came at all. Great conversations were possible for Vonnette with the latter people as they were usually open to having a new experience.

Hearing a Charleston tune play over the loud speaker, Vonnette began to dance. This time she was behind her display cases inside her booth. Glancing to her left she noticed a woman at the far end of her counters.

Laughing, this woman said, "It is a catchy tune, isn't it?"

Without speaking and shaking her head yes, Vonnette continued to move. Just because someone stopped to look into her booth didn't mean they would be interested enough to try on, let alone buy anything they were viewing. So, why interrupt their viewing with words?

While glancing over the jewelry in the display cases, the woman peered up over her half glasses and asked if Vonnette made everything here?

"Yes, I do. Even the beads you see I have strung along with having carved some stones as well. You just never know what I am up to in the creative department." All the while Vonnette moved with the music.

While chuckling mainly to herself the woman said, "One thing that is very apparent is the sense of humor you have in your work. I especially like the little sayings you have with your pieces. What do you mean when you say lapis helps decipher what's important?"

Vonnette stopped her dancing and began to explain her typed out cryptic notes. "Well, these summaries represent healing stone properties I have channeled."

Interrupting her verbal response momentarily, Vonnette studied this woman and then asked, "Do you understand what I mean by channel?" It was a question she'd asked and answered over and over again. Much the same as a musician sings the same song in many public appearances, she tried to make the explanation fresh each time she shared.

"I've heard the term and think I've read about it at some point, but please revive my memory."

"Well, channeling is something that can be done in a few different ways, but often is considered to have deep meditation attached to it. That was the case for me. I stepped to one side a bit psychologically while deeply meditating to allow other energies to step in and say something inside my head, or on paper. I used to do this for individuals but found it difficult to share my brain so much with outside sources. Guess that's why recreational drugs have never been on my hit parade. I like to know I'm in some form of control. That said, I did channel in order to gather information on the healing properties of stones.

"After I channeled a certain number of stone properties, I decided to write a book. My coffee table book combines that channeled information along with jewelry I've designed and created. Design symbolism is included as well as any actual dreams I may have had that assisted in the jewelry I made. It took many years to finalize that book due to the availability of stones along with all the time necessary to create each piece which had to be fit into my daily work. The book is for sale at your end of my booth.

"At this moment, you're asking specifically about the properties of lapis. The navy-blue opaque stone displayed above that note is lapis, and lapis helps you figure out what's important for you to pay attention to. However, I like to follow up with the fact that it is also *the family issues stone.* Family members know better than anyone else how to push your emotional buttons. I believe we are here on earth to learn. From the time of birth till the time our bodies give up and our souls move on we are in school. If you haven't learned how to deal with the issues your family supplied as possible lessons, then friends and work associates can push all those same old buttons for you.

"With lapis, you learn how to view those buttons for what they are, literal emotional pressure points. Better than that, lapis helps you see your way clear of how they got pushed either today or from many years back and now how to stop them from being pushed anymore! That's what I mean by decipher what's important. By learning how people have pushed your emotional buttons, you can see how to step away from all that, and when you do, it's exciting to find freedom."

"Are you serious? Can it honestly be that simple?"

This woman had responded so quickly Vonnette was caught off guard. It was normal for people to take their time to let what she said sink in before asking more questions.

"Personal belief gets me into things maybe other people are not ready for, but to answer your question, yes, it can in fact be that simple. As we age we can view those old emotional buttons as just that, buttons! See how people have pushed them both in the past as well as today to gain a certain response from you. When you see your own response to these buttons being pushed, you know it's an old knee jerk reaction. You can then move forward out of that old pattern with clarity. What a great gift to yourself to have such clarity, right?"

"So, if people see you coming with lapis on, do they automatically know what you are trying to accomplish?"

Laughing, Vonnette replied, "Honestly, many people have written books on stone properties over the years. When I began writing this book, I chose not to read what other people were coming up with for stone energies to make certain there would never be any overlaps, even accidentally. Each of the properties you see typed out here I have channeled. To this day I have not looked at other books to see if their concepts on energy match or come close to what I've written. To answer your question . . . who knows what other people think about stones, their energy, or if they even give credence to such an idea when they see real stones on you or anyone else. Possibly people would think about something they've read elsewhere. Or, maybe they don't even know about energy trapped in stones. If so, they could simply think you have exquisite taste in jewelry. You can't go wrong with that! Let's face it, nice jewelry makes you feel good about yourself with or without knowledge of healing properties."

"That's true. However, with my luck everyone would know I was coming into the room trying to break old patterns."

"Obviously, it's your choice if you want to take the time to explain what lapis is doing for you. Perhaps, though, you could get going on your personal growth and tell people you bought the lapis jewelry for its beauty. Isn't that what attracted you to begin with anyway? From there, any healing properties the jewelry might possess would be an added bonus. Does everyone really need to know your inner workings? Let others think what they will. You can then go on your merry way with new knowledge and inner growth."

Response to questions such as these came in an almost mater-of-fact manner for Vonnette. Interestingly enough, people at one given show could be drawn to the same stone all day and even ask the same kinds of questions. She had explained channeling twice thus far today, so that could be the main question of this show for Vonnette. Maybe the stone of choice at this show would be lapis.

"So you really don't know what other people have come up with for stone properties?"

"As I said, I didn't investigate what other people have channeled or written for healing energies. I didn't want to feel I was possibly plagiarizing, or so off the mark of what someone else thought. Instead, I chose to do my homework in my own way. Over time I tested my properties out on both myself as well as my clients!"

"Okay, that sounds dangerous."

"It most certainly has not been even remotely harmful in any way or, I would not have done so. After maybe channeling ten stones at a sitting, I never recalled what was written. Putting the written sheets away, I eventually made something with most of those stones. Writing down how I felt as I made the new jewelry, I later cross-referenced that with the information I had channeled. Interestingly enough, the information came up almost the same each time. After feeling comfortable with these self-tests, I later allowed clients to read the information written.

"First, I watched people choose one or two particular stones over and over again in any one visit. Generally, people will naturally be drawn to whatever stone or stones they need at any given time. Noticing that, I then asked if certain types of events were happening in their lives? When they said yes, I let them read the channeled information. Once they finished reading the stone properties, they usually looked more calm than when they came into my studio space. Telling them they chose the right stone to assist in their continued growth for right now, they generally found the process enlightening and fun. Please hear me, I would never knowingly place someone in a dangerous or uncomfortable position either physically or emotionally.

"Don't know if you've ever heard of or paid attention to this idea, but children automatically know what color suits adults without any education on the subject. Carry that idea forward and in my opinion, we know instinctually what stone or stones we need at any given time. It's the same inner voice I think that we possess as children."

"Does your family know what you are doing when you wear lapis to functions? Or maybe you have all your issues solved and wear lapis only for the beauty now?"

"I'm not sure if my family knows what lapis is for, or why I might wear it to family functions, but here's the thing.... There are moments

I wear stones because I love the design I created with that piece of jewelry. There are times when I wear a piece for the colors that coordinate with what clothes I've chosen for the day. And, there are times I wear stones for their healing properties. Anyone who knows me wouldn't know what I was doing from one minute to the next with the jewelry I wore. Don't forget, I said anyone can push your old buttons, not just family. So, I don't wear lapis simply because I am around family.

"Friends, family and even complete strangers can and do press buttons that allow each of us to see those buttons more clearly at any given moment. It's not their fault you respond the way you do. It's up to you to remove the emotion you've attached to that button and move on through it into some new way of response and perhaps even have some form of inner comprehension as to why you've reacted a certain way all these years.

"Lapis has helped me muddle through what I view as family issues and move into a clearer thought mode. Moreover, when we are young, we are easy marks for people to get at emotionally on all levels. As adults, we are, hopefully, willing to see life full of opportunities to grow and to learn."

Thinking over what she had just shared, Vonnette then added, "Jewelry is emotional. When a connection is made with a piece of jewelry, the feeling is undeniable. We always remember when and how we came to possess pieces of jewelry. Honestly, when I feel emotional about a new piece of jewelry, I feel as though it's telling me not to only get involved with it spiritually for growth purposes, but also to get on board with the idea that it's good for me to treat myself. It's positive reinforcement that I've progressed a certain distance to find comfort in who and what I am right now. Putting it simply, I am complete just as I am, in this moment.

"I've found that women often have great difficulty with how they justify spending money on themselves. Generally, they feel men ought to buy their jewelry for it to be emotional. What I feel is, we spend money on our clothing, handbags, shoes, gloves, hats and home furnishings, why not spend money on jewelry? If I only bought costume jewelry for myself then what message am I sending out to loved ones? I'd be telling them I feel I'm not worth the price of genuine jewelry, authentic metal and stones. Or, I'd be saying that I really prefer costume jewelry over real. When I buy the real McCoy, I tell those around me how worthwhile I am! That can even be another button. Feeling worthy I mean."

"Guess I never thought about it that way before. I have bought costume jewelry for myself over the years and waited for a loved one to give me the real stuff. Then there is the inheritance element. My mother left me a couple pieces of real jewelry that I love because I know they belonged to her."

While mentally pondering the words she'd just uttered, the woman stood silently for a moment in front of the booth with her bottle of water in hand. Suddenly, looking for a place to put the bottle down, she asked if she could in fact try the lapis necklace on she had been eying?

Vonnette lifted the pendant off the white neck form while pointing to where this possible client could place her bottle. It was an oval lapis cabochon set horizontally with a cushion cut cobalt druzy underneath that then had a long, moving teardrop shaped lapis drop at the very bottom. The pendant was on a 17" yellow gold box chain. Explaining as she came around the corner of the booth to place the necklace about the woman's neck Vonnette said, "This is natural, undyed lapis from Afghanistan as top and bottom stones. In the middle is a cobalt druzy that changes color between navy blue and maroon depending upon the light you are in at the time. On the outer ends of this pendant are gold starfish. Where the pendant attaches to the chain is a conch shell also in gold. The whole piece is in a combination of 18Ky and 14Kw/y gold. This is part of what I call a *Sailors' Valentine* design."

The woman lifted her chestnut colored hair so Vonnette could clasp the pendant. When it was in place, she dropped her hair from her hands and automatically felt for where the piece landed on her chest. Vonnette went behind her cases to pull up her large mirror. Holding it up over the top of a display case, the woman could then easily view the necklace.

After a moment or two of looking into the mirror, the woman asked if she could try the pendant on with the lapis beads as well?

Silently, Vonnette opened the case again then handed the 8mm lapis beads to her and asked if this woman knew how to use the pearl clasp on them?

Nodding a no back, Vonnette opened the clasp to demonstrate how the fishhook design wound around one end crossbar and then slipped into the body of the hollow clasp to click into a locked position. "By slightly squeezing the ends together, the fishhook part of the clasp can slip out of the stable end. If the clasp ever comes undone, the beads won't drop off because of the crossbar catching the fish hook in the middle. This style clasp originated for pearls and as such is termed a pearl clasp. Today, I use it on most strands of beads I string for the security element."

Feeling confident with the demonstration and explanation, the woman placed the 31" strand of 8mm lapis beads around her neck as a double wrap. Sitting as a choker length, the beads landed just above the chain holding the lapis pendant. It looked perfect from the designers' standpoint.

"This could be a chance worth taking," Vonnette thought as she removed the oval lapis earrings from the display case. Teardrop shaped lapis dangled off the bottoms of each stud earring. Holding them up to the woman's ears for her to view in the mirror without saying she made the earrings to match the pendant, she felt that was already obvious.

Moaning, the woman looked over at Vonnette and called her evil. Laughingly, she seemed anxious to try them on with the two necklaces. Removing the earrings from their stand, Vonnette then raised the mirror up again so the woman could see where her pierced earring holes were.

Motioning with wide eyes, this woman held her hands out to the side and said, "Voila. Now that is what I call a statement!"

"They do hang perfectly on you. Something worth mentioning is, all the lapis you have on right now is not dyed. Most stones today are treated in some manner. Some are heated to enhance color;

some are actually dyed, and still others are irradiated. Personally, I don't work with irradiated stones. That could be a conversation for another day. When I find undyed lapis, I happily work with it. This particular color of druzy is dyed however."

"Guess this is what they would call a selling point? Undyed lapis I mean. Don't think I have ever seen druzy before."

Taking the que, Vonnette began. "Druzy is spelled either druzy, drusy or drusie. It's a method to describe tiny crystal formations that are either part of the base mineral or that have attached themselves to a base mineral as they all form in nature. So, when you hear two or three words together with druzy you'll know the mineral as well as the crystal structure. My calling this a cobalt druzy quartz tells you that the cobalt color has been dyed into a druzy quartz based mineral. Larger, sort of chunky crystal formations, are usually called a mineral specimen, not a druzy.

"More examples of different kinds of druzy are druzy psilomelane, druzy chrysocolla, druzy hemmimorphite, druzy chalcedony. For many years stonecutters removed these crystal formations. Back in the seventies I bought some druzies because I loved their individuality.

"Healing properties vary according to what the base mineral is. In this case the base mineral is quartz, which provides clarity to the family issues stone of lapis."

Though she was filling air space while this woman was possibly deciding if she would purchase any or all of the jewelry she had on, Vonnette had to stop from sharing too much information. Discovering years ago that when new people got into a place of information overload, she found they often walked away without making any purchase.

Though it was a chance, Vonnette opted to break the silence again. "Have you ever heard of Sailors' Valentines before?"

Admiring herself in the mirror the woman delayed slightly before she shook her head no.

"It's believed that when ancient mariners were out to sea, they would create wonderful shell mosaics on odd bits of board. Once back home they presented the mosaics to their loved ones as gifts.

Over time these pieces have come to be termed *Sailors' Valentines*. That's the design element I have going in this pendant and earring set. My shells are made in different colors of gold and are usually alongside tiny 18Ky gold starfish. Though these pieces are not mosaics, it's my concept of a theme. I've always loved shells. Something that a mollusk creates for their home fascinates me. The shell lives on long after the mollusk is finished with it. You can view shells as an art form as well as something really fun to work with in designs."

Vonnette was almost lost in thought remembering all her childhood years walking the shoreline searching for shells. Breaking that train of thought, the lapis woman offered, "I hadn't heard about Sailors' Valentines before today, but I think I have seen shell mosaics before. That's a lovely concept, mariners bringing created gifts home to their loved ones."

"There are major discrepancies as to whether the mariners made those shell mosaics. Mostly it's assumed they discovered them on a tropical island, bought or traded for them, and took them home to their loved ones. That thought comes about due to the idea that sailors didn't have down time to create such things as mosaics.

"Personally, it doesn't matter to me if they created these Valentines or not. However, I do love the idea of their sitting and making these things while out to sea. I go with that image."

"Yes, I'd agree with that idea myself.

"Well, gosh, I don't even know your name, and maybe it's time for me to inquire what the cost is of all these fine pieces?"

Both women stuck out their hands to shake. Names were exchanged. The woman in the booth was Nancy. Giving the mirror over to Nancy for a moment, Vonnette pulled up the calculator. After she added the tax into the total cost, she showed the calculator amount to Nancy as she mouthed it almost silently. "$2,996.00 covers all three items with sales tax included. I don't ever like to say prices loudly in case someone is listening close-by. It's no one else's business what you might or might not spend here today."

Coyly, Nancy's eyes met Vonnette's as she asked if that was the best price she could do?

Smiling, Vonnette suggested a price of $4,200-.

Swallowing oddly and blinking repeatedly Nancy spoke in almost a panic. "But I thought you just told me the price *with* the tax would be in the twenty-nine-hundred-dollar range. Did I miss some-thing the first go-round?"

Outwardly laughing Vonnette said, "You asked if that was my best price, and the answer to that question is no. I can do much better if you're willing to go up. Seriously, I've said these are one-of-a-kind pieces with natural, untreated lapis. Cobalt druzy is different each time it is dyed, which makes each piece there unique as well. Ulti-mately, these pieces cannot be replaced, so if I was to do better on the price I would be charging more than the prices they're marked."

Physically calm now, Nancy joined in. "I did notice your sense of humor when I first got to your booth. Guess I am receiving that end of your personality now. So, it's up to me whether I want to spend this amount of money on the set.

"While I ponder this purchase, can I ask you a couple more questions? Would you mind?"

"Have no idea if I'll mind until you ask, so shoot."

"Are you what I've heard call a sensitive? Not one-hundred per-cent sure exactly what that is, but you are maybe the only person I've ever met who comes close to what I thought it means."

"It's all very interesting, Nancy. I mean what you ask and how you feel comfortable enough to ask. A simple answer is yes. I am a sensitive as well as an empath. Hope I'm not confusing you here. Most people don't know the difference between a sensitive and an empath. Generally, a sensitive is someone who is usually an intro-vert. And though there are loads of times I feel I might be, I'm not completely that. I do enjoy being alone and in my own head, but I also crave to be around other people. Large crowds are generally too much for me, though, as I fear I might short circuit internally as well as physically. The stimulus takes a toll. I then need days to recuperate from such an experience.

"I won't say I have never entered into large crowds before, because I have. Even shows like this can and often do attract large numbers of people. The difference between being in a large crowd and working in my booth at a show with many people about is that I've got space behind my displays to move around and be somewhat alone. What happens to me in mass gatherings is that I take on some of the energy that I feel being exuded from all of the people. My emotions go into overdrive and over-load. It feels as if I may go crazy and physically spastic all at the same time. In a quieter world, I can hear internal voices as well as external ones, and if someone wants or needs a word from me I can give it. With too many voices externally, it gets confusing. Quiet environments provide me with a richer life.

"Back to your original question, an empath is someone who often cannot deal with extra emotions from others. I do, and then I take it one step further. I want to know if there is some way I can help appease those emotions. It's as though I feel inside my heart what others are feeling and then I want to heal their woes."

"So, if I am understanding correctly, this is maybe how and why you have channeled all this information on the healing properties of stones. In order to help others to heal, right?"

"Yes. You're right."

"Have you always been this way? A sensitive, or an empath I mean?"

Chuckling a bit while feeling surprisingly safe enough with Nancy to continue this conversation, Vonnette went on. "Honestly, you can learn to be intuitive, and as women I believe we all have that ability. Actually, I think a lot of men have this ability as well. Though we might live in a world that isn't ready for them to express that side openly yet. Women can and do have more opportunities to be sensitive and intuitive. To be an empath, you are born to it and cannot make it go away, though there are times when you wish you could."

"Seriously? I would think it was such a gift! Why would you want it to go away?"

"The easy answer is, we always want that greener grass over that fence than what is growing in our own yard. The harder answer is this: it can be and is painful to experience what others feel all the time. I know things. There are times when I least expect it where information comes to me. Though it's been part of my life since childhood, when I share knowledge, I still find it challenging when a facial expression of extreme distrust, or a desire to run and hide shows up on the face opposite me. I don't care what age I am, or how long it's been part of my world, these are not fun things to experience. As a younger woman having these experiences with others was a challenge. There were times when I felt alone and even ostracized as a teen. Now, I have the advantage of age behind me and the experience of dealing with it all for this long. Seeing horror on someone's face when I share too much of what I know doesn't scare me so much today. Of course, it does still bother me when something I say upsets another person. What I'm suggesting is that I've grown to understand the different looks I receive when I choose to share. Whereas, as a young woman I didn't comprehend it all so much.

"Knowing something and making the conscious choice to share that with another person is up to me. What I reveal could in fact emotionally affect another person and that can be a big burden. So, my choices need to be weighed carefully because the consequences can be dire for the recipient as well as with whomever that person may choose to share anything with once they leave my space. There are times, though, I feel directed to communicate and usually trust those instinctual moments.

"But, as I said, with age comes a certain amount of understanding of how to deal with all this, as well as inner growth in what I choose to share, and when. Maybe someone can handle information in bits and pieces. Or, maybe they need to be somewhat hit over the head in order to get whatever message that comes through me.

"Part of my purpose in this life is to share information. Being a sensitive I always want people to take it well, so I try to be gentle with whatever. Even so, we each respond in our own way and in our own time. I have to let go once I have revealed and let the universe do its thing.

"It's a ripple effect. You know, as when a pebble is thrown into a calm pond and that action creates ripples that circle outward. When I give out information, the ripples that are created from that sharing now affect other people or things because of that one bit of input.

"In taking responsibility for myself, I sometimes do not say what I know spiritually some entity wants me to say. Then, there are moments where I cannot do anything about what just came out of my mouth. And what do I do with that pain when it appears I've emotionally hurt another? I feel that pain both before I share and after I have shared! I feel the suffering. That's when people might be afraid to be near me for fear I may disclose something else that person wishes to keep buried deep inside."

"Wait, wait. Are you suggesting that you hear voices telling you what to say and or do? Am I understanding correctly?"

"Sometimes that's it exactly. When I hear things in my head about someone and am then guided to share it verbally, it's almost as if an energy has control over me. That energy pushes me to follow through. I trust those moments are Divinely guided and are maybe given as an opportunity for someone listening to my words to do whatever they are supposed to do with what's said. I don't share because I want to feel I know something or want to tell someone how to live their life differently. When this happens, it feels as though whomever needs to be reminded of something in order to make a shift to possibly move onward or even through some experience. Who knows, maybe that person has even been asking for an answer and coming across my path provided the opportunity for growth. If that's the case, then I am simply a conduit for them to see something through a different lens.

"Guess I'm sounding vague and am sorry for that. But here's the thing . . . I used to hate the fact that I was physically alone as much as I am. But, being around others all the time is too much stimulation and even bombardment for me. I need time to recharge my batteries. My emotions lay very close to the surface. Maybe that's why I can and do feel what others feel. What I do with that is to try to suppress it, or let it out in a safe way. But when it comes to emotions, who is to say it's ever safe? Maybe that's why I am so good at knowing who is right for a certain piece of jewelry and who might need something else entirely. Maybe it's why I paint and write and, and, and."

"Wow! Is there anything you don't know?"

Outwardly laughing, Vonnette shook her head and replied, "There is *soooo* much I do not know in this universe of ours.

"For some weird reason, I just remembered an exercise I did when I was younger. Maybe it came to me now because I'm supposed to share it with you. Maybe you're going to have your own guided moment through me."

"Oookaaayy," came slowly and with trepidation from Nancy, unsure if she wanted to know anything more than what she had already heard today.

"No, it's not anything bad. It's a seemingly harmless and simple question. What do you want?"

"What do I want?"

"Yes, what do *you* want?" Vonnette was nodding her head as she answered with a broad smile. knowing this was not a simple exercise at all.

"I want all these pieces of lapis jewelry, but . . ."

Cutting Nancy off before she finished her thought, Vonnette quickly said, "Okay. Now, what do you want?"

"I just told you."

"Yes, and once you have that, what do you want?"

"Oh, so I'm supposed to say what's next on my want list now?"

"Yes. What do you want?"

"Is this where I say world peace or something spiritual?"

"Nancy, this is an endless question with endless answers. That's the point I think. That we are all trying to figure out just what it is that we want in life. Here, today, you want the lapis jewelry I have created. After that, the possibilities continue onward. You might say you want to experience inner confidence when others push your buttons not to have the same reaction you've had in the past."

Nancy was nodding in agreement.

"Then, you could say that you want others to see the inner you that is strong, vibrant, and full of inquisitiveness of what life can bring."

More nodding.

"Next you might want a new car, a new house, a new job, a raise, new friends. Who knows? The answers are endless."

"If the answers are endless then what is the point of the exercise?"

"It's to get past the surface stuff and reach down inside to your core to see what it is that you really want in life. You see, we deal with surface all the time, like new cars. Say I am a Genie and magically grant you everything you claim you want each time you name something. When you dig deeper past the new car, and whatever else you come up with over the next hour or so, do you eventually find that what you want is actually peace of mind? And if so, what can give you that peace of mind? That's why I said that once you have the lapis, do you want to have others see the real you without pushing old buttons? Picture whatever it is that you want as happening, I mean really happening, and it can come your way as magically and as simply as asking for it to come."

Obviously deep in thought, Nancy didn't respond in any verbal manner. Her mind was off in some direction or other prompted by the conversation.

Vonnette stood and smiled knowing how Nancy must be feeling at this moment in a far off mental place because she'd been there so often herself. It's infinity.

Coming back to center, Nancy wanted to say something. Felt she ought to say something but still, her mind kept moving too quickly for her mouth to catch up with any words. After opening and closing her mouth a few times she did finally speak. "You know, I thought I stopped in your booth to look at pretty jewelry. Look at all the information I have at my disposal now because I stopped to talk to you! You really are a gift. I'm impressed and appreciative for sure. Thank you for everything.

"My mind is going a mile a minute. Not sure where it will land, but one thing I do know is, I feel connected to this jewelry. Guess I need to decide about taking one piece over another. How on earth will I decide?"

"Please do not feel I passed along information to make you buy jewelry from me Nancy. Information is always yours to keep. What you do with it is up to you. This goes for the use of lapis in resolving old button pushing in your daily world, too. Many good things come from us when we choose to move forward with new understanding in our world."

"I cannot leave here without taking all three pieces. I just can't!" almost burst out of Nancy.

"Well then, I cannot do anything but write up a receipt for your purchases and wrap them."

Vonnette made a hand motion for Nancy to hand over the jewelry. Obligingly, she removed each item from her personage but had to ask, "Why wrap? These items are just for me."

"My belief is to wrap all items unless the client wants specifically to wear the jewelry out of my booth. It's a gift for you, from you, and that's special. Remind yourself you deserve what you are doing and that is to treat yourself." Vonnette was wrapping as she spoke.

"Well, the thing is, I don't know if I will ever be the same after walking away from your booth. What an unexpected experience it has been for me. Guess you hear that sort of thing all the time, or is this something you chose to share with me alone and no one else?" Nancy pondered as if the answer wasn't important anyway she sliced it.

"If people want a pretty piece of jewelry, I have no problem selling them exactly that. If people want to discuss all the other things in life I find interesting, then we go into that territory as well and see what comes of it. I never know how far in any direction a conversation will lead. I learn from others, too, you know, and that's a gift while living here in our worldly experience."

"Vonnette, I need to ask something else before I leave and that is, what do you want? Have you ever gotten to the end?"

"You know, I did find the end which turned out to be the beginning for me." Looking at Nancy, Vonnette realized she was totally confused. "I can share with you what I found and perhaps shall in a moment, but first let me say that what was my answer most certainly will not be yours. This exercise took me years to get to the bottom of. Not that I asked myself this question everyday over years. Rather, off and on I pondered the question and eventually came to terms with what I really wanted."

"Was it world peace?"

They both chuckled a bit, breaking the tension that comes with serious questions in life.

"No, not world peace. For me, getting to the bottom was finding I wanted freedom. A seemingly simple thing to say and yet quite another thing to have in my life."

"But, I'm confused. Isn't traveling about doing shows a type of freedom? Isn't having your own business a freedom?" Nancy was quite interested, and her questions seemed astute and yet there was a need to go even deeper.

"Maybe having my own business and doing shows are a form of freedom when I think of one alternative as having a physical storefront. For me, freedom is not having to be anywhere that is set up timewise by another, like these show schedules. Freedom goes so deep that I can perhaps only share tidbits with you here today. I crave to be able to get up in the morning and do exactly what I want each and every day."

"Like being retired you mean?"

"Maybe that's what *you* would call it, Nancy. As an artist, I constantly reinvent myself and my art forms, so for me there will not be a normal retirement. What I'm trying to say is this, there are many things in our past that cause emotional restrictions that eventually come out physically and play into our everyday world. These are almost badges of honor, or even dishonor that plague each of us. Maybe you'd call it our conscience or subconscious life. In there, we bring about restrictions, maybe even welcome these places where we hold ourselves back from living the full life we all wish for in our dreams. My freedom stems from one such moment in my life where I discovered many things about restriction. Now, I am finding freedom from that one moment that then overlaps into all aspects of my life. My own ripple effect is created when I can see that what I think about can and is becoming my reality as long as I hold my thoughts up and don't falter.

"At this moment in my life I am reinventing myself, slipping backwards, and then rediscovering what I knew deep inside, maybe even since before birth. This is the reason I am suggesting that for me getting to the bottom of the question of 'what do you want' was actually the beginning. Since I believe in continuous life, I feel we all have missions while we are here on the earth plane. Part of *my* mission while here in body is to experience restrictions beyond the beyond. And then to find a way to free myself from those bonds. To find a way to live in a place I feel is *emotionally* free.

"What's important is this, Nancy, when you find that you have what it is that you crave, you will discover something new to crave."

"Are you saying that freedom is not the end for you then?"

"Yes, that's my point! And aren't you good to get it straight off like that! What I'm finding is this; once I got to the bottom, which I felt was actually the beginning for me, the emotional freedom, I found that I then had been wanting more. Freedom was a doorway that has allowed me to see where I want to be today and on into the future. It has become the bottom, the top, and the everything I guess. I hope that my personal freedom is going to lead the way to assist others in finding their freedom in whatever way they crave it to be. Perhaps even today I have helped you to find some form of freedom through lapis being in your life."

"So, let me ask, has lapis brought this freedom into your world?"

"Yes, lapis along with all my other stones. I change my jewelry daily due to the color of my clothing or even a dreamed-of message."

After a very brief pause, Vonnette looked very seriously at Nancy and began again with a slightly different tone to her voice.

"Nancy, I'm feeling guided to share something else with you. Certainly, you are on information overload. Trusting my inner voice, I feel there is a reason you need to hear this and that it can be of some use to you. Early in my life I experienced a master at manipulation. Who that person was along with what that person did is not important at this moment. What you need to hear is that people who manipulate, just like bullies, only have strength if you allow them to have power over you. When you face your fears it's a gift on all fronts. A woman in the late 1920's wrote affirmations for people. That was how she earned her living. Her name was Florence

Scovel Schinn. There was a person who was in great need of money and went to the bank to take out some cash. She was deathly afraid of walking under a ladder. When she reached the bank, there was a ladder up over the doorway. Walking away at first due to fear, she found a phone and called Florence who gave her this affirmation, 'Face a situation fearlessly and there is no situation to face.'

"Lapis can help you with that element if it's present in your life: fear and/or bullies or manipulators. It's not that I am picking up on anything. Please don't feel I am outing you in some way here and now. However, when I hear something in my head, I pay attention. This could be something that is coming at you from a work front, or it could be from a more personal level. As I keep saying, lapis can help you see button pushing for what it is. Once you fully recognize how people get at you emotionally, you can then see a new doorway out of that behavior. Manipulators change bodies and minds over the years until you finally see bullying and manipulating clearly and find your own way into a new life-path. I don't judge those who were the manipulators or the bullies. I am so happy those people all came into my life because I learned how to live my own truth. Each person who was an antagonist has actually helped make my beliefs stronger."

"Can't guess what energy you're seeing associated with me. Is it possible you are picking up on someone else right now instead of me?"

"Could be. It could even be that a child of yours is experiencing this kind of energy and through you I am feeling guided to share now. Sincerely, I do not have any idea of why this needed to be said, just an inner voice told me to share. If it is a child, and we haven't even discussed if you have children, this idea carries over to them. What I'm saying is that when a loved one is under the scrutiny of a bully, or is being manipulated, you will have new ammunition from utilizing your lapis. You can be a sage of information on how to shift that energy into something that needs to be learned from, or let go of, in order to move ahead in life.

"You won't feel the need to lord information over another. Lapis is not like that. You will have wisdom and the willingness to share as you learn about the energy of stones. It's something that another might learn from you just as you feel you are learning from me here today. This information becomes a ripple in your pond. How you affect others from this moment forward is part of that ripple. So, your lapis lessons can overlap onto another, or maybe even many. It'll be interesting to see what kind of effect it has on you over time."

"This whole day has taken on new meaning for me with buying the lapis. Vonnette, I pray I can find the same dignity you display in walking your talk."

"Once you decide what your truth is, then when others push your buttons, you might be set back emotionally for a moment or two. In the end, trust that you will find your truth and a way to combine it all so that you are comfortable with your choices, especially with the use of lapis as a terrific tool! Life brings us new experiences all the time. As I said before, I believe we are in school while on this earth plane. What a shame it would be to stop learning!

"When we let go of existing in a certain way, as in an old pattern I mean, I feel we are tested to see if in fact we are sincerely done with whatever. It's as if the universe asks, 'Are you done? Are you really done? Are you really, really done?'

"When you know intuitively that you are finished with certain patterns or behaviors, and are really, really done, you find a deeper and richer you. I stand before you as a more liberated woman than I was before I utilized lapis and got rid of manipulators and bullies from my life. What's left after these moments is the idea of forgiveness."

"Gee, I'm almost afraid to ask what you mean by that."

"Part of my being human is that I want to learn lessons from life. Over time, I have put myself in harm's way with bullies and manipulators. Instead of experiencing any kind of loathing for either the giver or receiver, finding forgiveness allowed me to move forward without the emotional baggage I might carry onward from those kinds of experiences.

"Forgiving is an act of freedom. It's something I've done for myself, always. Forgiving another is actually easier than forgiving yourself, at least it has been for me. Absolving never means excusing an act of injustice. By choosing to move forward with life and not be stuck in that fateful moment whatever it might have been, that is then liberating. Once I really forgave the manipulators and bullies in my life, I was able to move on. Bullies have no place in my world now, nor do manipulators. I'm sure that I attracted all that because I had fear of people knowing I held beliefs of the unknown. Taking responsibility for attracting this attitude into my life brought me to the place of forgiveness. Now I can share openly with confidence that you either believe, or not. You can accept lapis as a friend to help your personal growth, or to simply view it as a pretty stone. Once you walk away I will dance for the joy of life bringing us together, and you know I will dance!"

They both laughed about the idea of her dancing in her booth again.

Nancy became a bit serious and asked, "I know I've asked this already, but do you share like this with every customer? If so, it must be exhausting."

Shaking her head while chuckling a bit outwardly, Vonnette expressed now with words what she was already physically saying. "No. I only share with people who seem to want to know something I feel I know. Or who might be looking for answers to something I feel I have learned over the years. There are even moments when I share because I need to hear my own words spoken out loud. By doing so I can hear and connect some dots I've been working on. We are honestly, individuals, and as such need different things at different times. Being sensitive, I have to remain conscious of my own energy levels. Sharing can be tiring, stressful, or exhilarating. You are obviously one of the latter types of people."

Once the three pieces of jewelry and sales slip were handed over the counter, Nancy and Vonnette vowed to connect again in the future to compare notes. She would check Vonnette's web site to find a show and come see what there was in the way of new designs. Vonnette felt in her heart that they would meet again at another show, but there was no way to tell here and now if or when that might come to pass.

Nancy then walked off spiritually lighter. Watching her walk away, Vonnette thought of how she never knew who she might connect with nor where the conversation might lead.

Before Vonnette could do a happy dance in her mind let alone physically in her booth about making the sale of three pieces of jewelry, a woman stopped in front of her. The gray clothing and hair color reflected negatively on her skin tone. She was a bit plain overall in image. Looking past her clothing, Vonnette immediately noticed her intensely blue eyes, similar to what many Irish people have. But that was not the first thing that stood out today. She was simply a cloud of gray. No distinctive jewelry or handbag in tow, Vonnette wondered if she would be more of a tire-kicker than someone who would actually be interested in her creations.

When Nancy left her booth, Vonnette had a good feeling. She did not expect the tidal wave that was about to come her way. Even an empath can and does get caught off guard.

"Do you make this jewelry?"

"Yes. Is there something you would like to see or try on?" Vonnette asked.

"I'm wondering how it is that you were accepted into this show when I was not!"

Stunned by this remark and attack, Vonnette tried to keep a calm demeanor while inside she wanted to scream. Didn't she just get through claiming there was no room for bullies in her life now? In an effort to comprehend, she inquired in a low voice, "I take it you are a jeweler?"

"Yes, I am. I do what you do and yet, this show refused me. It's not right that you are in the show and I'm not!" Clearly incensed, this woman was not going to let this show refusal go lightly.

"Why don't I call the show promoter and have her explain why it is that you were refused? She's walking the show floor today along with the judges. I saw her about an hour back and am sure I can reach her by phone. I mean, speaking to me is not going to get your questions answered. Not being involved beyond being a participating artist, I cannot guess why you were not accepted." Certain this statement and offer to call would stop the angry and frustrated woman from being in her booth, Vonnette pulled out her flip phone to dial the sponsor's number.

Waving her hand in a no fashion, the woman stopped Vonnette from completing the call. "No, I'm angry and you can tell me all I need to know. I make jewelry. I want to know what you did differently from me that got you accepted? I sent off pictures of my work. I sent in the completed application along with the show deposit fee. I just don't understand how it is that you are here and I'm not!" Her questions were a rant.

"I'm not sure what to say to your questions. That's why I want to call the promoter. She can give you answers." Working to remain calm, Vonnette's first concept was that maybe this woman was off her meds and could do something crazy to her display cases, or even her jewelry if she didn't remain focused and willing to talk. In an effort to turn the conversation around she asked, "So, you make jewelry like me. It's always great to meet a fellow goldsmith. Where did you go to school?"

"School? Oh, yeah, I took a course in bead stringing at Michaels last year. Since then I've been applying to shows and not getting accepted. It's not fair. It must be political!"

Vonnette now had a better idea of where this woman was coming from. Mustering up all the communication skills she'd read about over the years, she began to mirror the questions back at this woman. "Looking at my work you are feeling the show has done you wrong. You're upset about that. Personally, I've been doing shows for ten years. There are many shows I get refused to as well. Some that I have done before and for some reason on that go 'round they didn't accept me; sometimes they even place me on a wait list. Weird, but jewelry is the most competitive category in shows these days. Seems everyone feels they can and do make jewelry. It's interesting that in my booth you only see the strung beads and not all the gold jewelry. I am a *goldsmith*. I make the pieces by hand that are displayed here. Almost every strand of beads act as an accent for my gold work because I do like and wear beads, too."

"Yah, yah, I get it. You think I'm just a bead stringer! Well here's something for you to chew on, I also took a wire-wrapping course at Michaels. So there, what do ya think of that? Just like what you have here, wire wrapping on that ring there and that pendant behind it." Exasperatedly, she was now pointing to one of the beach stone pendants that had continuous prongs, and then the beach stone ring with the same type mounting. She was in attack mode with no sign of stopping.

Feeling trapped behind her booth Vonnette took a deep breath and as calmly as possible she responded, "This ring and pendant are not wire-wrapped. They are something I call continuous prongs. They are soldered. As you know from your class, there is no soldering in wire wrapping. Wire wrapping is a great art form. I'm sure your pieces are terrific. Keep applying to shows. There's room for every type of art in this world."

Like a dog with a bone protecting its possession, this woman was not calming down and not going away. "Those pieces are wire-wrapped!"

It suddenly felt as if a mad dog was grabbing hold of Vonnette's flesh. Every form of abuse experienced in this life suddenly came to mind. Being molested took first place. Being bullied came in second. Losing her battle with patience, Vonnette's voice became low, stern and unforgiving. "Enough! You need to stop attacking my creations. These pieces are not wire wrapped! As I stated already, wire wrapping does not use solder. These pieces *are* soldered. I ought to know, I've made each one of them!"

While taking another slow, deep breath in an effort to regain control, Vonnette noticed the expression on this woman's face. It was suddenly very clear she had no idea what solder was or even the jewelry making method called soldering. Vonnette then found her center again. The woman had taken two quick courses, one on how to string beads and another on how to wire wrap and felt that was all she needed to know in order to make jewelry for fine art and craft shows. Surely, it never crossed her mind that Vonnette had taken *years* of jewelry making courses and beyond that had been making jewelry since childhood. This woman could only see what she felt was injustice. Unless she was some sort of goldsmith savant, it was literally impossible for her to make jewelry similar to what Vonnette made after two short courses of study.

In that moment, maybe because her senses were heightened, a vision came clearly into Vonnette's mind's eye of this gray woman cowering on her kitchen floor as her husband repeatedly struck her with a sock filled with coins. There was a horrifying fury on his face. Seeing this as a transparent movie-like moment flashing before her eyes, Vonnette felt empathy for the woman. This information also spoke volumes as to why she was literally gray from head to toe. Obviously, the abuse this woman endured manifested outward today to help her become a bully towards others. It was the grey woman's ripple effect of what was given to her, she was now giving back out in an effort to gain control of an absurd situation that could never make any sense.

With understanding and even forgiveness she did not possess earlier along with a smile on her face, Vonnette tried one more time to reason with the woman. While speaking, Vonnette visually sent all kinds of white and pink light towards this woman's solar plexus. White for pure energy, pink for love, and then Vonnette spoke in a different tone. "Certainly your work is great. I am not the person you need to talk to about why you were not accepted into this, or any show. Perhaps you have pictures on you where the promoter might review them. You could then see what her reaction is. You have value. I have value. Being fellow artists I would have loved to have been of assistance to you today. Clearly, I cannot answer your questions. Since you do not wish for me to call the promoter, I thank you for your interest and wish you all the best in your search for shows. Excuse me now, I need to make a few phone calls. Bye."

Stunned, the woman didn't want to let go of her seemingly trapped prey and leave. It was as though she was standing guard in front of the booth. Carrying her injustice forward, she'd trapped Vonnette and tried to victimize her. Vonnette flashed back to the time dogs came after her while on a casual walk at a friend's home. Thankfully, instructions read years earlier flooded into her brain all at once on how to deal with a dog attack. *Don't look crazed dogs in the eye or it can be mistaken as confrontation. Keep breathing slowly and steadily. Move as normally as possible. Animals can smell fear.* She continued walking to the best of her abilities. The dogs seemed to lose interest at one point and dropped back a bit, but then came back at her again in full force. It was a warm summer day. Vonnette had on cropped pants with ankle socks and sneakers. These dogs were right behind her breathing and barking. Feeling their angry hot breath on her ankles had never left her memory bank in all the years since that day. One false move and she would have been bitten for sure, and once that happened she might have fallen, and then who knows what might happen to her body?

No one came out from their homes to assist. She was alone then like now. It took everything she could muster to be calm that day, and eventually the dogs did fall back. After she got to safety, she discovered these dogs had been dumped in the woods and abandoned. They were now wild. Today, if this woman in attack mode was allowed control of the moment, Vonnette could have been emotionally bitten and then how would she recover from that tension for the remainder of the day at the show? That exchange of energy was not invited on any level, nor would Vonnette tolerate it.

Vonnette made a decision not to give over to the moment. She picked up her flip phone to call a friend if necessary in order to stop the dead-end conversation. It worked; the woman wandered off. Vonnette began to breathe a bit more regularly. Surprised by this woman, she did understand a bit of her quest due to the fact that there had been many shows where Vonnette had not been accepted. Beads can be an art form when the beading involved has say, seven strands, or cords, that eventually weave into some form of a scene. That type of beading may have been approved; whereas, simply strung beads would not. Perhaps if the woman had shown her wire wrapped pieces to the jury, she would have been accepted. Of course, that would depend upon her ability at wire wrapping and the quality of her photographs.

Why was Vonnette giving any further thought to such a problematic person? It was due to the vision she'd had of the woman being beaten by her husband. Seeing such a thing was awful. Living through such horrors at the hands of another must be indescribable. Being an empath wasn't always easy especially when she saw such injustice to another human being. However, in one quick meeting where this woman decided to take her negative energy and concentrate it on Vonnette, there was nothing she could have possibly said that would make things right. That woman attacked like those wild dogs that came after Vonnette that summer day.

Vonnette kept telling herself to let go of this experience. What that woman was suffering in her life was horrid. In Vonnette's vision, this woman was still with her husband. As with any injustice, the person on the receiving end has to take the first step towards freedom. If no effort is made, then no one can possibly assist.

Vonnette couldn't fix everything. Honestly, there was so much in life she had no control over. And there was no way she could reveal what she saw for fear of being confronted further today. No, this was a time to step back, take care of herself, and let this woman go.

What Vonnette knew *this* day was that a bully is a bully, is a bully. There was no longer a need to subject herself to such treatment. Lapis had helped her with that life lesson over time, and she had no intention of going backwards. Feeling tested yet again, Vonnette heard words spoken in her head, 'Are you done? Are you really done? Are you really, really done?' Handling all that lapis may have triggered such a test. But, today, she was really done!

It was great to have her booth quiet again. Amazingly, it was closer to closing time than she had realized. Fussing a bit with her bags of equipment and straightening and organizing before the time came to actually pack up her jewelry and head home filled some time and energy that allowed her to refocus.

While thinking about heading home, Vonnette suddenly had a realization she had not expected. Her conversation with Nancy about forgiveness helped create a bolt of light! Vonnette had never forgiven herself for being in harms' way when she was molested as a child. Emotional birth happens when least expected.

Being molested took so much away that day. The inability to be a true child ever again from that moment forward was in the forefront of her mind. Youthful attitudes had been given up as Vonnette shifted into a child-like adult mode to care for her inner emotional wounds. Having never admitted something crazy had happened to anyone for years, Vonnette was just now wondering if perhaps on some level she'd invited, or deserved, such treatment from another. Searching her mental archives, Vonnette knew she was a child, and children are not expected to take responsibility for being attacked. However, Vonnette was an empath as well as a sensitive. Not that she grasped all that as a child; however, as she was remembering today, she had sensed something was wrong that unfortunate day.

Being eleven when the molestation happened, Vonnette knew enough not to go anywhere with a person she didn't know even though she had never been told why. But then, to some degree, she thought she knew her attacker because he had the puppies she played with in a box on his front lawn each day. Her guard had been dropped because of those puppies along with her desire to have one to call her own.

Frozen behind her booth as others were in process of shutting down for the day, Vonnette's mind had shifted into overdrive. She was that child again, sitting on the grass on a front lawn, holding and playing with a litter of puppies, thinking only of how much she wanted one.

Everything about the moment read innocence.

Everything changed when she went with that man.

He asked her to accompany him while he carried the box of puppies into his garage workshop. Her father had a workshop, too. Vonnette loved tools, so there was a lot to talk about with this man besides the puppies. She trusted that older man to be like other older men in her world. Adults are supposed to keep children safe. They are supposed to be guides. This man guided her from his workshop up into a bedroom, under the guise of showing her around the house, and then, onto a bed. He used those puppies as a lure for just that moment in time. He wanted her innocence and being innocent, she didn't have any experience of what was about to happen.

Thankfully, discomfort did eventually help Vonnette climb out from underneath that man. Once she was up and off the bed, she put her clothes back in place, and left that house.

She was too young to have had the sex talk even if her parents felt comfortable about doing such a thing back in the early 1960's. Which of course they didn't do or feel was ever necessary. Vonnette had no comprehension of what had just happened. On some level, she felt responsible, shameful after the fact. Dirty. Wrong. And yet she didn't know why. Without the mental tools to understand how wrong this molestation was, or how to handle the experience, her brain never completely processed what or why it had happened. This was what caused Vonnette at age eleven to do to dolls what that man did to her in an effort to psychologically work her way through the emotional and physical trauma of that day. Somehow, she did grasp that the responsibility and shame elements could eat her up from deep in her core because she could feel all that in her belly. It turned into the emotional quicksand that retarded her complete growth and self-love. What she knew was that something had gone horribly wrong in her world that day, and she had no idea of how to make it right.

Hiding her feelings of responsibility and the shame of being manipulated drove her not to trust her parents to protect her, even after the fact. That same shame lead her to distrust men in general to this very day and was how and where her craving for sweets began, though she had never made the association until just now.

Keeping this act secret for many, many years became a shadow element on her soul. Desire for light in that part of her was strong. Even with all her spiritual work, sadly, she hadn't known how to let the light in until, maybe, this moment.

Vonnette's mind flashed back to college where she had first opened up with friends about being molested. She'd heard that some had endured similar fates. One woman had even suffered at the hands of her priest. While sharing, a couple people claimed that working with a psychologist brought forth the understanding as an adult that they didn't have as a child. Unfortunately, Vonnette had never found that comprehension when she saw a psychologist.

Years later, while working on finding her inner spiritual light as a metaphysician brought forth forgiveness for her attacker. Vonnette found forgiveness for that man was actually easy. Maybe he was abused himself and didn't know any better. In the end, it didn't matter how he was brought up. What stayed with her long after she'd found forgiveness for her perpetrator was the blame, guilt, responsibility and shame she placed upon herself. This was all illogical. It was the kind of guilt and responsibility that children often feel when they know something is horribly wrong. Something they participated in but didn't comprehend just what *it* was. That unnecessary guilt and shame had held Vonnette back emotionally most of her life. How could she forgive something that really wasn't her fault? She was a victim! But, on some deep level, she felt responsible for being in that exact place at that exact time especially since she had sensed something in her belly that day. Unable to wrap her brain around that feeling back then, she *did* go inside his house anyway.

Even though Vonnette was working at a show, she knew enough as an adult that things happen when they happen. Reliving that moment in her mind from the past was vital to complete the act of self-forgiveness. Today she had to grasp hold of all her emotions to say inwardly that her innocence brought her to that awful experience. Today, as an adult she could and would forgive that childhood moment of inquisitiveness. Mentally wrapping her arms about that younger form of herself, Vonnette whispered in her ear, "I forgive you for your innocence. I forgive you for your belief that all people are good and that they will take care of you. I forgive the belief that some adult should have protected you. I forgive your being in the wrong place at the wrong time. I straight up forgive you!!!" As she spoke those words to her inner child, warm, cleansing tears streamed down her cheeks.

Often when one emotional door opened for Vonnette, additional doors revealed themselves. Frozen in place, Vonnette realized she had never forgiven her parents. Deep inside she felt they should have protected her, and yet, they had not. Tears still flowing, Vonnette forgave her parents for not explaining fully about possible dangers when dealing with strangers. She forgave them for never having any comfort in giving or providing a sex talk. She forgave them for not being there for her on that ill-fated day. Vonnette had chills and felt her parents' energies close. Her heart had fully opened, and she knew these acts of forgiveness were supposed to happen. As emotionally difficult as it was to relive that day in order to actualize forgiveness of herself and her parents, Vonnette was happy to have such a birth moment.

Being the person she was and craving complete closure, Vonnette mentally replayed this day. She needed to fully comprehend how this most serious moment of inner growth came to fruition. Once she had gone through the day again Vonnette hoped the absolutions for herself as well as her parents would be forever fixed in her heart as well as her mind. And, total comprehension was a necessary part of who Vonnette was deep inside her soul . . . . After suggesting the concept of self-forgiveness to Nancy, who bought the lapis jewelry, Vonnette at first followed a similar mental thread by pardoning the gray woman's lack of jewelry making knowledge. That woman had been a victim of her husband's rage. That woman tried to make Vonnette her victim as she laid blame for not being accepted into the show. All that helped the dominoes line up concerning Vonnette's own childhood. If the gray woman had not followed on the heels of Nancy today, maybe Vonnette would not have received mental clarity on where distrust, victimization and un-forgiveness existed in her world. By shifting from a place of distrust into forgiveness, Vonnette had created a ripple affect into her own pond that provided an unexpected closure. She was washed clean of the illogical guilt of being attacked along with the childhood guilt that had been buried deep within her soul and placed on a file card marked *forget this moment*. Today, she pulled that file card out from the emotional basement where it had been locked away. Today that card had been dusted off and stood clearly in the daylight. Vonnette faced what had been hidden away and then wrote on the huge blackboard of life claiming fault for being in the wrong place at the wrong time and now used the eraser to wipe that slate clean. The act of molestation would always be a part of her inner make-up, but *he* could now be forgotten. As an adult, she knew the child was not at fault. The child was the victim. However, the child *in* her felt that insane shame, responsibility and guilt most of her life.

In this evolving moment, Vonnette felt that this whole day *and* early-life experience could have been chosen before she entered her physical body this time around precisely for her to learn. At this age, she firmly believed that not only could life happenings be chosen before birth, but the people who participated in those educational moments could also be pre-chosen. Meaning, her molestation may have been decided upon long before it came about. And if so, then she needed to completely grow from that experience or it was all for naught.

Vonnette realized there had been some closure for being molested when she long ago forgave her attacker. Today, she experienced further closure by forgiving herself and her parents. Shuddering at what had just transpired emotionally, she felt stunned this day had turned into what it had. Snapping her mind out of that far-off land, Vonnette began the task of shutting down her booth. The thought that kept rolling around inside her brain was, "I hope I can hold onto this forgiveness of a childhood moment where I did *feel* I shouldn't go inside with that man that day."

Able now to see everything as both an adult and a child, Vonnette knew the act itself, from this moment forward, would become part of her spiritual development, a building block. One where all things were possible. One where her glass was more than half-full. One where light and love of self, as well as others, could live freely. Feeling magnanimous, Vonnette blessed the event. By blessing the molestation, she would completely clear the blackboard allowing her soul to take a giant cricket leap where karma could not carry that event forward into any other of her future life existences.

While walking to her car Vonnette thought, "I wonder if . . . in the life we are living, are our experiences really pre-ordained; and if so, then can our daily free will choices significantly shift that roadmap?"

Mentally, she was on overload. By focusing on last night's dream and the crows seen this morning Vonnette hoped to connect everything and then really let it go. In the dream she wore a pink, see-through blouse. Feeling a bit exposed at the very end of the day by that unnamed gray woman, Vonnette did use pink and white light to help her move away from the booth. Or, that dream could have suggested that what had transpired as a child was now more transparent. Five crows were a sign of wealth and sales had thankfully, turned out well. Then, seeing seven crows had been a sign for Vonnette that she would receive news from a distance. Melinda Bronson's grandson Justin had called with news about his grandmother. Four crows represented birth on some level. Vonnette felt hopeful she'd resolved a core issue today with her need to forgive herself for being in the wrong place at the wrong time that lead to her molestation along with forgiving her parents for not being able to protect her from the perpetrator.

Even her choice of jewelry had been correct. Pink pearls provide a sense of comfort and self-love. Pink spinel is the tactile stone that can give information on whether hands are touching something wonderful like Egyptian cotton, or ashes. Today, Vonnette touched cotton with many of the people she came across, including the man, Tony, the walk-in. The ashes concept came front and center with the final person of the day. That woman proved to be someone who did not know the meaning of soldering in regards to goldsmithing techniques.

All in all, she correlated her dream message, stone choices and number of crows seen on her drive into the show with everything that had happened throughout the day.

Joy took over this day. Especially once she was able to clear her booth of the mad-dog woman who could have turned even more ugly. Similar kinds of people had come into her booth in the past. Usually Vonnette let them spout off and then later kicked herself metaphorically for feeling like a trapped wimp when she didn't lash out in some manner. Vonnette happily stood her ground today. She was also especially happy she sent the woman white and pink light instead of reflecting the anger and frustration back at her.

Today, Vonnette stood up for herself!

Today, she turned the tides on bullies and molesters.

Today, she reclaimed her physical and emotional space, her right to have opinions and her right to have a life!

Suddenly, Vonnette tasted thickly frosted cake when there was none around. In the parking garage at this point, she knew this was not a place for the scent of baked goods because the smell of gasoline was too over-powering. Tasting cake made her think of how sweet life can be when a very deep inner emotional connection is made. Perhaps this oral sensation was to let her know spirits were happy, and the taste of cake marked a birthday celebration. Vonnette needed some sweetness about then. She thought how wonderful it felt to receive oral sensations like frosted cake when no calories were involved! Maybe this day would be a forerunner for her not to crave sweets whenever things went awry in her world. That, too, would be a birth and a wonderful gift!

CHAPTER FIVE

Valentine

October 29, 2008, Wednesday

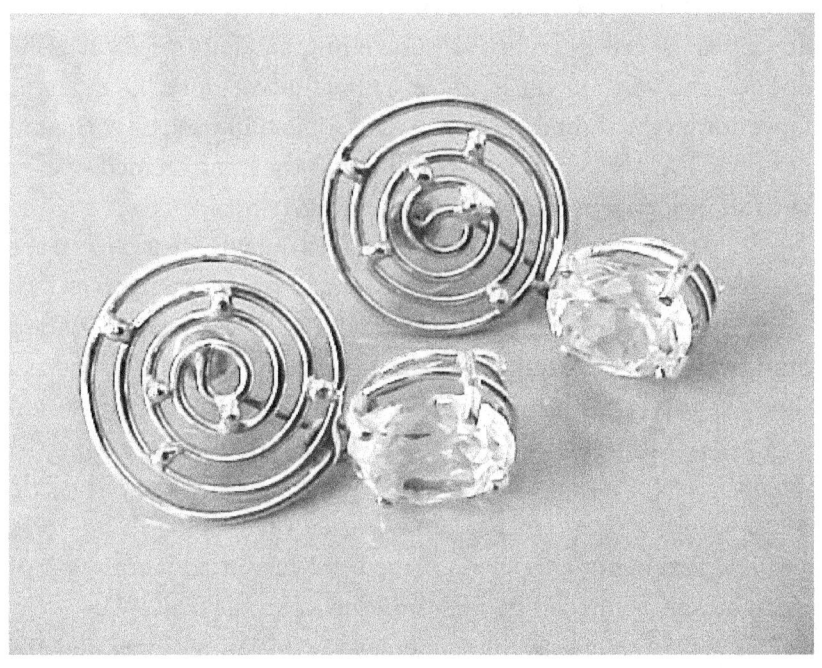

Spiral & Dot Stud Earrings with White Topaz Drops

Waking up this morning was an incredible challenge. Twice during the night Vonnette had gotten up for a bathroom run and climbed back into her cozy bed. Feeling the covers wrap around her was like being in a cocoon. Dreams escaped her. The show had ended Sunday night. Four day shows including set up were exhausting under normal circumstances. Coming off of four back-to-back shows, it was no wonder her bed was the best place to be.

It's easy to procrastinate. Not wanting to know a negative answer held her in sort of a trance this day. But Vonnette needed to contact Boston for an appointment. Around nine a.m. she slipped into her old terry cloth robe for emotional comfort, began to run a bath with the water just trickling out of the spout because she didn't know how long the next step of the day would take. She headed downstairs to call and schedule a mammogram. Last week when she phoned she was put on hold for at least a half hour. Deciding it must not be the right time to have this looked into, she gave in and hung up. Today was different. She thought the lump seemed smaller but still needed it to be looked at by a professional.

The phone rang on the Boston end and quickly went over to the recorded message, "Please hold as your call is important to us. We will answer your call in the order in which it was received." Weird music that was supposed to be calming came next but no sound at a time like this could bring Vonnette peace. The same recorded message played again, and then, more music. Vonnette wondered if she would hold for a half hour today or give up as she had last week. More recorded message and more music, the ringing of a phone, and low and behold, a person picked up! Putting down the bit of cold chicken she had in hand, Vonnette began the drill.

"This is Vonnette Webber and I was wondering if you had any cancellations for this week?

"My birth date is 10/30/50 ...

"Yes, I had an appointment scheduled for September that had to be canceled ...

"Yes, that was redone for January twelfth ...

"The thing is, I have found something in my left breast that I am unsure of . . .

"No, I don't understand. Why can't you see me as a regular appointment?"

Teri, on the other end of the phone, informed Vonnette that a diagnostic exam would be necessary which would not come with a normal mammogram. "First, go to your primary care physician and then they will call to schedule an appointment with the ultra-sound department. *Then* an exam of that breast alone will be done. You also need something written from your primary care to bring in, in person."

Taking a couple moments to breathe, Vonnette tried to hold back the tears that had begun to bubble to the surface. Exhausted from the show schedule and unable to control anything medical around her, she knew tears could very quickly send her into a dark emotional place. "I think it might be a cyst as the size seems to be different on different days. Can't I just come in and have it looked at to get it over with?"

"Believe me, you are going to want that paper the doctor will give you for health insurance purposes. In case your fears are warranted, and something more needs to be done," Teri explained with total detachment as if she hears the same thing many times throughout any given day.

This was Vonnette's first time experiencing this sort of issue, and Teri's detachment didn't help with getting an immediate answer.

"Okay . . ." was the weak response that came from Vonnette feeling she was up against a bureaucratic brick wall.

Hanging up, the well of tears with no more room to hide bubbled out. Letting some go, she then grabbed her purse to locate the number of her nurse practitioner. Once that card was in hand, she began to dial. The clock on the small antique table across the room said it was 9:33. The answering service on the other end of the line claimed otherwise when she reached the Jamestown practice.

"Office hours are from 9:30 a.m. to 4:40 p.m. Monday through Friday with lunch being from noon to one each day. If this is an emergency, please hang up and call 911. If you need immediate assistance, but this is not an emergency, please remain on the line and someone will connect with you."

Another machine. How and when did this world get to be so impersonal? She needed to be seen by someone professional in order to get the answers she so craved, Vonnette stayed on the line. When someone finally spoke, she was informed the office would be picking up in another five minutes, to please call back at that time. Obviously, they had a different idea of what qualified as being in need of immediate assistance than Vonnette.

Having settled into a spot on the end of the couch closest to the phone, Vonnette hung up and said loudly into thin air, "Fine, just fine!"

As she got up off the couch to replace the phone into the book-case where it normally sat, she then reverted to the only thing that brought her comfort at such stressful times as these, the refrigerator. Opening the freezer with purpose she reached into the back where she had stuck a dark chocolate bar two days ago hoping she would forget it was there. It was now 9:40 a.m. and chocolate seemed not only logical but necessary to calm her raw nerves. To justify having chocolate so early in the morning Vonnette thought, "It must be later in the day somewhere!"

While opening the chocolate bar, Vonnette felt disappointed that sweets were, sadly, still part of her existence. "Guess my big reveal and act of self-forgiveness has not yet completely stuck," she pronounced to the ethers as she climbed the stairs to her now full bath.

⁂

October 30, Thursday 2008

Once awake, Vonnette lay in bed allowing her dream messages to gel before heading to the bathroom. This method of waking had been with her since she couldn't remember. College honed her skills of dream recall but having dreams, full on color dreams had been part of her life always. Reviewed dream details suggested what the day would bring along with what jewelry, and more specifically, what stones she should wear for the day.

DREAMS

1. Outside Vonnette's actual home in Newport men were working on a new stone foundation. The trench had been dug. They were carefully laying down new stone as if a wall was being constructed in the ground. It was very neat and stood about two feet outside the original foundation. Going out the door and around the corner of the house Vonnette went straight over to these workmen and asked, "Why are you doing this? We discussed the idea of expanding the house, but you never gave me an estimate. I love what you are doing, it looks great, but I need a price!"

In a dismissal tone of voice along with the flick of his hand the head contractor replied, "We'll work out the price later. We had the time, so decided to start your project now."

2. Gold ring with a Connecticut state quarter as the focal point. Gold vine work formed the ring shank twisting up and around a faceted blue topaz sitting next to the coin.

The coin ring from her dream was quite attractive. Being a jeweler, goldsmith, artist, jewelry designer, whatever: Vonnette never did know how to describe herself, it was quite normal to dream of jewelry, some made and some to be made at a future date. Back in the eighties she had created a coin ring for herself that had a dragon on the surface. Vonnette designed and formed gold bamboo work along the sides of the ring to compliment the Asian element of the coin's origin. Blue topaz did not play into that ring. Noting the stone reference Vonnette knew she had to wear a blue topaz today even if it meant stuffing a loose one in her bra. Blue topaz brought forth verbal and bodily fluid flow. Why the coin ring or a new house foundation was significant she had no idea as yet.

Back in August Vonnette had met with carpenters about house

repairs. Some said wooden gutters needed replacing. Others claimed the gutters just needed a bit of reworking. The roof over the backdoor mudroom definitely needed replacing along with a window and a troublesome door. For that matter, that whole rear entrance structure had appeared to Vonnette as a space that Jack had built. It was made of bits and pieces of wood that didn't match up on one side over the cement slab floor. An old wooden business sign had even been incorporated into that wall structure. All this created an open invitation for bugs, mice, and yes, even the occasional garter snake.

Two carpenters in particular gave Vonnette creative suggestions on how the space could be extended to include a half bath, something she always felt would be proper for the house. Friends of hers had changed closets into half baths in their homes in town. Built in the late 1800's Vonnette's house never had anything in the way of real closets let alone a second bath. Vonnette consistently tried to come up with creative ways to store her clothes. Storage in the basement was out of the question. Holes in the old stone foundation allowed water in. Lack of storage and a damp to wet basement meant that creating a half or full bath inside the house or basement was not possible.

Concepts of expansion often occupied her mind. Having another room for either an office or a painting studio would be such a treat. The shower in her existing bathroom was on the fritz again for the third time in twenty years. No time to handle the shower repairs over the course of this year left Vonnette with use of the bathtub alone. Thankfully, she liked baths so this was a non-issue, unless she was in a hurry.

Eventually, time needed to be made for her to repair her shower and then find the time, money and energy for the mudroom to be handled or changed. Overall cost, along with the idea of increased taxes, stopped her from jumping into making the expansion ideas come to fruition. Well, there weren't any return calls from carpenters with estimates anyway, so alterations were a moot point for the moment. Why then did she dream of the foundation of the house being expanded? It never occurred to Vonnette that her emotional foundation would be in need of expansion today. Instead, she trusted an answer to this question would come with the help of the coin ring and a blue topaz contained in her brassier.

⚜

Fifty-eight years ago, today, Vonnette had been born. According to her mother, financial difficulties, her fathers' health, along with condemned buildings kept her from being born a full week earlier. Her mother, father and sister had been living in condemned army barracks while building their house in Hopkinton, Massachusetts. Her father had come down with a strange illness and was taken into the hospital. Unscheduled illness can be a problem at the best of times. At that moment, the family had no time to waste. The barracks were about to be demolished. Nine months pregnant her mother opted not to falter on her mission with or without her husband. One call to the American Legionnaires and the plumbing issue was under control. Simca was then able to move her little family into their new home finished or not!

Walking up the wood plank known as the front steps on the twenty-third of October with what felt like labor pains, Simca quietly said, "No. No. Not yet. Not yet! Your father is not here. I have no one I can leave your sister with while I run off to deliver you. Please wait a bit longer. PLEASE!!!"

Intuitive connections between mother and child grew stronger from that instant forward. Eventually they would drive other family members to distraction when answering one another's partially asked questions. No one else knew what these two were talking about. It was a secret language, one of psychic connection born that connective day fifty-eight years ago.

One full week later Vonnette entered this world. Her father had *just* been released from the hospital. Doctors didn't know it was spinal meningitis until after he was home. Infectious, they would not allow him back into the hospital to visit his wife and newborn child. Simca had the freedom to choose the name she wanted for this not so little girl of ten pounds. The book she was reading at the time took place in Canada. Born in Canada herself, Simca connected with the book and the main character's name was Vonnette.

Vonnette grew up hearing this story of delayed birth, illness, no money, no plumbing, and the need for safe shelter. A secret pact could have been formed that day on the wooden plank between mother and unborn, empathic child. If so, Vonnette would have an explanation about why she never had enough money, why her housing was shaky, in serious need of assistance, and, yes, even why plumbing issues were a big part of her daily existence.

When finished going over her dream messages and flashbacks, Vonnette climbed out of bed and headed for her bathroom ritual.

Thinking not only of her birthday but also of the lump found on the eleventh of this month in her left breast, she wondered why she kept seeing crickets around the house. Vonnette felt much needed answers seemed to be just out of reach these days.

Vonnette paid attention to signs, all signs. Keeping track of these signs would be exhausting for most people. For Vonnette, paying heed to them had become part of *her* sense of normal. Seeing crickets symbolized giant leaps forward. How could a lump in her breast be considered a giant leap forward? Fear crept up inside her throat strong enough to make her breathing a struggle. "Why does the universe give me such signs when, obviously, there is no immediate correlation?"

After checking on her bath water, she headed into the jewelry studio down the hall from the bathroom. Pulling out a clear plastic bag that contained unset blue topaz, Vonnette chose one round cabochon she thought would be comfortable in her bra for the day. Turning and walking over to a shelf, she pulled out the bamboo dragon coin ring from a box sitting there. Around that time the phone rang.

Stone and ring in hand, she grabbed the phone in the studio, answered, and heard the song, "Happy birthday to you. Happy birthday to youuuu. Happy birthday deeear Von-neeette. Happy birthday toooo youuuuuuuu," in a familiar voice. Her sister Aurelia was on the line.

Vonnette felt her emotions flood to the surface as she told her sister about the lump found earlier that month in her breast. Her guard down, she cried. Each sister went silent remembering how their mother had passed from breast cancer twenty some odd years earlier.

Her dream about building a new foundation could have referenced Vonnette's relationship with her sister. It could also be that her emotional foundation needed to be rebuilt beginning today. Signs for emotional wealth along with the balancing of bodily fluids from dream messages had already shown themselves. No surprise to Vonnette the coin and blue topaz had been correct choices for the day. What surprised her was how early in the day she discovered the connection to her dreams.

Though it was her birthday, there would be no celebrating for Vonnette today. Not that she ever really celebrated her birthday in a big fashion, but she did usually enjoy phone calls and cards. Cards received by mail sat patiently on her side table in the dining room. No interest in opening them yet, Vonnette told herself there was no expiration date on birthday cards. A couple times throughout the day, the phone rang with well wishes from friends. Once or twice she answered, other times she let the answering machine pick up.

Self-absorbed, she opted to remain quiet and watched a couple of old romantic comedies. Lying on the couch with her two cats was comforting and the best she could hope for today. Her body as well as her mind needed time to stop and simply exist. Since speaking with Aurelia earlier, Vonnette thought about their mom. She'd been a fighter, had a full mastectomy only to have the cancer return in her back after five years of being clear. Today procedures were quite different. Perhaps she would have lived longer if her cancer had appeared now. Maybe she wouldn't have had to suffer through a full mastectomy. No one could know that.

The dream message of men building a new foundation outside the original one came back into her mind at some point during the day. Vonnette decided the concept from that dream could work if she built a new emotional foundation for herself. She had been rattled to the core with the breast lump and today her thoughts had been running wild. Over-tired, and overwhelmed, whenever she began to think, Vonnette opted to stop and either eat or nap. It was either that, or she might be sitting in a puddle of tears. Vonnette had a brain over-load kind of birthday. Telling herself tomorrow would be better and more focused, she allowed the day to be simple. She had called the Jamestown practice back yesterday and scheduled an appointment for tomorrow, so for today, she allowed herself to be emotionally and physically lost.

⁂

October 31, Friday 2008

DREAMS

1. After making a gold chain with round links and white topaz, Vonnette looked it over carefully to decide if she ought to make the links oval or leave them alone. Upon careful consideration, she decided it might be best if the links were left more round.

2. Telling someone about leaving laundry that was damp on a warm radiator. Not only did the laundry dry, but it added moisture to the house.

3. Working in the studio with someone who was learning about jewelry making. One minute he was drilling something, the next he pushed pitch around on a flat surface. (Pitch is a black tar-like substance used when doing chase or repoussé work. It holds metal in place. Using specific tools, metal becomes bowed in some places while more flat in others depending upon the artists' intent.)

4. Valentine's Day. Red paper heart cutouts were all around the room. Each one had white lace along the outer edges.

Upon waking, Vonnette thought the warm radiators and clean clothes dream might suggest she ought to send off a warm note to friends as an update. Friends were being wonderfully supportive and concerned as they reached out through steady e-mails. Vonnette welcomed each one. Later she would respond to these kind people.

The round chain links gave Vonnette hope beyond what she had been holding onto. The nurse practitioner told her on the phone yesterday, that if the lump in her breast was more round, it could most certainly be a cyst. As it was not round, she felt it could be something else. Right this minute Vonnette held onto the thought that the dream message meant the lump was actually more round than what she had been feeling.

While going over the healing properties of white topaz in her mind, Vonnette felt hopeful. "Use white topaz after the mental or emotional fog has lifted to breathe more easily. Relax in any new-found knowledge that comes due to relaxation. White topaz is for the weary traveler who begins to see his/her way clearly now and wants a bit of R&R, much deservedly so."

Taking this week to heal emotionally as well as physically, Vonnette napped when she needed it, ate when that seemed a good idea, and made better food choices than she had been doing in quite some time. By making this shift in food, Vonnette felt she made every effort to heal inwardly as well as psychologically.

Still, Vonnette worried about the shows she'd applied to that had either refused, or wait-listed her. Most of those shows were scheduled for February 2009 on through to the beginning of May. Could this be a sign she would be needing time to heal well into the New Year perhaps after having surgery?

Torturing herself with thoughts of the need to heal with no shows and therefore no money coming in, Vonnette felt she might lose her mind. God only gave each person what they could handle at any given moment is how the saying goes, but no money *and* cancer? Wasn't that over the top? Vonnette knew she was a strong person except that she didn't feel that strength right now at all.

Sincerely, she wanted to know something from the other side.

Couldn't God tell her *something*?

What good were all these gifts everyone thought she possessed at a time like this if she couldn't ask questions and then receive answers for herself?

Today, she glanced over at her park with monuments and saw it just as it was, an old cemetery. Emotionally, Vonnette couldn't hold onto her normal hopeful base.

"Wasn't this considered the Day of the Dead? Or was it called All Saints Day," she wondered?

Maybe she had the term wrong but the image right. People dressed up as if they were skeletons who painted their faces in that image, too. Photos of deceased loved ones and skeletons decorated mantels and even gravesites. If memory served, people even held competitions for how they decorated their homes as many do at Christmas. Only at this time it's a celebration of their dead, similar as to how some view Halloween here in the US, while others here view it as a time for tricks or treats.

Talking out loud, she began asking questions to thin air. "Must look the day of the dead up today. I cannot recall if it coincides with Halloween or not.

"Where did that originate anyway?

"Didn't it begin in Mexico?

"Wasn't that about one day a year where spirits came back to life? Where the deceased unite with the living?

"If that's so, then why can't I reunite with spirits today to know beyond a shadow of a doubt whether I will survive this breast issue? You all come visiting when I don't ask. I'm asking now. Who will come in and tell me what I need to know?"

Drifting into a sad place, Vonnette wondered why she dreamed of a work studio with some man using pitch. Utilizing pitch to create jewelry was a long process of heating a black substance that becomes the consistency similar to cold black molasses. Waiting for it to cool with a flat piece of metal embedded into the surface of the pitch took patience. Once the pitch hardened, the gold or silver would be repeatedly hammered, or pushed, as much as possible with special steel tools to create a low relief protrusion from the back side known as repoussé. While hammering, the metal becomes hardened and then needs to be heated to make it malleable once more. The metal has to be removed from the pitch. After annealing and placing that metal back into the pitch, time is necessary for the hot metal to cool in place again. Work on the opposite side or front would then be done to add detail, outlines, and to smooth out the rippling edges to what had been started from the back. That part of the process is known as chasing. A jeweler spends a lot of time waiting in between each process. Each procedure has to be repeated many times before whatever is being worked on looks like a finished product. Chase and repoussé were common methods used to create items like tea and coffee pots with matching sugar and creamers for centuries. Though Vonnette had experimented with this method from time-to-time, it was not a choice procedure for her to make jewelry today. As she pondered, she realized that dream didn't involve metal. The man was simply preparing the pitch for use by heating and spreading it about. Feeling this dream had to be a message about work, Vonnette let it take over her mind. Anything to do with work was better than thinking about her health.

Maybe it meant that she would soon be in the black with work.

Maybe that dream was some sign of hope for such a day.

Maybe she wouldn't need the shows she was being refused to or wait listed for.

Maybe on some other plane she would be getting the work she needed without all the traveling.

If that were true, it would certainly take a load off her mind! Then again, maybe the dream meant she was supposed to be malleable with herself right now. At this moment, Vonnette recalled the jeweler in her dream had also been drilling something. Fear was back in her throat as she felt the drill might symbolize her need to have a biopsy on the lump.

Dressed after her bath, Vonnette decided to work up estimates for clients in the studio. Once there, she placed spiral and dot stud earrings in her ears along with detachable white topaz drops. While putting her earrings in, the phone rang. It was a call back from the last show she had done in Providence. The man asked if she still had a pair of earrings that were a combination of 14Kw & yellow gold in a shell motif? Once she established that in fact the earrings were still available, Vonnette told the man she would hold them for him until he could pick them up in a week.

Vonnette loved it when she got such specific answers to her dream messages. The black pitch and the studio dream symbols quite obviously meant money through work, being in the black financially. Letting go of the drilling element of that dream, Vonnette felt one dream was figured out! Carrying forward on a line of hopefulness, Vonnette wondered if the dream with the round link chain could be about her having a cyst rather than something more tragic. As healthy food choices were once again in place, Vonnette felt certain the white topaz dream meant she had in fact done her homework and was hopeful the rest and relaxation process would follow.

This morning before heading into the studio to figure job estimates and waiting for her hair to dry, she saw the man come to do the lawn. It was the final cut of the season. Using his blower tool, he made sure all the leaves were off the lawn and into the boarder gardens. Vonnette went out and told him she didn't like the blower. The grass seed would spread into the gardens along with the leaves. Weeding grass as well as weeds became a tougher job in the spring. He had just finished blowing everything but understood what she was saying. He would, she hoped, retain this request for the following season. Learning how to ask for what she wanted in life instead of burying what she hoped for was all new to her. And by asking for what she wanted in life, Vonnette held onto hope that she would be creating a healthier life emotionally as well as physically. It felt good to say out loud what bothered her. Freeing in fact. So much so that she hoped food might not be used in the future to suppress her feelings.

At eleven o'clock Vonnette needed to make the trek across the Newport Bridge to the next island for her appointment in Jamestown. Meeting a nurse practitioner three years back became a Godsend for her state of mind. Vonnette did as much holistically as possible. However, if she had something serious like pneumonia, she knew it and went to the local clinic for the drugs necessary to conquer that illness. The first time she experienced pneumonia she didn't know she had it. After four times with that dreaded disease, she not only knew she had it, she knew she had it before anything showed up on an x-ray. Owning a business meant Vonnette had little time for illness. Calling to make appointments at any doctor's office meant she had to call, schedule something, drive, and then wait in an office to be seen. The clinic on Valley Road in Middletown always had a shorter wait time, and Vonnette preferred that over any lost time in a normal doctor's office waiting room when an issue appeared such as pneumonia. Once finished, and if necessary, she would be close to a pharmacy as well as a grocery store. Collecting supplies before heading home to bed would be a total time and energy saver because she lived alone and had no one to run errands for her. Other than such an emergency visit, Vonnette went once a year to see the nurse practitioner for blood work and a physical.

Today would be one of those moments where she would have to wait in an office to be seen by the nurse practitioner. Though she only called this nurse for normal yearly visits, Vonnette liked the woman much more than any doctor she had met to date. To Vonnette, most doctors had little patience for anyone who didn't treat them as gods. While sitting alone in a doctor's office as a younger woman, Vonnette found herself reading the degrees displayed on the wall. Each time she sat waiting for that person to enter the room, she wondered just where this doctor graduated in their class. Did he graduate first, in the top ten, or at the bottom of the class of a thousand or more? If the doctor graduated at the bottom of his class, then how would Vonnette know if his assessment of her issue would be correct?

No, she never treated doctors as gods.

After gathering up a magazine and word puzzles, Vonnette left the house for her appointment with destiny, whatever that might be.

While driving over the Newport Bridge today, Vonnette's breathing became strained. She hated what happened in her body when very stressed. She would tend to breathe in and not completely breathe out each time, which lead to a buildup of oxygen in her system that had nowhere to go. Moments such as these resulted in painful gas pockets. Of course, they were working on the bridge today! Why wouldn't they be? Traffic was funneled into one lane in each direction instead of the normal two lanes. When movement began to stall and then completely went into a standstill, one of those gas pockets began to bark at Vonnette. Like having a caged animal trapped inside her body, the pain pushed to somehow escape. Rubbing her right side, she began to belch. Glad to be in the car alone and not in the doctor's office while this was happening, she kept rubbing and belching. Once the traffic began to move again, she placed both hands back on the steering wheel but continued to belch.

Once she arrived at the offices of three doctors and one nurse practitioner, Vonnette stepped out of her now parked car and headed inside while telling herself to stop belching. Happily, the other two possible elements had not reared their ugly heads this morning. Often after the belching came hiccups and/or then the passing of gas through an orifice other than her mouth. Checking in with the front desk was mandatory. After that was a waiting game until her name was called.

Removing her jacket, Vonnette settled into one of the twenty matching uncomfortable chairs lined up as though there would be a game of musical chairs later. She pulled out the word puzzle booklet from her bag. Feeling as though she was actually involved in a game of musical chairs, she glanced about the room in readiness. Certainly, if piped-in overhead music stopped, a chair could be removed and another player would be knocked out of the game. Right now, in her mind, she was one of the two remaining players, she and someone by the name of *Cancer*. She sat waiting. Not for the music to stop, but rather for someone to tell her she had won the game of life. And cancer was in fact not only knocked out, but kicked out of the playing field.

Pen in hand and reading glasses on Vonnette began to circle words with a large oval outline when a man came inside the waiting area, checked in with the front desk, and sat two chairs up from her. "There was a whole room of chairs. Why did he choose to sit two seats away," Vonnette wondered? Feeling as though someone was looking over her shoulder, Vonnette glanced up every so often. When she did, he smiled at her. After three of these moments in time, he spoke.

"Nice day," came with a nod of his head towards the window opposite them. Vonnette nodded back in a yes fashion.

"Hope you're here for a normal checkup?" Came his next attempt at conversation.

Vonnette shrugged her shoulders and said, "We'll see." Ever hopeful this would be the end of these attempts at conversation!

"I come here for my yearly as well as any kind of cold thing that won't go away."

Nodding and slightly smiling again, Vonnette wished he would cease and desist.

"So who is it you see here?" He questioned.

"The nurse practitioner," Vonnette replied while keeping her eyes focused down on her puzzle.

"I just live up the street at the cross road. It's nice to live in James-town, isn't it?"

"Wouldn't know, I live in Newport."

He seemed calm, sincere, and interested in conversation. Too bad he chose this day to talk to Vonnette. Her mind was not here in the waiting room, it was in that examination room, a space beyond reach at the moment. Any other day and maybe they could have struck something up. Today simply would not work!

"Guess that's why I haven't seen you before now."

Looking weirdly at this man, Vonnette wondered if she had missed some part of the conversation.

Realizing her quizzical glance, he continued, "I mean, I've lived in Jamestown my whole life and rarely go over to Newport. Guess that's why we haven't met before now. When I leave town it's usually in the opposite direction, over to the mainland."

"Oh." What brilliant repartee Vonnette thought. One-sided conversation with someone she would never see again on a day when she least wanted it. Inside her head she was screaming, "I'm here for a possible cancer issue. I don't really want to be hit upon thank you very much!"

Oblivious to her inner voice, he went on.

Honestly not hearing his next statement, she suddenly realized he asked a question. What was he saying, and why was she even trying to pay attention?

Realizing she had not heard him, the man repeated himself: "My name is Frank, Frank Parson." His hand was out for an introductory shake.

Automatically Vonnette placed her hand in his and they shook. She gave her first name only. Finished now with the introduction, she was surprised he kept talking.

"I'm sure you think this is highly unusual being where we are and all, but would you consider having dinner with me?"

Her voice almost shrieked in response. "Tonight?"

Chuckling, Frank shook his head in a no fashion, stopped and then said, "Well yes, why not tonight? Hit while the iron is hot I always say."

"Not tonight." Vonnette heard her mouth reply. In her mind, she was saying, "Not tonight, not ever." But her lips announced, "Tuesday night will work for me."

"Okay, shall I pick you up, or do you want to meet me someplace?"

"I will meet you. You said you don't go to Newport, so I guess you would rather we have dinner here in Jamestown?" Forcing her mind to function, she was thinking about restaurants.

"I'll come to Newport. It'll be fun! You choose where and what time works for you, and I'll be there. Let me give you my number as well, just in case something goes awry."

He stood and got one of the doctor's business cards from the reception desk and wrote down his personal number. Handing the card over to Vonnette, she absently took it and suggested a restaurant on Washington Square called Yesterdays. It was a place where she knew the owners as well as some of the bartenders. If the date went horribly wrong, she would have back-up. They could sit at the bar and then if conversation went into a dead zone they would at least have distractions. They agreed. Vonnette would make the reservation under her first name not wanting to let him have her last name as yet. Safety first was the plan.

Suddenly, her name was called by a nurse who appeared in the door that lead to the examination rooms. No need to but the nurse almost yelled out her full name, "Vonnette Webber." Why she yelled, who knew, since there were only two people in that waiting room this morning and one was a male. But yell she did and all those safety precautions Vonnette had put in place for allowing Frank to only know her first name came to a tragic halt. Oh, well, good plan, lousy carry through. Standing quickly, Frank and Vonnette shook hands again and off she went with the nurse into the maze of exam rooms.

Right turn, then left and coming to a stop, Vonnette was told to go inside, remove clothes from the waist up and put on the dressing gown so the closure was in the front.

Following instructions, Vonnette finished and sat on the side chair. Pulling out her magazine, she began to leaf through it casually. Thoughts of, "What just happened? Was this some sort of cruel joke from on high? Imagine meeting a man in the doctor's office while waiting to find out if I have breast cancer or not," circled her brain. It was beyond her at this moment. The magazine would have to do its trick for distraction when suddenly, and unexpectedly, the door swung open and her nurse practitioner came inside. It was then that the hiccups appeared.

Pleasantries were exchanged. Hiccups were front and center. The nurse practitioner asked if the hiccups were why Vonnette was there today. Shaking her head, no, Vonnette tried to ignore her momentary uncontrollable physical ailment. As she began the discussion of what she had found in her breast, the nurse recalled the phone conversation they'd had yesterday. Amazed at how calm she was at this moment in spite of the hiccups, Vonnette said she felt it might not be anything, but it had to be addressed. Continuing, Vonnette suggested the lump might not be cancer due to her beliefs in metaphysics. Egged on by the nurse who seemed interested, Vonnette went on to say that she had precognitive dreams all the time. Yet when it came to this lump, there seemed to be a serious lack of information. Trusting the old adage of "no news is good news," Vonnette implied the lack of information on the metaphysical front had to be a good sign, right?

"Let's get you up on the table to have a look and a feel. I'll give an opinion after that as to what you're calling hope."

Serious prodding came next. Some of which was extremely uncomfortable. Vonnette did expect a certain amount of that. Laughter came with one very uncomfortable probe. Eyes met with queries so she explained. "Years back, I saw a doctor who began poking at my shoulder blade. It was very painful. But, I didn't say anything. I didn't even let out a moan. Suddenly he asked if I was experiencing discomfort? I told him yes. He then asked why I wasn't complaining? Honestly, I said, I'm a woman. Pain is part of our existence. He got so frustrated he threw his hands up in the air and walked out of the examination room. The pain I'm feeling now with your prodding reminded me of that moment with that doctor. Recalling his reaction that day made me laugh."

Both women now chuckled. Glad for a moment of levity, Vonnette waited for the probing to stop. Once done, she was instructed to sit up. By this time, her hiccups had become that ugly sort where so much air was gulped in with each breath that her whole body shook. Why she didn't have the cute hiccups was forever a question when these kinds of moments appeared in front of others. To say it was embarrassing would be putting it lightly, but then, there was also the pain involved. Actual physical pain. Such violent hiccups expanded her chest quickly. The uncontrollable jerking of her whole body with each sudden intake of breath made Vonnette feel as though she had Turrets Syndrome. With each spasm, even her brain was feeling like a pincushion where pins were being shoved into her skin. Even the bottom of her rib cage felt sharp pains with each sudden lurch. Putting all that to one side, she was thrilled the nurse had not spoken more about these ugly hiccups. Focused on the task at hand, she began to discuss the probing.

"I do feel what you're talking about and cannot be sure. The next step is for a mammogram and/or ultra sound. I can set that up for you to have later today at Newport Hospital."

"No, thanks," Vonnette replied, "I have been going up to Boston for about ten years. They have all my records. Since they specialize in breast issues, I prefer to go there. Actually, they have ultrasound and mammogram machines all in the same building.

"What I do need from you is . . . a letter to bring to Boston. I was told they require a letter of confirmation from a doctor in order to see me quickly. Something about insurance protocol I guess."

Feeling she was talking entirely too fast, Vonnette took a breath to slow her speech. "So, I know you can't be held to anything, but what would an educated opinion be at this moment?"

"Won't give one. I can appreciate your need to know, or need to hang onto hope at this moment, but I cannot go there without more information. I'm concerned enough to say this needs further investigation. Are you sure you don't want to me to set up the mammogram for here rather than your having to drive to Boston?"

"Thanks, but no. I'll go to Boston. They'll give me results immediately. If I have it done here, I might have to wait a week to know anything."

"Okay. Let me have their phone information. I'll get this appointment scheduled for you as quickly as possible. Perhaps then you won't have to travel emotionally to the dark places we all tend to go at moments like these."

Vonnette rummaged through her handbag and found the number for The Faulkner Saggoff Breast Center in Massachusetts. Upon handing it over to the nurse practitioner, she was then instructed to get dressed and wait while the call was made.

Following instructions, Vonnette dressed then sat back down on the side chair and pulled out her magazine again. During her time alone, she tried to slow her breathing down more and more to stop the hiccups. It was beginning to work. Within ten minutes the nurse came back in the room and amazingly enough, she had scheduled an appointment for Vonnette for the coming Monday in Boston! They'd had a cancellation and would fit her into that with both an ultra-sound as well as a mammogram. With those two methods of observation, there ought to be some form of answer. Feeling informed, she still needed a letter from the doctor to bring with her. The necessary paperwork was brought into the room by another nurse and handed over to Vonnette to take with her to Boston. The nurse practitioner had also placed a request with Boston to be notified of the test results by way of a phone call.

It was then the nurse chose to address the irritant in the room no one had been speaking about until now. "So, these hiccups of yours. Why don't you tell me about them?"

"What's to tell? They're hiccups. Doesn't everyone get them?"

"I'm thinking your case is unusual, Vonnette. They seemed to get worse and worse through our exam today. Do you also have gas when these appear?"

"Wow, psychic as well as medical input. Color me impressed!"

"Not psychic. Purely medicinal, I'm afraid. Long term hiccups are not good. To have them occur once in a while is okay, but yours today have been on the side of intense. So, tell me, is this normal for you? Is this something that happens all the time? Is this only today? What?"

"Honestly, I've had these occasionally since childhood. I have the tendency to breathe in and not completely breathe out, especially when I get nervous, I guess. Gas pockets lead to pain. Once I rub the painful area, I belch and belch. Sometimes after the belching, hiccups occur. Today they've been more intense than usual."

"Okay. This sounds like it's due to the stress you're under at this moment. If they continue, we'll need further investigation. For now, I have some patients who have told me of similar experiences with their breathing patterns when upset or stressed. They've shared with me how probiotics have helped. That's something you can get at the health food store in Newport. Take it at the end of the day before bed. They will help control excess gas in your system naturally. I think you'll be amazed!"

"I'll give it a try. Thanks for the additional input. Who knew? I am in and out of the health food store often, so will ask as to what brand or what amount I should take. Thankfully, they seem to be very knowledgeable about all things health oriented. Honestly, it never occurred to me to ask about my hiccups before."

Nods, handshakes, and hugs were exchanged before Vonnette walked out of the examination room to the outer office where she paid for the visit. There was an obligatory ten-dollar co-pay which Vonnette paid in cash. She then walked through the wooden door into the waiting area to see that Frank had left his chair. He must be in his appointment with the doctor. Relieved not to be facing him again at this moment, she continued through the front door and on to her car.

Driving home she went over everything again in her mind. Thoughts of dinner with Frank would take last place for her this day. Getting everything ready for the drive to Boston on Monday was top priority. Stopping on the way home for gas was the first step. Magazine and word puzzles were already in her handbag, so that was good. Vonnette thought about her sweet tooth at times like these, being so stressed. Opting to skip that food moment and head home after filling her gas tank, she knew she had to stay busy so as not to break down again emotionally.

Thinking back over meeting Frank made her realize what a gift it had been. By keeping her mind occupied with his questions, she didn't have time to retreat into that dark emotional place and blubber all over her nurse practitioner. The red hearts in the dream message were front and center in her head. Overall, she did have a type of Valentine's Day.

Suddenly, the studio dream and black pitch being moved about crossed her mind. That dream may have been about Frank giving his *pitch* for further acquaintance. And then he drilled home his invitation of a date. His seemingly irritating distraction at the time became a gift.

❧

November 3, Monday 2008

Sleep escaped Vonnette last night. Dozing on and off on the couch with her two cats was the best she could do under the circumstances. Thank goodness she had the cats at times like these. Wordlessly, they snuggled and gave comfort without demanding anything in return other than food, water and love.

At seven a.m. Vonnette gave up, got up off the couch and headed upstairs for her bath. Even without benefit of dream messages, she was certain today would bring forth answers on some level. The elephant sitting on her chest would either crush her or move on.

Dressing for comfort and for the almost two hour drive each way, Vonnette decided on a light-weight tee shirt under a cashmere sweater and then a jacket. Stretch pants were in order for sure. Sweater, bra, tee and jacket would end up in a locker. Pants would remain on, and stretch pants didn't have zippers. Years back, Vonnette had been informed that metal could confuse any X-ray/mammogram machine readout. No zippers on her pants, no metal pins in her hair, no jewelry on either, hopefully meant a clear readout today.

Mother Nature provided a good distraction for her this day while driving up to Boston. It was fall and the leaves off island had shifted. In Newport, the colors had not changed yet. Vonnette was nervous on her drive as to what the machines would claim. After seeing the nurse practitioner, she had gone into the health food store and began taking probiotics. Pleasantly surprised, Vonnette discovered her body was not betraying her with strange noises or jerks this day! Instead, she was actually appreciating the fall colors on the drive.

Her appointment was scheduled at Faulkner for ten o'clock.

Vonnette pulled into the parking area at nine fifteen. Walking into the building and then the elevator, she pushed the button for the fourth floor. It all seemed to be happening as if in a dream segment, slightly blurred and outside her body. Stepping out of the elevator and turning into the office space to the right was known territory. Experience told her to take a white sheet of lined paper, write her name and time of appointment down and then place it in the black perforated bin sitting on the desktop. Going over to an empty chair, she waited for a woman to call her name to collect insurance information, any necessary updates, and who knows what additional questions.

Soon enough Vonnettes' name was called. She was motioned over to a cubicle on the left and asked to sit. Paperwork had to be cross-referenced with information on the computer. Date of birth, home address, name of doctor, insurance card, and reason for appointment had to be checked and rechecked. She was then informed the mammogram would be first today, not the ultrasound as she had been told last week over the phone. Once everything was recorded, Vonnette went back to her seat in the waiting area. Within twelve minutes Vonnette was called along with six other women to enter the next room. There they were told to enter a dressing room, remove clothing from the waist up, place all in any empty locker, put on a hospital gown with the opening in the front, and go out into the next waiting area with any valuables in tow.

Being a larger breasted woman, Vonnette had never found a hospital gown that closed properly across her chest on exam days. Constantly tugging at the fold over element of the gown made her feel she was only partially dressed and, in fact, she was. Sitting around in cotton hospital gowns was never fun, fashionable, or comfortable. Vonnette wondered, "Whoever named these things gowns didn't have a clue, seriously!"

So far this day was familiar.

Sitting in the waiting area for her name to be called again, Vonnette began to reflect. Sometime after their mother had passed, Aurelia had found this hospital specializing in breast issues. Since

Aurelia and Vonnette shared a family history of breast cancer, Aurelia suggested they both go to the same place for mammograms, just in case. At least if there was an issue all their information could be easily accessed. Vonnette wondered if this appointment would lead to such a moment where their family history would indeed need to be correlated.

Once a year she made this trek and did exactly the same things she had done thus far. This second waiting area had a TV tuned onto the *Today Show* where the television people were interviewing a guest chef. Not paying attention Vonnette found a seat directly under the TV. Within seven minutes her name was called again. Jumping up to attention, Vonnette exchanged hellos with the technician and followed her into the room three doors down on the left. Breathing a bit easier, Vonnette felt slightly better knowing this tech was one she'd had numerous times before. Stressful instances such as these were somewhat held at bay by familiarity. The technician was perhaps five years older than Vonnette, usually had a smile on her face, and presented a calm demeanor. All the techs dressed in drab uniforms but chose their own shoes. This woman wore clogs. For some reason clogs made Vonnette smile. She never knew why.

While looking over the paperwork on file, the tech asked why she was there today.

Vonnette suddenly had a lump in her throat that felt as if it was the size of a city. Speaking slowly, she hoped the lump in her throat would dissipate, and she would not tear up. "I had an appointment but had to cancel it, then I found a lump. Following procedure, I went to my nurse practitioner to get an exam and have her write a letter for the insurance. She called here. There was a cancellation, and so I'm here today."

"Okay. Give me the letter from your nurse, so I can place it in your file."

Vonnette reached into her purse and pulled out the letter as instructed.

"Thank you. Show me where you feel the lump."

Opening the top of her gown Vonnette displayed with her right hand where the lump was.

"I'll mark it with this tape that won't be uncomfortable at all, but it will show up on the X-ray for the doctor to use as a reference for easy identification. Now, remove your left arm from the gown. Let's get going with this to see what shows up."

The attendant continued placing Vonnette's left breast into the machine to be squished beyond recognition, like an egg out of its shell spread over the hot frying pan surface. "Turn you head to the right and hold your breath. Hold. Hold. Okay, breathe," came the instructions.

The machine let go of her flesh and immediately Vonnette felt that freedom. The attendant then shared information on medical procedures. "According to the insurance companies, we are supposed to do the mammogram on one breast alone when there is a question. Over time we made the decision here to do both breasts just in case, insurance coverage or not. That way we can be sure if it's something that has developed quickly and spread, or is clear except for in that one spot."

"That makes sense to me. I do have an appointment scheduled upstairs with the ultra sound people after I get through with you. It'll be a relief to know if there's nothing in my other breast today, though. So, thanks, I'm happy to hear that you will do both breasts at once."

Not knowing why, other than the fact that it was good manners, she thanked this technician. She was hurting Vonnette in a way beyond imagination with these machines, so why would someone thank that person? Meanwhile, Vonnette was instructed to stand in another position that was slightly sideway, had her left breast moved around a bit to the side, and then squished again. As the machine came down tighter, tighter and tighter, Vonnette felt her whole-body slide downward a bit. Her knees almost collapsed as she tried to deal with the pain.

Noticing what was happening, the attendant told her to push her caved in shoulders back, to stand absolutely still, to breathe in, hold it, hold it, hold it.

When told to breathe as the machine released its grip, Vonnette could stand upright without much pain. Massaging the breast a tad, she began to put her arm through the arm hole to then remove her right breast when she heard those dreadful words, "No, not yet," come from the attendant. "The film is not clear enough. It all needs to be redone."

Fighting with all her might, Vonnette held back the tears gripping her throat. Every time the nurse repeated each step on her left breast, Vonnette winced as the machine tightened its grip on her soft flesh. Feeling embarrassed she said, "I'm not normally such a wimp, but Friday my breasts were poked and quite seriously prodded by my nurse practitioner. They haven't had enough time to recuperate and then today to be squished to this degree, it's fairly unbearable."

"Understandable for sure. Please do remember, though, you could be catching something in a very early stage that could save your life! So, some pain is doable, right?"

Nodding, Vonnette felt this woman was correct, however, it was still extremely uncomfortable.

Feeling some form of conversation would be a good distraction, the technician shared that under these kinds of circumstances, they often did an ultrasound first, and then a mammogram. Vonnette would have these treatments backwards today due to scheduling. Vonnette now understood the change in appointments today. The attendant then began to speak about Newport. Once a year she went to Newport for an overnight stay with her daughter. Talking about her trips helped break up the pain and discomfort. Any mental distraction was a good thing at a time like this.

Everything went along much the same on the right breast only without as much intense pain. Hospital gown wrapped over both breasts again, Vonnette was instructed to go into the waiting room to be called. The normal procedure was to see a physician after her films were developed; however, today Vonnette would have the ultrasound instead of seeing a physician. Originally, the ultrasound was planned to be done one floor up. Today, she would remain on this floor for that procedure.

The waiting room was almost empty at this point. The medical center workers were about to break for lunch, so no new patients were waiting to be called in for mammograms. Only four other women sat pensively. One by one they were called in to see the physician, get dressed, and then schedule an appointment for next year before leaving the building and continuing on with their lives for the day. Finally, Vonnette heard her name called. She was shown into a room down the hall, around to the right, and then straight ahead. The only light in that room came from a very large, overhead, blue viewing screen. Furnishings and equipment were tightly fit into a small space she guessed used to be a closet. A hospital bed with only very slight padding, no mattress, was positioned at an angle with the foot at the door, something that was unable to be closed due to where the bed thing was positioned. And, an extralarge and movable metal arm hung over the stylized bed. One really big machine to the left side of the room stood out and was presumably for readouts. Overall, this space reminded her of a science fiction film, or novel.

Instructed to lay upon the bed that felt more like the steel table that in fact it was, and wait, Vonnette did as she was told. While waiting, she called upon the healing angels and whoever was hanging about spiritually in the white light energy department to enter the room and help her. "I'm scared and in need. Can you please bring in healing energy while I'm here? Will healing angels please come forth this day for me?" She repeated these lines a few times totally uncertain if anyone would come forth since she couldn't recall how to specifically call in those angels.

Only recently Vonnette had been informed about angels after an experience while meditating where archangel Michael showed up in a big way. His giant wings were open. He suddenly stood right there in front of her without warning. She even felt his physical presence that night. This was a very new concept to her. Of course, she'd heard about angels and their omnipotent powers, but feeling and seeing a huge one in front of her brought all that to life. One might hope that he imparted some form of great wisdom at that unscheduled meeting, but no, it was simply a meeting.

Archangel Michael had opened Vonnette's mind to possibilities. Although confused, she headed off to the nearest *Barnes and Noble* to find books on angels and, archangel Michael specifically. There were way too many books on angels, and too many names of angels for someone who didn't grow up hearing about them all the time. Leaving the store that day empty-handed, she felt the amount of information was just too daunting. After some time passed, she went back and tried again. That time she came away with a couple books that explained in simple terms how to call upon angels when in need. Being on this table at this time constituted an in-need kind of moment. Calling forth, and then seeing white forms without specific shapes fly about this closet-size and shaped room gave Vonnette some of the peace of mind she craved. Feeling these forms were in fact angels, she watched as they flew in a circular fashion overhead. As difficult as it was to relax in a situation such as this, she began to feel watched over and did feel her muscles give way a tad.

Within minutes of seeing these energies flying about, a woman came into the room and began to spread a cold gel on Vonnette's left breast. She did not speak other than to instruct Vonnette to open her "gown." There was that term again. This was not any type of formal social gathering she'd ever known before, so why on earth was this called a gown? The woman seemed to be in her thirties and came across as cold as the gel she applied. Image wise, too, she felt unapproachable. Then something happened. This cold woman called out to an attendant in the hall to turn the heat down in the room. It had felt quite cool, so Vonnette had no idea at first why this cold as a fish-like woman felt that the temperature seemed warm to her.

As the technician began using her tools for the exam, she called out to the attendant once again, this time to request the air conditioning be turned on.

All this made Vonnette more nervous. Thinking it was already quite chilly in the room and the woman wanted it to be more cold was unnerving. Was this part of the exam? About that time, she noticed the woman actually began to show signs of sweating, something Vonnette was surprised to see in this very cold and dark room. Focusing on the angels floating above her gurney or examination table thing, she tried to remain calm and breathe slowly, deeply. Gritting her teeth while suffering through the deep digging into the left breast with the smooth, ice-cold ultrasound wand, Vonnette suddenly remembered something she'd read about healing angels. When they come in, the room is often heated up. It could be that, or the person doing the medical work, or psychic healing, or what-have-you gets hot, or it's all elements at once. Almost chuckling, though suffering from all this probing on top of the squishing from the mammogram and then even before that the nurse practitioner having a serious go at the same breast, she knew beyond a shadow of a doubt that her healing angels were there doing their thing. Grateful beyond comprehension, Vonnette began to really feel calm for the first time since she'd entered the room.

She kept trying to breathe her way through the pain. And then, out of nowhere, Vonnette asked if there was a reason she was in this room instead of upstairs where ultrasounds were normally done. Vonnette hoped the technician would warm up in some small way by being asked a question.

In a robot-like manner, the woman responded: "You're here because this will be part of your normal exam this year. If there is something we need to pay closer attention to, you will in fact go upstairs." Pausing briefly, she kept probing as deeply as she could. Staring mainly at the machine screen in front of her and keeping emotionally distanced, she made certain no questions would distract her from her job. The wand continued to probe seemingly of its own volition. All words spoken could have come from a recording rather than this human technician. "Do you remember being hit here by anything?"

Unclenching her teeth from the pain she was trying to hide, Vonnette considered a moment and then answered. "Nooo . . . not that I can think of." Vonnette kept thinking about the question but her thoughts were interrupted.

"You have bruising in this breast tissue. I don't see anything that needs a biopsy or to be looked into further unless it doesn't eventually go away. You'll know, and can then call again and be seen if that's the case."

With that statement, the technician stood, wiped off her tools, replaced the wand back on top of the larger machine and turned to leave the room. Stopping briefly, she said with her gaze elsewhere, "Get dressed and make an appointment for next year. There's no need to be seen by the doctor today. We've covered everything in here that's necessary. The mammogram will back up my findings."

She left. The air behind her was as frigid as she was. It always amazed Vonnette how women in such a personal field could manage to be so cold to another woman in such emotional turmoil. Maybe if they were warm and had a caretaker personality they would suffer burn-out quickly. Or, maybe if they cared, they would become a richer person for the experiences. No matter how Vonnette looked at it, this woman was as cold as ice all the way through the appointment and the air conditioning only emphasized her seeming lack of concern or even interest. What fascinated Vonnette about this whole ultrasound experience was . . . the technician had no idea healing angels caused her to feel hot in such a cold room.

Shocked, Vonnette lay still for a moment while pulling her gown closed. Did she honestly hear what she thought she heard? Was it a bruise for sure, not cancer? If so, when could that bruise have happened?

It hit her like a bolt of lightning! Sitting up on the table, Vonnette had a clear picture in her head. One night she had climbed into bed and lay down on her back. While getting settled and adjusting the covers to a comfortable position, out of nowhere her small black cat, Rose, who was pure muscle, came flying up the stairs and leapt onto the bed straight onto Vonnette's left breast! Oh, my God! That was it! Rose was the culprit! It all came rushing into Vonnette's mind at once and felt like a blood rush that could trigger a migraine. She felt a bit dizzy. Then she heard the words, "bruised breast." Words the ultrasound technician had mouthed. What a fantastic day! This was indeed a miracle!

Could it all be this simple?

Could everything she'd been experiencing emotionally be gone with the blink of an eye like this?

The reality of how wrong she had been, now sank into her mind very slowly, into her psyche, and onto her muscle structure.

"How wonderful to be wrong," she thought.

How different the day was right now than what she had expected it to be. The dread was gone!

Smiling, she was still somewhat frozen in place upon that very cold table in that very dark room. Realizing that she had not moved off the table, she began to do so. Inwardly, she leapt for joy! Outwardly she was being methodic, looking about to make certain she had not left something behind other than her fear, and that could remain there forever as far as she was concerned. After taking hold of her handbag, she moved out into the hallway maze of rooms she had never seen before today and hoped she would never have to see again. Moving was automatic and most definitely an out of body experience. Some other technician stood in the hall and directed her to the changing area after noticing a look of confusion displayed on Vonnette's face. The look was easily read as Vonnette stood still at one point, looked forward, then back, then forward again.

Once she found her way back to the locker housing her clothes, she took them in hand and closed the curtain to dress. Here she looked up and thanked all who had been with her this day. Smiling, she couldn't believe that she'd never called upon angels before now. Vonnette told them that from now on she would remain in close touch. "Thank you! Thank you all so very much! I needed you and you came to do your magic! I believe. I believe. I believe!"

Dressing and making next years' appointment all seemed to happen in a fog. Emotionally, she was floating. Even traffic jams on the drive home didn't darken Vonnette's mood. She was high up in the air, as though she was in her body, and above it at the same time, like astral traveling while being fully awake and aware.

On her drive home, she composed a group e-mail in her head to be sent out to all her friends.

Great news everyone! I just left Boston and found out the lump in my breast is actually a bruise. After everything I have been through with my nurse practitioner and examinations these past few days and weeks, it's a miracle I remember Rose's jumping and landing on that breast some time back. Yes, my little, loving, black cat is the culprit that caused all this uncertainty in my life. Knowing that at this moment is a good thing. Loving her in spite of all the worries she caused is even better. Cats are pure unconditional love. She didn't mean me harm, and I don't wish any for her. Right now, I feel like the weight of the world has been lifted off my shoulders and I can begin living again. As time and energy allows, I will give each of you a call and we will catch up. For now, it has been a whirlwind with back-to-back shows and medical issues. Emotionally and physically I'm drained. Happy, but drained. Thank you all for your well wishes and prayers. I accept them with sincere gratitude. That each and every one of you are, and continue to be part of, my life; I am forever humble!!!!

Be well.

Love Vonnette!!!

There was an answer to Friday's dream about warm radiators and laundry being placed upon them. Keeping her friendships warm with a note, and then to follow up later with a personal call at her leisure, Vonnette was gliding along. The white topaz also helped with her need for rest and relaxation now that the fog had lifted! The chain dream she'd had was front and center as well. To Vonnette each link clearly formed in that dream was round, and not an oval shape to mark cancer.

Vonnette was ready to be home and not have to think or to be filled with fear, but simply to BE. Once she did arrive home she gave Rose extra special hugs and kisses. Yes, Rose was the cause of this cancer scare, but she didn't mean to hurt Vonnette. Rose deserved acknowledgement for this blessing today.

Although still wondering why all this had happened, Vonnette was thrilled it was over.

Was it over though?

Could she simply pick up where she left off a few weeks ago when all this began?

Could Vonnette ever know what lesson she needed to learn from the experience of possibly having cancer? Forever in school Vonnette couldn't shake the feeling she was still in learning mode about something big that had to do with being alive, and existing on this planet in her body. Maybe it was all to understand why people freak out when diagnosed with serious illnesses. Perhaps she needed to be more compassionate with those who had diseases, though she didn't know how she could be more sympathetic when it came to others' being ill. Being an empath and a sensitive, she often sensed what pain others felt. Maybe she had to learn more about living in the here and now. As a serious thinker, she would ponder these concepts for some time because that was what she did. Vonnette was someone who needed answers as to why things happen on all fronts.

<hr />

November 4, Tuesday 2008

Vonnette was happy, honestly happy all day! Everything that had happened since finding the breast lump seemed so far in the past. Today seemed as though she had just gotten out of a long sentence in a solitary prison.

Tonight, she would have her date with Frank and enjoy it.

Throughout the day she did little things like stare out the window at her park with monuments and look at her back yard. Interestingly enough, the cemetery was back to being a park in Vonnette's mind. Everything had seemingly brighter colors. All sorts of birds were in her yard, including the wonderful cardinals with their sweet chirps. Even the food Vonnette chose to consume came at a normal pace instead of one with urgency or addiction. She felt free, sincerely free for the first time in weeks. Had it only been weeks she wondered? It seemed like a lifetime ago she began this nightmare scare of what-if.

Thinking about her mom and her experience brought a momentary frown to her face. Vonnette knew first hand now how life must have been for her mother all those years ago when she first went in to have her lump looked at. Unfortunately for Simca, that lump was in her lymph nodes under her right arm. Taking as much as they could then and following up with chemotherapy and radiation were normal procedures at that time. Though she was a fighter, Simca ultimately lost that battle. How alone and lonely her mother must have felt.

Shaking her head Vonnette opted to think instead of her mom as a vibrant woman in spirit, whole again. Speaking out loud as if to no one, Vonnette actually spoke to someone in particular. "Once you enter spirit, I know you become whole again. Soooo happy for you Mom to be complete after everything you went through. Sorry you had to experience a massive mastectomy in your lifetime this go 'round. Hope whatever lesson you were supposed to learn, you did, and have moved on. For that matter, I hope whatever lesson I was supposed to learn from my experience has been learned, too."

Around 5 p.m. she began to ponder what she might change into for her date. It was a casual restaurant, but it was also a first date. Always nice to be a bit dressed, yet not overly so. No need to make Frank feel out of place in case he wore casual clothes. A couple items from her closet came out and were dismissed for one reason or another. Settling on a white, long sleeve jersey, she chose a simple pair of light green, loose fitting pants to go with the top. Frank was at least a few inches taller than Vonnette, so she could get away with wearing high heels. In the end, she opted to wear a low-heeled shoe for comfort. After picking out a pink and green shawl, Vonnette felt her clothing choices were complete. Fall nights in New England can become quite cool. If she was chilly in the restaurant, she could use the shawl. Otherwise it would serve as a scarf inside her jacket.

Deciding on jewelry would be a different matter. Tonight she felt light and free. A three-strand necklace of faceted rainbow moonstone beads came out of her jewelry box, and she placed it around her neck. The pair of white topaz spiral and dot earrings she wore a couple days ago went into her pierced ears. A long, black silk cord that housed a three-inch clear natural quartz crystal came out next. Last was a dendritic quartz ring that she put on her left index finger.

Looking in the mirror, Vonnette considered the healing properties of the jewelry combination she had chosen. Rainbow moonstone connects rainbows of possibilities to the inner lunar cycle. White topaz helps the weary traveler who sees the way clearly after doing their homework and wants a bit of rest and relaxation. Clear or white quartz helps to find clarity, and dendritic quartz provides cool clarity while thoughts come in a relaxed frame of mind instead of racing around. Feeling this combination of stones would bring about an interesting evening emotionally she was ready to meet Frank.

Instead of having them sit at the bar as she first planned, Vonnette asked for a table. With a little more privacy, they could actually get to know one another without constant distractions. Their table sat on the left side of the main room. Not knowing one another, and by not sitting at a center table, neither of them would feel on display. Frank arrived. Food and wine orders were placed and delivered in a timely manner. Loads of smiles came easily from each person as conversation never seemed to lag. Feeling as if she had a new lease on life after such a health scare, Vonnette decided to share some of her recent experience with Frank. Might as well find out what he's made of emotionally was her thinking.

"When we met in the doctor's office, Frank, I was in the middle of a traumatic moment."

He stopped eating to listen better, a good sign.

"After discovering a lump, I had to get it checked out here and then follow up in Boston making sure it was not cancer. My mother died from breast cancer that eventually went throughout her body. Obviously, when I discovered the lump in my breast, I felt very connected to her experience. My appointment in Boston was yesterday. I am happy to say it was a bruise, not cancer!"

He exhaled as she finished her last sentence. Smiling at him Vonnette thought he was a nice man, someone worth getting to know better.

"So, when I met you on Friday at the doctor's office you were there in pursuit of answers about this?"

"Yes, and I have to thank you."

"Thank me?" He almost choked as he repeated her words as a question. "Why would you want to thank me? I'm sitting here blown away that I asked you out at such a traumatic moment in your life. What gaul!"

Chuckling a bit, Vonnette reached across the table and touched his forearm momentarily in reassurance. "Seriously, Frank, you were such a gift to me Friday! I was in a bad place feeling as though at any moment I would and could sink into a crying jag. You pulled me out of that place with your conversation. So much so that I didn't even cry when I got into the nurse's office. Something I'm still amazed at quite honestly." Vonnette chose not to share the element of uncontrollable hiccups. She felt that was not something pertinent to their conversation at this time.

"If I had only known."

"If you had known you would never have spoken to me that way nor would you have asked me out. I'm saying I'm glad on all accounts. Let me thank you and please accept my appreciation," Vonnette pleaded.

Noticing the look of either shock or sadness, she just stopped talking to give him a moment to process what she had been saying.

"I think this is not normal first date conversation." Came after about two minutes of empty silence. "My dad passed away from cancer a year ago. His was pancreatic. I never saw anyone so brave in all my life. Watching over him, I tried to help as much as I could, but really, he had to face it on his own. I felt how alone he was and it killed me. We had a good relationship. It's taken me a long time to process that experience and move on. People want to be shoulders for you to lean on at times like that. Honestly though, we each go through whatever alone, too. You're the first person I felt ready enough to ask out, and be out with since all that happened. Once he passed, I felt like life was too short, and nothing much mattered.

"Of course, we all expect to die at some point. The thing is, my dad was a vibrant man who liked life and even chopped his own wood for the fireplace until maybe four months before he went. Seriously, I began to think he would outlive me!"

Switching gears a bit he asked sincerely, "So, you're sure this was not cancer then?"

Smiling and reaching out once again to have human contact between them, she affirmed his question with a "Yes."

The rest of their date went along quite well, well enough, in fact, for them to schedule a second date for the next night, something Vonnette had never done before. Two nights in a row was highly unusual for new daters, but then who knew at that time they would have such a short shelf life?

❧

November 10, Monday 2008

DREAM

Vonnette wasn't sure you could call this message a dream, more like an event during the night. She became semi-conscious at some point to hear someone say out loud, "Give him up."

Vonnette had been asking about her developing relationship with Frank before sleep for almost a week without getting any answers, until now that is.

Vonnette replied to whomever it was that she was talking to from the ethers. "He's a nice man, and I deserve a nice man!"

Her answer was immediate and quite strongly presented.

"Walk away. Your time is over. You've had your moment; now do the right thing."

Vonnette woke fully from this experience feeling sad and a bit as though her heels were dug emotionally into the ground. Why should she give this man up? He was the first man in her life who actually seemed to get her. He honestly understood who she was and liked her for it! Why should she give him up?

No, she wasn't in love with him as yet; however, she knew people who had been in love and after time fell out of love, and then back into it again. Couldn't some version of that happen to her with Frank?

Frank was great. He found Vonnette's psychic images and dreams fascinating. When it came out in normal conversation that Vonnette had written a book, actually two on the healing properties of gemstones that she had channeled, he seemed genuinely intrigued! Could she possibly ever find someone else who would do that? After many years of testing out dates and all of them failing miserably, it seemed highly unlikely!

They had been together three times in one week. They e-mailed and phoned numerous times daily. Vonnette looked forward to their connecting each time on whatever level. Verbally there was never a dull moment in their conversations. They seemed to be getting closer, really getting to know one another. During this short dating phase, Vonnette realized she had never allowed a man to see the real her until now. Normally, men in her life would go kicking and screaming out of the room when she began conversations of how she spoke to the dead, or spirits. Amazingly, conversations of her life experiences of communicating with spirits came pouring out of her easily with Frank. All her quirks, her psychic ability, her visions, spirit guide explanations and the overall meaning of metaphysics were each discussed over a short amount of time and never once did he flinch.

Claiming he had had some spiritual things happen after his father had passed lead Vonnette to believe he understood some of what she was telling him. This was a whole new experience for Vonnette something she was not ready or willing to kiss off.

Confiding even that her ability to talk with the spirit world could be done by everyone if they allowed themselves, he was intrigued enough to ask what she meant by that. "To me, it's like when you drive up the road at night. Coming upon a house that belongs to friends, you see the lights are on inside with their car parked in the driveway. Deductions are made from the lights being on and the visible car that your friends are home. That's what it's like for me having visits with people from the other side. They see my lights are on, and my car is in the driveway. They know I'm home and can come visit! When spirits realize that you are open to receiving them, their energy I mean, and even welcome their visits, they come fairly regularly. At least they do for me."

Frank didn't run away screaming.

Taking the cue, she continued almost without the ability to stop herself. "Of course there is what I call trickster energy in spirits, and that energy needs to be dealt with firmly. Letting that kind of energy know you will not accept or welcome it is vital to your own health! At one time, I had to take severe action, such as putting Kosher and sea salt around the outside of the house. Eventually it washes into the earth and dissipates, so it doesn't look like a crazy person lives wherever. In the beginning, though, it acts as a ring of protection keeping out unwanted energy. After completing that act, I took a long, very sharp knife and waved it about the air inside the house including the corners all while I was saying out loud that only white light energy was allowed in this place! Of course, I did the American Indian method of smudging the house afterwards in order to get whatever plasma remained out, too."

"Okay, smudge, salt and a knife?"

"Yes. Guess when it gets blurted out like this it sounds nuts. Honestly, when you have trickster energy around, you'll use any tools you might hear of at your disposal to get rid of it.

"A smudge stick has herbs tied together like lavender and sage. It can be anywhere from a few inches long to many inches. You can buy these at the health food store and were originally created by American Indians. When using a smudge stick, you light one end on fire. Once it gets going you blow out the fire and are left with cinders from the herbs. While waving that smoking wand about the house from one corner to the other, you ask out loud for all negative energy to be removed from this house and allow only white light energy to remain. Always do this while heading towards either an open door or window, so it gives the negative energy an exit point, and that's something you definitely want. I actually begin at an open window, and then end there as well. Within two or three days after you've completed this act, you'll notice a sincere difference in the energy surrounding you in your home."

Though Frank's mouth stood ajar while Vonnette presented instructions on how to deal with trickster energy, he was still not running, so she went on.

"My trickster energy was doing things like opening water valves in the basement. I would come home to the sound of running water along with three inches of water down there. When I went to turn off the valve, I had to turn it eight times, something that could not have happened on its own over the course of time, as some people suggested.

"Friends of mine have experienced more violent energy than I have, though, such as spirits tripping them on their way up or down the stairs. Turning on or off electrical appliances, or even having books fly about the room. When something like that happens, you need tools such as what I have just spoken about to turn the energy either around or away!

"Opening the door to *all* energy is never a good thing whether you are dealing with warm humans or cool spirits. When it's serious trickster energy, you need to pull out the sage, salt and the big sharp knife. Simply put, you need to let energy know you are home and ready for visitations but will only accept white light energy."

Only a couple other times had she expressed this version of how easy it was to commune with the dead. But with Frank, it came out of her mouth so quickly and effortlessly. Perhaps she was comfortable for the first time in her life with a man, feeling he accepted what was normal in her day-to-day existence. He even seemed interested. Maybe Vonnette was testing to see if this seemingly understanding man would in fact be there when she finished telling her life story, or if he would go screaming as did so many others.

Frank appreciated the explanation. He didn't run. He stayed.

Their next date also had an element of the supernatural to it.

"You mean that when you are working, these spirits visit? How do you concentrate? Even more, how do you know one is friend or foe, as you mentioned before about those trickster energies?"

Completely pleased and impressed that Frank was not only paying attention, but that he was also retaining what Vonnette had been sharing these past three times they'd been together in that week, she happily went forward with confidence. "Over time, I've discovered that spirits find it easier to communicate with me when I'm working. These sudden appearances no longer disturb me. Actually, I welcome them when I have invisible or transparent visitors while at my bench. They've shared how it's much easier for them to visit when I'm deeply concentrating on one thing like my work. Guess it's similar to how our brains work on many things at any given time. As when we are deeply concentrating on one thing, another part of our brain suddenly comprehends some other element than what we were thinking directly about. Spirits used to come visit me when I was in deep meditation. Now it's easier for them to come in when I'm working. I generally feel energy comes in from our left; however, spirits appear on my right side because I work with a left-hand torch. If they came in on my left, the flame would interfere with their energy. Don't know the proper terms here, maybe it's called ectoplasm? Anyway, they suddenly show up off to my right where I see them out of the corner of my eye. Remaining centered on the job at hand, I talk to them inside my head, and that's how I hear them respond as well. In intense moments of such deep concentration, it's actually comforting to have someone I knew come in to say hello even for a moment. That way my intensity is broken and . . . I don't ever feel alone; I mean really alone in life.

"Maybe because I've been seeing these spirits since childhood I don't find sudden appearances odd, disturbing or scary."

"Think I'd find it very scary! But then, I'm not you."

"Knowing you the little that I do, it's doubtful you'd be that disturbed by someone you knew in life that you liked appear as a spirit. Most likely they have come visiting already. Maybe in your sleep. Maybe when you awaken some mornings a deceased relative is on your mind without reason? If so, then perhaps they came calling during your sleep when your brain was relaxed enough to accept their visitation."

"You have an uncanny way of making something I would find extremely uncomfortable sound almost logical."

They both laughed. Finding their way through the discovering phase of a new relationship was in a very different realm for each person, at least in this particular dating experience. Vonnette was openly sharing and Frank wasn't sure what he believed any more. What he did know was that being with Vonnette was not dull.

At the end of the second evening together, yes, he began kissing her. Tender kisses. Inviting kisses. Lovely kisses actually. However, Vonnette didn't seem to get into them emotionally in the way that Frank did. What was wrong with her? Why wasn't a chemical connection happening? On so many other levels they seemed to be perfect for one another.

Vonnette sat and meditated. Deep breathing through her third eye charka helped to get her into a place of relaxation. Once there she began asking questions on the instructions she'd been given in the middle of the night.

Why was she supposed to give Frank up?

Why wasn't he right for her?

Would she ever meet someone who got her as much as Frank? If not, she might not give him up.

The questions were coming too quickly for responses. She felt the answer to the first question come, but the others might need to be asked of the pendulum.

While still breathing deeply Vonnette heard one question repeated in her head: "Why was Frank wrong for her?"

"Because it would be selfish if you hang onto him when you know you don't love him. You could be preventing him from finding his true, life mate."

This answer was not what she wanted to hear, nor was it something she would make up inside her head. But there it was staring her in the face each time she asked. Who was telling her this she did not know.

For the first time in Vonnette's life she wanted to be selfish and keep what was given so easily and willingly.

Opening her eyes after meditating, she knew she could not live with herself if she kept another person from finding who and what they were looking for. That was just not who she was. If she clung to someone or something that was not hers, truly hers, then she would not be walking her walk or talking her talk. So, telling him would be the next step. How could she present this to him? It would not be easy. Obviously Vonnette cared *for* him and *about* him. Now that she knew they had to go different ways she had to wrap her brain around that fact and then present it to him however she could.

Though a decision was made after meditating to tell Frank, Vonnette did not feel peaceful yet about that pronouncement. Pulling out her pendulum, Vonnette felt the need to do her homework and make sure she had confirmed answers through many means before acting upon anything. Her pendulum was a faceted round, glass crystal with a long thread attached. Something she had bought years back and used when she wanted immediate answers about health issues, or whatever.

Using the pendulum was a bit of a ritual. The thread attached to the crystal was about sixteen inches long. After wrapping the thread three times around her two, right hand first fingers, she would hold the exposed end thread in place between her thumb and index finger. Placing her left-hand index finger and thumb around the thread up next to the index finger of the right hand, she would pull her finger tips down towards the crystal quickly three times. Clearing the energy this way each time she made use of it allowed her to ask her questions without any energy hangover from the last usage.

Next, she placed her left hand flat on top of the kitchen counter close to where the pendulum hung in a still position slightly above the counter between her left-hand index finger and thumb. Vonnette could then begin asking her questions in earnest.

"What will you give me for a yes? What will you give me for a yes? What will you give me for a yes?"

When she had first discovered the pendulum and possibly how to use it, the suggestion was to sit on a straight-back chair and place her right elbow on her right knee. Allow the pendulum to hang in between slightly open knees. Then, begin by asking, "What motion will be given for a yes?"

After that is established then ask, "What pendulum motion will be given for a no?"

Over the years Vonnette had shortened that process and just asked what she would be given for the yes answer. It could be a clockwise circle swing of the pendulum. It might be a counter-clockwise swing. It could be a left to right movement in a straight line. It could move right to left, or even top to bottom. No matter what the response, Vonnette had a yes base line to work with for today. Simply put, she felt that anything other than that first yes response would obviously indicate a no, so there was no reason to go further than what the sign was for a yes. Today her yes was a counter-clockwise circle.

Sometimes the pendulum wouldn't move when she was asking for a yes baseline. When that happened, she would close her eyes and keep repeating her question, "What will you give me for a yes today? What will you give me for a yes today? . . ." By closing her eyes, she hoped she would not be psychically influencing the outcome of the swing as to what movement might be given for a yes. Someone had once shown Vonnette how she could make the pendulum swing in whatever direction she might desire simply by concentrating on it moving in one direction or the other. All that sounded a bit like "Let the Force be with you" to her. So, by closing her eyes while asking for a yes, Vonnette removed any idea of the pendulum's swinging specifically in one direction. When she did eventually reopen her eyes to find the pendulum swinging in one direction or another, she felt assured it was an authentic yes. Today, she thanked the powers that be for the core response and then waited for the pendulum to come to a full stop before asking a new question.

Standing absolutely still, she went into shallow breathing mode to make certain the pendulum didn't swing due to her breath. Leaning into the counter edge was an effort to stop any possible body movement that might influence the pendulum action. Last, Vonnette held her right elbow tightly up against her right side so her arm didn't move. All this was in an effort not to influence any motion of the pendulum.

"Is it the right thing I tell Frank I'm not feeling more than I am for him emotionally?" The pendulum swung in a counter-clockwise circle.

When it came to a full stop again she asked, "Should I wait to tell him this weekend when we are scheduled to get together?"

The pendulum took a wide swing in a clockwise direction. It had such a wide swing the answer could not be mistaken. Vonnette had a no answer.

After thanking it and waiting for the full stop again she then asked, "Should I tell Frank over the phone?" Counter-clockwise.

"Thank you. Should I tell him about how I was told to let him go?" The pendulum swung quite widely. No.

"Soooo, I get that I'm supposed to let Frank go. That there may be someone better for him than I, but is there someone out there for me?" Almost not moving, the pendulum swung in an almost undetectable counter-clockwise direction.

"Okay, thank you. I get it. Any break-up is painful. If we continue, it would be even more difficult after a longer period of time to say good-bye. That said, I do only wish the best for Frank and hope he does find the right woman quickly! He's too nice a man to miss any opportunity for real love."

In one of those ah ha moments, Vonnette quickly asked, "If I were to stay with Frank longer, would he or *could he* miss this woman?" The pendulum gave a direct yes answer.

Not wanting to become dependent upon use of the pendulum, Vonnette never asked it too many questions. Trusting this was it for now, she ran her index finger and thumb down the thread three more times to clear the energy and took hold of the crystal in the last swipe and said, "Thank you." After placing it with the cord wound up in circles in its own drawer in an antique clock maker's cabinet, she closed the drawer and felt certain she was on the right path. Vonnette had confirmation come from on high during the night, then again this morning while meditating, as well as from the pendulum of what she should do about Frank. There was nothing else she felt she could do other than end the relationship.

Sitting down on the couch for a moment, Vonnette felt sad and happy all at once. Sad that she and Frank would no longer be in one another's lives daily. Sad to have to say all this out loud to Frank when she knew he was already in that emotional place that transcends friendship. Happy, though that he had been in her life at all.

For this little segment in time, a full week really, she had connected with a man in ways she had not done before. By being completely herself, Vonnette was totally honest with him, up till now. Honest about her abilities. About her past experiences with men. About being abused. About when she was emotionally driven to scream at people. And even about how her right-hand index finger would uncontrollably go up when she was seriously angry. Sharing more with this man in a very short amount of time than she had done in years with even her closest friends left Vonnette wanting more! Unfortunately, it was not the same *more* that Frank wanted.

It would be sad not having her daily contact with him. How quickly she let this man into her world! Frank had been such an unexpected emotional gift to her at a time when she didn't know she needed it. Facing cancer at any time is difficult and she had felt so alone.

Vonnette hoped that she had been a gift to Frank, too. She had been the icebreaker companion after his father had passed away. Maybe she had shown him that possibilities existed in the romance department for him as well.

"Darn," she thought, "being true to your inner self can be one of the most difficult paths you travel in this life! Well, maybe next to cancer and any other possible death-related illness."

Unexpectedly the phone rang. Frank called earlier than usual. They caught up on normal conversation of what each wanted to accomplish for the day. He wondered if they might get together that night. Knowing this was a new week, one where Vonnette had a show coming up and time was getting tight for her, he figured the answer would be no. As it was a new relationship, and Frank was in that undeniable phase of *I still can't get enough of you*, he felt he had to ask even if the answer was no.

Vonnette began with what she had no idea how to say. "Frank, we have been getting very close very quickly. It's been wonderful on so many levels. Personally, I'm extremely grateful, but I am not feeling what you are when we kiss. Since we've been up front about so many deep issues, I feel it's important to discuss this."

Knowing instinctually where this conversation was headed, Frank interrupted. "That's something that will come with time. You're just learning to trust me and as such are holding yourself back a bit emotionally. With everything you've been going through of possibly having cancer, I'm sure you're still on edge. I'm not bothered by that and I don't think you should be either."

"The thing is, Frank, I do usually feel something when I kiss a man I am involved with. God, I know this is painful to hear. It's also painful to say!"

His words up until this point had been in a kind and calm voice. Now his verbal response came forth with a bit of anger and frustration attached. "So then don't say it."

"Frank, I would not be honest to who I am if I didn't say this out loud and then let you go forward with your life. That would be slighting you as well as me, to say nothing of the fact it would come between us for the rest of our time together." Vonnette was fishing to find words that would be gentle, sincere, but also honest. No such thing when it comes to a break up.

"Listen, I feel you are not giving us a chance here. Unless I'm wrong and you are not trying to break up with me? I mean, whenever we're together we can't stop talking. We haven't even had enough time together to go dancing, to a movie, or even antiquing yet. You're not giving us a chance!"

"I hear what you are saying, Frank, and I appreciate it all . . . but my emotional state won't shift. I'm not in my twenties. At this point in my life I know myself well enough to realize that if the emotional side has not jumped out to be front and center as yet, then it won't. Trust me, I wish it had. I enjoy your company so very much. Our time together has been important for us both, but it's time to let go of it now."

These moments are never easy for either party. Even if she was not an empath or a sensitive, having been on both sides of this kind of conversation, Vonnette could feel his pain deeply. There was an invisible element in the air that was not being spoken of by Vonnette. Though they had come so far and so quickly in communicating their beliefs, how could she convey that this message came to her from the other side?

He interrupted her thought pattern with shear agitation in his voice. "Vonnette, I don't get it. We can't stop talking on multiple levels either when we are together or when we're apart. I know it's only been a week, but we can't seem to get enough of one another. I mean when we are on the phone or by e-mail. How can you dismiss this, whatever it is so easily?"

"That's it, Frank, I am not dismissing this easily! Please don't think I'm letting go without a lot of serious consideration."

Frustrated with his need for information, Vonnette felt a slip coming. She couldn't help it. She did care. Having no desire to hurt him, she wanted Frank to know there was a reason, a very good reason for all this. "It's just that . . . it's just that I was told to let you go. Frank, I would not be walking my talk if I didn't pay attention to these kinds of messages! I was told during the night that our time has come to an end."

"If you want to end things I think it's because we've gotten close very quickly. I think you're frightened by it. If you want some space and time, then let me know that. You don't have to make things up like you've received a message about me."

Hearing Frank's last statement Vonnette wondered if in fact he had really understood her? He wasn't hearing what she was saying, or maybe he didn't want to hear it. Feeling backed into a corner emotionally with no conceivable way out of the conversation, she honestly didn't know what to say next. There had been no time for a rehearsal before he called. Maybe a story would help. It was the only thing in her head at this moment. Perhaps it was the right thing to do.

"We have been talking about how I have visions, Frank, and talk to spirits. You said you found everything about my visions very interesting. Let me tell you about a previous time I got involved with a man. For the longest time one vision kept appearing to me while I was fully awake. It expanded over the course of a few years into larger scenes. Everything began while working innocently in my garden at home here. Living across the street from a graveyard, I dismissed the visions at first, thinking I was seeing something that had taken place in the past. I was sure it was someone else's life. An apparition given by someone buried across the street. Soon, though, it became apparent this scene was supposed to be my life! These images were scenes of an outdoor wedding.

"During these moments of visualizations, it was like having a dream while being wide-awake. Perhaps having this kind of experience once or twice I could have dismissed it as a fluke. Over the next four years it became a weekly vision. Something I would see when I least expected it. I could be inside the house looking out the window. Then again, I could be in a car driving and see it all flash before my eyes in a transparent fashion. Eventually, I saw a house on the side of a road midway up a mountain. Parts of the exterior and interior of that house worked their way into my waking dream. At one point, I shared these visions with a friend. Before I even finished describing the images, she told me details about that same wedding dress I had been seeing. My friend as well as I thought it amazing that we both saw the same dress. I had not met any man at that time that even caught my attention let alone someone who struck me as a person I could spend a married life with. Nor did I ever see the face of the man in all those images.

"Unexpectedly, after those years of experiencing the same visions, I met a man while walking in and out of stores downtown. We began dating and felt we had a lot in common emotionally. In a very short time we became close. One day he was supposed to call and didn't. When he did choose to call, I was hurt. That emotion came out as anger directed towards him. Yelling, I said I didn't deserve to be treated in that way, nor would I accept it.

"Following that ill-fated moment of lost temper, I waited for him to call me back.

"He waited for me to call and apologize.

"By the time I did call to apologize, it was done, over.

"To this day I stand behind what I said, but hated my delivery.

"Yelling never resolves anything.

"In the end, the apparitions from my garden stopped. He was the opportunity from my visions that I didn't trust. Beating myself up for a few years, I thought I ought to have done something differently to bring forth an outcome that connected to my daydreams, if you will. Feeling I had let the universe down with my being stubborn, I pulled back from dating. That man and I had a deep connection, too, and the emotional side was there for us both. After that fateful phone conversation, our heart connection went away.

"The point in telling you this story is . . . all the dreams and visions I had back then could not make something happen. He was still a gift for me as he came into my life after years of my not dating. Honestly, I thought I would never find someone to connect with on that level again. I had given up. Learning after such a long time I could care deeply for a man was great. Believing in myself enough not to accept crap from a man was terrific. What wasn't wonderful was how long it took me to understand that my dream messages and visions were in place to bring me the experience only. They did not magically tell me of an end result. What transpired between him and me was like a marriage that happened in a split-second. That was all part of my life lesson. It took a long time for me to grasp that this man had provided a lot for me in the way of gifts. Now I am living more in the moment . . . like any other mortal," they said simultaneously.

Frank had been quiet through this whole story seemingly interested in every word. Perhaps he thought the outcome would be different if he waited till the end. He chose this moment to chime in. "Your visions really stopped when that other relationship ended?"

Nodding, yes, Vonnette realized she had to say it out loud as they were on the phone. She took a sip of water and said, "Yes."

"You feel he was a gift in a few ways. I get that idea and can agree. However, I don't understand the years of visions beforehand."

"Since I rely so much on dream messages for guidance in my life, I think my spirit guides wanted to make sure I didn't miss that opportunity for growth or the actual connection. Maybe if we had both been younger we would have actually married one another. Maybe we were married in another life. Being of a certain age provides some wisdom. My point is . . . in a weird way I think we were married for a moment in time on this plane emotionally. Hopefully, we each learned something from one another. What he learned from me is none of my business. I learned that not only do I *deserve* to be treated better, but now I also *believe* I deserve to be treated better. That situation took place over the course of a few months in actual physical time. The dreams and visions had all happened over the course of a prior four-year period.

"The problem I had from this gift, Frank, was that I turned back to eating sweets again after being off them for over seven years. Somehow I felt I had let the universe down with not being able to follow through on all those visions. Punishing myself physically with food became a norm. Eventually, I came to understand the visions were like exclamation points, something provided for me to catch the importance of the connection no matter how brief. The gift is always what you do with what life places in your path. It can be a dung heap, a bed of roses, or even in between. At that juncture, I had thought my visions were telling me I was supposed to have married that man. Now, though, I feel the visions were about the intense time spent together. Like a marriage of sorts."

"Have you had any visions of us?" Frank asked thoughtfully. "You said you had a message to break up. I hear that. What I'm asking is ... have you had visions during the day about us like you did that guy?"

Smiling, Vonnette wished she was looking into Franks tender eyes. Knowing without seeing him in the physical that he was searching for a way to make a connection happen beyond what they had at this moment. "Frank, I have not had any day visions. What I have had is a straight forward message during my dreamtime. I was awakened by the messages coming through."

His emotions were close to the surface and that caused Vonnette to drop her guard a tad. Feeling his need to interrupt, she began speaking a bit more quickly to stop him. "Last night, specifically, I was wakened by Spirit if you will, to hear someone telling me it was time to give you up. I fought with that instruction. You are a nice man, and I deserve to have a nice man in my life and said so to Spirit. I put up a fight. Once I was fully awake I realized I would not be walking my talk if I did not walk away from us.

"Please know this has been a very challenging decision on my part. You've been wonderful to me. Not to keep repeating myself, but you have been a gift. Knowing there might be someone out there who will love you as you deserve to be loved is my consolation in letting you go.

"And, I feel our connection, however brief, has run its course, just as that other relationship had. You and I were wonderful together for the short time we've shared. You told me you had been closed down emotionally after your dad passed, and that I had swung that door open again. If you can look at everything from that perspective, it's lovely really. I'm thrilled I could in some small way have been a portal for your emotions."

"I just do not get this. You are fighting with spirits about not letting me go, and now you are doing just that?" Came his plea with a sincere edge.

It was hitting her just then how she should not have informed Frank of everything that transpired during the night. But, she had. So, now she had to deal with the fallout from letting that cat out of the bag. Spirit had told her not to tell him, and yet, here she was doing exactly that!

"Since I was wakened during the middle of the night, Frank, I have been wrestling with this idea of holding on or letting go. Please hear me. I am blessed to have found you for this brief moment in time. You've shown me there are wonderful men out there who can possibly understand and support me emotionally. To me, that means so very much. With all the different conversations we've had to date, you know I listen to the messages given from on high. Since I've not had an emotional reaction to your gentle and giving kisses, I have to trust the messages are right. And that it's time for us to part before we get to a place of comfort. If we get there, then it'll be so much more difficult to walk away."

Vonnette hoped she was not being hurtful.

"Don't you think you're putting up road blocks not to get involved with me? It's just that we've only been seeing one another for a week. We've spoken every day and night. Numerous times even each day, but still, it's just been a week."

"No, Frank, I feel sad not to continue on with our relationship. Don't you think it's better to find all this out now? I mean rather than to have it happen after a few months where we've seriously begun to share daily lives?" Vonnette hoped she was connecting on some deep level with him at this moment.

"It seems your experiences in dating are on a whole other level than anything I've ever known. Maybe you know more than most. Maybe you're cheating with additional information we mortals are not privy to." Frank seemed to be thoughtful with this response.

Chuckling, and thinking he was kidding with her, Vonnette asked, "So I'm not mortal?"

"I'm not sure, and feel under qualified to answer." His voice sounded deeply wounded. "This was not where I thought today would lead." He began to sound despondent.

After a moment of silence where Vonnette thought they were each deeply contemplating losing one another, he almost yelled, "Are you serious? Are you really breaking this off? All this because of some message you received last night? After the story you just told me, how do you know that the message from last night was true and not just another one of those messages telling you to pay attention?"

"I've fought with wherever the message came from during the night. I've meditated. I've pursued this from different angles to make sure I received the message correctly, that I'm not mistaken. If we remain together you might miss out on a true love. What if we stayed together for a period of time and still fell apart in the end? Wouldn't I be a selfish cow if I kept you from meeting another woman who was perfect for you?" Vonnette felt she was fighting an uphill battle and her tone showed it.

"No. Unacceptable. Unexpected for certain after what we've shared together verbally thus far. I don't believe it, that whatever this is isn't supposed to go further. You're just putting up roadblocks not to have a true relationship. This is unbelievable. I cannot believe you, this . . ."

As his words trailed off a bit, Vonnette took the opportunity to repeat what she was claiming. No matter how difficult it was to do, she felt she had to carry forward. "My message was so clear. Spirit woke me, so I wouldn't allow the message to be pushed into the back recesses of my mind. You are wonderful. I have enjoyed our time together. I don't believe in being with a man who seems to be right for just this moment. I believe in forever love. Unconditional love. Love that gets you through the hard times people share together. Don't you think you deserve that?"

If she stopped now the tears that were taking shape would win. As Vonnette took a deep breath, she continued, "Frank, unfortunately it has been made very clear to me that you have been a gift for me for the brief moment we've shared. Hopefully, I have been one for you as well. We opened each other's eyes up to what is possible. Now it's time to let go and move on. Certainly, you don't believe me as I say I'm not pleased with this message. I would not be walking my talk if I didn't heed that message and let you move on. Seriously, you are a wonderful man. You've given me hope that someday I will find another nice man. The next woman you care for will possibly be the one whom you are supposed to be with. Maybe at some point you'll come to view this moment as a true psychic reading instead of a break up."

Suddenly silent and emotionally spent, Vonnette sat with her eyes fixed on the living room wall. He was angry and felt betrayed.

"If you want to end something, just end it. There's no need for all this message stuff." Frank was now speaking in a dismissive way. Feelings hurt, he wanted his emotions to be known. How could he fight with an invisible force such as Spirit? He did the only thing he could think of; he dissed her life method.

Maybe it was all the hurt feelings speaking right now and not his true self. Her heart was breaking for both of them. But if she didn't break it off, she wouldn't be honoring her true self. She wouldn't be honoring her visions, her dreams. She would not be honoring how she enjoyed his company, but was not in love with him.

It was unpleasant as most break-ups are, but they did call it quits that day.

Sadness results from any relationship difficulties. People from Vonnette's inner circle felt they'd been there and gave voice to understanding but, how could they? Simply put, not everyone lived their dream messages the way Vonnette did and most of her friends couldn't grasp her letting go of a seemingly nice man due to a dream-type message. Vonnette did fight with the powers of that message only to be told to let go in no uncertain terms! She would have to live with that decision and trust it was time to move forward.

When the story was shared with her friend, Jennifer, she thought Vonnette was brave to have fought with Spirit. She guessed it took a Scorpio to have stood her ground in such a way.

Vonnette simply thought she was standing up for what she felt was her due. After that, Spirit convinced her it was indeed time to move on before things got ugly. This ending was dreadful enough for her. Maybe if they had hung on longer, their break-up would have been even worse than it was at this time.

Pondering her decision to end their relationship over the next few days, Vonnette was grateful she left out the very end of the story about Joseph when she shared it with Frank. Feeling strongly that it was not finished between she and Joseph after many months had passed, Vonnette was amazed when they unexpectedly ran into one another downtown in Washington Square.

Agreeing to have a casual nosh around the corner at The Brick Alley Pub, it seemed as though no time had passed. He still looked good to her even though those steel gray eyes of his said, "Trouble."

He was in town visiting a friend who owned a boat moored at the end of Banister's Wharf. They had been school chums of some sort. Light repartee` such as this had been the main course of their conversation over appetizers and a drink for him, while Vonnette ate a bit and drank her water. Being the middle of the day and hopeful of an approaching auspicious opportunity, she didn't want to have alcohol blur her mind.

Pessimistic they would eventually get around to the past, she waited and waited to no avail. He somehow seemed nervous all the way through their get together. Unable to really get a word in, Vonnette felt the kismet moment of their running into one another was for naught. This wasn't going to turn into something she had long hoped for, an in-person apology for that ugly day when she had screamed at him.

There simply was no correct time to bring that incident up. Giving up, she excused herself for a ladies' room run upstairs. When she came out of the lounge, she was caught completely of guard at the sight of Joseph standing in wait. He had paid the bill when the waitress asked if she could have the table back since there was now a line waiting to be seated. He wanted to make sure Vonnette didn't feel deserted by going back to an empty table. Thinking that was all there was to the moment, she was taken by surprise when he then leaned in towards her as if to kiss.

They'd had good chemistry when they first connected, but time had passed and this meeting was not about that for Vonnette. Placing her hand on his chest was an effort to stop him from completing the pass. Maybe it was the actual physical contact with Joseph at that second, or perhaps it was this quiet space on the second floor that somehow afforded Vonnette the opportunity to see their relationship clearly. It was now crystal clear why he was so nervous through their time together today and why their relationship came to such an abrupt halt. He couldn't handle how she spoke with the dead, knew things before they might happen, and how over the long term their relationship could be more one-sided in her favor rather than his. Balance of power is a funny thing. His machismo ultimately couldn't take living in her world. It was another of her vision moments where she couldn't deny what she saw.

Here, Vonnette found her voice for the first time since they had run into one another. "You know, Joseph, I suddenly get it. Why we couldn't carry forward all those months back. It's because you can't cope with how my life functions. That's okay. You're not the first, and most likely you won't be the last. But here's the thing, we had good chemistry. Maybe that's all you're looking for in a relationship. What I'm looking for is someone who accepts all of me, *and* who shares good physicality with me.

"Perhaps you think this unknown energy affords me an unfair advantage.

"Maybe you think this metaphysical involvement on my part threatens your masculinity.

"Honestly, that's none of my business. However, I finally grasp the real reason why we came to an end months back, and for me, that's a win, win. Thanks for the reunion and the appetizers. It was great to see you, but I need to go now."

She made a motion of leaving the space he'd created with his arms on either side of her and the wall when without warning, he grabbed a serious hold and kissed her with a probing tongue that was seriously searching for something.

Though Vonnette allowed the kiss, even enjoyed it, she wondered just why he felt the need to complete the pass. Maybe, Spirit was telling her it *had* been completely physical between them. Maybe he couldn't handle that she knew precisely why he chose to leave their relationship. Maybe he had to feel he had physical power over her just then to boost his lack of verbal control.

Whatever spell had been holding onto her about their relationship was broken that instant. Seeing their end clearly allowed her also to grasp why the backyard wedding visions had ceased. Even though she'd held onto some weird thread of hope, she realized now that they were actually over before they began. Finally, she had an answer to what had happened. It might not be a complete answer, nor was it one she expected in any manner, shape, or form. The answer she had, though, was enough to ascertain that whatever their relationship had been; it sincerely was over, and that the real reason had nothing to do with the outburst on her part that fateful day of screaming.

Conveying this event to her closest friends later that week, she was honest about what had happened. How running into him had felt as if it was meant to be on one level, and how it turned into another unexpected form of completion entirely. In any case, she couldn't control what she knew or when understanding might come through any more than she could control the tide. Lovers she'd had thus far had not been able to accept her one-hundred percent. It was vital for Vonnette to know that she was not only accepted, but was also lovable at any given moment, just as she wanted to love and accept whomever she was with the same way.

Sharing this experience with friends only solidified her resolve that things were over.

As Vonnette thought back about Joseph now, it was with clarity. They had come together for that moment when they were supposed to. Vonnette had the full closure she'd craved.

At this interval, she had to deal with Frank and all that he had meant to her during their short time together. Though it was just a week, their story was intense on many levels, too. Today, she saw that Joseph and Frank shared one common denominator, neither of these men could really cope with Vonnette's communication with the dead and how she would unexpectedly know things.

Maybe each man thought she would one day see through them and know they had fears and insecurities. Vonnette thought, "It's funny how being human is never enough. Each person in a relationship feels insecure about one thing or another. Fear their partner could see who he or she is deep inside is the doubtfulness that could hold each party back from all that might be theirs."

Maybe she would never meet someone that filled the bill she desired, chemistry along with communication and room for all her beliefs. Even if another partner didn't share her beliefs, Vonnette had to hold onto the thought that there could be a man out there who respected her beliefs as well as the fact that she did walk her talk. Certainly, she could and would give another man space to have his own beliefs if different from hers. It was also important for this other person to be interested in life outside their relationship, and that would help keep them interesting to one another. There needed to be common ground through communication inside and out of the bedroom, or it wouldn't last. And Vonnette was looking for a relationship that would last.

⁂

After a few days of tears and thoughts of calling to see how Frank was, Vonnette told herself she had done what she needed to do. Instead, she called one of her close friends who usually had an interesting slant on things.

Jennifer was a woman whose hair had turned white when she was in her twenties. Of course, now that she was fifty it was almost fitting. That thick white mop contributed to the glow Jenn had and partly what people were attracted to. No one ever mentioned the white aura surrounding her or the snaps of light that popped off her as she spoke for fear that no one else saw them. But, it was also partly responsible for what made people want to be near her, to see if perhaps those pops would somehow land on them to create some form of magic.

While sharing the experience of Frank with Jennifer once again, face-to-face now, each woman understood how the split had to happen once Spirit gave Vonnette the message to let him go.

Jennifer also understood how it must have been a difficult thing to do knowing what Vonnette had been going through with the cancer scare and all. Suddenly, Jennifer began to do her white light popping thing, and her eyes sparkled like stars meeting sunshine as she said, "You know, this is good! I mean really good!"

Caught off guard at how the conversation had energetically shifted, Vonnette portrayed her query all over her face.

"I mean, you've had a bunch of experiences with men over time where physically you couldn't get enough of one another. And this time, you had serious, open conversations and communications with Frank. A man you were interested in being more than friends with. Even though he said he understood what you were talking about, and in the end, he didn't really, the two of you were able to talk outside the bedroom, if you will. That was serious growth for you! So, what, if your time together was short. You got what you needed from that moment. You grew! And, you and I both know that it only takes as long as it takes!"

Jennifer was right, of course, but Vonnette wasn't through licking her wounds as yet. Noticing the still sad look on Vonnette's face, Jennifer's voice went soft. "Oh, I'm sorry. This is not what you wanted me to say right now. But here's the thing . . . you and I both feel we are here to learn and that all this education is carried with us from one life to another. So, growth is important. This guy Frank allowed you to learn something about yourself. You were vulnerable physically just then with the cancer scare as well as psychologically, and yet you let him in. Not only that, you were willing to allow him to see the whole you, including the parts of you that are normally hidden from the men you date out of fear of their bolting. And, when you were told to let him go, you did! In spite of your arguments with Spirit, you did the right thing and walked away.

"I still can't believe you had the gumption to argue with Spirit! You Scorpio you! However, this means that not only did you grow, and you did eventually listen to Spirit, but you also allowed Frank to learn something that he can carry forward to his next relationship. That is, that there are other types of people in the universe who have different points of view and experiences than what he has had thus far before meeting you. Now when he gets together with the woman he is supposed to be with, he will have a wider range of comprehension of who any woman can be at any given moment.

"I really do think this was good on all fronts. And I believe you should take the time necessary to heal the emotional wounds you have right now. But, in the end you'll see what I see, and that's a brighter future all around."

Her pops of white light suddenly faded as Jennifer said she would like some tea, indicating that the serious conversation was finished.

Vonnette obligingly got up off the couch and made tea for them both knowing she still had things to process emotionally from this break-up. At this moment, she needed to have tea, change the subject, and spend some quality time with her enlightening friend.

After Jenifer left that day, Vonnette thought about how her life progressed through visions and dream messages from the other side. The other side of what, who knew for sure?

Once, when much younger, she'd asked her father (a self-proclaimed agnostic) if he believed in continuous life? After such a long pause on his part that she thought she would not receive an answer, he did finally speak. "I'm not sure what I believe, but I don't think this is it."

That was enough for Vonnette to have hope that the family she'd chosen to be born into this go 'round had some qualities of connection to her belief system. Her mother had been gone for so many years at that point and their relationship had been a strain before she parted, so Vonnette had long given up on that kind of bond with her parents. It was nice to know that door had not completely closed.

Yes, she was home, and the lights were on. She talked to her mother and maternal grandfather even though they were departed; she always wondered though, if they all were still in body would they have these kinds of conversations?

Many different kinds of spirits came to visit Vonnette. What she really wanted to know was how did that help her now? Even though she took great comfort in the fact that spirits spoke to her, she had no idea just who had told her what to do about Frank. Maybe it was the same energy who screamed at her on her drive up to Northampton to the Paradise City Show. Most likely, none of that really mattered in the end. What did matter was the fact that she had received the message, paid heed and walked her talk. Following through with the guidance given, time would have to bring in whatever was next.

Speaking out loud to whomever, Vonnette said, "It's interesting how you cannot ever tell if someone will affect you in an emotional and chemical way or not."

Frank had affected her. He touched her heart and her soul. He was a port in the storm for her during that trying time of possibly having cancer. Somehow a nice man had come into Vonnette's life when she thought she was on the downside of health. Somehow that relationship was a sign that she had turned a corner in the men she would accept, or invite in. Vonnette hoped she would no longer be attracted to the bad boy mentality and only accept healthfully spirited men.

Once again, speaking to the invisible. "When I care about someone, be it through love or friendship, I want only the best for them, no matter what that might be. And, if I was not the best for Frank, then I do sincerely hope he finds that true love with someone else who really appreciates him and his kisses more than I did. Doubt I'll ever know if he does find that person, but at least I am walking my talk! I've got to make peace with it all now."

Welcoming the what's next concept in her daily life, Vonnette sincerely hoped the message she received was true about Frank meeting the right person once she gave him up.

It was here she shrugged her shoulders to let go of all the wondering that came with any breakup where the mind overthought all decisions made and roads taken. Content with life being slow at least momentarily, she chose a movie to watch to forget and to stop thinking!

CHAPTER 6

Marlborough

November 14-16 2008
Set up Thursday the 13th

14Kg Stelagtite Quartz Ring, 22Ky Turquoise Ring

Candace L. Sherman

DREAMS

1. Turquoise and clear quartz were dancing about in Vonnette's face as if some form of human life existed inside each stone.

2. Entering a door to a business location with Bruce Willis. He was appalled the door had a top section while the bottom two-thirds was missing. That top portion of the door was propped up in place. Bruce and Vonnette went off together to get a new door that he would install.

During her almost two-hour drive from Newport, Vonnette had plenty of time to review her dream messages. Use clear quartz to promote mental clarity while turquoise represents some form of birth. A famous person in a dream means help from an unexpected source.

Vonnette's set up in Marlborough today was done with high hopes. Everything went smoothly as her booth took form. Lights were working correctly. She opted to leave them turned off as well as unplugged just in case the artist behind her began to plug and unplug things as what had happened in Northampton. Once burnt, twice shy was her thinking there. While walking outside her booth to form a client perspective, Vonnette thought out loud, "If I don't learn from the past with my lighting plugs, then shame on me." Already experiencing clarity through wearing quartz today, and a possible birth from her turquoise ring, Vonnette felt her stone messages connected to her booth lighting.

This well-established indoor show was the second one for the same promoter who organized the Northampton show. Both were known as Paradise City. Their two show events ran for three consecutive days. The one in Northampton was Saturday, Sunday and Monday over the Columbus holiday weekend. Size wise, it spilled out into numerous buildings, so attendees needed the supplied map especially if they wanted to return to a booth after pondering a purchase. This Marlborough show would be open Friday, Saturday and Sunday. Being a Veterans holiday weekend, the extra day off for

most people could be either a Friday or a Monday. The show promoters felt that even if Friday was not their holiday, many people
would still take that day off to attend. One building alone housed
this event, so the show itself was smallish. No map was necessary
although one was still provided.

It was only a few short weeks back when her booth in Northampton was across from the donation table for cancer where Vonnette
thought she, too, had cancer. She felt good about the possibilities
for this show even though it was her first time participating. Being
run by the same organizers, their invitation mail-list would be the
same, so there ought to be a similar attendance. And, a smaller
venue meant less competition from other jewelers. Perhaps this
show would harvest even better financial results without that possible death sentence of cancer hanging over her head.

Finished with her set-up surprisingly ahead of schedule, Vonnette opted to go back to her hotel room and straighten something
out over the phone. A notification that claimed she'd been denied
credit when in fact she had not applied for any credit lately came
through the mail this past week. With the company on the phone,
she went over the notification bit by bit. Under the reason for refusal
of credit a box had been checked off claiming Vonnette didn't have
enough collateral. According to the records the woman was looking
at, Vonnette had refused to apply for this credit card, which was
true. Why then did she have this refusal of credit in her hands?
Information was not forthcoming. Vonnette asked for a manager.

Inability to handle difficult customers was never a good thing for
these phone representatives. They didn't want to hand any phone
client over to a manager. They were supposedly trained on how to
deal with all kinds of customers and as such, should have no need to
bother their managers. No matter what, Vonnette knew a manager
was hired to manage!

Vonnette worked at not losing her temper and waited as long
as it took to get a manager on the line. Eventually a man came on
claiming that the mail out Vonnette received was not worth the
paper it was printed on. In fact, Vonnette had not applied and

therefore was not refused credit. And, no, this supposed refusal of credit would not be going on her credit report. Not trusting this man's word because she was staring at this weird statement, she asked for a written apology to be mailed. He was taken aback and couldn't understand the need for such a thing. Vonnette told him she was in business for herself and should anything like that happen between her clients and her, she most certainly would follow up with a letter of apology. Ultimately, she wanted the letter in case something did ever show up on her credit report. Such a letter of apology would null and void it.

He said he would do as asked.

He had provided help from an unexpected source, so the dream about Bruce Willis was now in front of her fully answered. Except... there was a door element in that dream, too.

Though the end result made her glad she'd made time to call and follow through on this false statement, it also made her think about money yet again. Having a paper trail was always a good thing, but why had this false statement happened to begin with? Money was a life-long issue for Vonnette. Sometimes she felt her problems with money resulted from pre-birth: all the struggles her parents had had with money when she was in the womb carried over to Vonnette's existence even today.

Yes, artists had difficulties with money since the beginning of time. However, some artists had steady income, so why wasn't that the case for Vonnette? What could she have possibly missed in the gene pool for success?

Lack of money had to be a learned pattern! Anything learned could be shifted. Just as Vonnette had begun to shift the type of men she dated. After a lot of inner personal work, Vonnette did finally feel ready to accept good men into her life and that she *deserved* good men in her life. Wasn't Frank a perfect example of that concept? Why then couldn't she wrap her brain around this whole money thing?

Somewhere along the line Vonnette either read or heard inside her head that it wasn't about the end result. Rather, it was the process that counted. Often wondering just who would make such a claim, she was sure it could only have been made by someone with money. What Vonnette did know was that once she could locate the root to an old inner issue, a new behavior pattern could then be created.

Was her half-door in the dream a message concerning her ideas about money? Would more help from an unexpected source provide a new door on that front for her today? Maybe standing up for herself on the phone gave birth to new ideas of how Vonnette felt she *deserved* to be treated concerning finances. Ever hopeful, Vonnette's thoughts focused on how clear quartz and turquoise could possibly provide clarity for her and then birth on how to create financial bliss.

November 14, Friday 2008

DREAMS

1. Vonnette was talking on the phone with someone while a friend stood in the room. Noticing a squirrel jump onto the side of the house, she attracted the friends' attention. Though she continued speaking on the phone, she became agitated and yelled as the squirrel climbed up inside the house. Her friend, Todd, grabbed a stepladder and put it up towards the board blocking the attic. Certain he would not be able to get up into the attic with that ladder as it was a bit short, she tried to motion for him to wait until she hung up the phone and found the taller ladder. Not seeing her, he forged ahead anyway. When she looked away and then glanced back, Vonnette realized Todd had made it up into that upper level with the smaller ladder and was now in search of the squirrel. Next thing, he commented on how much space there was up there and how it could be made over into a perfect room!

2. Vonnette watched as a woman told Oprah Winfrey to open her handbag. While picking up the handbag, Oprah asked if the woman meant this one? Nodding the answer yes, Oprah opened it up slowly, glanced inside, then reached in and pulled out a Publishers Clearing House winning entry. Everyone looked with glee as the woman nodded yes again, meaning Oprah had won. Everyone proclaimed joy knowing that Oprah would be taken care of financially for the rest of her life with the sweepstakes win.

In general, though both dreams were fairly straight forward, Vonnette still wondered what the squirrel dream could represent other than some form of aggravation coming her way this day.

In real life, tiny ants had begun to invade her kitchen once again. When these sugar ants appeared in her life, they always seemed to mark a difficult period of some sort to Vonnette.

Over many years of gardening, nests of ants would be disturbed and then they would reestablish themselves. While stepping over them as much as possible, she would tell the ants that as long as they remained out of doors she would let them live as peacefully as she could.

Eventually though, they came into the house through each floor in different locations searching for food in the kitchen, trash bin, countertops, empty food plates waiting to be washed, and even the cats' food on the second floor. Trails came in around the front door, crossed the hallway into the living room and under the couch. Vonnette even spotted lines of them out on the front porch where no food could be found. These tiny dark spotted trails appeared to be coming in from behind electrical outlets, from under the stove, from behind the radiators and through windows. Any miniscule hole in her house was subject to their armies. Marching in full formation their sheer volume was to be reckoned with. These ants seemed to be oblivious to her efforts to make them leave the premises.

In years past Vonnette's cats brought fleas in her house after they would go outside. Having fleas jump around on the floors and then on to human skin is an experience no one should have to go through.

Tiny ants crawling everywhere in her home including her couch made her feel invaded upon; she also hated how the ants felt being in her hair. They hitched a ride on the fur of one of her cats and somehow climbed over onto Vonnette's long hair and then onto her head.

This was war! Vonnette had tried to be nice and talk them out of her world but without success. Experimenting with any known method, she began with store-bought ant cups. Once, she had carpenter ants come into her dining room through a window. Knowing how destructive they could be, she immediately took action. Ant cups worked in that instance. Unfortunately, sugar ants were impervious to ant cups or even the wiping down of any and all surfaces with Windex to remove any scent they might experience in their tiny world. Food was never left out. Utilizing tiny bags for garbage, Vonnette took those out to the yard bin once or twice a day. Even the cats had to wait to be fed instead of a steady dish of dry food on the floor. No trash, no food about, and still these relentless armies marched on in.

Eventually she gave up. She called the exterminators, and they came to do their thing. Vonnette was nervous the poison sprayed about the floor and baseboards of her home would kill her cats. Reassured that such a thing would not happen, she still went around after the exterminator left and washed down the floors close to the edges of the baseboards in an effort to keep the poison away from any tiny feet that might walk on top of, be touched by, and then later licked off their paws. It was unbelievable she had paid for this service and yet, here she was removing some of what she had just paid for. Vonnette knew she was acting nuts. She also knew how much she loved these four legged children and, wouldn't be able to live with herself if in some way that poison caused either of them harm!

The ants seemingly knew danger was afoot and stayed away for a few days. Then, they came back.

One day while explaining her frustrating situation to her beloved aunt, she was given a sure fix that sounded so simple. "Use a product called *Terro*," her aunt said, explaining that Vonnette should place a drop or so in the path of these tiny efficient invaders; somehow, that would be all that was necessary. They would take that clear, thick liquid poison back to their nest, eat it as well as share it, and slowly would stop their long line coming in and throughout her home. Having tried everything else she could think of, Vonnette felt this new idea was worth a visit even if it sounded simple.

For some reason her ants seemed to ignore most of the tiny drops suggested by her aunt. Vonnette had to become fiercer. After collecting bottle caps from her almond milk cartons, she placed many drops of Terro inside and put these caps as far under where ever the ants were crawling in from to keep the caps out of reach of her cats. This method worked! As the caps were emptied, she either refilled them and repositioned them, or Vonnette would use new caps. Her decision to refill or replace caps depended upon if the tops were full of dead ant carcasses or simply empty of the liquid poison. Each year she had to revisit this method. For some weird reason the ants took vacations during the cold winter days and then returned each spring.

Though seemingly gone, the chilly fall weather brought the ants back in full force without warning, entering from under her kitchen sink. The line went on and on. In this go-round, they spread all over her kitchen. No surface safe from their coming on into her food preparation, Vonnette wondered if this could be, in some weird way, a reference to her cancer scare. If so, she thought they should be long gone since that experience had ended.

No such luck!

Vonnette reflected on her dream message from the night before about the squirrel entering her house and the fact that there seemed to be more space in her attic than she knew of. Maybe while she was at this show the ants would vacate her house. Or, maybe the squirrel meant there would be an aggravate at the show, and the discovered space represented a shift of her mindset away from whatever issue was presented. Always hopeful for good end results, Vonnette clung to the thought that extra space in her attic must be a benefit.

Somehow, now at the show venue and while setting up her booth for the day ahead, Vonnette's mind shifted gears and went back to a time when she had participated in past life regressions. Why hadn't she thought to ask about financial blocks when she did those hypnotized sessions? In one session she was able to discover who some people were in her life today, who also existed in that other life. Making those associations of the past with the present allowed Vonnette to gain insight of why certain relationships existed. So, why then, didn't she learn how to be out of a financial dead zone in this life, since some of those past lives had been okay financially.

Seemingly on overload, Vonnette couldn't wait for the doors to open to be mentally distracted.

While working to come back to reality, Vonnette reminded herself it was Friday morning. Looking over her booth she felt everything was displayed well and looked inviting. When people began to walk through, she realized she recognized a few faces from Newport. Surprised they traveled almost two hours to view the show, she thought about people who follow antique shows, so why not do the same for fine art and craft shows? About that time one recognizable person entered into her booth. Smiling, Vonnette welcomed her into the space and show.

Sharon Blount had been an occasional client over many years. With short blonde hair and honey colored brown eyes, she had a yoga-type body with nice tone. Sharon pulled out a small cloth pouch, placed it on top of one of the glass cases, and began to open it. While doing so, she explained that one of the prongs on the boulder opal pendant had snapped. Frustration was written on her face.

Once the pendant had been handed over for examination, Vonnette smiled and told Sharon it could be fixed. Price would run approximately $100 due to the fact that the stone had to be removed from the mounting in order to complete the repair and then be remounted.

Seemingly on the edge emotionally, Sharon demanded an explanation. "But why did this happen? The pair of earrings you made for me hasn't ever had any issues."

Feeling as well as hearing her frustration, Vonnette began a possible explanation hoping it would smooth the ruffled feathers. "Okay, here's the deal. Your earrings go on in the morning, and I'm guessing you don't play with them as you do your pendant. I've watched you fiddle with this pendant over many years. That causes wear and tear. Also, the pendant is on a long cord that can either be hit or caught in things. This particular pendant has numerous prongs going up and over the stone to protect it from being bumped and scraped. The stone has not broken, which is a testament that the prongs are doing their job. Better to have the metal wear or break away than the stone to crack, break, or possibly even disappear out of the mounting.

"Here's what I say when things like this happen to mountings, think of your pendant as you would a car. They're both metal. You use your car daily. You take it in for service every few months. Often times there are bits that give way from wear and tear. That's considered normal. Usually, we all go along with whatever estimate an auto place suggests without much questioning. Yet, somehow, with gold jewelry, people think it ought to never need another look or work done on it when in fact, it's metal, just like your car is metal. If I recall, you bought this piece when I was in my store on Bellevue Avenue. If so, then you've had it for twelve years. How many cars have you had in that amount of time?"

A look of understanding began to cross Sharon's face. "I've had two, and honestly need to think about a new one."

"Okay, then, you've had two cars and are ready for a third. In all that time, you've had countless visits to the mechanic for work. In twelve years, this is your first visit to me in need of a repair. Look at this from my perspective. These are not bad odds for something made out of metal that is used almost daily like a car."

"You know, I came here today because I saw the show listed on your web site along with your booth number. Honestly, I was feeling angry with you for faulty workmanship. Now I'm thinking you do such a terrific job that I have only needed work done on the pendant once in twelve years! And, you're right, I do wear this pendant almost daily because I love it so. It also feels good to touch. It's like a worry stone for me. Actually, I haven't had anything done to my earrings in all that time either. Guess your work surpasses anything else that's metal in my life! Thanks for making me see this experience through different eyes!"

"Not a problem. I always say you should never ask a question you don't want an answer to. You got an answer to your question and are, thankfully, happy about it. Sincerely, I have numerous clients who've had similar experiences. Generally, I use the car analogy. Most everyone gets the point because we are an automobile-oriented society. To spend a hundred dollars in twelve years to maintain this pendant I sincerely don't think is asking too much.

"There are jewelry designers who make their pieces with such thin metal there is no way they could last many years without repairs. The logic is that once the jewelry breaks you'll stop back in to have it fixed and will then buy something new to take the place of whatever piece is broken. I like to make my jewelry to last for as long as possible.

"I know I do good work that lasts. I also know what practices are in place with other jewelers and don't feel intimidated when someone seems a bit miffed over having to pay for a repair." Feeling this was a bit of a diatribe, Vonnette could see the client not only got the point, she now understood the pieces she owned were of exceptional quality and in fact even better than any car she had owned!

"Everything happens for a reason," Vonnette said as she wrote up a receipt for Sharon. Facing down a possible irate client with respect showed Vonnette she was standing up for herself and that in itself was a very good thing! Placing Sharon's opal pendant safely away in the rear of a showcase, Vonnette handed the repair slip over to Sharon and they said good-bye.

Sharon came thinking she was going to be angry and was now pleased with what she had, and how it could be repaired. Vonnette's dream message about a squirrel coming into the house was staring her in the face. The attic space in the dream was, maybe, Sharon's mind being open to an explanation and new understanding. Her emotions had space to accept a new point of view.

Both stones from yesterday's dream message came front and center. Quartz provides clarity. Today Vonnette brought clarity for Sharon who had felt ill of her workmanship until an explanation was given. Turquoise brings forth birth or rebirth. Emotionally, a birth had happened. Though the stone element came yesterday, all information stood valid. Ironically, dream messages were meant for herself, not clients. Obviously, today was proving to be a bit different.

No sooner was Vonnette completing that thought when a young woman walked into her booth wearing an odd, miss-match of clothing and jewelry. The woman made a statement with her manner of dress, but exactly what kind of statement Vonnette had no idea. She wore thigh-high, black leather boots with bold, almost seventies style paisley stockings visible between the boots and the light green, leather skirt. A red, ruffled blouse with a small black check in it made a sharp contrast to the huge purple felted beads about her neck. Over-sized spikey silver earrings stood out clearly beneath her short curly brown hair. Gold rings were stacked up on each finger and appeared to have the same simple bezel type mounting. Nothing matched on her, except for the rings all having the same size stones and same metal style. But then, each ring had a stone of a different color so, they, too, didn't really match.

Walking about the booth she stopped in front of the blue topaz display and claimed, "Your work is very detailed."

Something about the way she spoke those words gave Vonnette an inclination there was more. Guessing, she asked, "Do you make jewelry?"

"Yes, my booth is over two aisles and up seven spaces, I think. This is my first time doing this show. I had no idea what to expect. There are more people than what I thought might be here for a Friday."

While nodding in acknowledgement, Vonnette recognized something in this woman. Internally, she didn't seem to understand just who she was. Something Vonnette felt about herself almost her whole life! How did she fit into the world while searching for her artistic style and personal identity? Over the course of her career, Vonnette hoped some internal comfort came despite the feeling that she almost never fit in with society. Maybe that was a gift in itself.

Watching this young woman was painful for Vonnette because

she wore her personal discomfort in such a bold manner. If this girl grasped who she was as an artist, her choice of earrings might not have been so sharp and pointy when combined with the soft, felted beads about her neck. Add in all the rings, and her three distinctive styles in jewelry choices did not flatter one another. Maybe she didn't make all the jewelry. If not, that could be a poor choice to wear another artists' work at a show when trying to sell your own creations. No, her jewelry and clothing choices would confuse anyone, and that overlapped onto her as an artist and person.

Feeling confused, Vonnette asked, "Do you do custom work?" Hoping the woman would point out what jewelry displayed on her body was hers while answering.

"Not *per se`*. If someone wants a different color in my bead design I will do it."

"Oh, so your jewelry is felted then. The earrings and rings, did you make those as well?"

"No. Well, actually I made the earrings and the beads. So, both the felted and silver jewelry is what I make. It's a lot of polishing when you work in silver. I'm guessing all your pieces are gold?"

"Yes, my pieces are gold. I switched over to working only in gold many years back. Gold is more forgiving in the polishing department than silver.

"If you made the felted beads and the earrings, who made the rings?"

Sounding almost prideful she looked at the rings, smiled and said, "My booth neighbor makes these rings. Feeling there is energy in stones I asked if I could wear some to help advertise her things. My creations don't have stones. The color in my work is from the felting I do. I see in your cases you also feel there's energy in stones."

"Yes, I do," Vonnette offered while watching the young artist view a few more designs.

Over the next few minutes, they conversed about stone energy and jewelry designs. Looking about at the people touring the show, the woman decided to return to her booth. She handed a postcard showcasing a few pieces of her felted and silver jewelry to Vonnette as a parting gift.

While contemplating this young designer, Vonnette almost felt sorry for her. Between the flouncy red-checked blouse and the giant purple beads, there was conflict. These could be a stand-out features if she showcased her felted pieces alone. However, her mixing the bold, pattered clothing with the softness of felted beads, the hardness of pointy silver earrings along with the fact that she was wearing rings she had not even made, and that indicated her confusion about what style she connected with.

Was she a biker chick with the boots and skirt?

Was she a flower child with those tights?

Was she a punk rocker with the earrings?

Standing out is always good for people to remember particular artists' work at a show. But if the creations are not what stands out, then everything can and usually becomes lost in the effort. And, if Vonnette felt confused, as a fellow artist, she could only imagine what clients thought when they viewed this young woman.

According to the photos displayed as postcard images, her felted designs were generic in style. There were different sized and shaped felted beads, along with a few styles of felted pins. Her silver pieces were all very sharp edged and each had a completely different look. Not one item crossed over into the other to make any form of connection other than the fact they were all jewelry. If she had even one piece incorporating her spikey jewelry with felting, that alone would show some form of unity. These postcard images came across to Vonnette as though a few artists may have come together to form a co-op of some sort.

Vonnette suddenly thought about something that had until that very moment escaped her . . . her brand! All the years of traveling and participating in fine art and craft shows Vonnette heard repeatedly how she ought to have or develop a brand.

What was a brand anyway?

What kind of clients could she attract as part of her brand?

Suddenly, Vonnette felt she had to thank this young woman who just left her booth for her personal revelation! Yes, that young artist had brought about a birth and a great, unexpected gift today.

Vonnette smiled as she thought about her client base clearly for maybe the first time in all the years she had been making jewelry. People who did not know who they were could never be comfortable wearing Vonnette's designs. Men and women had come to Vonnette for her creations over thirty odd years who had some sense of who they were, and what image they wanted to present through the jewelry they purchased and wore. It didn't matter what their income level was. What was inside of them emotionally became their form of distinction. If unable to find their inner voice, most likely they would not seek Vonnette out for jewelry. Each of her pieces made a statement on its own, and even more so on a woman or a man who knew herself or himself.

Unconsciously, perhaps Vonnette knew all this, but today she understood it all in the very front of her cerebral cortex. Dots connected and provided clarity. Birth was indeed happening. Vonnette's designs and her clients were connected, centered, and very comfortable living in their own skins and their own worlds. This realization had to be associated with the dream of Oprah and the sweepstakes win! Have a famous person in a dream and help can come in from an unexpected source. That young jewelry designer had given a terrific bit of exactly that, unexpected help.

Vonnette saw her brand had an organic base, but all things were tied in together with the use of beads, different colored stones, different colored and karat golds. She made jewelry that had identifiable designs such as shells, dragonflies, roses, swans, butterflies, trees and onward. Many pieces formed filigree designs in gold, too. Those pieces stood out by her having incorporated different colors of gold with different size and shaped gemstones and pearls. Using raw crystals in her work only accented her desire to create one-of-a-kind jewelry because no two natural crystals are formed alike. The solid gold designs Vonnette created could almost be considered a bit heavy by comparison to her organic looks. However, stones always acted as a core design element in each piece she crafted. The beads she strung usually complimented her pendants, so each creation became a complete package. Thinking outside the box, Vonnette even loved taking beads normally worn as a necklace and forming temporary bracelets out of them. Along that same line, fashioning jewelry that could become something different was a passion. Her clients loved when a piece they purchased could shift over time if say, they changed their hairstyle, or neckline, or even their choice of inner lifestyle. Clients understood that as their lives shifted, their jewelry that Vonnette created could change along with them. Money spent on Vonnette's designs became well worth the investment from many angles.

When trying to grasp her brand in the past, Vonnette always thought her many designs were confusing compared to what she saw as brands by others. Normal branding was almost minimalistic. A jeweler would incorporate many different colors of stones into the same pattern. Like the rings that young artist had had on her hands today. Each ring she displayed contained the same size stone mounted in bezels in simple, thin, band-like rings. Vonnette's creations varied in style motif, and she mounted all her stones differently. Some were in bezels. Some were in prongs. Some had gold wire going completely over stones to form what she termed *continuous prongs*. Stones were a variety of shapes and sizes along-side different symbols and that translated into the fact that Vonnette's jewelry was uniquely created and not all of one image, shape, or color. Still, there was an undeniable crossover connection to her creations where clients always recognized her work on others.

Women and men who knew themselves well enough to make a statement with jewelry understood Vonnette's creations would be an accent of who they were personally, metaphysically, emotionally, and physically. Unique jewelry for unique people *was* Vonnette's brand!

Vonnette suddenly understood why women would look at her work at shows and comment, "Oh, so this is where the real jewelry is." Always wondering why those people would give such accolades about her jewelry yet not stop long enough to shop and possibly purchase, Vonnette heard it all today in a very new way. Anyone spending time looking over her work understood Vonnette's passion for designing unique gold and stone jewelry. If the passers-by didn't feel unique themselves, or want to stand out as being different, they would not want to purchase. Vonnette suddenly thought, "Leave generic jewelry for the men and women who are not yet comfortable with who they are, their placement in the world, or their ability to stand out. Perhaps they crave to stand out, but don't know how to do it yet." No, Vonnette's client base was built on women and men who welcomed standing out, in fact, shouting out in whatever way to the world that they were individuals who deserved attention.

Turquoise from her dream yesterday came across in a big way to Vonnette this morning. After deciding that dream message had associated with her client; birth, or rebirth, circled in the air now of how Vonnette created her own brand. What a great, unexpected gift the young artist with miss-matched clothing turned out to be for Vonnette as she understood her own brand!

The rest of the day at the show took on new meaning for Vonnette because she understood her clients better. The usual passers-by did not affect her emotionally. She decided that many of those people didn't know their inner workings and as such might purchase something from a young designer who made more generic jewelry. Pieces that looked the same and would in no way help them stand out as individuals. They could still walk away from making such a purchase claiming they had just bought from a designer and would be correct. Maybe that was the first step to eventually becoming a Vonnette client. Her clients were miles beyond a generic place. They didn't want to blend into the crowd. They already knew they stood out and reveled in that fact. Vonnette's designs simply became an exclamation point to that fact.

Clients continually reported back how the jewelry purchased from Vonnette garnered great attention no matter where they were. One claimed she was at a social affair in one of the naval captains' home in Newport where a few women compared their pieces purchased from Vonnette. Each loved one another's designs, and the fact they were hand made just for them! Another client shared a year ago how she couldn't make it through the grocery store check-out line without being stopped by the cashier's asking about a ring made by Vonnette. One other client in particular traveled often for work where she entered into many conversations with strangers due to her jewelry. Strangers craved what they saw on that client in the way of creative jewelry designs. Some even followed up by calling to see if perhaps they, too, could have something made just for them.

Vonnette thought of how she could hear things repeatedly but still not have whatever heard fully register until she was ready to hear it. Today, Vonnette heard and connected with branding concepts that she'd heard repeatedly over many years. If that could only overlap into understanding money, she would be more than grateful! Sincerely, she would be over the moon!

⁂

After the show, and as she was getting ready for bed, Vonnette would normally ask for something wonderful to happen financially the following day. This Friday night, she tried something different. Vonnette asked what lesson she had not yet learned about finances. Perhaps an answer would come forth during the night that could clear the way for money to come into her realm more steadily.

⁂

November 15, Saturday 2008

DREAM

A mass-produced engagement ring that didn't have a center stone mounted in it. Most rings form a complete circle. This ring was open across the top. Overall, the design looked like a large, open U shape. One end of the ring floated up over the top of the pinkie finger. The middle of the ring wound down under the ring finger with the other open end coming up and over the middle finger. The ring appeared almost like a tiny, moving snake that had been frozen in gold while winding its way over and around three fingers. Smaller diamonds mounted along one outer, top side of the ring gave a nice sparkle as it moved. The ring finger held the open-ended ring in place. There was no need to worry about this ring turning around from top to bottom on any hand as it couldn't possibly shift accidentally.

Carl brought this ring to Vonnette asking her to set his square, loose diamond in it. That larger diamond, he suggested, could be attached to one side of the ring to then overlap the ring finger. While she contemplated his request, he went on to claim that once the ring was complete, he would make it her engagement ring.

Although not pleased with his assumption of an impending engagement, Vonnette did what was asked and mounted the stone because she was, a jeweler. While trying on and looking at the finished ring overlapping her three fingers, Vonnette decided the center stone was too small to be her engagement ring. That fact, along with the knowledge that she had not made the whole ring, told her this man was not for her either. If Vonnette had made the ring completely, the design would have been different. This ring was unique. But she could never be comfortable wearing such a significant piece of jewelry that someone else had designed and made. When removing the ring from her hand, she considered the possible engagement seriously.

Decision made, the ring would be returned to Carl at the next opportunity. He could hold onto it for another fiancé. This ring seriously had someone else's name on it. Vonnette could not be with a man who didn't respect her talents enough to have her make the whole ring.

The Carl in her dream was a man Vonnette had actually dated in college who found drugs more important than their relationship. Why he popped into her dreams she could only guess. Men with addictions were part of her lessons in this life. What Vonnette had discovered was that these men were reflections for her to see her own addictions with food. What she still didn't understand, though, was how to permanently remove the problematic men from her life.

In the beginning when Vonnette first tried to comprehend why she attracted and was attracted to such men, she felt they could be a reflection of her parents' addictions to smoking cigarettes and alcohol consumption. Perhaps she was so accustomed to being sur-rounded by addictive people that dating them was simply a contin-uation of a theme. Over time she realized the fault was with her own addiction to sweets.

Friends and family didn't understand how difficult food could be in her life. Food was her Achilles heel. Sweets stood tall at the head of the list, but then, she could consume any food in vast quan-tities whenever stressed, and she felt stressed all the time! During the daytime while occupied with work, she did well with food. Eve-nings spent alone however, became her downfall.

There had been a seven-year stretch where she was off sweet foods. Gaining control of her eating during that time created a great moment to be thin again and for her to like her figure.

Enter Joseph. Relationships that come so quickly and so strongly often crash and burn as did theirs. Finding sweets again after that break-up was a pleasant renewal at first. Eating sugar after a sev-en-year break did not add on any weight, at least not right away. Vonnette felt she had crossed some invisible threshold. Addictions are funny like that. They came back into her world at the very moment she was certain they had left the building for good. Why couldn't she get rid of that addiction again when she had success-fully done so in the past?

While showering, and dressing for the day, last night's dream became clear. She viewed the mass-produced ring as representing something made by someone else, not her. The dream reminded her how being a walk-in, Vonnette had to accept, or at least deal with what the prior Vonnette had as addictions in her life. Carl stood in her dream as a representation of her addictions to food. In the dream, Vonnette finished the ring as asked but opted to return it. If the present Vonnette could successfully get food addictions under control and see them for what they were, a crutch left over from the original Vonnette, she would be returning that issue to the original Vonnette and, peace of spirit could then replace strife. Maybe even financial woes could be shifted as well.

This dream analysis might be Vonnette's answer to the question she asked before bed last night on lessons not yet learned concerning her finances. On the drive from her hotel to the show parking lot, Vonnette realized that stress was the main cause of her downfall, so stress had to be managed in a new way. Instead of allowing stress to rule her and her addiction to food, she would now choose to let go and enjoy food when stress was no longer a factor. Understanding the trigger, and the fact that it was not really *her* choice in this life to have this issue but rather the first Vonnette's, was a new facet in understanding herself as a walk-in. Vonnette felt she had just discovered the missing ingredient from when she lived sugar free for those seven years before. In the dream, Vonnette had released the ring back to Carl. Perhaps that part of the dream indicated she needed to release stress, not internalize it somehow.

About a block before the show site, she recalled something her white snaps friend Jennifer had suggested years back. "When you feel stressed, with each exhale, moan! Do that until the stressful situation or moment subsides, and you'll feel much better!" For the remainder of her ride to the show, Vonnette moaned as she exhaled. While moaning, her muscles relaxed, and she felt hopeful for a new and much needed resolution for stress. Four crows appeared out of nowhere above her car while at a stoplight. Four crows stood for birth!

⁂

Saturday brought more fulfilled moments in the work arena for Vonnette. Design techniques and her ability to create for the individual stood out to the show clientele.

A couple perhaps in their mid 60's, was walking hand-in-hand. Smiling broadly as they stopped in front of the booth, they took great care to see everything. Once finished, eye contact was made with Vonnette as they asked if she had in fact created all these wonderful pieces of jewelry.

Nodding, yes, she waited to see where this question might lead.

"Can we see this ring here with the diamonds and a green stone? What *is* the green stone?" The man asked.

"It's a green sapphire. Sapphires come in all colors of the rainbow except the true red which is called ruby. Most people don't know that ruby and sapphire are the same mineral, corundum. Every color including the pink is called sapphire. Colorless or white sapphires exist as well, then the colors go all the way up to black.

"Believe it or not, the red, or ruby, is usually more expensive than other corundum's. That's generally due to rarity." Vonnette spoke with sincerity as she handed the ring over to the couple. "This ring is a size six at the moment, but can be sized if you want it and it doesn't fit. Looking at your hand, though, you do look like a six. Alongside the sapphire are two round white diamonds that are VVS in quality."

Seemingly not hearing her, he slowly slipped the ring upon his partners' left-hand ring finger as a perfect fit smiling all the while. Her gaze was focused upon the ring.

Feeling her words would be wasted at the moment, Vonnette stood watching over her design. The couple gazed upon the ring on the woman's finger a good minute or two before looking up to ask the price.

Vonnette informed them the price was $3,800 before sales tax. No one seemed to flinch at the cost, always a good sign. Vonnette surmised this was a newer relationship and perhaps they were getting engaged.

Heads close together, they appeared to be whispering to one another though their conversation was louder than an actual whisper. Each person across the counter was smiling at one another while nodding at the ring. Vonnette stayed focused. Though she wanted to give them a bit of privacy to discuss this possible purchase, her ring was still on a stranger's hand.

After a few minutes the man spoke. "If this turned out to be too tight or too loose, what is the procedure for such an event?"

Repeating what she said a moment ago, Vonnette replied, "I can and would alter the size for you most certainly, but it seems to fit nicely right now. Do you live in a very warm climate that you feel it will be too tight once home?"

For a moment, no answer came from across the counter and then the woman spoke to Vonnette in an actual whisper. "Men don't get hearing aids."

Vonnette knowingly nodded. The two women understood one another completely. Vonnette wondered inwardly why men feel it is some form of debasement to their masculinity to either wear hearing aids or to have baldness? Over countless years of dealing with the public, she had noticed many men who could not hear what was being said, yet would not admit they had any form of hearing issue. By the same token it amazed her how many men wore baseball caps in an effort to hide their baldness. What their partners thought might be another thing entirely, but Vonnette felt most men looked great bald.

While Vonnette was lost in thought, the woman spoke to the man and there seemed to be an understanding of some sort.

Looking over the counter at Vonnette the man said, "We're going to walk about and have some lunch to think this over." As he said that he winked at Vonnette and handed the ring back over the counter, which usually meant he would be back to get the ring without the woman in tow.

Vonnette was unsure how much this man could hear, so she silently smiled and handed over a business card. Speaking perhaps a bit more loudly than was necessary, she told them to enjoy their lunch as they left the booth.

While placing the ring back into its clear plastic stand and then inside the display case, Vonnette was hopeful this man would in fact return to buy it. That one purchase would not only make her day financially but it would also give her positive reinforcement of the connection she felt she was making with her dream. The universe can and does give answers when the mind is open and/or the correct question is asked. Today, Vonnette felt she had connected some major dots by figuring out that as a walk-in she still had to deal with the addictive behavior of the first Vonnette. And, by understanding her brand she was perhaps eliminating financial blocks.

One nicely dressed woman in her fifties stopped to look over the jewelry. Vonnette let her peruse. Eventually she looked up at Vonnette and mentioned that her feet were hurting. Any conversation that began this way at a show never went well. Vonnette opted not to respond verbally. Instead, she just shrugged her shoulders as a response hopeful that would be the end of it.

"This is my first experience attending one of these shows. Having no idea how much walking was involved I opted to wear my Manola Blahniks. Now I feel as though I need a cab to get to the end of the show."

Vonnette was unsure how to respond to this comment so casually suggested that perhaps she could wear sneakers in the future.

Clearly outraged by such a suggestion the woman replied, "My Manolas are staying put! Perhaps I won't attend such a show in the future." With that she left the booth and was soon out of sight.

Unexpected conversations such as these were part of every show, and yet they always came as a shock. For a brief moment, it left Vonnette not only stunned, but also confused. Shaking it off was the only way to move through the blind-sided situation.

Since Jennifer had been on her mind early this morning, it was understandable she popped back in just now. Some conversation Vonnette had with her produced a chant-like suggestion. Jennifer said, "When someone does something to wrong you, forgive them, then lose them, and let them go." Jennifer claimed she had learned this trick from the now famous Louise Hay.

Having that suggestion in her head, Vonnette followed that advise. Thinking about the woman who just walked away, she forgave her ignorance of what shoes to wear at a show of this kind and then, she let her go. Repeating this in her mind a few times did the trick. Vonnette felt centered again and was ready for the remainder of the day.

Sitting quietly for a few moments, Vonnette watched people mill about the show when a woman in her forties approached the booth. Her hair was slightly unkempt and her clothing was run of the mill in style. Looking about she focused on a pair of 14Ky lever back *Flying Pig* earrings. When she bent over to get a closer look through the display case, Vonnette opened the case and removed the earrings still on their clear Lucite display stand.

"Oh, I can't see them really without my glasses," came as a response.

Vonnette had a pair of readers behind the display cases. Something she'd been using at shows to read her own price tags for years. Handing the pair of glasses over for the woman to use, Vonnette noticed that once the glasses were in place, this woman looked straight at the price before taking a close up look at what the earring detail actually was. While passing the glasses back she said, "You know, I make almost all of my own jewelry. I cannot justify buying these."

Being a keen observer, Vonnette knew the price was the deciding factor, not the fact that this woman made her own jewelry. Just nodding her head in acknowledgment Vonnette replaced the earrings inside the case while accepting her readers back in hand. Locking the display case door, she was certain the woman would now be leaving her booth.

Surprisingly, she stopped in front of a rose gold, pink sapphire ring that had a small white pearl and diamond along one side. Pointing to it the woman asked, "What about this ring here? Can I take a picture of it?"

Artists are no strangers to people who try to duplicate their creations for less. Vonnette had experienced such practices with her creations more than once herself. Certain she wanted to either make a copy of the ring on her own or have someone else do it for her, Vonnette wouldn't have it. Slowly she said, "Noooooooo." Feeling an explanation about artistic copyright laws would be lost at this moment, she also felt the woman had no intention of making a purchase now or in the future. And, "No" is a complete sentence.

Clearly incensed, the woman now stood very upright and asked, "Why not? Who makes this jewelry?"

"*I do*." Came rolling off Vonnette's lips at a very fast clip along with an all-knowing smile that suggested the woman was not going to win.

Who knew what the woman wanted, but to Vonnette it seemed it could be blood on some level.

"All of it? You make all the jewelry here?" Flailing her arms about widely with an equally wide glance this woman clearly didn't believe Vonnette.

"Yes," popped out so quickly from Vonnette's mouth that if spit had come forth with the word it would have had enough force attached to hurt when it landed firmly on the lady standing opposite her.

With one and two words responses, the woman realized she would not be getting anywhere with Vonnette just now. With no recourse left, the woman turned on her heels and walked out of the booth in a clear huff. Had there been dust around, that would have been flying because of how she stamped her feet in departure.

Vonnette followed up with forgiving her and letting her go while wondering if this was how the remainder of her day was going to be.

⁂

Casually dressed, an elder gentleman approached Vonnette. On his pinkie, he wore two yellow gold ladies' rings. One bore a round white stone. The other was a wedding band. A few minutes into the conversation it seemed clear he wanted the two rings made into something he could wear in remembrance of his now deceased wife.

Vonnette asked a few questions as to where on his body he intended to wear this newly created piece of jewelry? Would it be a ring, a lapel pin, a pendant?

He suggested that some form of pendant as well as a chain would work well.

Pulling out paper and pen she began to do some sketches. As she sketched, her head was down. Concentrating on her drawing, everything around her became a blur. Speaking out loud to this man while in this deep concentration, she had no real concept if perhaps she was talking to thin air.

"I call this *Freeform*. It's where I cut up your gold into smaller pieces and fuse it all back together. By that I mean, the metal gets slightly melted but not enough so that it becomes totally liquid. Each bit of metal adheres to one another. There are holes, if you will, where multiple pieces of metal get attached to another piece. I think of this gold work as being like water running about on a countertop. You never know exactly where it will go. There are always breaks in that escaping water. How it all bridges together both in liquid and in gold becomes unique. Each time I do this it comes out differently, which is part of who I am as an artist. The interior as well as the outer edge of this design is abstract. All that adds to the piece being one-of-a-kind. When I'm finished, the fluid form of the gold is nice to the touch as well as the image.

"To make the diamond appear more masculine in this design, I might suggest placing it in a bezel instead of the six-prong style mount it's in now. That's where there is a rim of gold encircling the stone. Some people feel that look makes a stone appear smaller. Personally, I don't feel that way at all. Sometimes it makes the stone stand out even more than it does in prongs. The best part of doing this freeform design is that I will for the most part be working with your metal. Which keeps more of the sentimentality in tac and your charge for my work is mainly for labor. What I charge for in addition to my labor will be the metal I use for a bezel and whatever we decide ought to be a correct chain for you. Though I do make chains, I think on this piece having a ready-made chain will suit nicely for you, and a manufactured chain will cut the cost element from something I make by hand.

"If this is amenable, I will work up an estimate and we can get going." Speaking while sketching was a norm for Vonnette. Turning the paper around often for the client to see where she was going with the design was courteous. Otherwise, whomever would be looking at her sketches upside-down.

The man seemed interested enough to want to go ahead.

Normally, Vonnette looked through her jeweler's loupe at all stones someone wanted remounted before sketching. Today, Vonnette reversed that procedure and turned in her booth to grab hold of her invoice slips as well as her 10x jewelers loupe. The stone was only slightly dirty from wear. However, she still needed to have a closer look into the stone to make sure there were no serious cracks or chips. If such issues were visible, she would need to discuss those with the client before removing it from the mounting as well as write all information down on her sales slip. God forbid she cleaned the mounting with the stone in it only to discover issues afterwards. Any client could then claim she switched the stone out. Having dirt in place on a stone in a mounting meant no one could ever dispute her changing stones on them.

Bringing her loupe up to her right eye with the left one closed, Vonnette then brought the ring up closer to the loupe until it all came into focus. Turning the ring around and then on its side to see underneath, she put her loupe down on the velvet pad and began to speak again.

"What are you going to tell me about this stone sir?"

"What do you want me to tell you about the stone?"

"You need to tell me what you know about this stone before we go further with a new design or my even accepting the job."

Fidgeting a bit, the man began to ponder if he was going to come clean or not. "Why don't you tell me what it is that you want to know and then I can say if you are correct or not?"

"Please sir, do not try to play with me. I am a professional goldsmith slash jeweler. Starting my business in 1976 gives me many years of experience where I've seen more than I could possibly tell you. At this moment, it's important for you to be honest with me or I won't take the job."

"Okay, okay. It's not a diamond."

"Yes, I know that. Please continue."

"It's a man-made diamond. My wife never knew. Guess I ought to have told her, but when we got engaged we were facing a lot of other expenses. It was a second marriage for each of us. Wife number one got everything. Maybe I should say I gave her everything. When I proposed to this wife, we were already living together. I had to make a decision, spend the money I had on a diamond or on all the other things we wanted. I opted to purchase an Airstream and truck. That was so we could travel together since we were each retired. Feeling it was the right decision at the time I always felt badly I never told her it was a fake." Looking downward clearly embarrassed, he fell silent in thought.

Listening intently, Vonnette bit her tongue. Literally, she bit the very tip of her tongue. It hurt, it hurt a lot . . . . She even tasted blood. How bad was it she wondered? No time to investigate, she knew the tongue issue and this man were interconnected. What should she say and not say right now? Clearly he was upset. Vonnette felt that biting her tongue was either a sign for her not to keep silent or to bite her tongue in this conversation metaphorically. She had to be as honest as she could be at this moment with this man.

Through her personal pain, she remained centered, figuring she would deal with her hurt tongue later. "Thank you for being honest with me here today. In some way that maybe makes up for what you never said to your wife years ago. Maybe she knew it wasn't real. Maybe she loved you enough to never tell you she knew. But why I have to be above board and honest about all this now is because later on you could see the new mounting and claim I switched the stone on you."

Noticing he was about to wave his hand in dismissal as if to say, "I would never do that," Vonnette stopped him before the words came forth.

"You may not say such a thing, but look at this from my perspective. You never told your wife about the stone, so why should I trust you would be truthful when it came time with me? We don't know one another, so there's no reason for me to believe it could be anything other than what I have explained. For that matter, if your wife were alive and came to me asking for an appraisal, I would have been honest with her and would have said it was an imitation stone."

His mouth fell open a bit in surprise and perhaps of a dawning realization.

Taking in all his physical reactions Vonnette connected psychically to his ah ha moment. "Yes, you are realizing now that your wife most likely did know it wasn't real because certainly over all the years you were together she went into a jewelry store in a mall where they offered to clean the ring. It's something they often do to check prongs to see if the ring needs repairs. Once clean they would certainly say the stone was not real. Maybe she even took it into the place where you bought the ring because of the label on the original gift box. Who knows?

"My point is this; you never told your wife about the stone. Obviously, she loved you enough to keep your secret. That's also why she kept the ring as clean as it is now because once a fake diamond gets really dirty, the sparkle is lost. If this were a real diamond, no matter how dirty the stone would become, the twinkle would still be there!"

His mind was on overload and Vonnette tried to take that into consideration before continuing. Shoulders rounded, he no longer appeared to be a fine elder gentleman, rather a simple man, caught in his own snares of secrecy. Letting him have his dawning moment along with his emotional reconnection with his lost life mate, Vonnette felt deep passion coming from this man for the wife he had lost however long ago. His sorrow, his regret, and his realization were felt deeply by Vonnette. Something she couldn't help if she tried due to being an empath and a sensitive.

When his physical stature came back upright, she felt it was okay to continue. "I know this has been a lot for you to take in all at once, but I'm willing to and can make this into a pendant for you even with it being a non-diamond. Jewelry is sentimental and I feel this new piece of jewelry could have more meaning for you than you originally thought. Having knowledge is good. Your wife is maybe telling you today in her own way that she knew about the imitation stone and didn't care because she loved you that much. That could be why you came to me at this moment. Another jeweler would not be explaining all this.

"You see, I believe in continuous life. I also believe we have spirits around us all the time. Some are people we've known in this life. Some spirits are guides that provide answers if we give them half a chance. Those spirits help steer us in the right direction. Most people call them angels, and I do believe angels check in on us often.

"Of course, we also have visits from loved ones who have passed over. It's very possible your wife pushed you to be here today for this stone issue to be resolved. Allowing you to let go of the guilt you have been carrying all these years. Let's face it, not only did you come to me to have this new design made, but I also made you confess that the stone was not a diamond. Something that you wanted to tell your wife, at least that's what you said."

The man's facial expression before now had been fraught. He finally began to speak after nodding yes. "Interestingly enough I have had this very question on my mind lately. I felt it was because I needed to have these rings made into something as a reminder of my wife.

"Think I always felt she knew the stone was a fake diamond, but I never had the courage to talk it over with her. When she became ill, it felt too much like I was trying to make restitution, so in the end I never opened up. I have felt guilty. Today you said some things to me that I obviously needed to hear. For that I am most thankful! Guess, to use your terminology, my angels brought me here today to the right place for the right reasons."

"Good. What we can do now is begin again. You can choose to walk away with this knowledge and a lighter heart feeling your wife has forgiven you for not telling her, or for not giving her a real diamond. Or, you can choose to have this made into the necklace we have been discussing. You can then wear the new piece guilt free!"

Waiting for him to catch up, Vonnette thought about his love for this woman no longer on this plane and she wondered if in fact she would ever find such a connection herself.

His head bobbed again. "Yes. I do wish to have this pendant as an even deeper connection with my wife. And now, thanks to you, the necklace will take on new meaning without guilt."

Taking hold of her sales book once again, Vonnette began to write up a receipt for the man who now claimed his name was Evan. As part of the description Vonnette wrote the ring she was receiving had an imitation diamond along with a wedding band. All this was an effort to protect herself and her business. Glancing up from her notes as she was almost finished writing, she noticed his eyes had watered a bit. When something simple turned into a nice connection for the client, she loved knowing she'd had a small part in that special moment. Little did this man know today would be a greater connection for him to his deceased wife than he had felt it would be. Even his skin tone looked a bit brighter now than when he had walked into Vonnette's booth.

They smiled at one another with deep sincerity, even shook hands before he walked away.

⚜

Two women approached the booth who had to be a mother and daughter as their features were almost mirror images of one another at different ages. The mother asked very quickly to see a ring over to the right.

Opening the case Vonnette reached in and asked as she pointed to a white moonstone ring that had five rubies surrounding it, "Is this the ring you would like to see?"

Smiling, the woman said, "Yes" while she reached her hand up and over the counter to have Vonnette slip the ring on. When people did that, Vonnette felt like a shoe salesman, but she did slide the ring on her finger. Both mother and daughter were ogling the ring when the daughter, who was maybe in her twenties said, "Mom, this is the happiest you've been all day!"

Laughing, they looked at Vonnette and felt an explanation was necessary. "You see, I had a fight with my husband earlier today over the phone. He works for Verizon and has to travel a lot. Somehow he feels he can control me from a distance. I don't understand why after all these years of marriage he feels that way. Sincerely, he has never been able to control me. Well, maybe in the beginning of our marriage he did rule the purse strings, but never me. Why is it that men are attracted to strong personality women before marriage, and then try to put a net over that same personality after marriage?"

Vonnette's head bobbed as she smiled in a knowing fashion.

The mother asked if there was something the daughter liked. After pulling out an amethyst ring that was a nice deep purple color Vonnette handed that over to the daughter. While these two women had their heads together comparing the two rings on their hands, Vonnette felt it would be a good time to interject a bit of information. "Deep color amethyst is the preferred tone. You know it was the stone that royalty as well as clergy used to wear to denote power. As for white moonstones and rubies, well, personally, I feel that combination in this piece is a true visionaries ring. The energy that emanates from it is a terrific internal high. Moonstone connects with lunar energy, as with the twelve cycles of the year. Ruby starts with the kundalini and goes straight up to the heart."

Realizing there was a quizzical look developing across the counter she explained further: "The kundalini is the energy center found at the base of the spine. If I'm correct, in yoga practices, they feel all energy stems from there. I feel the energy generated from rubies begins there and travels up through your heart region. Your heart is what pumps the blood through your veins. It's what gives us true passion, be it love or hate because, I feel they are flip sides of the same emotion."

Interrupting the roll Vonnette was on, the mother said, "Yes, anger is where I'm at. He needs to expand his **horizons**! That's what I say at times like these."

All three women laughed. Mother and daughter did not seem surprised. So, Vonnette felt this statement was not anything new for the mom.

"Is there anything else I can give you in the way of information?" Vonnette asked.

Slight shoulder shrugs began to pass back and forth between the two women now as if to say, "We can't think of anything." And then something else popped into the elder woman's mind. "You are very creative."

"Thank you."

"No, seriously, I see even by the way you dress and wear your jewelry you are creative."

"Thank you very much."

"Do you think one is born to be creative? I mean, I don't feel I have a creative bone in my body, especially when I stand before someone such as yourself."

"Don't know how you can say such a thing! I mean look at this woman here who is obviously your daughter. You literally created this woman!"

"Well, not really. I mean, yes, my body formed hers, but I feel birth is something other-worldly, not something I really can say I had a hand in."

Chuckling outwardly, Vonnette found this conversation interesting as well as entertaining. "You are cracking me up. Seriously! Not only did you give birth to this woman, which is the biggest form of creative energy known to man, or womankind, but you also helped her formulate along the way to become the woman she is here and now! You need to take credit for having that creative energy."

"Well, guess I never thought of childbearing or childrearing in that way before." Looking her daughter over from head-to-toe, she surmised she maybe had done a good job. Her facial expression said it all.

The daughter laughed at how she was being scrutinized. Both their heads bobbed as if they agreed she had done a good job helping to create this young woman, and then laughed at themselves.

"You know, people continuously underestimate their gifts. I see it all the time while traveling to do these shows. Your opinion of not being creative is a perfect example of that. I think each of us has some form of gift or gifts. You took an egg and turned it into this lovely young woman. I take gold and turn it into fine jewelry to celebrate how we are each one-of-a-kind. What's important is that we each take credit where it is due. Your daughter here either knows her gifts already, or will discover them as time goes forward."

With that came a proud momma moment.

The two rings chosen fit their fingers well. Something Vonnette confirmed with her normal on/off testing method. Watching as the client pulled a ring off a finger and then as she put it back on, she could tell if it fit well or not. When a ring fit perfectly, it went over the knuckle with a bit of a nudge and then came off with a bit of a tug or twist. If someone was about to lick a finger to get a ring off, it demonstrated the ring was too tight. That was something Vonnette tried to stop before it happened. If she didn't catch it, she then had to clean the ring of their saliva. God forbid someone else would want to try on that ring with someone else's spit on it!

Once it had been established the rings were a good fit, the mother decided they ought to have both rings to prove her husband did not control the purse strings or her personality. And that these rings celebrated how creative they each were. It was maybe a birth moment for them today. Money was exchanged. Each ring appeared to be permanently on a finger so, no wrapping was necessary. The two women left the booth almost singing to one another delighted by their new purchases.

⁂

Hungry, Vonnette pulled out a tuna pouch, plastic fork and a paper towel when she saw a familiar face rushing towards her. Quickly the man made a motion by pointing to the green sapphire ring before he was even fully into the booth area. Placing her lunch on her chair and on hold, Vonnette picked up the sales book to write up the purchase. A full description of the ring along with the karat of gold, the carat sizes of all the stones along with clarity and color of diamonds was included on the sheet. Amused over how the karat of gold was spelled with a K and the carats marking stone sizes were spelled with a C, Vonnette was about to make that association with this new client when she remembered his hearing issue and opted to leave it off for now. It was more important that they get the money situation straight than for her to entertain him with light repartee. In an effort to make certain there would be no confusion about the money owed, and what was about to be on his charge card, Vonnette wrote up the sales slip, added the sales tax and then physically showed the slip to the client. Not being able to communicate easily due to the client's inability to hear, this was the nearest reliable alternative.

Nodding in agreement to the amount written, the man pulled out his credit card and handed it over the counter to Vonnette. While she was taking care of the charge information, the man enlightened Vonnette on how he planned to present the ring and pop the question. Almost bursting at the seams to tell someone his plans, he said he was a master gardener in charge of a local botanical garden that was also the location of their first date. He wanted to propose there under the glass dome with a candlelit dinner.

Upon hearing this possible presentation of her design, Vonnette grabbed a heart-shaped, white, fabric-covered box to wrap the ring in. Inside the box was a fabric roll attached on one end and a snap on the other end. Once Vonnette pulled that rolled fabric through the center circle of the ring, she snapped the roll back in place. During transport, the ring would not shift position. Looking up she was no longer fearful of this man's hearing her or not and explained, "I've been holding onto this wonderful box for a very special occasion such as this."

Handing the heart shaped box over the counter inside a plastic bag for the man, she explained how women are usually very sentimental. "Women not only recall how and where they are proposed to, but also what any sort of box looks like."

He thanked her for being so helpful. "I have to hurry to get back before she knows I didn't just go to the men's room."

Vonnette picked up her lunch items to sit and eat while watching the man hustle out of sight and back to his lady love. It was great to know both parties seemed pleased with a ring when a proposal was imminent. Happy, she sat and considered how she was making sales. This show was turning out to be good not only financially but also wonderful for input on what her brand was.

On her third mouthful of tuna, Vonnette was still thinking about the green sapphire engagement ring couple when she realized and said out loud to herself . . . "I haven't had any time to research about Jackson, to see if he is in fact Sophie Belle's brother as he claimed to be! Think he's supposed to be calling this next week. Who might I call to ask if he really is who he said he is?"

For a moment, her thoughts drifted off and were now about his wavy brown hair and piercing blue eyes. Vonnette didn't know why but that combination was always attractive to her. Most of her lovers had light hair color with blue eyes. This made them all appear to others a bit more like relatives since she had long blonde hair and blue eyes.

Interrupted by a few women coming into her booth to look around, Vonnette not only put her lunch on hold again but her thoughts about Jackson, too.

There had been so many shows where it was beyond slow, at least in her booth. Shows where it was like watching paint dry while waiting for someone to demonstrate any interest. She felt delighted to be busy with attentive people. Since she had already made sales, Vonnette felt calm and would be full of joy throughout the remainder of the show whether she made any more sales or not.

While staring out into the crowd, she pondered how fine jewelry can be a spontaneous purchase, but usually it was an acquisition that came with thought and serious financial decision-making. Always taking that into consideration, Vonnette knew calls after the show when she was home could come in, and sometimes did. Those call-backs may level the playing field financially if she didn't make sales during the show. So far, this show was not of that ilk. Sales were being made and were good ones to boot! Her mind was stimulated as well as joyful over all that was happening.

People wandered in and out of her booth throughout the afternoon, which made the show day go by more quickly. Some were simply looking, some asked to try things on. Being distracted by visitors in her booth was so much better than being alone with her thoughts at any show. Because of all these interruptions, Vonnette eventually finished her lunch at 3:30.

Suddenly alone, her mind wandered to Jennifer for some reason and those snaps of white light that shot off her and into thin air. In some way, she felt comfort seeing her friend in her mind's eye. Something Jenn suggested was to live *as if.* This term came up in a conversation one day while Vonnette was confiding how difficult it was to keep all the financial balls in the air she felt were necessary to remain in the business she loved so. Mentioning how friends took vacations, Vonnette wondered if a vacation would ever be part of her existence due to lack of funds. Jenn said that living *as if* could mean many things. But to her, at this juncture of their conversation, living *as if* meant for Vonnette to find a way to be on vacation without spending the money to actually take one. When she'd had a vacation at a younger age, Vonnette felt she existed in an altered state because she had no stress. She had no place to be at any specific time. Between her creativity and living with spirits Vonnette wondered if perhaps she always lived in an altered universe, so maybe a vacation wasn't necessary anyway. Still, it would be nice to have enough money come in not only to pay her bills but also to get far enough ahead to have a savings account again. The last time she had such a thing was before she opened her business when she was in college. A time when she dreamt about owning a business.

Well, she had established a business and as people constantly pointed out to her, she did travel. However, she never saw anything outside her hotel room, the show venue, or highways to and from each show.

Vonnette felt it was entertaining how people thought she could work whenever and wherever she wanted while having her own business. Jennifer proposed at one point that all those people who thought she had tons of time and money to enjoy such freedom of working whenever she wanted were ultimately providing help from unexpected sources. Jenn explained, "Positive thoughts, are positive thoughts no matter who gives forth the energy." That if other people thought Vonnette could afford to work whenever and wherever she wanted, then why fight all that positive energy? So, these people were actually giving Vonnette a helping hand energetically. Jenn felt Vonnette should accept their good wishes with open arms.

Hearing Jennifer's ideas in her head right now reminded Vonnette that outside sources could help to manifest what she felt was lacking in her existence. Though, she didn't want to think about that just now. The idea of living her life *as if* circled her brain instead.

When Jennifer had recommended Vonnette live *as if* that one day, the words sounded simple. Attainment of this seemingly simple exercise appeared easy. But, how does anyone begin that kind of journey?

What's the first step?

And then, can anyone really know when they're living *as if*?

Vonnette had spent a very long time trying to grasp exactly what living *as if* meant, and then how to do it. Jenn said the idea of living *as if* had been placed in the Universe by someone, who knows who, to mean one thing and then became adopted by New Age thinking. Over time, the term, living *as if*, had turned into the law of attraction. A way to manifest on a metaphysical and physical wavelength. Making that notion an actual part of her life was proving much more of a challenge than Vonnette had expected.

How could Vonnette live *as if* she had money when she didn't have anything extra financially?

How could Vonnette see her home paid for when it was a struggle to meet the mortgage each month?

The more she thought about it, the less Vonnette felt she grasped the concept.

At this moment, her thought was, "When I'm stuck, emotionally, mentally, even creatively, the only way out is through." Possibly, this concept of getting through something would be Vonnette's saving grace. Proceeding along that mental thread, she connected how self-worth and judgement can be major players for negative inner reflection. Taking a deep look internally, Vonnette wanted to understand how judgement and negativity were manifesting as a possible way to learn what needed to be shifted.

Debt can associate with shame. Being molested as a child had caused severe shame that had carried forward for Vonnette. Certain she had forgiven herself and her parents now, as well as the man involved then, she'd hoped to be through with that element of her past. But then she wondered if she could ever be through with her past? All in all, moments that produce shame helped formulate her at the very core of her existence and secrecy had helped develop Vonnette's shame. Since she had begun to share that incident with people in her close circle, at least one tiny bit of that shadow was lifting.

Was it her addiction to food that now held Vonnette back from having everything in her life run smoothly? And, if elevating, or living *as if*, was a way up and out of all these learned patterns, then she had to be creative on how to raise her inner beliefs to manifest what she knew she wanted externally. Topping everything off she was a walk-in, and as such, these were the original Vonnette's issues she as the new Vonnette had to resolve.

A couple entered her booth space at four o'clock and pulled her out of this internal reflection. Looking as though they might be that kind of slow-to-spend show visitors, she held back at first. Conversations got going where they asked about different pieces of her jewelry. The woman then asked why there were typed sayings below certain rings inside the cases?

Looking at this as a possible lead in for at least a sale of one of her books, Vonnette began to explain about the healing energies she felt were present in all stones, and metals too for that matter. Thinking Vonnette saw interest appear on their faces, she went on to describe how she channeled these properties over a serious amount of time. After a few years, she was able to find all the stones she felt were necessary to make the jewelry and finish the book she had for sale here today.

Pointing over to the book on display, Vonnette added, "There are design symbolisms included in the book as well as healing properties of stones."

Leafing through the book, the wife remarked on how there

were *dreams* highlighted on some of the pages and wondered how dreams could have anything to do with making jewelry?

Feeling a bit more comfortable with the couple, Vonnette described how she had very detailed dreams nightly for most of her life. Often her dreams even suggested what stones for her to wear for the day along with what possibly to work on in the studio. Paying attention to these messages had become an important part of who she was as a person as well as an artist.

"Does this mean you are RICA then?" The woman questioned.

"I believe you mean WICA, and the answer is no, I am not a witch although it's quite possible I was one in a previous life." Laughing slightly, her intent was to lighten the mood that can and usually does surround people talking about witches. "Sincerely, I don't even know what those initials stand for, but I believe they pertain to white witches. My dream messages suggest ways to utilize stones and their energy to bring forth beauty, inner growth, and understanding on many levels. Accepting these messages from the other side, if you will, is a method of choice for me to feel I'm not alone. I am guided."

Almost in a singsong voice the woman asked, "Soooo, if I heard correctly, you feel there are other lives?"

Meanwhile, her husband had been looking around the booth and then became visually fixated on Vonnette. Not a new experience for her, although there was one moment when she looked up and thought she saw the husband wink in her direction. Hopeful the wife didn't see, Vonnette continued while trying to dismiss this man.

"I do believe in continuous life. Honestly, I feel we come into this earth plane as human beings to learn whatever lessons we are supposed to learn. When we are done, we move on. Our souls leave our bodies. We are then free to move about the universe and perhaps beyond."

"If I understand, you are saying that if I die tomorrow my soul moves out of my body and takes off to somewhere, who knows where?"

Feeling a bit uneasy with this woman's sudden shift in tone,

Vonnette decided to move forward a bit more cautiously. "We all have life experiences. Yours will be very different from mine of course. By the same token, we all have different beliefs. And we all have different opinions about religion and politics. These are things we could discuss or debate for a very long time. My personal experiences tell *me* there is life after life. Your experiences might tell *you* something very different." It was here that she felt she should have stopped. For some reason, Vonnette couldn't seem to stop herself from talking. "I see and speak with spirits. Usually there's no need to call out their names because I recognize them from when they were alive. Then there are what I call spirit guides, whom I have not known in the physical on this plane. I see them often enough to accept their visits as well. Honestly, the only way I can explain to myself that I see them is if in fact there is continuous life and as such we do not actually die when we leave our bodies, but rather our spirit moves forward."

"Oh, my God, Paul, are you hearing this woman? She *is* some sort of witch! She sees ghosts and feels they are talking to her. Do you believe it?" Getting his attention fully with her tone of voice, the woman went on to make sure she had a rise out of her husband. "We came to this show today for art, not some hocus pocus on spirits and ghosts. I'm horrified! So much so that I intend to let the people who run this event know just who and what you are! Trust me, I am very upset and feel you have no place being here. Paul, let's get out of here before she begins to tell us she sees our future as well as our dead relatives!"

Leaving her booth space the man turned around and yelled back, "Witch!" Loudly enough that other artists turned around to see Vonnette standing alone in her booth.

Physically shaking, Vonnette stood in her booth clearly unnerved by this couple. It all began as an innocent conversation. How did this turn and go so wrong? These two people obviously didn't have enough to do. They had come and rained their Puritanism on Vonnette.

Could their conversation, their attitude and report to the show promoters have some effect on her being accepted into future shows? There was always talk of blackballing artists who irritated show promoters in one way or another. Though these shows are nation-wide and run by different promoters everywhere, it was still a small community where an artist could in fact be banned if one person opted to make their life difficult enough.

An artist came over to Vonnette who made ceramic mugs. Her set up was two booths away. Unsure of where this might lead, Vonnette stood as still as she could, trying not to show how shaken she was by this latest encounter.

"Are you okay?"

It was a sincere inquiry. One which Vonnette wasn't sure of how to answer as so many thoughts were flying through her brain every instant since that couple had left her space.

"Honestly, I don't know right now. We seemed to be having a nice conversation when suddenly, bam! Who can figure what the public will say or do?" Vonnette offered, hopeful that if she down-played the couple, the incident would somehow dissipate.

"Did you say something to cause such a reaction?"

Shrugging a bit Vonnette told her they had been discussing jewelry as well as healing properties found in stones when suddenly the woman blurted out the word, "witch."

"Do you believe there's energy in stones?"

Vonnette didn't utter a word but screamed inside her head, "Yes," while she also considered, oh, no, here we go again.

"If you believe that, why don't you look at it the same way I look at politics? No matter what anyone says or believes, a conversation about who you believe in or why is a no-win situation. Usually everyone walks away mad. Overall, I think it's a waste of time and energy.

"Looking about, I see that you have healing properties listed in your cases. Can you remove those blurbs and let your beliefs go, so you don't have a similar thing happen?"

"I agree with you about politics," Vonnette replied, "and for that matter about religion as well. However, we all have the right to have opinions and beliefs. I don't force my beliefs on others. However, I'm willing to share when asked. That woman asked me questions and I answered honestly. Healing properties in stones is something I've shared now with clients for more than twenty years. This is the first time someone ever reacted in such a manner. Most people find my ideas interesting and fun."

Not even hearing what else this artist was saying, Vonnette was in her own head and that was all she could concentrate on for this second. Flashes began to happen. The four crows she saw this morning she felt stood for birth. Over years of reading, loving and studying actual crows, she had of course read how a group of crows is called a "murder." Usually people would only share such a thought when there was a flock of crows together, but in fact, any number of crows from three on up could be termed as such. Never having used that terminology for crows before this instant, she was seeing her research appear in her third eye. Supposedly, the term came about due to crows' being scavengers who will eat just about anything. The couple who just left her space had murder in their hearts and Vonnette was their scapegoat. While they were acting as scavengers with her carcass as a target, they had in all honesty provided a terrific moment for Vonnette to see things more clearly than she had in her lifetime since that fateful childhood day.

Vonnette regained her mental wind and decided she was being asked one more time by the Universe, "Are you done? Are you really Done? Are you really, really, really done?"

"Yes," she thought, "I am soooooo done!"

Right here, Vonnette had a defining moment, a birth. Vonnette suddenly came out of a caged existence where her cup was more than half-full. Where she would never allow herself to be trapped under a man, in a car, or anywhere unless she *chose* to be there. Even this 10x10 foot show booth would no longer define or contain her spirit! She was bigger than this tiny space marked STORE.

She was suddenly full of self-love, of joy, and of belief that anything was possible. No one even remotely like the couple that just left her space would ever be allowed to steal her power again! If the show promoters did hear their complaint and came to discuss it,

Vonnette would hold to her beliefs and tell them they could choose either to stand with their artist or not. If they didn't want her to participate in their show, that would be fine. New opportunities would be waiting if the shows no longer wanted her to be there.

From every fiber of her being Vonnette proudly realized that she had choices to make and feelings that counted along with the belief that she did deserve to be treated with kindness, love and respect in this world. Come rain or shine, she was Vonnette, and Vonnette mattered!

She felt as if she could jump for joy, and run around the whole show screaming out loud how she was free! After doing that she wanted to tell her friends how not having cancer allowed her to look deeply inside. By letting go internally, Vonnette felt she was causing the domino effect of shifting externally, too.

Shows would become the showcase for who she was as an artist. Or she wouldn't do them.

Yes, she was born anew today all due to being called a witch. How liberating it was to be reminded she deserved better. Now, she was going to live *as if* she had better. Even though everything came into her head at once, she felt liberated.

Every bit of this revelation had taken place in a matter of seconds, and while she wanted to leap with exuberance, she realized the ceramic artist still stood in front of her. Time had stood still long enough to collect and assemble her new mindset. Looking this other artist in the eye, she began, "It's fascinating how people feel they can come into your booth space and rain over your spirit when in fact as artists, we have so much heart to give if they'd only ask. This is what they want to buy from us. What they cannot see or feel for themselves. Our minds don't stop. Our creative spirit doesn't quit. If it did, we would have to find other careers.

"Those people that just left my booth couldn't think outside the box and as such had to find a label for me and most likely others here today as well. What's wonderful is how I feel sorry for them. I see color where they could only see gray. My soul wants to soar every minute of the day and night. So, I'm fine. Actually, I'm better than fine! I'm elated to have had them come into my space today. My eyes are so open right now along with my heart. I thank them for their negativity. It's exactly what I needed.

"You see, I feel when weird, odd, upsetting, crazy, even wonderful things happen to each of us in life, it's like throwing a stone into a calm pond. That stone creates ripples. Those people threw their gunk into my pond. Some people might carry their negativity forward. Which is, of course, in my opinion, a complete waste of energy. No, for me, what my ripple will be is this . . . to thank them for opening my eyes! I'm not upset. I'm happy! My ripple is to take their negativity, turn that around and see them now as an opportunity for inner spiritual growth."

Obviously stunned by this response and uncertain of what to say, the ceramist stumbled a bit. "Oh, ah, okay. Just remember there are lots of crazies in this world. Don't take it personally." This was the last thing that neighbor said as she left Vonnette's booth and headed back to her own space.

During times where she was unstable and at the mercy of an uncertain public, Vonnette kept a strand of emerald beads in her travel pouch. Taking them out she began to hold them between her two clasped hands. Breathing slowly, she drank some water and then held the emeralds in her left hand while realizing that for the first time she was vibrating energetically due to her own awakening and not because of some abusive client.

After about five minutes her breathing became more regular. The shakes had subsided. Vonnette looked under her counter to see it was almost five. One hour before closing time.

A young woman perhaps in her twenties came in to peruse. Being a young and attractive woman, it was obvious to Vonnette that she had insecurities. How else could you explain her lips being filled with whatever at such a young age? It always amazed Vonnette how many women came through these shows who recently had facelifts or fillers of one sort or another done. For older women these enhancements usually meant that person didn't like how they were aging. Vonnette was seeing wrinkles on her own face so understood that concept completely. However, younger women having that kind of work done normally meant they had physical or emotional issues or even both at the same time. Something Vonnette could certainly identify with before this magical day. The problem with someone who just had their lips filled at any age was that they could not speak normally. As a show vendor, Vonnette had to pay extremely close attention to what that person was trying to say without being obviously horrified by their Daffy Duck-type speech pattern.

After reading some of the stone properties, this girl asked, "Do you know the healing pwopaties for Moganite?"

"Over here," Vonnette said as she walked to the other end of the booth. "I have a large portion of healing properties written in a book for sale." Feeling a bit gun-shy after that last couple she was unsure about discussing her book, but she was determined to be her whole self now and not a prisoner to anyone. All that along with the fact that she was directly asked, she flipped open to the alphabetic page for morganite and stepped back to let the girl read.

"You say that moganite is part of the barrow family. What is barrow?"

Deeply concentrating to catch everything this young woman was trying to say, Vonnette carefully attempted not to mimic her speech pattern. This was something that as an empath Vonnette had issues with. Like when she went south, Vonnette always came home with an accent calling people *Chile*. There was no malicious intent, Vonnette simply made every effort at total comprehension towards anyone with an accent different from her own.

Mustering whatever was necessary from deep inside, Vonnette remained focused on the current question. "Beryl is the mineral or crystal classification. Most likely you've heard of emerald and/or aquamarine that are also part of that same beryl family. Generally speaking, beyond the three stones thus far mentioned, any other color stone found in the beryl family are simply called beryl.

"Think of quartz. Most people know about clear quartz, or maybe even rose quartz."

The girl nodded in acknowledgement.

"Stones like jasper and opal are also part of that same quartz family. Different minerals shift the content within the quartz and make them into jasper or opal. Beryl is no different really.

"Might I ask, do you have a piece of jewelry made with morganite? Or are you thinking about purchasing one since you're displaying such interest today?"

"Ah, no, I don't have one. Saw one somewhare and thought it could be quite attwactive. Didn't have the money to make the purchase at the time, though. My name is Chandwa by the way."

"Hi Chandra, lovely name. I'm Vonnette."

"Lately I have been paying more attention to enageez. Maybe I ought to buy your book to look things up. Think I can afford that today. Yah, I will take one, pwease."

"Okay Chandra, thanks. I'll write up a sales slip and get a bag for you."

"Where did you come up with the stone pwopaties? Was it another book?"

"No. I channeled these properties myself over a few years. Then I went about creating the jewelry to go into the book for reference."

Feeling a tad more comfortable, Vonnette was still not coming forth with any kind of answers to unasked questions. At this time, it was not due to feeling defensive but rather it was enough to grasp what this woman was saying let alone add anything on to or possibly begin to copy her speech pattern.

"Holy cow! You made the jewry *and* channeled the pwoperties? Color me impwessed! I'm having enough twouble getting a thesis paper finished let alone white a book. Although, it would be a good thing for me to think about as I'm into my masters pwogram white now. Hey, here's a thought, how would you feel about collabawaiting with me on a thesis? It could be on healing enageez in stones."

"Let me think about that one, Chandra. It's a lovely thought to get the message further out there on the possibilities of stone energy. Tell you what, after you read the book you're purchasing today, and if you still want to collaborate, we'll talk again, okay?" Hopeful that by that time Chandra would be speaking normally again with her new lips, it would also give Vonnette time to consider being that involved in another writer's work.

"Yes, that'll work for me. Thanks."

A look came across Chandra's face that Vonnette felt she knew. A look that wanted another question answered. Which one she had no idea of. "Can I ask one more question before I go?"

"Ask away. If I know the answer I'm happy to reply."

"I beweave I wead somewhare how to cleanse jewry and/or loose stones of negative enageez. Cannot wecall where I wead that or what the suggestion was. Do you know? Is it compwicated?"

With one question, Vonnette returned to her twenties when she had all the same questions without the benefit of being able to ask even one person for an answer. For that matter she couldn't find books available with any of this information either. It was perfect timing after that last couple had blind-sided Vonnette by calling her a witch that gave her a life-changing, inner discovery kind of moment. This young woman was refreshing, open and sincere. Even if she couldn't speak clearly with these newly filled lips of hers that looked a bit like the red wax lips Vonnette used to buy at the penny candy store when she was a child, Chandra was thankfully someone Vonnette could let her hair down with once again. Maybe she was really, really, really done.

"There are a couple methods on how to cleanse stones and/or jewelry and each are listed in the book on page 269. Why don't you tell me if the stone slash jewelry in question has built up energy, or if it is in fact your energy that is in need of cleansing?"

"Oh, guess that's diffwent. Hadn't thought of that, good question; Well, I believe it's the jewry. Wecently I went true a bad bwake up with my boyfwiend. He was turning into a stalker. I was nervous at the time that he would shift and become more than a stalker. Sad to say, I kept twirling a wing of mine awound and awound on my finger. It became a habit. One day the wing fwew off my hand. Don't know how exactly because it was a tight fit up til then. Thankful it happened while I was at home, I still couldn't believe it, even though I was there and saw it happen. Told a couple fwiends about the wing fwying across the womb. Their take was that the enageez had built up to a cwescendo and had nowhare else to go. Since then I have almost been afwaid to wear the ring. Someone suggested I cleanse it of the bad enageez. Would you agwee?"

"Yes, most definitely. Before I get into the cleansing process you need, can I ask what happened to that guy?"

"He was awested for stalking another woman. Guess I wasn't enough." Just then, nervous laughter escaped her. "After that he went to twial and is in pwison in another state, thankfully. By the time he'll get out, I hope to be secuwa in a job and have evwewone awound me know about him just in case."

"Hmmmm. That's a lot on your plate for someone so young. Sorry you have had to deal with all that. Amazingly enough you sound centered at this moment for someone who has been stalked by an ex-boyfriend. No wonder you have been attracted to morganite because it helps you to chew on life and embrace new developments."

Mentally digesting what Chandra had just shared, Vonnette thought that her boyfriend experience most certainly could be why she'd had her lips done. Having difficulty taking in what she needed in the way of useful energy, Chandra was unable to digest what was coming her way. Insecurities over feeling safe inwardly had her question what was going on externally even on her own personage. And, all that added up to how she was interested in morganite.

Pulling herself back into the moment at hand Vonnette began, "Okay, back to the question asked. There must have been a build-up of some sort of energy in that ring for it to fly off your finger and across the room. Things like that happen to me, too. When it does happen, I always tell Spirit I will not wear the ring or whatever it might have been for a certain amount of time, like a month, let's say. During that segment of time away from wearing whatever piece of jewelry it was, I cleanse the piece and recharge it. All that information is in the book, as I have said, but let me give you a crash course.

"What I recommend is to take a small bowl and put a bit of

warm water in it along with some sea salt. Place your ring in that water. If it has a stone like amber, pearl, opal or emerald, then don't leave it in for very long. And by that, I mean only leave it in for a couple minutes. If the ring is plain metal, you can leave it in for as long as you like. When you remove whatever from the salty water, make sure you pour that water down the drain to eradicate negative energy. Rinse the ring off with clear water while asking for any negative energy to be removed and allow it to continue moving forward into the light, and then pat it dry with a clean dry cloth."

"Do I use bottwed water? Can I do all this with tap?"

"Good question. You can use tap. You're clearing energy with salt mixed in with water and then rinsing off any residue afterwards, so tap works quite well.

"Now, where was I? Oh, yes, place your piece of jewelry on a white cotton cloth or even a white paper towel in the open-air sunlight for any length of time you feel is correct. Again, if it has a pearl, amber, opal or emerald please only leave it in direct sunlight for a few minutes. The sun might cause damage if left out longer.

Placing the ring in a window with glass in between the ring and the sun won't do. It needs to be open air. This recharges the metal and stones with positive energy. You see, the window glass can magnify the sun's potency and ruin a stone because it can refract light incorrectly. So, best not to have a window between your jewelry and any effort on recharging.

"You ought to notice an immediate shift in energy after doing all this.

"Other types of jewelry such as beads need to be cleansed in very specific ways, but you said it was a ring alone, so that's what we're talking about here today.

"Remember though, if you made a pact with the universe about not wearing something for a certain amount of time, honor that, even though you have cleansed and recharged whatever piece of jewelry in question. The universe is funny about broken promises.

"There are other methods for this process covered in the book, but this one works on so many levels. I feel it's the right way for you at this time. This is something that can work for you as well as your home or apartment, too. I mean, since you have experienced someone stalking you. That means they were outside your residence and can leave trace elements of negative energy behind, to say nothing of what you still carry emotionally from that experience."

Realizing she was listening closely and feeling a bit like a teacher where Chandra was her devoted pupil, Vonnette continued, "Take either Kosher or sea salt because those are pure salts. Nothing mucked about with by added iodine or whatever will do here. Sprinkle the salt around the exterior of your home. I like to do it once in a great while like an afternoon before I know it's going to really rain that night. Ask for the negativity to be removed and let only positive energy remain. The rainwater will wash the salt away taking the negative energy along with it.

"Do the same for yourself in a bath with either sea or Kosher salt. You can do this over the course of a few days or a week. You'll know when to stop as you forget to add salt to the water. Before you climb out of the bath, make sure to rinse with clear water and ask the same thing I mentioned before . . . 'Please remove all negative energy from my body and allow only positive energy to remain. Allow me to continue moving spiritually towards the light under grace, and in divine right, perfect, and healthful ways.' That will wash your auric field and allow you to continue moving forward with positive energy. It's a good thing to do every so often."

Chandra's face had a new look now. Perhaps it was surprise, maybe confusion? While running her hands up and down her arms she spoke. "Don't know why, but I have a sudden chiww."

"Oh, okay, I understand now why you just had such a strange look on your face. When you get a chill as someone is telling you something important, it's confirmation of a truth. The other side wants you to understand that what you just heard is true and ought to work well for you.

"Do you know what I mean by your auric field Chandra?"

Nodding her head in a yes fashion, Vonnette felt she must continue to the end of this for Chandra to be rid of the negative, stalker energy that Vonnette felt was attached to her.

"Okay, then, are you following what I said about the salt around your house or your apartment?"

"Yes. I have an apaatment white now. There are five apaatments in the same building. Should I do the salt when othaws are going to be asking me if I'm nuts?"

"Sprinkle the salt around the perimeter *inside* your apartment while paying special attention to the door and window areas on the floor. When finished, wait until you feel it's time, trust your gut instinct, and then vacuum it all up. Make sure to get all the salt up in the vac. Once you do, throw the vacuum bag out in the trash. If you have a bag less vac, make sure you empty it out into the trash, and get that trash bag out of the apartment. Follow up by washing out the bag less area of the vac, too. It's important to make sure you've trapped the negative energy and have then removed it from your environment as best you can.

"If this guy was being weird around your car, you can do the same thing inside the car with the salt and vacuum. By doing all that energy clearing of yourself, your environment, and the ring, you ought to create a new personal space energetically. There are times I suggest to use apple cider vinegar baths or showers, but I feel you are in need of the intensity of salt right now. Salt has the best cutting action for auric fields I know of. You told me you had the chills. That confirms I have given you the proper advice for the kind of energy you are walking around with.

"There is also an American Indian method of cleansing for your building that's called a smudge stick. These can be found in health food stores where you can also get directions for use. That's something you can do at night when you feel everyone in your building is in bed, so they don't think you're nuts as you walk about with this smoking thing that has a strong scent. If you decide to use a smudge stick, always work the smoke from the stick towards an open door or window. By heading towards an open window or door, the negative energy has a place to escape. And, make certain you are keeping it away from smoke detectors, or you could have another kind of issue to deal with there.

"Honestly, I think we nailed what you ought to do with your ring, yourself, and in your apartment with utilizing salt."

Seemingly in deep thought, she was smiling so Vonnette gave her a moment to digest everything.

"I'm so happy I stopped at yowa booth today. Actually, I'm happy I came to the show. Didn't have the enageez this morning to do anything. That's why I'm hewa so late in the day. Think it's about qwosing time now, isn't it?"

Glancing under her makeshift counter, Vonnette noticed it was 5:50. Nodding her head in agreement, she was happy this young woman had stopped in, too. It was an upbeat end to the day.

"Can't thank you enough, Vonnette. It has been enwhitening in many ways tawking with you. Think this was a kismet moment in time for me!"

"Chandra, I thank you. This book will give you a lot of information you are craving right now. Do work with the salt cleansing, too. I feel it's something you need to shake free of that negative stalker element. If you have questions, give a call. My number is on the sales slip. If I can't pick the phone up when you call, leave a message. I'll get back in touch as soon as I can."

"Thank you, Vonnette. I weawly appweciate all you have given me today for infamation. Sawwy I am not in the mawket for jewey at this time."

"No worries. You bought a book and that's something I very much appreciate. The book will give you information today as well as into the future. It's been nice talking and getting to know you. I wish you well. Take good care."

"You as weww. Be seeing you."

While packing up her jewelry, Vonnette went over the day. Two crazy people drove home an important message Vonnette had been working at fully grasping that not only were her beliefs valid, but so was she! In spite of everything, other people sought her out to ask questions about her beliefs. Chandra was a perfect example of that. "Connect the dots," was what Vonnette kept repeating inside her head. For a brief second, it seemed the murder of crows had won out but in the end, the four crows spied this morning provided a birth moment instead. Grateful and hopeful at the same time, Vonnette wondered if this feeling of validity would carry forward to allow her to see life with joy in her heart.

Looking about the show as other artists left their booths, Vonnette wondered if they, too, had such strange experiences as she had at these shows.

Did they have people call them witches?

Did they get into conversations with clients about metaphysical topics?

Shaking the day off, she repeated her booth neighbors' thought out loud: "'People are crazy.' But then, because of those nutty people today, I'm seeing life through rose-colored glasses. A very special day I think!"

✺

November 16, Sunday 2008

Not wanting to wake fully Sunday morning, Vonnette lay still recalling whatever fragments she could from her dream messages.

DREAMS

1. Twenty-two karat yellow gold was in her hands. While talking to a woman, Vonnette spread this gold out in her fingers making it thinner and thinner as if it was bread dough. The woman was saying she didn't trust the element of such high karat gold over the long haul of wear and tear. Whatever ring this was to be in the end, she felt it ought to be of a lower karat, more durable gold. Smiling, Vonnette was in her own space feeling this metal in her fingers and deciding it could actually be made into an overlay on top of and incorporated into a base ring of, say, 14K. She went on forming her design.

2. Some man was moving a spatula around on the top of a thickly iced chocolate cake. Noticing the tiny ants marching about in army formation along the floor, the man scooped a bunch of the ants up and spread them out over the white frosting. Now dead, they had become part of his abstractly designed surface. Asking why he had done such a thing, Vonnette stood and watched him continue with this odd method of decoration.

Feeling the ant design was a form of protein, he informed her they could be usable in any kind of cooking that didn't require boiling or over-heating them. That would destroy not only their shape but also break down their proteins and not in a good way.

More chocolate cakes with the white frosting appeared in the dream. Since the ants had been so plentiful, the chef incorporated them into each of his designs to create one-of-a-kind cakes.

Vonnette had to wonder what the taste would be of such a cake.

Once she felt fully awake, Vonnette thought about the dream symbol book she'd worked with for many years titled, *The Dreamer's Dictionary*. Many definitions in that book Vonnette had memorized, not on purpose, but rather due to constant usage. Calling up symbols from that book this morning along with associating her own life symbolisms was in an effort to comprehend what these two dreams might mean for her final day of the show.

Everything had been good financially yesterday. In her experience of doing shows of different lengths of time, she found that in a two-day show, one day could be better for sales than another. Three-day shows were a crap shoot. Promoters usually gave attendees an option of returning a second day during the course of the weekend without an entrance fee, so they could in fact buy. That, or, buy more than they had the first go 'round. Unfortunately, that could also offer people too much time to think about what they might purchase to the point where they might decide not to return and buy at all.

Tearing up, Vonette tried to figure out why she suddenly felt like crying!

Tired from doing this and all the previous back-to-back shows, along with the cancer scare and then dealing with Frank, Vonnette realized crying was simply a side effect due to exhaustion. This was really her fourth day for this event with her set up happening Thursday. Vonnette needed to gather enough energy to make it through the day and then pack up her booth and drive home. Though it was a mere two-hour drive back to Newport, a shorter distance than most shows she participated in, she already dreaded the drive and wished she could simply remain one more night so as not to be weary on her way home.

Fully up, she listlessly walked about her temporary home gathering belongings and packing her bag. Choosing something in the way of clothing that would not only look acceptable for the day at the show but that could also work as she packed her booth inside the show location, on into her car, and then whatever would be unloaded once home was the immediate focus.

Normally a morning person, something still needed to shift for her energetically today. Knowing what a treat it was to have a shower in her motel room instead of only a bath at home, Vonnette jumped in. She began to feel a bit more balanced with the steamy-hot water and thought some yoga stretches would be a good thing. Once dressed she did exactly that, making sure she was on top of a towel on the floor of the motel room. Certain these carpets had seen more than they might ever tell, she didn't want any part of it, whatever *it* was, and a towel would help to that end.

Stretching complete, she pulled out an apple along with shelled walnuts and sat on the bed to eat while rethinking the dream messages.

Thickly-iced frosting on cakes suggested happier times ahead. Both cakes and icing were a good sign. Ants however . . . . Their industrious nature stood for a change in business position. Not only did she have issues with ants at home in real life but according to her dream book, to have them on food meant frustration. In the dream, they were in lines until they were on the cakes and had been dead once placed there by the chef. Could that possibly mean she was entering a place of release since death was on some level a symbol for liberation in dream symbology?

It was a hopeful thought. One that Pollyanna could be proud of.

Forming that ring with her hands as if it was made out of dough was indeed odd. Bread dough could represent financial dough. Yes, Pollyanna was alive. Maybe someone at the show today would like a ring she'd made out of high karat gold and then wouldn't justify making the purchase due to the possibility of it not being durable enough. Flip sides of the coin, she guessed where one minute she was in a positive emotional place and suddenly back into that undesirable state of mind where sales would not come to fruition. Not really any final feelings about the day, she headed off to the show and whatever might come her way.

No crows were seen on Vonnette's way to the venue. Disappointing.

While setting up her jewelry this morning, her mind went on and on, seemingly incapable of focusing on any one thing.

The people who called her a witch yesterday were whomever they needed to be. Unexpected opportunity for personal growth was their gift to her though she was certain that wasn't their intent. Show promoters had not shown up to reprimand her for speaking to attendees as she had. Most likely if they were to do so, they would come before the show opened and it was now open. Efforts were made to lose and let those people go, but Vonnette was too tired for complete follow-through.

Being overtired did not help her to focus and be on top of the day.

One person, then two, then a group of women came through looking, pointing and dreaming of whatever piece or pieces they saw in her booth. Vonnette handed out business cards with whatever pertinent information written on them for easy recollection once the people left the show in hopes it would lead to a sale down the road.

Comforted by the sales she had made the day before, Vonnette would be able to get caught up financially with the last couple of show fees she had not been able to cover on her credit cards till now. The mortgage would also be paid this month. All that was good.

On her bathroom run before opening time, Vonnette located the food vendor booth. Eating a corn muffin gave her the ability she had been craving to focus on the here and now. It was then that she was somehow filled with the Belief that things would work out. Suddenly, she felt worthy of remaining in her home. This was something she had not ever thought about before, feeling worthy of remaining in her home even though it had always been a financial struggle to maintain. Having Faith that financial matters will thrive might mean that Vonnette was kidding herself, or it could be that she was Believing the universe would support her whenever necessary.

Shame on Vonnette for consistently accepting less than what she knew in her heart she was worthy of. Somewhere internally she had felt less was all she deserved. This was part of the magical word "Karma!" Where what she sent out energetically came back to her. In this case, as long as Vonnette felt she deserved not to be supported in her home, she wouldn't be. Without realizing it all these years, Vonnette had been canceling out any good financial energy by believing she didn't deserve it!

No wonder supporting herself financially had always been such a struggle.

"I need to stop criticizing myself, my lifestyle, my work, my home and my selling techniques because I'm only attracting negative energy by doing that."

For this minute, she was living *as if* and the universe was saying okay, you've got it. If Vonnette could maintain this kind of thinking, then she would be living *as if* with Belief and Faith that all would work out in her favor.

These ideas of maintaining positive thoughts, and the concept of living *as if*, both went along with the idea of *if you can think it, it can happen*. Yes, it was the same thread as her positive affirmations. Being able to really feel these ideas were already so in her life meant Vonnette could see them on some level as well. Since Vonnette was a visually-oriented person, seeing it was not an issue. No, her problem with finding the *as if* part of the equation was being able to feel in her core that money already existed in her life, just as it was right now from the sales generated yesterday. Because of those sales she didn't feel needy when people came into her booth today.

Vonnette suddenly heard herself and the white light popping Jennifer speaking together inside her head and then she understood the meaning of her dream with two different karats of gold. It didn't have anything to do with a client coming in to look at something. That message was about Vonnette's dressing up the top layer of her own thinking while having a secure base metaphorically of a lower, more durable, karat of gold. She was the gold in that dream and was molding herself into something with a sound base as well as a decorative top layer. That top layer could very well be her thought patterns being of pure gold.

Associating the *as if* element along with manifesting, she was bringing in money as if by magic. Maybe not every day, but then she was just beginning to really grasp the living as if element. Some dots were connecting on how she had been able to manifest not only her own business, but her own home many years ago. Vonnette's issue all these years since could be explained today with her new comprehension about the laws of attraction. Where like attracts like. Where Vonnette had so much difficulty attracting steady income due to her feelings she either didn't deserve to have the money she needed or couldn't see what her life would be like *with* the money once it came her way. Vonnette saw her life with the aggravation of ants today in a new light. These tiny creatures were a reminder of her own negative thoughts marching around in her brain. As long as she allowed them to invade her positive belief system, she would always be caught up in an army of negative financial issues. With Belief and Faith fully in tact Vonnette could achieve the financial stability she craved. In spite of everything, she did manifest her business as well as her home all those years back. They were already present in her life. All she had to do now was to keep the Faith that she deserved to maintain these wonderful manifestations.

With the unconditional love of her two feline children as well as human friends, she had everything in her life that she wanted. And, everything she had in her life was from her first imagining it, and then it all came into her world. Living in constant fear of it completely going away was her block to having everything she wanted and how to keep it in her life.

The fear of losing it all was holding her back!

How could she eliminate the fear? That was a question worthy of major effort.

"I know to meditate, to take long walks, to chant, to moan, why is fear still with me?

"Fear of the unknown is a heavy weight to bear when it grips me by the throat stopping me from doing almost anything I feel I should do. And yet, fear does help to keep me out of harms' way when in any major life threatening kind of danger."

Here she was doing her thing again, talking to thin air. This was a method of not only hearing what she said but to also think about what she was saying.

"Okay, so I have manifested some pretty heavy duty things in my life with the business as well as the house. For that matter, I paid my way through college, working almost full time as a waitress. So, this last bit of the puzzle ought to be doable.

"Each time I have manifested things like the business or the house, I have visually pictured it repeatedly, along with how I could feel inside when it would come to fruition. I also went so far as to picture myself inside each dwelling with my cats and friends coming to visit, or clients coming in trying on jewelry and buying. That means that being as visually oriented as I am I need to keep that concept going to incorporate positive thinking into my everyday world and not to allow fear to grip my throat every day.

"Hmmm. Okay, I'm picturing it. I see myself walking, talking, driving with a sense of peace and wellbeing. My stomach muscles are level and quiet as when I meditate or even go out for a walk. The more I picture this, the more my muscles relax. The more my muscles relax, the easier I will see myself living as if, because I will be manifesting a lack of fear into my mind, body and soul. I will be embracing a new me.

"This is my way to unblock the blocked.

"This is the way for me to create a new life pattern, one without stress being in control. One where I find peace and freedom all at the same time. One where I let go of age-old emotional blocks I created for myself years and years ago. Since I generated those blocks, then most certainly I can remove those images and make new ones that will fill any emotional holes."

Completely in her own space, literally as well as physically while these threads of thought were being woven together, she was thankful no one was in her booth. That gave her the ability to rant and see what she needed in order to have this show rapidly become one of her favorites.

Quickly this all spilled over in her brain on how to shift her existence from lack into an as if life style, as well as to realize what her brand was with her jewelry style. Yes, these thoughts and inner connections were wonderful so far today. And these concepts began to give her the energy she needed not only to complete the day at the show but also to pack up and drive home. Her vitality was back on que. There was almost too much going on in her head to remain centered for the rest of the show hours, but she would.

As the show wound down and all artists began to pack up their vehicles, Vonnette went into another recess and thought again about the ant element on the cakes in her other dream. Apparently that old, annoying pattern was on its way out because the ants were killed to become part of the cakes! Old patterns such as negative thinking would always be part of Vonnette's core. Part of an inner base that reminded her of how life used to be. Today, she moved forward, up and out of the negative thought base that had held her back for most of her life. Perhaps due to the overwhelming shame of that dreadful day at age eleven. Today, Vonnette was continuing to move forward, where she conquered the aggravate of ants, or people labeling her, or feeling trapped in a ten-by-ten-foot booth. Today Vonnette had a firm grip on how Belief and Faith played an important role in how she could, and would manifest everything she needed, and wanted in life. Today, she knew eating habits would in fact shift. Her new thoughts were on how proteins (the now dead ants), could literally be the icing on the cake known as her life! Yes, driving home would be okay tonight. Vonnette was filled with gratitude; of understanding her dream messages, of being able to cross-reference them into her daily life, of being able to see how living as if had brought the element of positive thinking into full comprehension to even connect with her ability to manifest money, of being healthy, of simply being! Her energy felt balanced once again. Tearful thoughts were gone, and they were replaced with hope, utter Belief and yes, Faith.

While driving home that night, Vonnette kept thinking about how the weekend had gone, on so many levels. There were sales made; in fact, good ones. She had sincere connections with new people with whom she hoped would be in touch again in the future for other creations. One couple in particular Vonnette felt would contact her for wedding bands. Chandra was a nice surprise as well on a slightly different playing field since she craved input, but didn't even comprehend on what level or how until they met and began talking. Vonnette trusted their conversation would bring in positive shifts for Chandra. Then, the "witch" people presented an opportunity for internal growth. Recalling different conversations between Jenn and Vonnette even brought forth the concept of living *as if.* Something Vonnette had not been able to wrap her brain completely around until this weekend and, what she anticipated would become part of her daily existence.

Revelations came in fast and furious to Vonnette's internal emotional base. One dream message had suggested to her that being a walk-in meant the previous Vonnette had the issues with food. Understanding she was the flip-side of the whole Vonnette walk-in coin gave her the impetus to Believe she could and would climb onto the other side of that addiction.

While reviewing so many incidents from the weekend, just under two hours had past. Almost home, Vonnette felt something else shifting, her level of trust. Uncertain if this past weekend had brought so many self-discoveries home to nest, or if perhaps the cancer scare pushed her emotions enough to grasp what had seemed beyond her reach until now, Vonnette pulled into her driveway feeling as though she had become a new, updated version of her better self. Belief, Faith and Trust were elements she had felt internally, although sporadically throughout her life. Tonight, she felt each element existed inside, and was there to stay!

CHAPTER 7

The Gift

November 20, 2008 Thursday

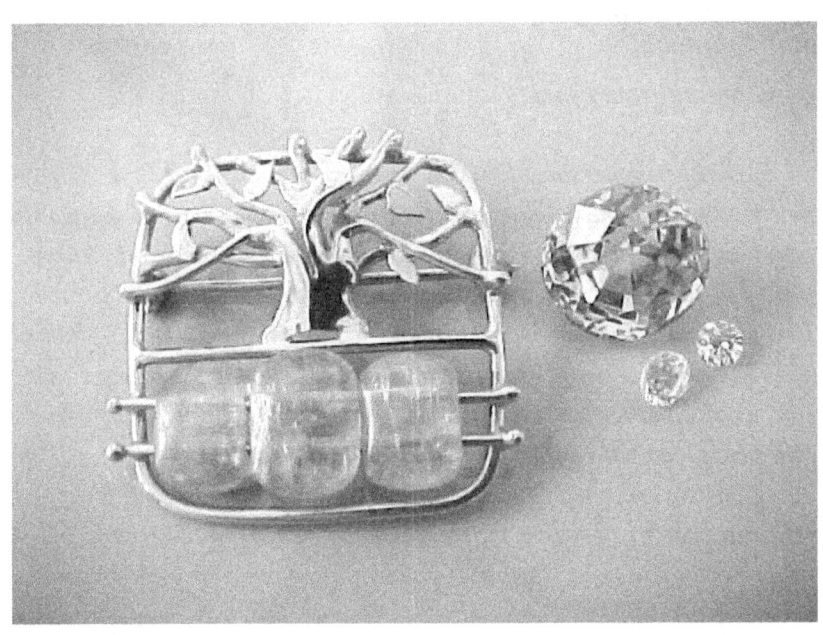

14Ky/w Green Kyanite Tree Pin with loose Yellow Sapphire & Diamonds

Candace L. Sherman

DREAMS

1. A gold wedding band being formed in front of Vonnette's eyes. The flat outer shape tapered down in the back. On the top section were two round bezels for smaller white diamonds. Another bezel appeared for a darker blue sapphire. Soon a fourth bezel appeared for a larger, round, yellow sapphire. Suddenly, the ring opened up lengthwise and turned into a very long path in a lovely garden. The stones that were originally scheduled to be part of the ring multiplied greatly and gathered together to form stepping stones along that garden path.

2. Some friend's birthday.

3. Being in a show where a third-place ribbon was being presented to Vonnette in her booth.

4. Seeing green kyanite everywhere.

5. Being in some sort of prison. There were many hallways. As Vonnette walked in one hall, her water broke and she realized she would be giving birth soon. Just then a doctor appeared. Vonnette told him she would be in need of assistance shortly with her birth. He was the actor who played a doctor and husband on the Donna Reed show. At first he didn't believe her until Vonnette told him where she would be meeting him and the others as a team while giving birth. Continuing on, she told him to fetch the others necessary to form this team.

Vonnette returned to wherever she had been in comfortable quarters and began to prepare for the birth. When the doctor came in, he said that once she did give birth, she would be released from prison.

Walking about her homes' upper level, Vonnette was talking out loud again.

"Whenever I receive messages from the other side, I do my darnedest to follow up on the input; that is, if I can figure the leads given out. None of this makes any sense to me. Why are you directing me in circles? I recall hearing a voice in the middle of the night telling me to *really pay attention today*.

"Don't I always pay attention? It seems as though I pay attention more than most people I know!"

For a moment, she lost her train of thought. A single crow was drinking in the wooden gutter adjacent to her skylight over the bathtub. She could see it through the window. Standing and watching she thought, "Okay, one crow, birth or new beginning on some level." Not wanting to disturb the crow she stood quietly as it took a good drink.

Another crow made itself known. Maybe it was on the telephone wires across the street. Moving slowly over to the other window and slightly opening the shade, she saw five crows on those wires interacting with one another. Observing them, Vonnette then saw the one from her gutter fly over to join the other five.

"Six crows! Love."

Dismissing that whole scene, she came back to her train of thought of how one dream was about a birthday, and yes, it was her friend's actual birthday. "I'll call and wish him a happy day.

"The third-place ribbon was maybe to remind me about the third book. It's loosely based on my travels while doing shows, about gifts we all have and come together to share. This is still in process of being written and could be the birth concept while in prison. Having someone famous in that dream suggested help from an unexpected source today.

"Who would give help about that book I wonder?

"Wedding band turning into a garden path that included faceted stepping stones could simply be my association with the title. I have settled on *Stepping Stonez* as the working title for this third book. I need to take charge of my life again and not only do what I'm directed to do with my dream messages, but also, I need to be living a dream! Choices must be made. I feel I need to make them without always referring to my dreams.

"Generally, I feel I make choices on my own and let the chips fall where they may. But of late, and being as tired as I am from the frantic show schedule along with the health scare, I think I've been more reliant on what the dreams have suggested. I get the message . . . I need to be first in my own life. We are here on this planet earth to learn!

"Smaller white diamonds bring more intensity to the larger blue and yellow sapphire. Blue sapphire gives the intuitive brain permission to open. Yellow sapphire is to stop moping, begin hoping. Green kyanite helps to peel away the layers of doubt and fear. Birthday is some form of celebration today. Being third could be a reminder of how I have accepted less than being first in my own life in the past.

"Amazingly enough, I feel I can give up the thought that I have to do something more, make something more, or be more for others in order to have the life I want and deserve! I'm the only one who has put myself in third place. Therefore, I'm the only one who can make myself first!

"Be who I am at each and every moment. Maybe this is the reason I had the lump in my breast. You Stupid Head! Maybe on some level I needed to stop running around trying everything known to mankind. Why not relax and be?

"What a concept!

"It's so simple!

"Why does it take a time like a near-death experience to bring this into the frontal brain lobe for me?

"Why am I so stubborn?

"Why do I need to literally be hit over the head to get messages like this?

"The dream about giving birth with someone famous in it maybe means actual mental birth for me, but with unexpected assistance. I wonder.

"Who understands all their dreams?

"I must be nuts to think I can figure out what these messages mean each morning before the day actually begins."

As the bathwater ran, Vonnette shook her head as if to rattle these dream segments out of her brain. Making a brief trip downstairs, she wanted to make sure the cats were fed and situated. While in the kitchen she grabbed a glass, filled it with water. Drinking a bit, Vonnette felt something had shifted in the room, but what. Slowly, she placed her glass down on the counter while she visually scanned the area. Picking up her glass again she began to shrug her shoulders.

"I must be losing it. Everything looks clean and in good working order."

Turning to head back upstairs she stopped in her tracks, rotated, and faced the kitchen again. "Oh, this is terrific! No ants! Don't know what I've done, but this is a great moment, and I appreciate it however it happened! Thank you, thank you, whoever helped me with this feat!"

With that, she turned back and headed up to the bathroom once again with a new appreciation for her home being pest free. "Maybe this was my birthday dream come to manifest. Maybe this is the help from an unexpected source today!"

Pouring a generous amount of sea salt into her bathwater and climbing into her antique, ball-claw tub, Vonnette stopped talking out loud for the first time all morning and sank completely into the warm water. Closing her eyes, she appreciated the warmth and clean water around and over her body. It gave her a sense of peace. Something she had not experienced for weeks with her hectic show schedule along with the serious health scare. Letting go a bit more and sinking a little further into the water she let her mind relax, too. Obviously, her mind was not completely shutting down on her this morning because she was now thinking about the stones in her dreams.

Although exhausted from all the back-to-back shows, she was thankful it had been hectic. Such a jammed work schedule kept her from completely sinking into the dark, emotional hole breast or any cancer brings. Especially since her mother had died from breast cancer that eventually went through her whole body.

Grateful to have that cancer experience behind her, Vonnette realized how wonderful it had been to meet Frank during that crazy time frame, too. He was a very nice man. It had been almost two weeks since she'd broken it off with him. He showed Vonnette that she had turned a corner in her world of dating. Accepting him quickly into her life with a sense of inner honesty caught her off guard. Until that time she had found sincerity on that level difficult in her dating world. Among personal friendships it was easier, but in dating it had most certainly been a challenge.

Vonnette pondered how the mind goes into strange places without warning. Since being molested as a child, she didn't speak about her own physical truth very often. Shame had controlled her, so how, then, could she have moved forward out of such an emotional hiding phase?

As an adult, she understood that many people are sexually abused for years before they either find the courage to stop it, or someone discovered what was going on and they then put an end to it. That concept had come as a shock to Vonnette. How would she ever know that others had such experiences when she never shared what had happened to her until college? "If I don't let others in to know the real me, then I have no idea of what their lives are really like either."

One thing she did grasp was that most people had had these horrid experiences with someone they knew. That was not the case for Vonnette. The man she had been with was a scruffy-faced, older man who smelled of the booze he'd drunk the night before. He had a litter of puppies, and she wanted one. Visiting them daily while pleading with her parents to let her choose one became his lure. All he had to do was wait for a moment when his wife left the house to go grocery shopping to attract her into his den of iniquity.

Being a sensitive, one might think she knew what was headed in her direction, but she didn't. And, being a sensitive as well as how vulnerable she was, that one molestation experience was more than enough. It had branded her for life. From that moment forward she never felt clean enough to allow good men into her dating world.

One good man did come calling when Vonnette was in her thirties but before the evening was over, Vonnette was crying in front of him. To say it freaked that guy out was an understatement. Vonnette couldn't help herself, though. She knew he was a decent guy. Maybe even the first of his kind to enter her life since that moment in childhood where she felt so unclean and unworthy. Those feelings of being unworthy were why she cried that night, on that date. The men she chose to date in the past always had issues with alcohol, drugs, or were simply cads of some sort or another. One thing was certain, and that was, that her lovers had been people who were incapable of giving unconditional love. The one thing she craved so very much.

None of that mattered now. What did matter was how that one event in her youth had taken away her childhood. It could be a challenge still, but Vonnette felt she had to be an adult and take care of the child buried deep within to never allow anything like that happen to her inner child again.

Perhaps that was how people developed multiple personalities. Suppressing the child within can make a mind go in different directions all at the same time, especially when there's need to find a safe place to exist.

In this moment, she felt that the rest was the rest, as she'd heard some people say.

Vonnette wanted people to be happy. It gave her hope that one day, too, she would find that kind of peace and joy.

In this bath moment, she was pondering how she needed to love herself first before anyone else could love her. Of course, she knew this psychologically for years and years but then, she was back in that rabbit hole of how could she begin what she didn't know how to do? The shame that stayed with Vonnette from that childhood day was like the scent that lingers after stepping into dog poo. Since she never shared what had happened back then, the child in her could never grasp that she had not done anything wrong, that she deserved love. Fear for emotional survival had stopped her from sharing her history and that same fear stopped her from being all she could be by actually living life instead of functioning, working, working, and working her way through it.

Yes, fear had become Vonnette's best friend in this life; something she understood well.

Fear was what drove her in childhood to run her fingers along the edge of a satin-lined baby blanket to find comfort when spirits were visiting and she didn't yet understand why.

Being the younger of two children, she was the first to go to bed, and those spirits came to see what she was up to while she was alone in bed. Eventually, she became accustomed to transparent people she didn't know who stopped in to visit. As time progressed, she did know some of these people like grandparents, an uncle, or a great aunt by the name of Foffee. Being very young when she had these kinds of experiences, Vonnette grew to accept them as her normal and began to feel at home with these sightings.

As she grew older, though, she realized her friends and family did not see the same dead people she did, and so she hid that element from them, too. By the time Vonnette had graduated college, she began to share some of her visitation experiences, and people often told her they felt uncomfortable. Even her family members didn't like her to talk about who and what she saw. It's no wonder she hid the molestation from everyone as easily as she did. Hiding from those around her was her norm. In childhood, her sister would have chided her for visiting with dead people. Who knew what she would do or say about her being molested back then? Vonnette didn't want to know, and so she never told.

Maybe while relaxing in the tub this morning Vonnette was connecting more dots, so-to-speak.

Maybe she was washing away whatever she considered her shame from that fateful childhood day with the salty water caressing her aura and skin.

When young, she didn't know of anyone who spoke of such things, so she never had an opportunity to regain any form of true emotional balance from that day forward, until right now.

This day she was enjoying a moment of quiet in the bath where she appreciated her immediate world without ants and any immediate show demanding her attention. The fact that she did not have cancer had given her sincere peace. That was something she recognized and appreciated! Emotionally she was giving birth in her tub with the help of physical health overlapping into mental health!

Maybe she would even find time to call a plumber to get her shower fixed.

"I love being me today," she uttered as her head slid underwater.

This was it. This was all she ever really wanted. Peace. It didn't matter if a man loved her. She knew her friends loved her. Her cats loved her. Certainly, God loved her. And she knew her family loved her, too. What really mattered at this moment was that she loved her! All the rest was just that, all the rest.

Visualizing her heart growing bigger to encompass this self-appreciation and love, Vonnette came up for air as if it was the first breath she had ever taken in her life. Maybe it was. One sure thing was that Vonnette felt something new. Something she had waited her whole life to hear inside her heart: She loved herself! It was the biggest and most important gift for which she could have ever hoped. Reaching with her left hand, she touched the lump and sent it so much love at that moment she thought she would burst while thinking, "I am like the stones I work with, multi-faceted and wonderful!"

At that moment, the scent of lilies filled the air, as if it were the middle of May after a spring rain had all the Lilies of the Valley come to full bloom with windows open to receive their lovely aroma.

Her taste buds were suddenly full now of spice cake with peanut butter frosting. Odd, that was her favorite birthday cake when young. Her mother Simca used to make whatever favorite cake and frosting she wanted when it was her birthday. That was a family tradition. Vonnette hadn't had anything like that cake in years, not only because she no longer baked, but also because she didn't allow herself to indulge in processed sugar any more. Yet, here it was in her mouth as if she had just eaten a big slice. It tasted good and came without any negative side effects of actual sugar being placed into her system.

"Hi Mom. Thanks for the cake. You remember that was my favorite. How nice. Hope you're doing okay. Funny, I don't see you, but smell and taste whatever is associated with you. Guess this is a birthday for me. If not, you wouldn't have made my favorite cake and frosting. Thanks."

Tears began to form in the corners of her eyes. "Mom, I've

thought a lot about you lately. Guess you know what I've just been through physically. You had such a struggle with cancer, and it went on and on for such a long time. I'm so sorry you had to have that as part of your physical existence while here in body this last time."

Within her mind she heard Simca speaking. "It's over for me now. No more pain I mean. No more suffering in the physical. And, I was with you as you went through your scare, every step of the way. I didn't want you to go through it alone, but I don't think you felt me there."

"Honestly, I didn't Mom. I felt alone. Alone, alone, alone, just like always I guess."

Tears now leaked out. How had such a relaxing bath turned so suddenly she didn't know, but it certainly had.

"Well, dear, please remember one thing; you are never alone! What you went through as a child, being molested, was part of what you agreed to as one of your many experiences to have while in body. When I was alive I couldn't understand how to talk to you during that time. When you were attacked, I couldn't be there for you in the way you needed me to be. I'm sorry for that, but I want you to know that you have come a very long way since that day, honey. You were stuck back then.

"You are wonderful!

"You have a wonderful spirit!

"You have the gift to feel deeply, empathically. With that gift, you may always feel a bit of anxiety about sharing, but sharing is something you must do in order to move ahead. It's part of your many lessons in this life."

Choking a bit as she allowed tears to flow, Vonnette didn't want to let go of the connection. "Mom, do you think I can learn to be more open and share with people? Do you honestly think I can move through this into some level of security when throughout my life I have felt there was none?"

"You've already done most of the homework necessary to go through the next doorway. Don't let fear hold you back from every-thing you want in this life.

"Fear can be a stumbling block.

"Fear can define you if you allow it to.

"Fear can be a great gift if you work through it and use it to be the lesson it was intended to be.

"Fear can produce wonderment in your life when you learn how to let it go.

"Fear has gripped you deeply, yet look at all you have done and all you are doing every single day. Hear and know this . . . fear is an illusion! I'm proud of you. I know you struggle with food. We all see your struggles on this side and feel your pain. Here's something to remember; when you overindulge, food shoves emotions down deeper and deeper. You have allowed yourself to become stuck in the fear of that childhood moment in your past. Today, you are moving forward. Today you are seeing your glass as half-full and your life through rose colored glasses. Please, remember one thing, when you believe it, you will see it and not only trust it will be good, but also know it will be!"

That was it, she let go completely and fully cried.

Sitting naked in the tub, maybe it was like being in the womb, but she was feeling that old connection with her mother where they could finish one another's sentences and yet today, they let each other speak completely. Though tears streamed down her face, Vonnette thought they were a bit happy, and not such sad tears.

Vonnette was happy for the renewed connection with her mom.

Happy to be safe and healthy.

Happy to think that on some level she was having a type of birth day.

"I smell cigarettes often when I'm in a shower and know you are with me, Mom. Today you are talking to me."

"Yes, I am. That's because you need to know how far you have come in this life. How wonderful you are as a being, and how very much you are loved from beings here on my side. Though you feel humans have not loved you in the way you would like, this day is showing you how that can shift if you allow it to.

"So, allow it to."

That was it. She was gone. Vonnette felt the connection close and knew her mother had left just as quickly as she had entered. She was alone again. Sitting for a few more moments in the warm water, Vonnette gathered her emotions and relished in the thought that her mother had visited with words of kindness today, and that was special.

Finished with her revitalizing bath, and while rinsing off with clean water, she asked to have any negativity removed while she continued moving on into the light where she belonged.

Once out of the tub Vonnette found a new way of placing lotion on. Today, she applied it in almost her normal way beginning with her feet, working up through the rest of her body, applying it everywhere. However, today she even put lotion on her breasts! It was a bit of self-love she had denied herself most of her life since that fateful day so many years ago. So, yes, this was a type of birth day even for something as simple as appreciating her full body, not just parts of it.

The day looked brighter somehow. It was like the rose-colored glasses theme had become her world. Her head was up, not down. That was a big part of it. Suddenly, she realized how much she had been looking at the floor for some time, and not at the horizon. It felt good to be looking up and around in her world. Just how long had she been looking downward, instead of up? Yes, today would be a horizon kind of day!

She loved everything.

She felt loved! Even if she knew the love she felt did not come from the all-important humans on this side of the spiritual realm, Vonnette was told spirits loved her. She loved her own self, too! The six crows predicted love, and that's what she experienced.

Pink and white light surrounded her completely. Vonnette's aura vibrated outward with the glow of self-love and love from Spirit.

Vonnette did her white light exercises as usual. Surrounding her car, her house, herself, her cats, even her work in white light was part of her prayer routine and a way to keep negative energy away from her, her belongings, even her cats for the day. Vonnette finished each of these visual exercises off with, "*Spirits go before me.*

Make my way safe, perfect and clear. Please don't let anything I consider even remotely negative come near me, my car, my cats, my home, or my my work all day this day and all night this night, under grace and in divine right, perfect and healthful ways. May only good come to me. May only good come from me. May I be guided in perfect harmony all day this day and all night this night."

Somehow though, this day the white light was brighter, as though the white light was coming from inside her and emanating outwardly instead of her usual visual method of picturing the white light surrounding her.

How was the light coming from inside?

She didn't know. Things were simply different today.

Who knew if this would last?

Who knew how this was even happening?

Vonnette didn't much care. It was a new experience, but then, most days were filled with new experiences for her. She'd accept it for what it was, and for however long it lasted.

Dressed, she thought about what her day might bring. Perhaps she would work on her latest book. Maybe she would simply sit on the couch and visit with her cats. Traveling so much of late, she did deserve a day of doing nothing.

Life this week would be about returning to a state of normal routine with a new twist, self-love with white and pink light everywhere. While seeing the white and pink light, she suddenly recalled the green kyanite from one dream last night. Kyanite is about peeling away the layers of doubt and fear. Look under a microscope at any created fear to figure out how it came to be, and then how to now develop a cure.

With her health issues, Vonnette had been facing fears along with whom she accepted as male companions. This last show had been a gift on a multiple of levels, facing fears being one biggie.

Talking with Simca while in the bath, she was further reminded about facing her fears. Her mother claimed that fears could be gifts. That was maybe something to ponder as the day progressed.

"Fear has been holding me back in general from moving into a place of emotional and financial security. I need to focus on my life as if I've already conquered these fears. Embrace what it looks like with that emotional freedom. Grasp that and I will sincerely have a birth day!"

The phone rang. A bill collector. Vonnette's throat tightened and her breathing became shallow as she grabbed hold of paper and a pen to write down with whom she spoke and take notes on where the conversation might lead in case at some later date these notes were necessary. Once settled in with what company was calling her, she asked again for the person's name. She would include it in her notes. Thinking she had not heard him correctly, she asked two more times, so he spelled it out for her. "A. S. I. F."

Repeating the name back to him, it registered on some deep level that this call was not about any bill she owed, it was Spirit letting her know something was up. The remainder of the call was not important to Vonnette, nor did it really register as anything vital. He was from the phone company. She had already mailed in their payment. After sharing that with him he asked for the check number and date she mailed it out. Not in her office at that moment, there was no way to convey this information, but she did recall mailing it off the previous week.

Somehow, that seemed to satisfy him and he left the conversation.

Laughing out loud, Vonnette stood still grasping what the message might be. *As if. As if.* Asif! Simca had spoken about fear and Vonnette had been working on living life *as if.* Was this her true birth moment for the day? Could this man's name, Asif, be the message received during the night where she was told to pay close attention today?

"Spirit is having fun with me. As if. Not sure what you want me to do with this, but seriously, you cannot make this stuff up, folks. Well, maybe you can, but I couldn't. Listen, whatever you want me to pay attention to, I will, but you've got to be more specific! I know, I know. How can you be more clear than to send me a bill collector named Asif?"

Moving about the house, Vonnette changed her direction completely and felt it might be time to investigate Sophie Belle's brother Jackson. Was he actually the sibling he claimed to be? It had been weeks since they met at the show in Newport. If they connected, would she still have the flip-flop stomach reaction she'd experienced when they first met? Was he really single? Vonnette felt a couple phone calls would resolve those questions. One thing she knew was that people always want to discuss other people.

While figuring out whom to call and ask for information about a possible new client, Sophie Belle, Vonnette decided she wouldn't let on about her emotional interest in Jackson. She thought, "Just get what information I can through casual conversation on both Sophie *and* if *he* really is the brother he claims to be. If in fact he is a brother, and I do begin to date him, maybe I will let him in emotionally, the way I had done with Frank."

Just then, she heard a knock at the door. Not expecting anyone she looked through her bay window to see who it might be.

It was Jennifer!

These two friends exchanged a warm greeting while Vonnette invited Jennifer inside.

"Shall I put the kettle on for tea?"

"Yes, please."

"Okay," Vonnette said, "tell me, why has your white light-self come to my door this day?" For some reason, Jennifer's aura today of white light seemed to be spitting out sparks that were like faceted diamonds shining in the sunlight. Vonnette knew her well enough to realize that this meant something was not only on her mind but also that it would be enlightening on some level once shared.

"I was compelled to come over, Vonnette. There is something in the air it seems."

"Interestingly enough, yes there is. My mother visited this morning. We had a nice chat about fear holding me back from all I want in life. Then, of course we spoke about the cancer scare I just went through. It all melded back into the conversation about fear, really."

"Ah, that can be part of it, then."

"Part of what, might I ask?"

Vonnette was in the kitchen pouring boiling water into the ceramic tea pot she loved that was white with navy blue swirls on it.

Something she had exchanged with a ceramist for at a show a few years back. The potter wanted a strand of cherry quartz beads for the teapot. It was a fair financial deal made between them for each artist to have what they wanted without money getting in the way. At shows, at least among artists, this form of barter system usually worked well with both parties gaining something they desired.

Vonnette knew Jennifer preferred chamomile tea so there was no need to even ask before she placed two tea bags into the pot. Next, she set the small antique pine table with a couple of mugs, cloth napkins, honey and the brewing teapot. Only two chairs could fit at that kitchen table. Jennifer sat comfortably waiting for Vonnette to join before getting into whatever she was going to share.

"I received a message this morning for you. I was informed to come and deliver it in person. You know I don't usually come without calling first, but I felt this was such a strong connection that I ought to get to it immediately."

Vonnette knew Jennifer was a wonderful person who only had anyone's highest and best interest at heart. Still, there was a little trepidation in her response. "Okay . . ."

"You have gone through a lot lately. It's almost like you have been taking a speed course on a computer or something. You've had this crazy show schedule. Then, the cancer issue came front and center. Add into the mix your very fast connection with Frank. Now, it seems your mom has popped in to give added information about fear possibly holding you back."

Nodding, Vonnette was listening intently and perhaps even let out a murmur that was her way of letting Jennifer know she was on board with all she was listing as what had been happening.

"Well, I'm here to add more onto that plate of self-discovery. I have felt for some time now that there was something you needed to hear, and today I was given the nudge to come and say it out loud. You have said to me over many years that you feel alone."

More nodding across the table.

"That's not true! Not only do you have two cats that adore you and whom you love very much, but also you have Spirit. I know when you have expressed the concept of being alone, you were in fact referencing human contact, but here's what I keep getting. That the last piece of your puzzle is to find the place inside where you feel worthy of whatever it is you really want in life. Somehow you manage to take care of people and sometimes yourself, but overall, you keep feeling alone. Yet, there are friends like me who are in your world. How is it you are alone when you have good friends? Is it that you feel the need to have a man in your life? If so, that's a different matter. But honestly, you have done, and do, so much everyday where your life is filled with Spirit, and you share whatever you learn with those around you. Even sometimes with those who don't want to hear it but on some level, must want to. If not, they wouldn't be in your face.

"I'm getting side-tracked. Sorry. You have Spirit, are not alone, and yet still feel as though you are. That really stems from self-worth. This can be something from your family background, or from when you were molested, or from people who try to pigeon-hole you into believing you need to have a man in your life to be complete. Only you can figure that part of the puzzle out.

"When you have self-esteem, and true self-worth, you know you are full to overflow with Spirit, even if you didn't believe in continuous life and all the spiritual contacts you have, let alone your dream messages, you would feel full.

"Somehow, you have to tell Spirit that you are ready now to walk through that door into being full, complete, and welcome the support from inside your emotional self to continue walking your walk.

"Once you do that, you won't ever feel the need to look outside for reinforcement that you are on the right path. You already have support that sometimes you don't hear because you've held yourself back with this feeling of lack on some weird level."

"So, if I'm following along correctly, you feel I misinterpret my feelings of being alone. That in fact, I am not alone, but feel like I am due to this lack of self-esteem?"

"That's it in a nutshell."

"Hmmmm. Self-esteem. Not something I really ever think about honestly. You could have something here.

"Then, in order to feel full and not alone, I need to look inward to connect with my self-esteem and then I will realize how not alone I am due to the people who are in my life. And what I got as you said this is that I will also discover how to connect with the financial world I need to be in."

Some hand movement suggested Jennifer was about to make an objection to what Vonnette had just said when Vonnette spoke up a bit more loudly to make her point clearer.

"No, no, I get it, you never mentioned money. However, it associates on so many levels of where you were dancing in this conversation. If I don't have the full self-worth I need to feel the connections with my friends, then I also don't have the emotional bit to hang onto what I have financially because, on some level, I don't feel I deserve to have all that is mine by Divine right."

"Ummm. You know, I didn't connect those dots but obviously, you have. And, they seem to be valid."

"Yes, I think so. Amazingly enough, at this last show I finally think I got on board with exactly that! Someone called me a witch. Actually, a wife and husband both. At first I felt horrified, and then thankful. It got me to a place where I knew beyond a shadow of doubt that I deserve better! Better treatment from others. A better financial status. Better relationships. Better food choices."

"Wow! That's impressive. What you need right now is a way to pull out from the inside what you already know then. You have some self-esteem, obviously. You know the jewelry you create is valid, beautiful, and helps people beyond being something lovely. Of course, I mean energetically. At this time, you need to find the rest that's necessary to know in your heart what you deserve. And that's a lot actually, knowing you deserve to have the connections you want in life. If it's with your friends, or your family, you not only can have these relationships deepen and be more fulfilling if that's what you're craving. And/or, you can talk to Spirit and let those powers know that you are ready now to have the financial support you deserve for the art you create. Maybe it's simply that you need to feel inside that you deserve all that you crave in order for it to manifest on the outside of your world.

"I know; it sounds so simple when I say it that way, but in fact it takes a lot of inner work to get to that very point where you know it's right, and you've connected the dots to produce the outcome you desire.

"One thing keeps popping into my head and that's to ask you, do you feel you deserve to have all the close connections you crave? Or, do you feel you deserve to be alone? Once you find the answer there, you will be on the right track to making the proper shift necessary to move on into the emotional place you desire.

"Maybe it's time for you to stop being so patient with Spirit about how you are asking for whatever. I'm suggesting that perhaps you need to be specific about how it's time right now to have Spirit produce sales in the way you want. That you are ready. I mean really ready to receive those sales now, right now!

"You don't have to be angry about it and stamp your feet, but tell Spirit you are there. You're on board with correct timing, and that time is now! You know you're worthy. You know you have self-esteem. And included with all that, say your work needs to sell immediately, so you can pay off your debts.

"Picture your debts as paid in full. Picture your life as it will be once all these things happen. The more you can picture that as already happening, the more you are seeing it in your life as being real. If you can feel it, see it, then *it* has to come in for you. Seriously! This is true for money as well as relationships.

"AND, I don't think you have any idea how much you affect other people both personally as well as professionally. Sometimes it's like you are an ostrich with your head in the ground where you cannot hear what others think or say about you and your creations. Let me just say this about that; people LOVE your work, Vonnette. Seriously! I overhear people talk all the time, even in the grocery store when I'm laboring over some decision or other on a product I'm about to buy. Two women inevitably will have their heads together talking about a piece you created that one husband bought for her. It's almost the same verbiage every time. Sometimes one woman mentions how magical your creation is, but that's to be expected. Not only are your pieces magical, but they are one-of-a-kind. With no two pieces the same, no matter what someone thinks, says or feels, they know it's theirs and theirs alone. That in itself is magical. Even if they feel a piece of jewelry you've created comes from some altered state and they attribute that to your connection with otherworldly energies, who cares. I know people push that end of things on you often. Or, when someone makes a purchase out of your cases, and it isn't something that was made specifically for them as custom, that person still feels as if you created whatever just for her! And that is magic because, as I said, it's one-of-a-kind. That also represents your connection to Spirit.

"So, why not use that connection to Spirit, to now say what you want in life. Clear away the junk and step into whatever it is you truly want. You don't need to be angry over how long it has taken you to get to this moment in time. Don't scream your demands out. Tell Spirit you're ready now to receive your highest and best. That you're worthy and open to receive whatever is yours. Ask for them to clear the path and part the seas for you right now! To lead you to what is yours. That you deserve every good thing without any negative setback. That this or something better is here now. Speak your truth *as if* it's already here. Thank Spirit for all that has been provided, even the crap, and move on into what you desire to exist now with full clarity, energy, love even of whatever.

"I'm not sure you know how special you are, and that goes into all of what I've been talking about with self-worth. People constantly say how lovely you are inside and out. They love your art. I'm sure there are many who would want to be you. And yet, here you are with no concept of any of that. I'm guessing you look in the mirror and see your faults. What I see is a light-worker who has almost everything together that she needs in order to move way ahead in the physical world. When you get the whole element of self-esteem up and running, goodness only knows where you will land, because manifestation is part of all that. Feeling you deserve, and then actually making whatever manifest are two sides of the same coin. Get that and there ain't nothing you can't do, girl! You are a light-worker who walks her talk. Not everyone I know in this field can say that."

After taking a long breath both in and out, one more thing was necessary to complete the errand for Jennifer this day.

"These are always old patterns and belief systems that we can and often do carry forward from past lives. The important piece is that once you find a way to solve these old patterns and problems, you carry the resolutions forward into future lives. The karmic pattern is then broken!"

Jennifer had a way of making whatever burning issue Vonnette was facing as simply being a thought away from eternal resolution! Vonnette had obviously been stuck on money issues for more than this life in order to have it be such a big weight to carry forward. She wondered if "faking it till you make it" as a simple act could override karma.

"Anyhow, that's what I've come to say today. What you do with this information is up to you. But, when you feel it, really feel self-worth, I think you can bring in anything."

Lost in her own thought, Vonnette was silent. After thinking over these suggestions first, she then spoke. "You know, it's interesting that you've come today to share this information with me. While I was in the tub this morning I honestly felt I loved myself. I mean, my whole body. Can't say I've ever really experienced that feeling before. I do love what I create in the artistic world. But sincerely loving myself has always seemed so very far off. Like something hovering on the horizon that I couldn't grasp hold of.

"Combine that with the people who called me a witch over the weekend, and I began to realize how much I deserve in life. More than I ever felt I did before. Those people did me a huge favor! Because of their negativity, I was pushed to look deep inside and know my life would shift from then onward. How I would live differently knowing I deserve better than whatever I've accepted as normal life in the past, or what I've even asked for in life until now. This is an important time for me obviously.

"I promise your visit today along with all you've said will not fall on deaf ears. Maybe this is one fear I've had that needs facing. Maybe what love I have in this life right now with my kitties, family, and friends is almost all I need. Moving into self-love is a new ball field, but one I'm willing to play in. Thank You!

"There is something else. Something that just happened before you got here that I need to share. The phone rang and it was the phone company asking about a recent bill that I had sent out last week. Obviously, they don't have the check yet. That's not the part I need to share. The guy on the other end of the phone was named Asif!"

Laughing burst out between the two women. They kept at it for a good couple of minutes while each shook their head in disbelief.

"Are you are kidding me?"

Shaking her head, no, Vonnette kept laughing.

"You cannot make this shit up!"

"I know, seriously! I made the guy repeat his name three times. He actually spelled it out for me. At that juncture, I knew it was a message but had no connection other than my mom's coming in today. Then you showed up and have been going on about self-esteem. Guess you and I are connected on some high plane today with Spirit, working magic through each of us, and all for me! Color me a lucky gal. And, one dream last night was about my giving birth with a famous man as my doctor. Famous people in dreams represent help from an unexpected source. Guess my mother, Spirit presenting me with Asif and you combined are the unexpected source today my friend!"

They laughed over this amazing connection between them and Spirit for a few more minutes. Conversations naturally trailed off into other subjects now that the serious one had come to an end. They enjoyed two cups of tea together before it was time for Jennifer to leave. By the time they were ready to part company, Vonnette noticed the white diamond-like sparklers had subsided around Jennifer. She was down to her normal white light auric energy. It was intriguing how when Jennifer was excited about something her white lights became sparkler-like.

After seeing Jennifer to the door, Vonnette stood in her living room and pondered exactly what self-worth and self-esteem meant to her. Not to leave out the news flash that she deserved more than she had ever thought to ask for before now, too. How to grasp these concepts completely was something she would have to work on over time. It was also imperative to learn how to make demands for her life to shift from one of a fear base to knowing from deep in her soul that she deserved what she was asking for from Spirit. On some level, deep inside, she had felt she hadn't deserved to have all she wanted until this day.

She was shifting.

"Wow, this is a lot today. I got the fear message from Mom, then Spirit jumped in. Now I have all this from Jennifer. Okay, I, Vonnette, am saying out loud that it's my turn, everyone. It's time my inner self finds all that I crave with sales of my finished jewelry, to come from a new, grounded place where I know I want financial success, am ready for it, am in a secure place of knowing it's rightfully mine, now! That on some inner level I maybe asked for all these experiences in life in order to learn; however, it's time for me to stand up, be counted and not shrink into the background with what I want. It's time for me to receive. It's time for me to know I have good relationships that are true and are with people who care about me: most importantly, that I deserve to have those wonderful relationships.

"It's time for me to care for myself.

"It's time for me to take back my power. To say no when I want or need to.

"To choose life, love of self, and then expand outward.

"To be confident enough to choose what I want at any given moment of any given day and Believe I deserve at least most of it to come my way. No, *all* of it to come my way. Mustn't shrink back now. Must get myself in complete alignment to receive all I deserve from this moment forward! This whole lack of self-confidence has to stop here and now.

"Okay, God and whomever might be listening who is part of the white light energy, I am ready to receive all that is mine by Divine right! It's time I let go of that moment in my childhood that has retarded my inner growth, stamped down my self-esteem to the point where I felt unloved, unappreciated, and unworthy. By releasing the pain and energy from the past, I live in the now. It's time for me to stand up and know from every cell of my being that I am worthy, that I am ready to receive, that I am going forward in life with a renewed spirit of gratitude for all I have been, all that I am, and all that I will become as I progress along this avenue of self-worth.

"It's happening! I'm living as if and I deserve!

"Guess that's a good enough start. Now I need to keep saying these kinds of things repeatedly in order for my cellular structure to completely grasp this new me, the one who touches ground and who finds being in body a blessing. Gratitude thinking creates abundance and I'm filled with gratitude now!"

As she stopped talking out loud, she stood still a moment letting everything sink in. Feeling confident she was getting this message from on high, she turned to the kitchen to clean up the tea items when the phone rang.

"Hello, Vonnette's Designs." Came forth with a slightly more exuberant voice than usual. Because at last, she was a new, or renewed person today!

Surprisingly, she felt an immediate gut reaction while waiting to discover who was on the phone when who was on the other end of the call became all too clear. It only took a couple of seconds of silence and yet, there was that unmistakable feeling. As her stomach was clenching up, she knew exactly who it was. It was Jackson.

No dream message.

No early heads-up warning.

No, there was no need to ask who was on the other end of the line, and then . . . there was his voice. Not that his voice had any particular inflection. Simply, his vocal tone sent Vonnette's physical self into another vibrational realm.

"Hi Vonnette, Jackson here. How's my timing today? Tried to

give you a few days beyond what our next agreed upon time to talk would be."

Without waiting for a response, and thankfully so as Vonnette was suddenly reeling, he kept filling the airwaves with conversation. "I'm actually in town visiting with Sophie. She's excited that we have made some form of connection and feels responsible for our meeting. I feel that if it's meant to happen, it will. The universe is weird in that way, don't you think?"

Frozen in place Vonnette didn't respond. For that instant, she didn't know how to respond nor could she physically even move. What happened to those feelings of self-love and confidence?

Lack of conversation on either end would have been difficult for most people. Lack of speech was actually a blessing for each of these parties right now, though. It gave forth enough time to gather thoughts and perhaps figure out what to say next.

Without acknowledging there had been a break in the conversation, Jackson began again. "I had a dream of you last night so felt it was time for me to get in touch."

Mumbling a bit unable to actually fully speak yet, Vonnette sat on her kitchen chair to gather herself. "A dream?" Only one other time in her life had she felt this physically disturbed by a man. He was a love like every woman ought to have at least once in a lifetime, all consuming and sexual. The kind where she knew hours beforehand she was about to run into him, and when she did, her adrenalin raced so much her skin jumped when he got close enough to have their auras collide. Her head felt as if it would implode when they did finally physically touch. With so much electricity running rampant around and between them all those years ago, words did not come easily. More thought could and should be given to this past relationship comparison. That blip from the past had ended years back. Every part of that connection took a lot out of Vonnette. Eventually she realized the relationship was meant to be only physical, nothing more.

Yes, this moment on the phone had an element of familiarity to it. Whatever this was between Jackson and her did, thankfully, feel different on a few levels from past relationships. They were connected, yet able to communicate thus far on multiple wave-lengths. You could not prove that through Vonnette's mumblings or actions in this minute, though. She heard words spoken on some distant plane but had not yet connected with them as her memories had momentarily consumed her.

The dream from October had suddenly begun to replay in her head about an explosion set to go off in 6 weeks. Didn't that dream happen in Northampton when she first discovered the lump in her breast? Wasn't that a dream message about the lump? Her brain was working overtime and making connections instantaneously. Or maybe time was actually standing still as she recalled the past. It had been fewer than six weeks when she discovered she did not have cancer so that dream couldn't have been about the lump. Had it been six weeks since she met Jackson? Could this phone call be the explosion to which that dream message referred?

Having entered an alternate universe, Vonnette was not aware of how long she had even been on the phone with Jackson let alone what he was saying, or better yet what he was not saying. Every-thing running through her head had only taken a few seconds but felt energetically like a complete day had passed.

Shaking her head to clear the explosion she was feeling physi-cally and to actually pay attention to the person on the other end of the phone, she began to hear, really hear. His words came through in delayed time. Yet, she thought she was actually hearing every-thing he had and was now saying.

"Yes, I had a dream about you last night. It was strange. You were in a summer dress with flowers on it; I guess it would be called a floral pattern. There were a bunch of layers to the bottom of the dress. Sorry, I don't know fashion so my description might be seri-ously lacking. It was lightweight, that's how I know it was a summer dress. Well that, and the fact you were in a garden full of flowers all in bloom. You were standing on garden stones. I think they're called stepping stones? But in the dream these were the types of stones you would make jewelry out of. Clusters of all these gemstones made up each stepping stone. Don't know names of stones so can't tell you that, but I knew they were jewelry stones because they were all cut like they were ready to be made into jewelry.

"Sparkling in the sunlight they were really quite beautiful. Still, they didn't hold a candle to the vision of your standing upon them. The dream was mainly of you standing there in this garden, on those stones, in that dress, with a great inviting smile on your face and bare feet. Who knows what all that means? Maybe you don't want me to say this kind of thing especially since we don't really know one another, but I don't often recall my dreams. This one was so specific that I felt it might be a sign that today was the proper day to give you a call. A long-winded way of asking is it okay, that I called today, I mean?"

"Did he just say he didn't know me," Vonnette wondered? Obviously, he connected in some deep way, enough so to mention a remembered dream. What were her dream messages again from last night? Trust your intuition with blue sapphire and to stop moping and begin hoping was the yellow sapphire. Visually the dreamed scene showed a wedding band that turned into a garden path with stepping stones. OMG, she had also dreamed of stepping stones. Then, someone had spoken out loud who told her to pay attention today. That message had been from some unknown spirit. Yikes! Thinking that dream was a clear message about her book, she had to wonder now about just how wrong she was.

Aware of the silence and deep thought, Vonnette began to gurgle out something close to words. "Dream, huh, and garden? Interesting."

Her speech finally began to formulate as she focused and made the effort to keep going. "I dream all the time, full color dreams actually. We could compare notes at some point I guess since you had a color version last night, too."

"Well, as I said, I don't usually recall my dreams, but I'd love to hear more about yours anytime."

"Careful what you ask for, Jackson. I have loads of dreams nightly."

"Anytime. The more the merrier. Seriously, Vonnette!"

There was something in the way he said her name that sent a vibration through her whole body. It was as if a tuning fork had just been struck on one of her vertebra. Though she was talking and hearing herself speak, she didn't feel as if she was in her body. It was more like watching everything from above it in a second or two, time-delay.

"Some of my dreams suggest what I ought to work on each day. Some tell me what I should do or not do, or maybe even who will be in touch that day. It's taken me years to learn to decipher what I see during the night. I think we're all given messages, and that during the sleep phase of the night is when it's easiest for us to receive these gems because we aren't blocking what's given then."

Watching herself in this out-of-body manner she wondered if she was seriously rambling like this? Somehow she couldn't stop.

"Last night I had a dream of being in my garden, too, and saw stepping stones. Guess the universe was telling me you would be calling today since you dreamed of a garden path as well. Of course, there were other dreams, not just that one."

"If you experience a rich dream life like that every night I wonder why on earth you would ever want to wake up and exist in the real world."

Smiling outwardly as well as inwardly, Vonnette felt his tenderness through his spoken words. Something was happening, and fast. Lightening had struck and she had hold of the bolt. The seconds, or minutes where no conversation transpired didn't matter somehow. Every color in the rainbow was melding into their energy.

Knowing there was a lot to say, and trusting there would be time in which to say it, Vonnette began to come to some sense of norm and took a different tack. "I've had some very strange experiences since we met. Maybe some time I'll share them with you. Right now, I think I must tell you I've not had enough time to check you out in any manner as we had agreed upon."

Feeling his energy drop on the other end of the line, Vonnette couldn't believe how connected she felt to this man whom she didn't yet know, or perhaps she knew him better than she thought.

"What I decided just this minute is that I'm going to trust, and all will reveal itself over the course of time between us. If you're not telling me the truth, I'll know it shortly."

Jackson began to breathe normally again and with that his energy came across as joyful. Unable to see one another, Vonnette felt his smile energetically, and she smiled as well.

Not remaining on the phone long, they set up a first date for the next night, Friday. He was in town already, so it would be easy to get together. Who knew, maybe this would be the first of many dates.

Reconnecting with her dream messages again she recalled the green kyanite. Kyanite helps to peel away the layers of fear and doubt. Look at any fears; figure how they came to be and then how to develop the cure! After what seemed like a lifetime lack of trust it surprised her how fear suddenly took a backseat. It was a giant leap of faith to meet Jackson for a date without checking him out to make sure he was not a repeat of so many unavailable men coming to court her. If Jackson were indeed like so many others in Vonnette's past it would become apparent very quickly.

Yes, between visiting with her mom, letting go of fear, talking with Jennifer about self-esteem, getting the as if message and speaking up for what she actually wanted this morning, Vonnette was peeling away layers upon layers already this day. How quickly the universe had responded to her actions of speaking up and out for herself was surprising, or was it? Maybe everyone on the other side had been waiting for that exact second where she did speak up and out and then they granted her desires all at once in celebration.

Trust was something new. Letting go and allowing life to unfold was an unfamiliar place for Vonnette to live, one that she felt she kind of liked thus far. In some way, it was exhilarating! Like floating through the air without benefit of an airplane. Like your feet could touch down to earth if you wanted them to, but then why would you want them to?

This was turning into a new type of day. Something Vonnette didn't know exactly what to do with energetically as yet, but she knew she would give it a go. Wasn't that what her mother had suggested while they spoke earlier? Wasn't that what Jennifer suggested as well?

Both women were important to Vonnette in this life. One was on the other side in the white light. The other was here on this plane shooting out white light like firecrackers. Each one spoke from her heart today. One about the fear holding Vonnette back and the other about asking for, or demanding, what Vonnette wanted, what she really wanted and deserved in this life. But, also on some deeper level, for Vonnette to find a place way down inside to connect with what she wanted as if it was already there! Vonnette felt she had to up her game today to speak up and out for what she wanted, deserved, and would accept now that her self-esteem was piqued.

Yes, this or something better was coming in fast. Vonnette almost didn't catch her breath enough to grasp it was all really happening.

Smiling throughout the day without any particular reason, she went on to call her friend to wish him a very happy birthday while feeling she was having one for herself.

Throughout the day Vonnette kept repeating, "He had a dream about me!"

Inside she knew that her dream was an overlap to his, too, since she had also dreamed about stepping stones. Thinking it all over again, Vonnette realized the stones in the initial wedding band were of diamond and blue sapphire. It was surprising how simple the connection was. Sophie Belle wants white diamonds and a blue sapphire for her engagement ring. "How did I miss that connection? But then, there was the addition of a yellow sapphire in that segment, too. Yellow sapphire reminded her to stop moping and begin hoping.

"Okay, I got the stepping stones, the birthday element, and then the actual stone connections. What was the deal with the prison and the third-place ribbon then?

"Hmmm, might have to let those elements go."

Just like that, for the first time in too many years to count, Vonnette let go of one of her dream messages without feeling she had missed something important about her day. This was something she maybe could learn to embrace. It did at least go along with the element of letting go of fear because she didn't stop to feel fearful of missing a message given from on high.

It was here that she remembered seeing six crows this morning. Six was her number for love. Suddenly, she laughed out loud. How funny it was that it never once occurred to her that a love interest would find her today. The reconnection with her mother and then with Jennifer would have suited love in her realm just fine and then, she recalled once more how a group of crows could also be called a murder and she laughed again. "Murder!" And she repeated herself from a few days ago, "Who would seriously call a group of crows a murder? They are true messengers. Thank you, Foffee, for introducing their energy to me at such an early age. Hope you're doing well. Love you."

⚶

November 21, Friday 2008

DREAM

Vonnette looked up and saw Jackson standing in front of her booth. His mouth was moving. She didn't think she heard his words as her ears were suddenly ringing. Coming a bit to her senses, she thought the words he was speaking were, "Don't you understand, you're in my thoughts, you're in my dreams and, you have total control of my heart!"

That couldn't be what she just heard! Head spinning, she wasn't sure if she was having a spell or a heart attack of some sort. Looking about she wondered if anyone else heard him say these things? Eyes darting to booth-mates across the way showed no signs of anything out of the ordinary. While visually sweeping the landscape around her booth, she tried to figure out if anyone next door had maybe heard him speak? For now, the coast looked clear.

Taking a moment, Vonnette wondered how anyone could be so pre-sumptuous in another person's place of business to spurt out such emotion that anyone could hear, even if it didn't appear that anyone else did hear!

Tango music was playing over the intercom. Vonnette wondered if she was actually hearing this music, or if it was only playing inside her head along with the ringing? Maybe she was having a nervous break-down, or even a psychotic break. So many of her spirit messages began through scent, but there were also times when sound made whatever connection was necessary.

She was in her dream while observing it all happening at the same time. Suddenly, Vonnette came back to some link with the dream message to realize Jackson was in front of her with arms held out in dance position. He asked, "Do you tango?"

Vonnette couldn't believe herself seemingly glide out from behind her display cases as though on some form of conveyor belt and slip effortlessly into his arms. It was the beginning of an out of body experience on high. He was at least five inches taller than she and yet their physical bodies seemed to fit well together in dance position. They began to Argentine tango to the music as if they had been dancing together forever. Words weren't necessary and actually had no meaning as their bodies had a synchronicity all their own. This moment was correct on so many levels in silence.

He stopped, stood in position a moment and then slid his right foot out to the side. He pushed her left foot out along with it as if their feet were attached. Vonnette melted into tango bliss as they continued to dance together. People stopped in their tracks to watch this unexpected event taking place at the show. Jackson and Vonnette didn't notice any of them. They were as they should be in one another's arms making their way through music.

⁂

Not wanting to wake, she moved slowly. Happy for no reason, she stretched out fully to remove any body kinks. That was when her dream became clear.

In the middle of a good stretch, unexpectedly and without warning, she shot straight up in bed to a sitting position and exclaimed out loud, "When we first met, did Jackson say he lived in New Hampshire?"

Vonnette had awakened both physically as well as spiritually this day. Working on two different mental levels all the cogs fell into place in her psychological wheel. From a deep, inner-core place, she knew Jackson was the man in her visions from years back. The ones that had happened over so many years and had stopped when she began dating Joseph. Clearly, Jackson was the man she married out in her garden, not Joseph! The man who owned a home built into the side of a mountain that was made of logs and had a swing built for two on the front porch was Jackson!

Why these visions of a marriage and a home in New Hampshire had stopped when she began to see Joseph all those years back, she had no idea. Unless, it was to tell her she was with the wrong man! Wow, her thought process was vibrant today and was answering questions she'd had for so long and had almost forgotten there were never any answers to them.

Why hadn't those visions picked back up again once she stopped seeing Joseph? No idea came to mind about that right now.

What was on her mind was how Jackson had dreamed that same garden vision.

Even though she had spontaneously agreed to see Jackson while on the phone, this connection to all those visions from so many years ago gave her positive reinforcement. Vonnette felt this connection to Spirit was what she craved to let her know in no uncertain terms that she and Jackson were meant to connect, that she was indeed on the right path. Interesting choice of words as she and Jackson had each dreamed of a garden path the night before they had spoken and decided to begin dating tonight. Having full recall from the night before, she knew this union was the reference to being told to pay attention. By accepting a date with Jackson, she was beginning the rest of her life.

In her soul, Vonnette knew for the first time since she could remember from early childhood that she was going to run *to* something and someone and not away from whomever. This new exuberance came from embracing life, not fearing or running from it.

Fear had had its grip on her for far too long. Vonnette stared down fear. Interestingly, she was no longer living as if. She was now embracing life.

Instead of working to exist, she was living with love overflowing from her heart and soul. What art came from that new place deep inside would be wondrous. It would feed her soul as well as others. And it would no longer be called work. It would now be called her *joie de vivre*.

Whatever amount of time she and Jackson might share together would be what that would be. It might be a blip in the radar of time, or it could last a lifetime. This, along with her other family and friend relationships, would be a gift. This connection with Jackson was something the spiritual realm had approved of and guided her to recognize when it was the right time. Even though she had waited so very many years for something to be right, none of that frustration mattered any more. It was not simply a relationship with Jackson that was making the difference in her world, it was her spirituality, her dream messages, her self-love, her self-esteem, her knowing she deserved and how she believed and she trusted that everything would work out! Having clarity and that connection to Spirit gave her permission to move on, on so many levels full of joy, full of bliss, simply full. Perhaps for the first time in her life, she felt food was not the way to feel full, it was internal bliss that finally filled that void. Who knew?

Her spirit and her heart were light. Vonnette felt as though her life had led to this exact moment where everything fit. This twinkle in time was so much more than her union with Jackson. This was when she met herself, her visions and her dreams. Where she had confirmation of her spiritual beliefs. Where she knew inside and out that living a New Age metaphysical lifestyle *was* the correct choice for her. Vonnette did live above and beyond the physical so much of the time it's no wonder that she questioned everything because everything was a mystery to her. However, the universe had given her a high-five moment she would not let go of any time soon. Walking her talk would no longer be a hardship; it would be a joy!

The End

Bibliography

"Metaphysics." Webster's Third New International Dictionary. 1976.

Robinson, Lady Stearn & Tom Corbbett. The Dreamer's Dictionary. New York, NY: Warner Books, May 1975. Is the book the author, Candace, utilized as a reference for her dream symbolisms and as such, the main character, Vonnette, did use in this book as well.

Sherman, Candace L. Dreams Made of Stone. Is yet to be published and is the coffee table book referenced within this book.

Stone Magic. Newport, RI: Crystal Books, 2018. Is the A-Z guide of stone healing properties book referenced within this book.

Under the Tuscan Sun. Directed by Audrey Wells, character of Katherine; Lindsay Duncan, Touchstone Pictures, 2003.

About the Author

Candace L. Sherman writes books on healing stone energies. *The Crystal Caves* is a fun adventure book for all ages and *Stone Magic* is an A-Z definition book on stone healing properties she channeled. Both books are available on Amazon.

Fascinated with stones and jewelry since early childhood, she made a natural transition after college to open her own business in 1976. Creating and winning awards for her fine jewelry, Candace became known as a Stone Whisperer. Being able to look at stones and know how they want to be mounted is a gift she doesn't take lightly. *Stepping Stones*, her new novel is loosely based on Candace's travels along the east coast while participating in fine art and craft shows . . . where a goldsmith and empathic artist, Vonnette, lives in a metaphysical world while sharing information on that lifestyle with possible clients.

As a renaissance artist, Candace creates one-of-a-kind fine jewelry, paints wall art with acrylics, makes fascinator hats, up-cycles furniture with her own designs and creates crystal pillows along with writing books. At the age of 69 when most people have retired, Candace keeps reinventing herself to remain creatively active. After living in Newport, RI, for over 45 years, she now resides in Fairhaven, MA, with her black cat where she combs the shoreline for creative inspiration.

Visit, write and buy her creations at www.clsherman.com + Instagram at Candace Sherman.